The Everlasting Arms

by
Joseph Hocking

The Everlasting Arms
by Joseph Hocking

Copyright © 2024

All Rights reserved.

No part of this publication may be reproduced, stored in a retrieval system, or transmitted in any form or by any means, electronic, mechanical, photocopying or Otherwise, without the written permission of the publisher.
The author/editor asserts the moral right to be identified as the author/editor of this work.

ISBN: 978-93-63051-90-4

Published by

DOUBLE 9 BOOKS
2/13-B, Ansari Road
Daryaganj, New Delhi – 110002
info@double9books.com
www.double9books.com
Tel. 011-40042856

This book is under public domain

ABOUT THE AUTHOR

Joseph Hocking was a Cornish author and United Methodist Free Church priest. Hocking was born in St Stephen-in-Brannel, Cornwall, to James Hocking, a part-owner of a tin mine, and Elizabeth (Kitto) Hocking. In 1884, he was ordained a Methodist minister. Working in various regions of England over the next few years, he completed his first novel, Harry Penhale - The Trial of his Faith, while in London in 1887. He saw fiction as a highly successful method for communicating his Christian message to the public, and he combined writing with church obligations until illness caused him to leave from the ministry in 1909. His final pastoral charge was the huge and important United Free Church in Woodford, Essex, which he helped rebuild by the skilled arts and crafts architect Charles Harrison Townsend. He continued to write, and in his career, he published approximately 100 volumes. Although virtually forgotten today, he was extremely popular in his day. His final pastoral charge was the huge and important United Free Church in Woodford, Essex, which he helped rebuild by the skilled arts and crafts architect Charles Harrison Townsend. He continued to write, and in his career, he published approximately 100 volumes. Although virtually forgotten today, he was extremely popular in his day.

CONTENTS

PROLOGUE

Chapter I
A Woman's Face 9

Chapter II
The Marconigram 15

Chapter III
The Shipwreck...21

Chapter IV
"The Enemy of Your Soul"..28

PART I
THE FIRST TEMPTATION

Chapter V
The Only Surviving Relative..33

Chapter VI
Wendover Park 42

Chapter VII
Lady Blanche makes her Appearance.............................53

Chapter VIII
Count Romanoff's Gospel 60

Chapter IX
Beatrice Stanmore...68

Chapter X
Uncertainty..76

Chapter XI
The Real Heir..83

Chapter XII
    The Day of Destiny 90
Chapter XIII
    The Invisible Hand 97
Chapter XIV
    A Scrap of Paper 106
Chapter XV
    Count Romanoff's Departure 110
Chapter XVI
    Riggleton's Homecoming 116
Chapter XVII
    Faversham's Resolution 122

PART II
THE SECOND TEMPTATION

Chapter XVIII
    Mr. Brown's Prophecy 129
Chapter XIX
    An Amazing Proposal 138
Chapter XX
    "The Country for the People" 143
Chapter XXI
    The Midnight Meeting 150
Chapter XXII
    "You and I Together" 156
Chapter XXIII
    The So-called Dead 163
Chapter XXIV
    Visions of Another World 171
Chapter XXV
    Romanoff's Philosophy 179
Chapter XXVI
    A Voice from Another World 188
Chapter XXVII
    Olga makes Love 196

PART III
THE THIRD TEMPTATION

Chapter XXVIII
The Count's Confederate 204

Chapter XXIX
In Quest of a Soul 213

Chapter XXX
Voices in the Night 221

Chapter XXXI
Dick hears Strange News 229

Chapter XXXII
Beatrice Confesses 237

Chapter XXXIII
Sir George's Love Affair 245

Chapter XXXIV
The Dawn of Love 253

Chapter XXXV
The Eternal Struggle 261

Chapter XXXVI
His Guardian Angel 270

Chapter XXXVII
At the Café Moscow 278

Chapter XXXVIII
The Shadow of a Great Terror 286

Chapter XXXIX
The Triumph of Good 293

Chapter XL
The Ministering Angel 301

PROLOGUE

Chapter I
A Woman's Face

"There may be a great deal in it."

"Undoubtedly there is. Imagination, superstition, credulity," said Dick Faversham a little cynically.

"Well, I can't dismiss it in that fashion," replied the other. "Where there's smoke there's fire, and you can't get men from various parts of the world testifying that they saw the Angels at Mons unless there is some foundation of truth in it."

"Again I say imagination. Imagination can do a great deal. Imagination can people a churchyard with ghosts; it can make dreams come true, and it can also make clever men foolish."

"Admit that. You still haven't got to the bottom of it. There's more than mere imagination in the stories of the Angels at Mons, and at other places. Less than three weeks ago I was at a hospital in London. I was talking with a wounded sergeant, and this man told me in so many words that he saw the Angels. He said there were three of them, and that they remained visible for more than an hour. Not only did he see them, but others saw them. He also said that what appeared like a great calamity was averted by their appearance."

There was a silence after this somewhat lengthy speech, and something like an uncanny feeling possessed the listeners.

The conversation took place in the smoke-room of a steamship bound for Australia, and at least a dozen men were taking part in it. The subject of the discussion was the alleged appearance of the Angels at Mons, and at other places in France and Belgium, and although at least half of the little party was not convinced that those who accepted the stories had a good case, they could not help being affected by the numerous instances that were adduced of the actual appearance of spiritual visitants. The subject, as all the world knows, had been much discussed in England and elsewhere, and so it was not unnatural that it should form the topic of conversation in the smoke-room of the outgoing vessel.

One of the strongest opponents to the supernatural theory was a young man of perhaps twenty-seven years of age. From the first he had taken up an antagonistic attitude, and would not admit that the cases given proved anything.

"Excuse me," he urged, "but, really, it won't do. You see, the whole thing, if it is true, is miraculous, and miracles, according to Matthew Arnold, don't happen."

"And who is Matthew Arnold, or any other man, to say that what we called miracles don't happen?" urged Mr. Bennett, the clergyman, warmly. "In spite of Matthew Arnold and men of his school, the world still believes in the miracles of our Lord; why, then, should miracles happen in Palestine and not in France?"

"If they did happen," interpolated Faversham.

"Either they happened, or the greatest movement, the mightiest and noblest enthusiasms the world has ever known, were founded on a lie," said the clergyman solemnly.

"That may be," retorted Faversham, "but don't you see where you are leading us? If, as you say, we accept the New Testament stories, there is no reason why we may not accept the Angels at Mons and elsewhere. But that opens up all sorts of questions. The New Testament tells of people being possessed by devils; it tells of one at least being tempted by a personal devil. Would you assert that a personal devil tempts men to-day?"

"I believe that either the devil or his agents tempt men to-day," replied the clergyman.

"Then you would, I suppose, also assert that the old myth of guardian angels is also true."

"Accepting the New Testament, I do," replied Mr. Bennett.

Dick Faversham laughed rather uneasily.

"Think," went on the clergyman; "suppose someone who loved you very dearly in life died, and went into the great spirit world. Do you not think it natural that that person should seek to watch over you? Is it not natural that he or she who loved you in life should love you after what we call death? A mother will give her life for her child in life. Why should she not seek to guard that same child even although she has gone to the world of spirits?"

"But the whole thing seems so unreal, so unnatural," urged Faversham.

"That is because we live in a materialistic age. The truth is, in giving up the idea of guardian angels and similar beliefs we have given up some of the greatest comforts in life. Because we have become so materialistic, we have lost that grand triumphant conviction that there is no death. Why — why —" — and Mr. Bennett rose to his feet excitedly — "there is not one of those splendid lads who has fallen in battle, who is dead. God still cares for them all, and not one is outside His protection. I can't explain it, but I *know*."

"You know?"

"Yes, I know. And I'll tell you why I know. My son Jack was killed at Mons, but he's near me even now. Say it's unreal if you like, say it's unnatural if you will, but it's one of the great glories of life to me."

"I don't like to cast a doubt upon a sacred conviction," ventured Faversham after a silence that was almost painful, "but is not this clearly a case of imagination? Mr. Bennett has lost a son in the war. We are all very sorry for him, and we are all glad that he gets comfort from the feeling that his son is near him. But even admitting the truth of this, admitting the doctrine that a man's spirit does not die because of the death of the body, you have proved nothing. The appearance of the Angels in France and Belgium means something more than this. It declares that these spirits appear in visible, tangible forms; that they take an interest in our mundane doings; that they take sides; that they help some and hinder others."

"Exactly," assented Mr. Bennett.

"You believe that?"

"I believe it most fervently," was the clergyman's solemn answer. "I am anything but a spiritualist, as the word is usually understood; but I see no reason why my boy may not communicate with me, why he may not help me. I, of course, do not understand the mysterious ways of the Almighty, but I believe in the words of Holy Writ. 'Are they not all ministering spirits, sent forth to minister for them who shall be heirs of salvation?' says the writer of the Epistle to the Hebrews. While our Lord Himself, when speaking of little children, said, 'I say unto you that their angels do always behold the face of My Father who is in heaven.'"

Again there was a silence which was again broken by Dick Faversham turning and speaking to a man who had not spoken during the whole discussion, but who, with a sardonic, cynical smile upon his face, had been listening intently.

"What is your opinion, Count Romanoff?" asked Faversham.

"I am afraid I must be ruled out of court," he replied. "These stories smack too much of the nursery."

"You believe that they are worn-out superstitions?"

"I should shock you all if I told you what I believe."

"Shock us by all means."

"No, I will spare you. I remember that we have a clergyman present."

"Pray do not mind me," urged Mr. Bennett eagerly.

"Then surely you do not accept the fables recorded in the New Testament?"

"I do not admit your description. What you call fables are the greatest power for righteousness the world has ever known. They have stood the test of ages, they have comforted and inspired millions of lives, they stand upon eternal truth."

Count Romanoff shrugged his shoulders, and a smile of derision and contempt passed over his features.

"All right," he replied, and again lapsed into silence.

The man had spoken only a very few commonplace words, and yet he had changed the atmosphere of the room. Perhaps this was because all felt him utterly antagonistic to the subject of discussion. He was different from Dick Faversham, who in a frank, schoolboy way had declared his scepticism. He had been a marked man ever since the boat had left England. There were several reasons for this. One was his personal appearance. He was an exceedingly handsome man of perhaps forty years of age, and yet there was something repellent in his features. He was greatly admired for his fine physique and courtly bearing, and yet but few sought his acquaintance. He looked as though he were the repository of dark secrets. His smile was cynical, and suggested a kind of contemptuous pity for the person to whom he spoke. His eyes were deeply set, his mouth suggested cruelty.

And yet he could be fascinating. Dick Faversham, who had struck up an acquaintance with him, had found him vastly entertaining. He held unconventional ideas, and was widely read in the literature of more than one country. Moreover, he held strong views on men and movements, and his criticisms told of a man of more than ordinary intellectual acumen.

"You refuse to discuss the matter?"

"There is but little use for an astronomer to discuss the stars with an astrologer. A chemist would regard it as waste of time to discuss his science with an alchemist. The two live in different worlds, speak a different language, belong to different times."

"Of course, you will call me a fanatic," cried the clergyman; "but I believe. I believe in God, and in His Son Jesus Christ who died for our sins, and who rose from the dead. On that foundation I build all the rest."

A change passed over the Count's face. It might be a spasm of pain, and his somewhat pale face became paler; but he did not speak. For some seconds he seemed fighting with a strong emotion; then, conquering himself, his face resumed its former aspect, and a cynical smile again passed over his features.

"The gentleman is too earnest for me," he remarked, taking another cigar from his case.

Dick Faversham did not see the change that passed over the Count's face. Indeed, he had ceased to take interest in the discussion. The truth was that the young man was startled by what was an unusual occurrence. The room, as may be imagined, bearing in mind that for a long time a number of men had been burning incense to My Lady Nicotine, was in a haze of tobacco smoke, and objects were not altogether clearly visible; but not far from the door he saw a woman standing. This would not have been remarkable had not the lady passengers, for some reason known to themselves, up to the present altogether avoided the smoke-room. More than this, Dick did not recognise her. He had met, or thought he had met during the voyage, every lady passenger on the boat; but certainly he had never seen this one before. He was perfectly sure of that, for her face was so remarkable that he knew he could not have forgotten her.

She was young, perhaps twenty-four. At first Dick thought of her as only a girl in her teens, but as, through the thick smoky haze he watched her face, he felt that she had passed her early girlhood. What struck him most forcibly were her wonderful eyes. It seemed to him as though, while they were large and piercing, they were at the same time melting with an infinite tenderness and pity.

Dick Faversham looked at her like a man entranced. In his interest in her he forgot the other occupants of the room, forgot the discussion, forgot everything. The yearning solicitude in the woman's eyes, the infinite pity on her face, chained him and drove all other thoughts away.

"I say, Faversham."

He came to himself at the mention of his name and turned to the speaker.

"Are you good for a stroll on deck for half an hour before turning in?"

It was the Count who spoke, and Dick noticed that nearly all the occupants of the room seemed on the point of leaving.

"Thank you," he replied, "but I think I'll turn in."

He looked again towards the door where he had seen the woman, but she was gone.

"By the way," and he touched the sleeve of a man's coat as he spoke, "who was that woman?"

"What woman?"

"The woman standing by the door."

"I saw no woman. There was none there."

"But there was, I tell you. I saw her plainly."

"You were wool-gathering, old man. I was sitting near the door and saw no one."

Dick was puzzled. He was certain as to what he had seen.

The smoke-room steward appeared at that moment, to whom he propounded the same question.

"There was no lady, sir."

"But—are you sure?"

"Certainly, sir. I've been here all the evening, and saw everyone who came in."

Dick made his way to his berth like a man in a dream. He was puzzled, bewildered.

"I am sure I saw a woman," he said to himself.

Chapter II
The Marconigram

He had barely reached his room when he heard a knock at the door.

"Yes; what is it?"

"You are Mr. Faversham, aren't you?"

"Yes; what do you want?"

"Wireless for you, sir. Just come through."

A few seconds later Dick was reading a message which promised to alter the whole course of his life:

"*Your uncle, Charles Faversham, Wendover Park, Surrey, just died. Your immediate return essential. Report to us on arrival.* Bidlake & Bilton, *Lincoln's Inn.*"

The words seemed to swim before his eyes. His uncle, Charles Faversham, dead! There was nothing wonderful about that, for Dick had heard quite recently that he was an ailing man, and not likely to live long. He was old, too, and in the course of nature could not live long. But what had Charles Faversham's death to do with him? It was true the deceased man was his father's stepbrother, but the two families had no associations, simply because no friendship existed between them.

Dick knew none of the other Favershams personally. His own father, who had died a few years before, had left him practically penniless. His mother, whose memory his father adored, had died at his, Dick's, birth, and thus when he was a little over twenty he found himself alone in the world. Up to that time he had spent his life at school and at college. His father, who was a man of scholarly instincts, had made up his mind that his son should adopt one of the learned professions, although Dick's desires did not lean in that direction. At his father's death, therefore, he set to work to carve out a career for himself. He had good abilities, a determined nature, and great ambitions, but his training, which utterly unfitted him for the battle of life, handicapped him sorely. For three years nothing went well with him. He obtained situation after situation only to lose it. He was impatient of control, he lacked patience, and although he had boundless energies, he never found a true outlet for them.

At length fortune favoured him. He got a post under a company who did a large business in Austria and in the Balkan States, and he made himself so useful to his firm that his progress was phenomenal.

It was then that Dick began to think seriously of a great career. It was true he had only climbed a few steps on fortune's ladder, but his prospects for the future were alluring. He pictured himself becoming a power in the commercial world, and then, with larger wealth at his command, he saw himself entering Parliament and becoming a great figure in the life of the nation.

He had social ambitions too. Although he had had no serious love affairs, he dreamed of himself marrying into an old family, by which means the doors of the greatest houses in the land would be open to him.

"Nothing shall stop me," he said to himself again and again; and the heads of his firm, realising his value to them, gave him more and more responsibility, and also pointed hints about his prospects.

At the end of 1913, however, Dick had a serious disagreement with his chiefs. He had given considerable attention to continental politics, and he believed that Germany would force war. Because of this he advocated a certain policy with regard to their business. To this his chiefs gave a deaf ear, and laughed at the idea of England being embroiled in any trouble with either Austria or the Balkan States. Of course, Dick was powerless. He had no capital in the firm, and as his schemes were rather revolutionary he was not in a position to press them.

On the outbreak of war in 1914 Dick's firm was ruined. What he had predicted had come to pass. Because they had not prepared for this possible contingency, and because large sums of money were owing them in Austria and Serbia, which they could not recover, all their energies were paralysed. Thus at twenty-seven years of age, with only a few hundreds of pounds in his possession, Dick had to begin at the bottom again.

At length a firm who knew something of his associations with his previous employers offered to send him to Australia to attend to matters in which they believed he could render valuable service, but payment for which would depend entirely on his own success. Dick accepted this offer with avidity.

This in bare outline was his story up to the commencement of the history which finds him on his way to Australia with the momentous marconigram in his hands.

Again and again he read the wireless message which had been handed to him. It was so strange, so unexpected, so bewildering. He had never seen or spoken to his uncle, never expected to. He was further removed from this representative of his family than the Jews from the Samaritans. It is true he had seen Wendover Park from the distance. He remembered passing the lodge gates some year or two before when cycling through Surrey. From a neighbouring hill he had caught sight of the old house standing in its broad park-lands, and a pang of envy had shot through his heart as he reflected that although its owner and his father were stepbrothers he would never be admitted within its walls.

But this message had altered everything: *"Your uncle, Charles Faversham, Wendover Park, just died. Your immediate return essential. Report to us on arrival."*

The words burnt like fire into his brain. A wireless message, sent to him in mid-ocean, must be of more than common purport. Men of Bidlake & Bilton's standing did not send such messages as a pastime. They would not urge his immediate return without serious reasons.

It must mean—it could only mean—one thing. He must in some way be interested in the huge fortune which Charles Faversham had left behind him. Perhaps, perhaps—and again he considered the probable outcome of it all.

Hour after hour he sat thinking. Was his future, after all, to become great, not simply by his own energies, but because of a stroke of good fortune? Or, better still, was his uncle's death to be the means whereby he could climb to greatness and renown? After all he had not longed so much for money for its own sake, but as a means whereby he could get power, distinction, high position. With great wealth at his command he could—and again a fascinating future spread before him.

He could not sleep; of course, he couldn't! How could he sleep when his brain was on fire with wild imaginings and unknown possibilities?

He reflected on the course of his voyage, and considered where the vessel would first stop. Yes, he knew they were to call at Bombay, which was a great harbour from which ships were frequently returning to England. In three days they would be there, and then——

Should he take anyone into his confidence? Should he give reasons for leaving the ship? Oh, the wonder, the excitement of it all! The discussion about the Angels at Mons, and the talk about visitants from the spirit world caring for the people who lived on earth, scarcely entered his mind. What need had he for such things?

But who was that woman? For he was sure he had seen her. Tyler, to whom he had spoken, and the smoke-room steward might say that no woman was there, but he knew better. He could believe his own eyes anyhow, and the wonderful yearning look in her eyes still haunted him in spite of the disturbing message.

It was not until towards morning that sleep came to him, and then he was haunted by dreams. Strange as it may seem, he did not dream of Bidlake & Bilton's message nor of his late uncle's mansion. He dreamt of his father and mother. He had never seen his mother; she had died at his birth. He had never seen a picture of her, indeed. He believed that his father possessed her portrait, but he had never shown it to him. His father seldom spoke of his mother, but when he did it was in tones of awe, almost of worship. She was like no other woman, he said—a woman with all the possible beauty and glory of womanhood stored in her heart.

And she was with his father in his dream. They stood by his bedside watching over him. His father's face he remembered perfectly. It was just as he had seen it when he was alive, except that there was an added something which he could not describe. His mother's face was strange to him. Yet not altogether so. He knew instinctively that she was his mother—knew it by the look on her almost luminous face, by the yearning tenderness of her eyes.

Neither of them spoke to him. They simply stood side by side and watched him. He wished they would speak; he felt as though he wanted guidance, advice, and each looked at him with infinite love in their eyes.

Where had he seen eyes like those of his mother before? Where had he seen a face like the face in his dream? He remembered asking himself, but could recall no one.

"Mother, mother," he tried to say, but he could not speak. Then his mother placed her hand on his forehead, and her touch was like a benediction.

When he woke he wondered where he was; but as through the porthole he saw the sheen of the sea he remembered everything. Oh, the wonder of it all!

A knock came to the door. "Your bath is ready, sir," said a steward, and a minute later he felt the welcome sting of the cold salt water.

He scarcely spoke throughout breakfast; he did not feel like talking. He determined to find some lonely spot and reflect on what had taken place. When he reached the deck, however, the longing for loneliness left him. The sky was cloudless, and the sun poured its warm rays on the spotless boards.

Under the awning, passengers had ensconced themselves in their chairs, and smoked, or talked, or read just as their fancy led them.

In spite of the heat the morning was pleasant. A fresh breeze swept across the sea, and the air was pure and sweet.

Acquaintances spoke to him pleasantly, for he had become fairly popular during the voyage.

"I wonder if they have heard of that wireless message?" he reflected. "Do they know I have received news of Charles Faversham's death, and that I am probably a rich man?"

"Holloa, Faversham."

He turned and saw Count Romanoff.

"You look rather pale this morning," went on the Count; "did you sleep well?"

"Not very well," replied Dick.

"Your mind exercised about the discussion, eh?"

"That and other things."

"It's the 'other things' that make the great interest of life," remarked the Count, looking at him intently.

"Yes, I suppose they do," was Dick's reply. He was thinking about the wireless message.

"Still," and the Count laughed, "the discussion got rather warm, didn't it? I'm afraid I offended our clerical friend. His nod was very cool just now. Of course, it's all rubbish. Years ago I was interested in such things. I took the trouble to inform myself of the best literature we have on the whole matter. As a youth I knew Madame Blavatsky. I have been to seances galore, but I cease to trouble now."

"Yes?" queried Dick.

"I found that the bottom was knocked out of all these so-called discoveries by the first touch of serious investigation and criticism. Nothing stood searching tests. Everything shrivelled at the first touch of the fire."

"This talk about angels, about a hereafter, is so much empty wind," went on the Count. "There is no hereafter. When we die there is a great black blank. That's all."

"Then life is a mockery."

"Is it? It all depends how you look at it. Personally I find it all right."

Dick Faversham looked at his companion's face intently. Yes, it was a handsome face—strong, determined, forceful. But it was not pleasant. Every movement of his features suggested mockery, cynicism, cruelty. And yet it was fascinating. Count Romanoff was not a man who could be passed by without a thought. There was a tremendous individuality behind his deep-set, dark eyes—a personality of great force suggested by the masterful, mobile features.

"You have nerves this morning, Faversham," went on the Count. "Something more than ordinary has happened to you."

"How do you know?"

"I feel it. I see it. No, I am not asking you to make a confidant of me. But you want a friend."

"Yes," cried Dick, speaking on impulse; "I do."

The other did not speak. He simply fixed his eyes on Faversham's face and waited.

Chapter III
The Shipwreck

For a moment Dick was strongly tempted to tell his companion about the wireless he had received. But something, he could not tell what, seemed to forbid him. In spite of the fact that he had spent a good deal of time with Count Romanoff he had given him no confidences. There was something in his presence, in spite of his fascination, that did not inspire confidence.

"By the way," ventured Dick, after an awkward silence, "I have often been on the point of asking you, but it felt like a liberty. Are you in any way connected with the great Russian family of your name?"

The Count hesitated before replying. "I do not often speak of it," he told him presently, "but I come of a Royal Family."

"The Romanoffs of Russia?"

The Count smiled.

"I do not imagine that they would admit me into their family circle," he replied. "I make no claims to it, but I have the right."

Dick was duly impressed.

"Then, of course, you are a Russian. You were born there?"

"A Russian!" sneered the other. "A vast conglomeration of savagery, superstition, and ignorance! I do not claim to be a Russian. I have estates there, but I am a citizen of the world. My sympathies are not national, insular, bounded by race, paltry landmarks, languages. I live in a bigger world, my friend. Yes, I am a Romanoff, if you like, and I claim kinship with the greatest families of the Russian Empire—but la la, what is it? Thistledown, my friend, thistledown."

"But you were educated in Russia?" persisted Dick.

"Educated! What is it to be educated? From childhood I have been a wanderer. I have taken my degrees in the University of the world. I have travelled in China, Japan, Egypt, America, the Antipodes. In a few days we shall call at Bombay. If you will accompany me I will take you to people in that city, old Indian families whose language I know, whose so-called mysteries I have penetrated, and who call me friend. Ecco! I owe my education to all countries, all peoples."

He did not speak boastfully; there was no suggestion of the boaster, the braggadocio, in his tones; rather he spoke quietly, thoughtfully, almost sadly.

"Tell me this," asked Dick: "you, who I judge to be a rich man, do you find that riches bring happiness?"

"Yes—and no. With wealth you can buy all that this world can give you."

Dick wondered at the strange intonation of his voice.

"It is the only thing that can bring happiness," added Romanoff.

"I fancy our friend Mr. Bennett would not agree with you," laughed Dick. "He would say that a clear conscience meant happiness. He would tell you that a good life, a clean mind, and a faith in God were the secrets of happiness."

Romanoff laughed.

"What makes a clear conscience? It is a feeling that you have done what is right. But what is right? What is right in China is wrong in England. What makes the Chinaman happy makes the Englishman miserable. But why should the Englishman be miserable because he does the thing that makes the Chinaman happy? No, no, it won't do. There is no right; there is no wrong. The Germans are wise there. What the world calls morality is a bogy to frighten foolish people. 'It is always right to do the thing you *can* do,' says Brother Fritz. Personally I believe it to be right to do what satisfies my desires. It is right because it brings happiness. After all, you haven't long to live. A few years and it is all over. A shot from a pistol and *voilà!* your brains are blown out—you are dead! Therefore, take all that life can give you—there is nothing else."

"I wonder?" said Dick.

"That is why money is all-powerful. First of all, get rid of conventional morality, rid your mind of all religious twaddle about another life, and then suck the orange of this life dry. You, now, you are keen, ardent, ambitious; you love beautiful things; you can enjoy to the full all that life can give you. Nature has endowed you with a healthy body, ardent desires, boundless ambitions—well, satisfy them all. You can buy them all."

"But I am not rich," interposed Dick.

"Aren't you?" queried the other. "Who knows? Anyhow, you are young—make money. 'Money talks,' as the Americans say."

Again Dick was on the point of telling him about the wireless message, but again he refrained.

"By the way, Count Romanoff," he said, "did you see that woman in the smoke-room last night?"

"Woman! what woman?"

"I don't know. I never saw her before. But while you were talking I saw a woman's face through the haze of tobacco smoke. She was standing near the door. It was a wonderful face—and her eyes were beyond description. Great, pure, yearning, loving eyes they were, and they lit up the face which might have been—the face of an angel."

"You were dreaming, my friend. I have seen every woman on board, and not one of them possesses a face worth looking at twice."

"I asked another man," admitted Dick, "and he told me I was dreaming. He had been sitting near the door, he assured me, and he had seen no woman, while the smoke-room steward was just as certain."

"Of course there was no woman."

"And yet I saw a woman, unless——" He stopped suddenly.

"Unless what, my friend?"

"Unless it was a kind of rebuke to my scepticism last night; unless it was the face of an angel."

"An angel in mid-ocean!" Romanoff laughed. "An angel in the smoke-room of a P. & O. steamer! Faversham, you are an example of your own arguments. Imagination can do anything."

"But it would be beautiful if it were so. Do you know, I'm only half a sceptic after all. I only half believe in what I said in the smoke-room last night."

"Perhaps I can say the same thing," said Romanoff, watching his face keenly.

"I say!" and Dick laughed.

"Yes, laugh if you will; but I told you just now that the world contained no mystery. I was wrong; it does. My residence in India has told me that. Do you know, Faversham, what has attracted me to you?—for I have been attracted, I can assure you."

"Flattered, I'm sure," murmured Dick.

"I was attracted, because the moment I saw your face I felt that your career would be out of the ordinary. I may be wrong, but I believe that great things are going to happen to you, that you are going to have a wonderful career. I felt it when I saw you come on deck a little while ago. If you are wise you are going to have a great future—a *great* future."

"Now you are laughing."

"No, I'm not. I'm in deadly earnest. I have something of the power of divination in me. I feel the future. Something's going to happen to you. I think great wealth's coming to you."

Dick was silent, and a far-away look came into his eyes. He was thinking of the wireless message, thinking whether he should tell Romanoff about it.

"I started out on this voyage—in the hope that—that I should make money," he stammered.

"Where?"

"In Australia."

"You'll not go to Australia."

"No? Why?"

"I don't know—something's going to happen to you. I feel it."

Dick was again on the point of taking him into his confidence when two acquaintances came up and the conversation ended. But Dick felt that Romanoff knew his secret all the time.

The day passed away without further incident, but towards afternoon there was a distinct change in the weather. The sky became overclouded, and the gentle breeze which had blown in the morning strengthened into a strong, boisterous wind. The smooth sea roughened, and the passengers no longer sat on deck. The smoke-room was filled with bridge players, while other public rooms became the scenes of other amusements.

But Dick preferred being alone. He was still hugging his news to his heart, still reflecting on the appearance of the strange woman's face in the smoke-room, and all the time he was under the influence of Count Romanoff's conversation.

Perhaps the great, dark, heaving waste of waters excited his nerves and made him feel something of the mysterious and resistless forces around him. After all, he asked himself, how small the life of a man, or a hundred men, appeared to be amidst what seemed infinite wastes of ocean.

After dinner, in spite of the fact that the weather remained boisterous, he again went on deck. The sky had somewhat cleared now, and although there were still great black angry clouds, spaces of blue could be seen between them. Here the stars appeared, and shone with great brilliancy. Then the moon rose serene, majestic. Now it was hidden by a great storm cloud, and again it showed its silvery face in the clear spaces.

"Great heavens!" cried Dick, "how little a man knows of the world in which he lives, and what rot we often talk. The air all around me may be crowded with visitants from the unseen world! My dream last night may have an objective reality. Perhaps my father and my mother were there watching over me! Why not?"

It is said that atheists are bred in slums, and amidst brick walls and unlovely surroundings. It is also said that there are few sailors but who are believers—that the grandeur of the seas, that the wonder of great star spaces create a kind of spiritual atmosphere which makes it impossible for them to be materialists. Whether that is so I will not argue. This I know: Dick Faversham felt very near the unseen world as he leaned over the deck railings that night and gazed across the turbulent waters.

But this also must be said. The unseen world seemed to him not good, but evil. He felt as though there were dark, sinister forces around him— forces which were inimical to what he conceived to be best in him.

Before midnight he turned in, and no sooner did he lay his head on his pillow than he felt himself falling asleep. How long he slept he did not know. As far as he remembered afterwards, his sleep was dreamless. He only knew that he was awakened by a tremendous noise, and that the ship seemed to be crashing to pieces. Before he realised what had taken place he found himself thrown on the floor, while strange grating noises reached his ears. After that he heard wild shouts and despairing screams. Hastily putting on a coat over his night clothes, he rushed out to see what had happened; but all seemed darkness and confusion.

"What's the matter?" he cried, but received no answer.

Stumblingly he struggled towards the companion-way, where he saw a dark moving object.

"What's happened?" he gasped again.

"God only knows, except the vessel going down!"

"Vessel going down?"

"Yes; struck a mine or something!"

Even as the man spoke the ship seemed to be splitting asunder. Harsh, grating, bewildering noises were heard everywhere, while above the noises of timber and steel were to be faintly heard the cries of frantic women and excited men.

Then something struck him. He did not know what it was, but he felt a heavy blow on his head, and after that a great darkness fell upon him.

How long the darkness lasted he could not tell. It might have been minutes, it might have been hours; but he knew that he suddenly came to consciousness through the touch of icy-cold water. The cold seemed to pierce his very marrow, to sting him with exquisite pain. Then he was conscious that he was struggling in the open sea.

He had been a strong swimmer from early boyhood, and he struck out now. He had no idea which way to swim, but swim he did, heedless of direction or purpose. A kind of instinct forced him to get as far away as possible from the spot where he came to consciousness.

There was still a heavy sea running. He found himself lifted on the crest of huge waves, and again sinking in the depths. But he held on. He had a kind of instinct that he was doing something to save his life.

Presently his mind became clear. The past came vividly before him—the talk in the smoke-room, the wireless message——

Yes, he must live! Life held out so much to him. His immediate return to England was essential. Bidlake & Bilton had told him so.

Where were the other passengers? He had heard women's cries, the wild shouts of men, the creaking of timbers, the grating of steel; he had felt that the great steamship was being torn to pieces. But now there was nothing of this. There was nothing but the roar of waters—great, heaving, turbulent waters.

He still struggled on, but he knew that his strength was going. It seemed to him, too, as though some power was paralysing his limbs, sapping his strength. He still had the desire to save himself, to live; but his will power was not equal to his desire.

Oh, the sea was cruel, cruel! Why could not the waves cease roaring and rolling if only for five minutes? He would have time to rest then, to rest and regain his strength.

Still he struggled on. Again he felt himself carried on the crest of waves, and again almost submerged in the great troughs which seemed to be everywhere.

"O God, help me!" he thought at length. "My strength is nearly gone. I'm going to be drowned!"

A sinister power seemed to surround him—a power which took away hope, purpose, life. He thought of Count Romanoff, who had said there was nothing after death—that death was just a great black blank.

The thought was ghastly! To cease to be, to die there amidst the wild waste of the sea, on that lonely night! He could not bear the thought of it.

But his strength was ebbing away; his breath came in panting sobs; his heart found it difficult to beat. He was going to die.

Oh, if only something, someone would drive away the hateful presence which was following him, surrounding him! He could still struggle on then; he could live then. But no, a great black shadow was surrounding him, swallowing him up. Yes, and the ghastly thing was taking shape. He saw a face, something like the face of—no, he could liken it to no one he knew.

The waves still rolled on; but now he heard what seemed like wild, demoniacal laughter. Once, when a boy, he had seen Henry Irving in *Faust*; he saw the devils on the haunted mountain; he heard their hideous cries. And there was a ghastly, evil influence with him now. Did it mean that devils were there waiting to snatch his soul directly it left his body?

Then he felt a change. Yes, it was distinct, definite. There was a light, too—a pale, indistinct light, but still real, and as his tired eyes lifted he saw what seemed to be a cross of light shining down upon him from the clouds. What could it mean?

It seemed to him that the sinister presence was somehow losing power, that there was something, someone in the light which grew stronger.

Then a face appeared above him. At first it was unreal, intangible, shadowy; but it grew clearer, clearer. Where had he seen it before? Those great, tender, yearning eyes—where had he seen them? Then the form of a woman became outlined—a woman with arms outstretched. Her face, her lips, her eyes seemed to bid him hope, and it felt to him as though arms were placed beneath him—arms which bore him up.

It was all unreal, as unreal as the baseless fabric of a dream; and yet it was real, wondrously real.

"Help me! Save me!" he tried to say, but whether he uttered the words he did not know. He felt that his grip on life became weaker and weaker—then a still, small voice seemed to whisper, "The Eternal God is thy refuge, and underneath are the Everlasting Arms."

The roar of the waves grew less, and he knew no more.

Chapter IV
"The Enemy of Your Soul"

When again Dick Faversham regained something like consciousness he had a sensation of choking, of a hard struggle to breathe, which ended in partial failure.

He did not know where he was, but he had a sense of warmth, of restfulness. He thought he heard the ripple of waves on a sunlit shore, and of wide-spreading trees which grew close to the edge of the sea.

But it was all indistinct, unreal, and he did not care very much. He was trying to breathe, trying to overcome the awful sense of choking, and after a while, dazed, bewildered though he was, he felt his breath come easier and the weight on his chest grow lighter. But he was terribly tired—so tired that he had no desire to struggle, so languid that his very efforts to breathe were the result not of his own will, but of some claims of nature over which he had no control. He was just a piece of machinery, and that was all.

He felt himself going to sleep, and he was glad. He had no curiosity as to where he was, no desire to know how he came to be there, no remembrance of the past; he only knew that warm air wrapped him like a garment, and that he was deliciously tired and sleepy.

How long he slept he did not know, but presently when he woke he saw the sun setting in a blaze of glory. Scarcely a breath of wind stirred the warm, fragrant air, and all was silent save the lapping of the waves and the screaming of birds in the distance.

He sat up and looked around him. Great tropical trees grew in wild profusion, while gorgeous vegetation abounded. It was like some land of dreams.

Then suddenly memory asserted itself, and the past flashed before his mind. Everything became clear, vivid.

"I am saved! I am alive!" he exclaimed aloud.

Again he saw the wild upheaving sea; he felt himself struggling in the deep, while his strength, strength of body, of mind, and will were failing him. He recalled the dark, fearful presence that surrounded him, and then the coming of the light, and in the light the outline of a woman's form. Nothing would ever destroy that memory! The face, the lips, the eyes! No, he should never forget! And he had seen her arms outstretched, felt her arms placed beneath him—the arms that bore him up, brought him to safety.

"I was saved," he murmured—"saved by an angel!"

He was startled by the sound of a footstep, and, turning, he saw Romanoff, and with him came back something of the feeling that some evil presence surrounded him.

"That's right, Faversham. I was afraid, hours ago, that I should never bring you round, but at length you made good, and then, like a sensible fellow, went to sleep."

Romanoff spoke in the most matter-of-fact way possible, banishing the mere thought of angels or devils.

"Where are we? How did we get here?" gasped Faversham. Up to now he had not given a thought to the other passengers.

"Where are we? On an island in the Pacific, my dear fellow. How did we get here? After the accident—or whatever it was—the boats were lowered, and all hands were got away. I looked out for you, but could not find you. There was a great commotion, and it was easy to miss anyone in the darkness. I was among the last to leave the sinking vessel, and the boat was pretty full. We had got perhaps half a mile away from the scene of the wreck, when I saw someone struggling in the sea. It was by the purest chance possible that I saw. However, I managed to get hold of—what turned out to be you. You were nearly gone—I never thought you'd—live."

"But how did I get here?" asked Dick, "and—and where are the others?"

"It was this way," and Romanoff still continued to speak in the same matter-of-fact tones. "As I told you, the boat was jammed full—overweighted, in fact—so full that your weight was a bit of a danger. More than one said you were dead, and suggested that—that it was no use endangering the safety of the others. But I felt sure you were alive, so I held out against them."

"And then?" asked Dick. He was only giving half his mind to Romanoff's story; he was thinking of what he saw when he felt his strength leaving him.

"You see the bar out yonder?" and Romanoff pointed towards a ridge of foam some distance out at sea. "It's mighty rough there—dangerous to cross even when the sea is smooth; when it is rough—you can guess. I was holding you in my arms in order to—give room. The oarsmen were making for land, of course; you see, we had been many hours in a mere cockleshell, and this island promised safety. But in crossing the bar we were nearly upset, and I suddenly found myself in the sea with you in my arms. It was fairly dark, and I could not see the boat, but I was fortunate in getting you here. That's all."

"That's all?"

"Yes; what should there be else?"

"But the others?"

"Oh, I expect they've landed somewhere else on the island—sure to, in fact. But I've not looked them up. You see, I did not want to leave you."

"Then you—you've saved me?"

"Oh, that's all right, my dear fellow. You are here, and you are looking better every minute; that's the great thing. See, I've brought you some food—fruit. Delicious stuff. I've tried it. Lucky for us we got to this place."

Dick ate almost mechanically. He was still wondering and trying to square Romanoff's story with his own experiences. Meanwhile, Romanoff sat near him and watched him as he ate.

"How long have we been here?"

"Ten hours at least. Look, my clothes are quite dry. By Jove, I was thankful for the hot sun."

"You saved me!" repeated Dick. "I owe my life to you, and yet even now——"

"What, my dear fellow?"

"I thought I was saved in another way."

"Another way? How?"

Dick hesitated a few seconds, and then told him, while Romanoff listened with a mocking smile on his lips.

"Of course, you were delirious; it was pure hallucination."

"Was it? It was very real to me."

"Such things don't happen, my friend. After all, it was a very matter-of-fact, mundane affair. You were lucky, and I happened to see you—that's all—and if there was an angel—I'm it."

The laugh that followed was anything but angelic!

"I suppose that's it," and with a sigh Dick assented to Romanoff's explanation. Indeed, with this strange, matter-of-fact man by his side, he could not believe in anything miraculous. That smile on his face made it impossible.

"I don't know how to thank you," he said fervently. "You've done me the greatest service one man can do for another. I can't thank you enough, and I can never repay you, but if we ever get away from here, and I have an opportunity to serve you—all that I have shall be yours."

"I'll remember that," replied Romanoff quietly, "and I accept what you offer, my friend. Perhaps the time will come when I can take advantage of it."

"I hope you will—you must!"—Dick's mind had become excited—"and I want to tell you something," he continued, for he was strangely drawn towards his deliverer. "I want to live. I want to get back to England," he went on. "I have not told you before, but I feel I must now."

Whereupon he told him the story of the wireless message and what it possibly might mean.

Romanoff listened gravely, and Dick once again experienced that uncanny feeling that he was telling the other a story he already knew.

"Didn't I tell you on the boat that something big was in store for you?" he said, after many questions were asked and answered. "I shall certainly look you up when I go to England again, and it may be I shall be able to render you some—further service."

Night came on, and Dick slept. He was calm now and hopeful for the future. Romanoff had told him that as the island was on the great trade route it was impossible for them to be left there long. Vessels were always passing. And Dick trusted Romanoff. He felt he could do no other. He was so strong, so wise, so confident.

For hours he slept dreamlessly, but towards morning he had a vivid dream, and in his dream he again saw the face of the angel, just as he had seen on the wild, heaving sea.

"Listen to me," she said to him. "That man Romanoff is your enemy—the enemy of your soul. Do you realise it?—your soul. He is an emissary of the Evil One, and you must fight him. You must not yield to him. You will be tempted, but you must fight. He will be constantly near you, tempting you. He is your enemy, working for your downfall. If you give way to him you will be for ever lost!"

Dick heard her words quite plainly. He watched her face as she spoke, wondered at the yearning tenderness in her eyes.

"How can he be my enemy?" he asked. "He risked his life to save mine; he brought me to safety."

"No," she replied; "it was the arms of another that were placed beneath you, and bore you up. Don't you know whose arms? Don't you remember my face?"

"Who are you?" asked Dick.

Then, as it seemed to him in his dream, Romanoff came, and there was a battle between him and the angel, and he knew that they were fighting for him, for the possession of his soul.

He could see them plainly, and presently he saw the face of Romanoff gloat with a look of unholy joy. His form became more and more clearly outlined, while that of the angel became dimmer and dimmer. The evil power was triumphant. Then a change came. Above their heads he saw a luminous cross outlined, and he thought Romanoff's face and form became less and less distinct. But he was not sure, for they were drifting away from him farther and farther——

Again he saw the angel's face, and again she spoke. "You will be tempted—tempted," she said, "in many ways you will be tempted. But you will not be alone, for the angel of the Lord encampeth around them that fear Him. You will know me by the same sign. Always obey the angel."

He awoke. He was lying where he had gone to sleep hours before. He started to his feet and looked around him.

Near him, passing under the shadows of the great trees, he thought he saw a woman's face. It was the face he had seen on the outgoing vessel, the face he had seen when he was sinking in the deep waters, the face that had come to him in his dreams.

He was about to speak to her, to follow her, when he heard someone shouting.

"Faversham! Faversham!" It was Romanoff's voice. "Come quickly. We've hailed a vessel; our signal has been seen. Come to the other side of the island."

PART I
THE FIRST TEMPTATION

Chapter V
The Only Surviving Relative

Dick Faversham made his way to the offices of Messrs. Bidlake & Bilton, Solicitors, Lincoln's Inn Fields, with a fast-beating heart. He felt like a man whose fortune depended on the turn of a die. If the lawyers had sent him a message for the purpose he hoped, all was well; if not— —And for the hundredth time he considered the pros and cons of the matter.

His rescue from the island had turned out to be one of the prosiest matters imaginable. The captain of an English-bound steamer had seen the signals made from the island, and had sent boats. Thus Dick was saved without difficulty. There were others who had a similar fortune, but Dick had no chance to speak with them. No sooner did he reach the steamer than he was taken ill, and remained ill during the whole of the homeward voyage.

After he reached Plymouth he began to recover rapidly, but he found on making inquiries that all who were rescued from the island had disembarked at the western seaport. This was very disappointing to him, as he wanted to make inquiries concerning the manner of their escape. Of Romanoff he neither heard nor saw anything. No one knew anything of him on the steamer, neither was he known to board it.

Dick was both glad and sorry because of this. Glad because, although Romanoff possessed a strange fascination for him, he had never been altogether comfortable in his presence. The man repelled him even while he fascinated him, and he felt relieved that he was not on board. On the other hand, he was sorry, because he had a feeling that this strange, saturnine man might have been a great help to him in his peculiar circumstances.

"It may be all a will-o'-the-wisp fancy," he reflected as he walked along Fleet Street towards the Law Courts, "and yet it must mean something."

His mind was in a whirl of bewilderment, for in spite of Romanoff's explanation he could not drive from his mind the belief that his experiences after the vessel was wrecked had been real. Indeed, there were times when he was *sure* that he had seen an angel's form hovering while he was struggling in the sea, sure that he felt strong arms upholding him.

"At any rate, this is real," he said to himself as he turned into Lincoln's Inn Fields. "I am here on dry land. I wear a suit of clothes which Captain Fraser gave me, and I have twenty-four shillings in my pocket. Whatever happens, I will at the first opportunity pay the captain for his kindness."

He entered the office and gave his name.

"Do you wish to see Mr. Bidlake or Mr. Bilton?" asked the clerk.

"Either, or both," replied Dick.

"Would you state your business, please?" The clerk did not seem to be sure of him.

"I will state my business to your principals," replied Dick. "Please take in my name."

When the clerk returned his demeanour was changed. He was obsequious and anxious to serve.

"Will you come this way, please, sir?" he said. "Mr. Bilton is in Mr. Bidlake's room, and — —"

He did not finish the sentence, for the door of an office opened and a man of about fifty years of age appeared.

"Come in, Mr. Faversham," he invited. "Do you know, I've been on tenterhooks for days about you."

"I landed at Tilbury only a few hours ago."

"Is that so? But it was this way: we, of course, heard that your boat had been mined, and we also heard that a number of the passengers and crew were rescued; but news about you was contradictory. In one list of the saved your name appeared, while in another you were not mentioned. Tell us all about it."

"Another time," replied Dick. He was in a fever to know why this very respectable firm of lawyers should have sent a wireless to him.

"Yes, yes, of course," assented Mr. Bidlake, leading the way to an inner room. "Bilton, you may as well come too. My word, Mr. Faversham, I *am* glad to see you."

Dick felt light-hearted. Mr. Bidlake would not receive him in this fashion had there not been important reasons for doing so.

"Well now, to come to business right away," said Mr. Bidlake the moment they were seated—"you got my message?"

"Twenty-four hours before I was wrecked," replied Dick.

"Just so. You'll tell us all about that presently. My word, you must have had a terrible time! But that's by the way. You got my message, and therefore you know that your uncle, Mr. Charles Faversham, is dead?"

Dick nodded. He tried to appear calm, but his heart was thumping like a sledge-hammer.

"Of course, you know that Mr. Charles Faversham was a bachelor, and—by the way, Mr. Bilton, will you find the Faversham papers? You've had them in hand."

"Yes, my uncle was a bachelor," repeated Dick as Mr. Bidlake hesitated.

"You've never had any communications with him?"

"Never."

"A peculiar man. A genius for business, but, all the same, a peculiar man. However, I think it's all plain enough."

"What is plain enough?"

"Have you the papers, Bilton? That's good. Yes, I have everything here. This is the last will of Mr. Faversham—a plain, straightforward will in many ways, although slightly involved in others. However——"

The lawyer untied some tape, and began scanning some documents.

"However what?" asked Dick, who by this time was almost beside himself with impatience.

"By the way, you can easily put your hand on your birth certificate, as well as the death certificate of your father, I suppose?"

"Quite easily."

"Of course you can. The fact that I have known you for some time makes things far easier, far less—complicated. Otherwise a great many formalities would have to be gone into before—in short, Mr. Richard Faversham, I have great pleasure in congratulating you on being the heir to a fine fortune—a *very* fine fortune."

Mr. Bidlake smiled benignly.

"My uncle's fortune?"

"Your uncle's estate—yes. He was a very rich man."

"But—but——" stammered Dick.

"Yes, yes, of course, you wish for some details. This is the position. Your uncle made a will—a rather peculiar will in some ways."

"A peculiar will?" queried Dick.

"Yes—as you know, I did a great deal of work for him; but there were others. Triggs and Wilcox attended to some things, while Mortlake and Stenson also did odd jobs; but I have made all inquiries, and this is the last will he made. He wrote it himself, and it was duly witnessed. I myself have interviewed the witnesses, and there is no flaw anywhere, although, of course, this document is by no means orthodox."

"Orthodox? I don't understand."

"I mean that it is not in legal form. As a matter of fact, it is utterly informal."

"You mean that there is some doubt about it?"

"On no, by no means. It would stand good in any court of law, but, of course, all such documents are loosely worded. In case of a lawsuit it would offer occasion for many wordy battles," and Mr. Bidlake smacked his lips as though he would enjoy such an experience. "But here is the will in a nutshell," he went on. "You see, his own brother died many years ago, while your father, his stepbrother, died—let me see—how long ago? But you know. I need not go into that. As you may have heard, his sister Helen married and had children; she was left a widow, and during her widowhood she kept house for your uncle; so far so good. This is the will: all his property, excepting some small sums which are plainly stated, was left equally to his sister Helen's children, and to their heirs on their decease."

"But where do I come in?" gasped Dick.

"Here, my dear sir. There is a clause in the will, which I'll read: 'Should not my sister Helen's children be alive at the time of my decease, all my property is to be equally divided between my nearest surviving relatives.' Now, here," went on the lawyer, "we see the foolishness of a man making his own will, especially a man with such vast properties as Mr. Charles Faversham had. First of all, suppose his sister Helen's children married and had children who were alive at the time of Mr. Charles Faversham's death. These children might not inherit a penny if his sister's children had been dead. Again, take the term 'equally divided.' Don't you see what a bill of costs might be run up in settling that? What is an equal division? Who is to assess values on an estate that consists of shipping interests, lands, mines, and a host of other things? Still, we need not trouble about this as it happens. We have inquired into the matter, and we find that your Aunt Helen's children are dead, and that none of them was married."

"Then—then——"

"You are the nearest surviving relative, my dear sir, and not only that—you are the only surviving relative of the late Mr. Charles Faversham of Wendover Park, Surrey."

Dick Faversham still appeared outwardly calm, although his brain was whirling with excitement. The words, 'shipping interests, lands, mines, and a host of other things,' were singing in his ears. And he—*he* was heir to it all! But was there some doubt about it? Was everything so definite as the lawyer had stated?

"I believe my Aunt Helen had three children," Dick said after a silence—"two girls and a boy, or two boys and a girl, I have forgotten which. Do you mean to say they are all dead?"

"Certain. Directly on Mr. Faversham's death I went into the matter. Two of the children died in England. The third, a son, died in Australia. I was very anxious about that, and spent quite a little fortune in cablegrams. Still, I got everything cleared up satisfactorily."

"Tell me how." Dick was very anxious about this. It seemed to him as the crux of the whole question.

"It was naturally a little difficult," and Mr. Bidlake smiled complacently. "Australia is some little distance away, eh? But I managed it. For one thing, an old articled clerk of mine went to Melbourne some years ago, and succeeded in getting a practice there. He was very anxious to oblige me, and got on the track almost immediately. Fortunately for us, the death of Mr. Anthony Riggleton was somewhat notorious."

"And Mr. Anthony Riggleton was my Aunt Helen's son?" asked Dick.

"Exactly. He was not a young man of high character, and I am given to understand that Mr. Charles Faversham threatened more than once, when he was in England, never to leave him a penny. However, he paid his debts, gave him a sum of money, and told him to go away and never to return again during his life. It seems, too, that Mr. Anthony Faversham Riggleton considerably reformed himself during the time he was in Australia, so much so that favourable reports were sent to his uncle concerning his conduct.

That, I imagine, accounts for his inclusion in the will. Whether he went wild again, I don't know, but it is certain that he met his death in a very suspicious way. It seems that he and some other men met in a house of bad repute not far from Melbourne, and in a brawl of some sort he came to an untimely end. His body was found more than twenty-four hours after his death, in the harbour at Melbourne. Evidently the affair was most unsavoury. His face was much bashed. A pistol-shot had passed through his brain, and there were some knife-stabs in his body."

"And his companions?" asked Dick.

"They had cleared out, and left no traces behind. You see, they had plenty of time to do so before the police were able to get to work. According to the latest reports I have heard, there is not the slightest chance of finding them."

"But the body—was it identified?"

"It was. Letters were found on the body addressed to Mr. Anthony Faversham Riggleton, and there were also private papers on his person which left no doubt. Added to this, the evidence of the cashier and of a clerk of the Bank of Australia was most explicit. You see, he had called at the bank on the morning of the night of the brawl, and drew what little money he had. When the body was brought to the mortuary, both the cashier and the clerk swore it was that of the man who had called for the money."

"That was settled definitely, then?"

"Just so. Oh, you can make your mind quite easy. Directly I got news of Mr. Charles Faversham's death I naturally took steps to deal with his estate, and I assured myself of your interest in the matter before seeking to communicate with you. I would not have sent you that wireless without practical certainty. Since then I have received newspapers from Melbourne giving details of the whole business."

"And my Aunt Helen?" asked Dick.

"She died before the will was made. I gather that her death caused him to make the new will—the one we are discussing—in a hurry."

"And my two other cousins?" Dick persisted. He wanted to assure himself that there could be no shadow of doubt.

The lawyer smiled. "Things do happen strangely sometimes," he said. "If anyone had told me at the time this will was made that you would come in for the whole estate, I should have laughed. There were three healthy people in your way. And yet, so it is. They are dead. There is not a shadow of doubt about it."

"But didn't my uncle know of their decease?"

"I can't tell you that. He was a strange man. As I have said, he had a regular genius for making money, and he lived for his business. He simply revelled in it; not because he cared about money as such, but because the accumulation of wealth fascinated him. He was, as you know, unmarried, and up to the time of his making this will, his sister, of whom he seemed to have been fond, kept house for him. But he would not have her children around him. He gave them large sums of money, but he had no personal knowledge of them. It is quite probable, therefore, that he, being in failing health for more than a year before his death, would have no knowledge that they died some time before he did. You would understand if you had known him. A most eccentric man."

Dick reflected a few seconds. The way seemed perfectly plain, and yet everything seemed intangible, unreal.

"In proof of that," went on the lawyer, "he did not tell either Mr. Bilton or myself that he had made this will. He simply gave a letter to the housekeeper he had secured after his sister's death, and told her that this letter was to be given to me at his decease. That letter," went on Mr. Bidlake, "contained the key of a safe and instructions to me to deal with the contents of the safe immediately after his death. Of course, I opened the safe, and among the first things I found was this will. The rest I have explained to you."

"And you say I am very wealthy?" asked Dick almost fearfully. Even yet it seemed too good to be true.

"Wealthy!" and the lawyer smiled. "Wealthy, my dear sir! I cannot yet tell you *how* wealthy. But if a controlling interest in one of the most prosperous shipping companies in the world, if the principal holding in one of our great banks, if landed estates in more than three counties, if important mining interests, if hundreds of houses in London and hosts of other things mean great wealth—then I can truly say that you are a very wealthy man. Of course, I cannot as yet estimate the value of the whole estate, but the death duties will make a nice fortune—a *very* nice fortune. Still, if you decide to entrust your legal business to us, as we hope you will, we shall be able in a few weeks to give you an approximate idea of what you are worth."

"Of course I will do that," replied Dirk hastily; "naturally there is no question about the matter. That must be settled here and now."

"Thank you," said Mr. Bidlake. "Naturally Mr. Bilton and myself appreciate this mark of your confidence. You may depend that neither of us will spare himself in order to serve you. Eh, Mr. Bilton?"

"Exactly," replied Mr. Bilton. It was the only word he had as yet spoken throughout the interview.

"And now," said Dick, "I want your advice."

"Our advice? Certainly. What about?"

"Well, owing to the wreck, I am at this moment in borrowed clothes. I have only a few shillings in my pocket— —"

"My dear sir," interrupted the lawyer, "that presents no difficulties. Let me give you an open cheque for two hundred—five hundred—pounds right away. Naturally, too, you will want to get clothes. You lost everything in the—the wreck; naturally you did. I had almost forgotten such things in the—the bigger matter. But that's all right. I have a private sitting-room here, and my tailor would be only too glad to come here right away. A most capable man. He would rig you out, temporarily, in a few hours, and afterwards— —"

"That's all right," interrupted Dick; "but what next?"

"Take possession at once, my dear sir—at once."

"But I don't want anything to get into the papers."

"Certainly not—if we can help it. And I think we can. Shall I ring up my tailors? Yes?" And Mr. Bidlake took a telephone receiver into his hand. "That's all right," he added two minutes later. "Hucknell will be here in less than half an hour, and you can trust him to fix you up and tide you over the next few days. Yes, he will be glad to do so—very glad. Terrible business this industrial unrest, isn't it? I'm afraid it's going to take some settling. Of course, it's world wide, but I say, thank goodness our people have got more sense and more balance than those poor Russians."

The words were simple enough, and the expression was almost a commonplace, but Dick Faversham felt a sudden pain at his heart. He thought of the dark, mysterious man who claimed kinship with the great Russian House of Romanoff, and in a way he could not understand; the thought seemed to take away from the joyous excitement which filled his being at that moment. He wished he had never seen, never heard of Count Romanoff.

With an effort he shook off the cloud.

"You suggest that I go to Wendover Park at once?"

"Yes, say to-morrow morning. It is your right; in a way, it's your duty. The property is undeniably yours."

"Would—would you—could you go with me?" stammered Dick.

"I was on the point of suggesting it myself, my dear sir. Yes, I could go to-morrow morning."

"Are there any servants there, or is the house empty?" asked Dick. Again he had a sense of unreality.

"Most of the servants are there," replied the lawyer. "I thought it best to keep them. I am not sure about a chauffeur, though. I have an idea I discharged him. But it can easily be managed. The housekeeper whom your uncle engaged on your aunt's death is there, and she, it appears, has a husband. Rather a capable man. He can get a chauffeur. I'll ring up right away, and give instructions. You don't mind, do you?"

"It's awfully good of you," Dick assured him. "I shall feel lost without you."

At half-past one Dick accompanied Mr. Bidlake to his club for lunch, attired in a not at all badly fitting ready-made suit of clothes, which Mr. Hucknell had secured for him, and spent the afternoon with the lawyer discussing the new situation.

"Nine-thirty-five Victoria," said Mr. Bidlake to him as he left him that night.

"I'll be there."

Dick went to his hotel like a man in a dream. Even yet everything was unreal to him. He had received assurances from one of the most trustworthy and respectable lawyers in London that his position was absolutely safe, and yet he felt no firm foundation under his feet.

"I expect it's because I've seen nothing yet," he reflected. "When I go down to-morrow and get installed as the owner of everything, I shall see things in a new light."

Chapter VI
Wendover Park

The end of April had now come, and a tinge of green had crept over what in many respects is one of the loveliest counties in England. The train in which Mr. Bidlake and Dick Faversham sat had left Redhill and was passing through a rich, undulating countryside.

"You feel a bit excited, I expect?" and Mr. Bidlake looked up from his copy of *The Times*.

"Just a bit."

"You'll soon get over your excitement, although, of course, you'll find the change very great. A rich man has many responsibilities."

"If I remember aright, there are several other big houses within a few miles of Wendover Park? Was my uncle on good terms with his neighbours?"

The lawyer coughed. "He did not go much into society. As I told you, he was a very eccentric man."

Dick was quick to notice the tone in which the other spoke. "You mean that he was not well received?"

"I mean that he lived his own life. Mr. Faversham was essentially a business man, and—and perhaps he could not understand the attitude of the old county families. Besides, feeling against him was rather strong when he bought Wendover Park."

"Why?"

"I daresay you'll learn all about it in time. Enough to say now that Sir Guy Wendover, the previous owner, was in money difficulties, and the feeling was that your uncle took advantage of them in order to get hold of the place. Personally I don't pay much attention to such stories; but undoubtedly they affected your uncle's position. Possibly they may affect yours—for a time." The lawyer appeared to utter the last sentence as an afterthought.

Presently the train stopped at a wayside station, where the two alighted. The sun was now high in the heavens, and the birds were singing gaily. Wooded hills sloped up from the station, while westward was a vast panorama of hill and dale.

"I don't think you could find a fairer sight in all England," remarked Mr. Bidlake. "Ah, that's right. I see a motor-car is waiting for us."

Dick felt as thought a weight rolled from his shoulders the moment he stood beneath the open sky. Yes, this was glorious! The air was laden with the perfume of bursting life. The chorus of the birds exhilarated him; the sight of the rich loamy meadows, where lambkins sported and cows fed lazily, made him feel that he was not following some chimera of the mind, but tangible realities.

A chauffeur touched his cap. "Mr. Faversham and Mr. Bidlake, sir?" he inquired.

A few minutes later the car was moving swiftly along beautiful country lanes, the like of which only a few English counties can show. Yes, Dick had to admit it. Beautiful as he thought the whole district to be when cycling through it years before, he had no idea it was like this. Every corner they turned revealed new loveliness. All nature seemed bent on giving him a great welcome to his new home.

They had covered perhaps half the journey between the station and the house when the chauffeur jammed his foot on the brake suddenly and brought the car to a standstill. In front of them stood a small two-seater, by the open bonnet of which stood a young lady with hand uplifted. Evidently something had gone wrong with her machine, and the lane at this point was not wide enough for them to pass.

Dick immediately alighted.

"I am awfully sorry to inconvenience you," protested the girl, "but my engine has stopped, and, try as I may, I can't get it to start again."

Her face was slightly flushed, partly with her endeavours to start the engine and partly with impatience; but this did not detract from her more than usually handsome appearance. For she was handsome; indeed, Dick thought he had never seen such a striking girl. And this was no wonder. It is only rare that nature produces such a perfect specimen of young womanhood as he saw that morning—perfect, that is, in face and form, perfect in colouring, in stature, in bearing. She was a brunette—great black flashing eyes, full red lips, raven-black hair, skin suffused with the glow of buoyant health. More than ordinarily tall, she was shaped like a Juno, and moved with all the grace and freedom of an athlete.

"Help the lady, my man," said Mr. Bidlake to the chauffeur.

"Sorry, sir," replied the man, "but I don't know anything about engines. I've only just learnt to drive. You see, sir, Mrs. Winkley didn't quite know what to do when— —"

"All right," interrupted Dick, with a laugh; "perhaps I can help you."

"If you only could," laughed the girl. "I haven't had the thing long, but it never went wrong until to-day. I know how to drive pretty well, but as for understanding the engine, I'm a mere baby."

She had a frank, pleasant voice, and laughed as she spoke, revealing perfect teeth.

Dick, who had quite a gift for mechanism, quickly found some tools, and commenced testing the sparking-plugs like a man conversant with his work.

"I'll have to take off my coat if you'll excuse me," he said presently. "I see you start the thing on a battery, and have no magneto. I'm sorry I don't know this class of car well, but I think I can see what's the matter."

"What is it? Do tell me," she cried, with an eager laugh. "I've been studying motor manuals and all that sort of thing ever since I commenced to drive, but diagrams always confuse me."

"The distributor seems to be wrong, and some wires have become disconnected. Have you been held up long?"

"Oh, a quarter of an hour—more."

"And running the battery all the time?"

"I'm afraid so."

"You must be careful or your battery'll run out of electricity; that would mean your being hung up for two days."

"They told me that at the garage a little time ago. But what must I do?" and she laughed at him pleasantly.

"If she doesn't start at once, get someone to adjust the parts. There, I wonder if she'll go now."

He touched a switch, and the engine began to run.

"She seems all right," he said, after watching the moving mass of machinery for some seconds.

"Oh, you are good—and—thank you ever so much."

"It's been quite a pleasure," replied Dick, putting on his coat. "It was lucky I came by."

"It was indeed; but look at your hands. They are covered with oil. I *am* sorry."

"Nothing to be sorry for. Oil breaks no bones. Besides, I shall be able to wash them in a few minutes."

"You are not going far, then?"

"Only to Wendover Park. Do you know it?"

"Know it! Why— —" She checked herself suddenly, and Dick thought she seemed a little confused. "But I must be going now. Thank you again."

She got into the car, and in a few seconds was out of sight.

"Remarkably handsome young lady, isn't she?" remarked Mr. Bidlake. "Do you know who she is?" he asked the chauffeur.

"Lady Blanche Huntingford, sir," replied the chauffeur.

"Whew!" whistled Mr. Bidlake.

"Anybody special?" asked Dick.

The lawyer smiled. "The incident is decidedly interesting," he replied. "First, she is cousin to Sir Guy Wendover who used to own Wendover Park, and second, she is the daughter of Lord Huntingford, the proudest and most exclusive aristocrat in Surrey."

"No? By Jove, she is handsome!"

"It is said that the Huntingfords rule Social Surrey. If they take you up, your social status is assured; if they boycott you— —" and the lawyer shrugged his shoulders.

Dick was silent a few seconds. Evidently he was thinking deeply. "Isn't she glorious?" he cried presently. "I never saw such a dazzling girl. Did you notice her eyes—her complexion? I—I wouldn't have missed it for anything."

The lawyer did not reply. Perhaps he had reasons for his silence.

The car dashed on for another mile, and then Dick gave a cry of delight.

"That's it, isn't it?"

"Yes; that's it."

They were looking at a lovely old mansion which stood on the slope of a hill. Stretching away from it were fine park-lands, and beyond these were wide-stretching woods. Looked at on that fair spring day, it was indeed a place to be proud of, to rejoice in.

"I never dreamt it was so fine!" gasped Dick.

"One of the finest places in England," was the lawyer's complacent reply.

Dick looked like one fascinated. It appealed to and satisfied him altogether.

"It's old, isn't it?"

"Three hundred years. It is said that the gardens are a wonder."

The car passed through some heavily wrought gates, and then rolled under an avenue of old trees. Dick could not speak; the thought of possessing such a place made him dumb. A few minutes later they drew up before the main entrance.

Dick was the first to leap out. He was eager to enter, to claim possession, to examine every nook and corner of his new home. He put his foot on the bottom step leading to the door, and then stopped suddenly. He felt himself rooted to the ground, felt afraid to move.

"I congratulate you again," said the lawyer. "I feel proud that I have the privilege to— —"

"Don't you see? There! Don't you see?" gasped Dick.

"See?" repeated the lawyer. "Of course I see one of the most beautiful houses in England."

"Yes, but nothing else?" he asked excitedly.

"What do you mean?" queried the lawyer.

But Dick did not reply. Although the lawyer had seen nothing, he saw in dim outline the face and form which had appeared to him when he was sinking in the turbulent waters of the Indian Ocean. Was this a warning that trouble was to overwhelm him again?

Dick Faversham had no doubts. Whatever he might think later, he was at that time certain of what he saw. The sun was shining brightly, and there was nothing in the various objects by which he was surrounded to suggest the supernatural, and yet he saw the face of the angel. She seemed to be hovering over the steps which led to the main entrance of the house, and for the moment she looked as though she would forbid his entrance. But only for the moment. Slowly she faded away, slowly he lost sight of her, and by the time the servant, who had evidently seen the approach of the car, had reached the door she had gone.

But he was sure he had seen her. The form he had seen hovering over him on the wild, turbulent sea was plainly visible to him at the door of this old Surrey mansion. The face, too, could not be mistaken. The same calm, benign expression, the same tender mouth. Goodness, purity, guardianship, all found their expression in those features. But there was something more. The eyes which had riveted his attention and haunted his memory for months seemed to convey something different to him now from what they had then. There was still the same yearning gaze, the same melting tenderness, but there was something more. They seemed to suggest fear, warning. Dick Faversham felt as though she wanted to tell him something, to warn him against some unknown danger. It is true the feeling was indefinite and difficult to put into words; but it was there. She might, while not forbidding him to enter the house which had so unexpectedly come into his possession, be trying to tell him of dangers, of possible calamity.

"And do you say that you can see—that—that you saw nothing?" he almost gasped.

"I can see a great deal," replied Mr. Bidlake. "I can see one of the loveliest scenes in England. I can see you standing at the entrance of—but what do you mean? You look pale—frightened. Aren't you well?"

Dick opened his mouth to tell what he had seen, but he checked himself. Somehow the thought of opening his heart to this matter-of-fact lawyer seemed like sacrilege. He would not understand. He would tell him, just as Romanoff had told him weeks before, that his mind was unbalanced by the experiences through which he had passed, that the natural excitement caused by the news he had heard were too much for him, and caused him to lose his mental balance.

"Yes, I am quite well, thank you."

"Well, what do you mean? What do you think you saw?"

At that moment the door opened, and the housekeeper, who had hurried to meet them, appeared, and the lawyer did not listen to his stammering reply.

"Good-day, Mr. Bidlake," smiled the housekeeper. "I am glad you got here all right. Winkley had quite a difficulty in getting a chauffeur. I hope the one provided was satisfactory?"

"It's all right, Mrs. Winkley," and the lawyer was very patronising as he spoke; "the man brought us here safely. This," and he turned towards Dick, "is Mr. Richard Faversham, the new owner of—hem—Wendover Park, and your new—master."

"Indeed, sir," and Mrs. Winkley turned and looked nervously towards Dick, "I hope you'll be very—happy here, sir. I bid you welcome, sir."

Dick smiled with frank pleasure and shook hands—a familiarity which pleased the housekeeper, but not the lawyer.

"You got my letter, Mrs. Winkley?" Mr. Bidlake said hurriedly.

"Yes, sir, also your telephone message yesterday. Wendover Park is a lovely place, Mr. Faversham."

"It is, indeed, Mrs. Winkley. This Surrey air has given me an appetite, too."

Dick was so nervous that he hardly knew what he was saying. As he glanced around the spacious hall and tried to realise that it was his own, and as he called to mind that for the last mile he had been passing through his own property, it seemed to be too wonderful to be true.

"Yes, the air is very good, and I am glad you are hungry. Lunch will be ready in half an hour. I have prepared a bedroom for you, Mr. Faversham. I have assumed you are—staying here?"

"Rather!" and Dick laughed as he spoke. "You must excuse me if I'm a little abrupt, Mrs. Winkley. You see, I imagine it will take me some little time to settle down to the new order of things."

"I think I understand; it must be a wonderful experience for you. But I think you'll find everything all right. I have taken great care of everything since the late Mr. Faversham died. It's all just as he left it. No doubt you'll want to look over the house?"

"Presently, Mrs. Winkley; but, first of all, I want to come to an understanding with you. I am a bachelor, and I don't think I have a relation in the world, so, for a time, I—shall make no changes in the place at all. What I mean to say is, that I hope you'll continue to be my housekeeper, and—and look after me generally. Mr. Bidlake has said all sorts of good things about you, so much so that I shall regard myself very fortunate if—if you'll remain in your present position."

Dick didn't know at all why he said this, except that he had a feeling that something of the sort was expected from him.

"I'm sure it's very kind of you to say so, sir," and Mrs. Winkley smiled radiantly. "Of course I've been a little bit anxious, not knowing what kind of—of gentleman the new owner would be, or what plans he might have. But, if you think I'll suit you, sir, I'll do my utmost to make you comfortable and look after your interests. I was housekeeper to Dr. Bell of Guildford when the late Mr. Faversham's sister died, and——"

"Yes, I've heard about that," interrupted Dick. "I'm sure he was lucky to get you."

"I did my best for him, sir, and he never grumbled. I lived in these parts as a girl, so I can get you plenty of references as to the respectability of my family."

"I'm sure you can," Dick assented. He was glad that Mrs. Winkley was of the superior servant order rather than some superior person who had pretensions to being a fine lady. "By the way, of course you know the house well?"

"Know the house well?" repeated Mrs. Winkley. She was not quite sure that she understood him.

"Yes; know all the rooms?" laughed Dick nervously.

"Why, certainly, sir. I know every room from the garret to the cellar," replied Mrs. Winkley wonderingly.

"And there are no ghosts, are there?"

"Ghosts, sir? Not that I ever heard of."

"I was only wondering. It's an old house, and I was thinking that there might be a family ghost."

Mrs. Winkley shook her head. "Nothing of the sort, sir, to my knowledge. Wait a minute, though; I did hear when I was a girl that the elm grove was haunted. There's a lake down there, and there was a story years ago that a servant who had drowned herself there used to wander up and down the grove wringing her hands on Michaelmas Eve."

"And where is the elm grove?"

"It's away towards the North Lodge. You wouldn't see it the way you came, and it's hidden from here."

"But the house? There's no legend that that has ever been haunted?"

"No, sir. I suppose some of the Wendovers were very wild generations ago, but I never heard that any of their spirits ever came back again."

Mrs. Winkley was pleased that her new master kept talking so long, although she came to the conclusion that he was somewhat eccentric.

"Of course, it was foolish of me to ask," Dick said somewhat awkwardly; "but the thought struck me. By the way, how long did you say it was to lunch-time?"

"Not quite half an hour, sir," replied Mrs. Winkley, looking at an old eight-day clock. "I'll speak to the cook and get it pushed forward as fast as possible. Perhaps you'd like a wash, sir? I'll show you to your room, if you would."

"Thank you. After that I—I think, Mr. Bidlake, I'd like to go into the gardens."

He was afraid he was making a bad impression upon his housekeeper, and he was angry with himself for not acting in a more natural manner. But he seemed to be under a strange influence. Although the thought of the supernatural had left him, his experience of a few minutes before doubtless coloured his mind.

A few minutes later they were out in the sunlight again, and they had scarcely reached the gardens when a man of about fifty years of age made his way towards them.

"Good morning, sir," he said, with a strong Scotch accent. "Have I the honour to speak to the new master?"

"Yes; my name is Faversham."

"I'm M'Neal, your second gardener, sir. I thought when I saw you I'd make bold to speak, sir. I've been here for thirty years, sir, and have always borne a good character."

"I've no doubt you have," laughed Dick. "You look it."

"Thank you, sir. I gave satisfaction to the late Mr. Faversham, and to Sir Guy Wendover before him, and I hope— —"

"That we shall get on well together. Of course we shall. I like the look of you."

He felt better now. The sight of the broad expanse of the park and the smell of the sweet, pure air made him light-hearted again.

"Indeed," he continued, "I may as well tell you right away that I intend to keep everybody that was here in my uncle's days. You can tell the others that."

"Thank you, sir. But I'd like to remark that this war has made food dear."

"I'll bear that in mind; you'll not find me unjust. All who serve me shall be well paid."

"We've all done our best, sir," persisted M'Neal, who was somewhat of a character, "but I'll not deny that we shall all be the better for a master. Personally I'm not satisfied with the way things are looking."

"No? I thought they looked beautiful."

"Ah, but nothing to what they can look. We are, as you may say, in a kind of between time now. We've not planted out the beds, although we've prepared them. If you'll— —"

"Of course I will," Dick interrupted him, with a laugh, "but you must give me time before making definite promises."

"If I might show you around," suggested M'Neal, "I think I could explain— —"

"Later, later," laughed Dick, moving away. "Mr. Bidlake, will you come over here with me? I want to speak to you privately."

"Do you know," Mr. Bidlake told him, "that your uncle discharged M'Neal several times during the time he lived here?"

"Why?"

"Because he followed him like a dog whenever he came into the grounds, and insisted on talking to him. He said the fellow gave him no rest."

"But why did he take him on again?"

"He didn't. But M'Neal took no notice of the discharges. He always turned up on the following morning, and went on with his work as though nothing had happened."

"And my uncle paid him his wages?"

"Yes. You see, the fellow is as faithful as a dog, although he's a nuisance. My word, what a view!"

The lawyer made this exclamation as a turn in the path revealed a landscape they had not hitherto seen. It was one of those stretches of country peculiar to that part of Surrey, and as Dick looked he did not wonder at the lawyer's enthusiasm. Beyond the park, which was studded with giant oaks, he saw a rich, undulating country. Here and there were farmsteads nestling among the trees; again he saw stretches of woodland, while in the distance rose fine commanding hills. The foliage had far from reached its glory, but the tinge of green which was creeping over every hedgerow and tree contained a promise, and a charm that no poet could describe. And the whole scene was all bathed in spring sunlight, which the birds, delighting in, made into a vast concert hall.

"My word, it is ripping!" cried Dick.

"It's glorious! it's sublime!" cried the lawyer. "You are a fortunate man, Mr. Richard Faversham. Do you know, sir, that all you can see is yours?"

"All mine?" Dick almost gasped.

"Yes, all this and much more."

For the first time Dick had a real feeling of possession, and something to which he had hitherto been a stranger entered his life. Up to now he had been poor. His life, ever since his father died, had been a struggle. He had dreamed dreams and seen visions, only to be disappointed. In spite of ambition, endeavour, determination, everything to which he had set his hand had failed him. But now, as if some fabled genii had come to his aid, fortune had suddenly poured her favours into his lap.

And here was the earnest of it!

This glorious countryside, containing farms, houses, villages, and wide-spreading lands, was his. All his! Gratified desire made his heart beat wildly. At last life was smiling and joyous. What a future he would have! With wealth like his, nothing would be impossible!

"Yes, and much more," repeated the lawyer. "On what chances a man's fortunes turn."

"What do you mean?" asked Dick, who scarce knew what he was saying.

"Only this," said Mr. Bidlake. "If that fellow had not been killed in a drunken brawl, none of this would be yours. As it is, you are one of the most fortunate men in England."

"Yes, by Jove, I am."

The lawyer looked at his watch. "Excuse me, Mr. Faversham, but it is lunch-time, and I must leave you at five o'clock."

"I'm sorry you can't stay a few days."

"Impossible, my dear sir, much as I'd like to. But I've made a little programme for you this afternoon, if it is quite convenient to you."

"Yes?" queried Dick.

"Yes; I've arranged for your steward, your head gamekeeper, and the other principal men on the estate to call here. I thought you might like to see them. There, I hear the lunch-gong."

Dick went back to the house like a man in a dream.

Chapter VII
Lady Blanche makes her Appearance

At six o'clock that evening Dick Faversham was alone. He had had interviews with his steward, his bailiff, his gamekeeper, his forester, his head gardener, and his head stableman, and now he was left to himself. Mr. Bidlake, after promising to come again in three days, had gone back to London, while the others had each gone to their respective homes to discuss the new master of Wendover Park and the changes which would probably take place.

Dick had also gone over the house, and had taken note of the many features of his new dwelling-place. He had examined the library, the billiard-room, the dancing-room, the minstrels' gallery, the banqueting hall, and the many other apartments belonging to this fine old mansion. Evidently many of the rooms had for years been unused, but, as Mrs. Winkley had said, everything was "in perfect condition."

His uncle belonged to that order of men who could not bear to let anything deteriorate for lack of attention, and he had spent his money freely. In a way, too, Charles Faversham had a sense of fitness. In all the improvements he had made, he saw to it that the character and spirit of the old place should in no way be disturbed. Thus, while every room was hygienic, and every fireplace fitted according to the most modern ideas, the true character of everything was maintained. Electric light was installed, but not a single fitting was out of accord with the age of the building. Modern science had in everything been perfectly blended with the spirit of the men who had erected this grand old pile centuries before.

And Dick felt it all. He was enough of an artist to realise that nothing was out of place, that it was a home to rejoice in, to be proud of. If John Ruskin had been alive, and had accompanied him on his tour of inspection, there was little that the author of *The Seven Lamps of Architecture* would have found fault with.

Most of the furniture, too, was old, and had belonged to the Wendovers. When Mr. Charles Faversham had bought the estate, he had taken over everything practically as it stood. Pictures, tapestry, antique articles of furniture which had been in the house for centuries still remained.

"Everything has such a homely, cosy feeling!" he exclaimed to himself, again and again. "The place is not one of those great, giant, homeless barracks; it's just an ideal home. It's perfect."

And it was all his! That was the thought that constantly came to his mind. This fact was especially made real to him during his interview with Mr. Boase, the steward. That worthy gentleman, a lawyer who lived in a little town, most of which belonged to the Wendover estate, made this abundantly plain by every word he spoke, by every intonation of his voice.

Mr. Boase unrolled maps and plans in abundance. He placed before him lists of tenants, with nature and condition of their tenancy. He told him how much each farmer paid in rent, how much the house property was worth, what amount was spent each year in repairs, and finally the net amount of his rent-roll. And this was all apart from his investments elsewhere. It was simply fabulous. He who had always been poor, and had often been hard put to it to pay for food and clothes, found himself ridiculously wealthy. He had money to burn. Aladdin of romantic renown was not so much filled with wonder when the slave of the lamp appeared, ready to do his bidding, as was Dick as he realised his position.

And he revelled in thought of it all. He was not of a miserly nature, but he gloried in the influence of the power of wealth, and he painted glowing pictures of his future. He saw the doors of the rich and the great open to him; he saw himself courted by people possessing old names and a great ancestry; he fancied himself occupying positions of eminence in the life of the nation; he saw proud beauties smiling on him.

Nothing was impossible! He knew he had more than an average share of brains; his late employers had admitted as much to him. He also had the gift of oratory. On the few occasions he had attempted to address his fellows this had been abundantly proved. In the past he had been handicapped, but now — —

After dinner that night he walked out alone. He wanted to see his possessions, to feel his own earth beneath his feet, to feast his eyes on the glorious countryside.

"It will take me a week," he reflected, "to get used to it all, to fully realise that it is all mine. I want to feel my feet, to formulate my plans, to sketch my future. Of course, I shall be alone for a time, but in a few days the neighbours will be sure to call on me. After that I must give a ball. Of course, it is a bad time just now, and it is a nuisance that so many of the young fellows have been called into the Army; but I'll be able to manage it," and then he pictured the great ballroom filled with laughter and gaiety.

Then the memory of Lady Blanche Huntingford came to him. He saw her as she had appeared to him that morning. What a glorious creature she was! What great flashing eyes, what a complexion, what a figure! And she belonged to one of the oldest families in England. The Huntingfords were a great people before half the titled nobility of the present day were ever heard of.

He called to mind what Mr. Bidlake had told him. If the Huntingfords recognised him, his social position was assured, for Lord Huntingford was the social magnate of the county. He was almost half in love with her already. He remembered her silvery laugh, the gleaming whiteness of her teeth. What a mistress she would make for Wendover Park! And he could win her love! He was sure he could, and when he did ——

He blessed the failure of her car to run that morning; blessed the knowledge he possessed whereby he had been able to render her a service. Of course, she would find out who he was, and then—yes, he would find the Open Sesame for every door.

For the next few days things happened as Dick expected. He was given time to view his possessions, to take stock of his new position, and then the neighbours began to call. By this time Dick knew full particulars of all the old families in Surrey, and he was gratified at their appearance. Evidently he suffered from none of the antipathy which had been felt towards his uncle. He was young, he was good looking, he had the education and appearance of a gentleman, and people accepted him at his face value.

One day his heart gave a great bound, for a servant told him that Lord and Lady Huntingford, accompanied by Lady Blanche Huntingford, were in the drawing-room. He knew then that his position in the society of the county would be assured. It was true that Lord Huntingford was poor— true, too, that his uncle had practically ejected Sir Guy Wendover from his old home, and that Sir Guy was a relative of the Huntingfords. But that would count for nothing, and the Huntingfords were the Huntingfords!

"This is good of you, Lord Huntingford!" he cried, as he entered the room.

"I came to give you a welcome," said Lord Huntingford somewhat pompously. "I trust you will be very happy here."

"I'm sure I shall!" cried Dick, with the laugh of a boy. "Wendover Park feels like Paradise to me."

"I know the place well," said the peer. "My Cousin Guy, as you may have heard, used to live here."

"Yes, I have heard of it, and I'm afraid you must feel rather bitterly towards me as a consequence."

"Not at all," replied Huntingford. "Of course, it is all ancient history now. We *did* feel cut up about it at the time, but—but I congratulate you on possessing such a fine old place."

"But for the fact that I so love it already," said Dick, "I should wish my uncle had secured some other place; but, for the life of me, I can't. It's too lovely. Anyhow, I'll try to be not an unworthy successor of Sir Guy. I hope you'll help me, Lord Huntingford, and you, Lady Huntingford and Lady Blanche. You see, I'm handicapped. I'm a bachelor, and I'm entirely ignorant of my duties. I shall look to you for help."

This was sound policy on Dick's part. Lord Huntingford was a vain man, and loved to patronise.

"You began all right," laughed Lady Blanche. "You helped a poor, forlorn, helpless motorist out of a difficulty."

"You recognise me, then?"

"Of course I do. I positively envied the way you tackled that engine of mine and put it right. Of course, I felt angry when I knew who you were. No, no, there was nothing personal about it. I only hated the thought that anyone other than a Wendover should live here. A family feeling, you know."

"All that Wendover Park has is yours to command!" and Dick looked very earnest as he spoke.

"Now, that's good of you. But don't be too liberal with your promises. I may take you at your word."

"Try me!" cried Dick. "I should like to do something to atone. Not that I can give it up," he added, with a laugh. "I simply couldn't, you know. But—but——"

"And how are you going to spend your time?" asked Lord Huntingford. "We are living in a critical age."

"I shall make something turn up!" Dick cried heartily, "as soon as I know where I am."

"And, meanwhile, I suppose you motor, ride, shoot, golf, and all the rest of it?" asked Lady Blanche.

"I have all the vices," Dick told her.

"You say you golf?"

"Yes, a little. Would you give me a match?" he ventured.

"I'd love to," and her eyes flashed into his.

The next afternoon Dick met Lady Blanche on the golf links, and before the match was over he believed that he was in love with her. Never before had he met such a glorious specimen of physical womanhood. To him her every movement was poetry, her lithe, graceful body a thing in which to rejoice.

After the match Dick motored her back to her home. He was in Arcadia as she sat by his side. The charm of her presence was to him like some fabled elixir. On their way they caught a glimpse of Wendover Park. The old house stood out boldly on the hillside, while the wide-stretching park-lands were plainly to be seen.

"It's a perfect place," said the girl. "It just wants nothing."

"Oh yes, it does," laughed Dick.

"What?" she asked.

"Can't you think? If you were a bachelor you would," and he watched her face closely as he spoke.

He was afraid lest he might offend her, and he wondered if she saw his meaning. He thought he saw a flush surmount her face, but he was not sure. They were passing a cart just then, and he had to fix his attention on the steering-wheel.

"Do you know," he went on, "it's a bit lonely there. I haven't many friends. And then, being a bachelor, I find it difficult to entertain. Not but what I shall make a start soon," he added.

"I think you are to be envied," she remarked.

"Of course I am. I'm one of the luckiest fellows in the world. By the way, I want to give a dance or something of that sort as a kind of house-warming."

"How delightful."

"Is it? But then, you see, I'm so ignorant that I don't know how to start about it."

"Don't you? That's a pity. You must get help."

"I must. I say, will you help me? There is no one I'd so soon have."

He was sure this time. He saw the rosy tint on her face deepen. Perhaps she heard the tremor in his voice. But she did not answer him; instead, she looked away towards the distant landscape.

"Will you?" he persisted.

"What could I do?"

"Everything. You know the people, know who I should invite, and what I should do. You are accustomed to that kind of thing. I am not."

Still she was silent.

"Will you?" he asked again.

"Perhaps. If you really wish me to."

She almost whispered the words, but he heard her, and to him there was something caressing in her tone.

They passed up a long avenue of trees leading to her home, and a few seconds later the car stood at the door.

"You'll come in and have some tea, won't you?"

"May I?" he asked eagerly.

"Of course you may. Mother will be expecting you."

As he rode back to Wendover Park that evening Dick was in Paradise. Nothing but the most commonplace things had been said, but the girl had fascinated him. She had appealed to his ambition, to his pride, to his admiration for perfect, physical womanhood. She was not very clever, but she was handsome. She was instinct with redundant health; she was glorious in her youth and vitality.

"I'm in love," he said to himself more than once. "And she's wonderful — simply, gloriously wonderful. What eyes, what a complexion, what a magnificent figure! I wonder if — —"

I am dwelling somewhat on this part of Dick Faversham's life because I wish the reader to understand the condition of his mind, to understand the forces at work. Uninteresting as it may be, it is still important. For Dick passed through some wonderful experiences soon after — experiences which shook the foundations of his life, and which will be more truly understood as we realise the thoughts and feelings which possessed him.

As I have said, he was in a state of bliss as he drove back to Wendover Park that evening, but as he neared his lodge gates a curious feeling of depression possessed him. His heart became heavy, forebodings filled his mind. It seemed to him that he was on the edge of a dreadful calamity.

"What's the matter with me?" he asked himself again and again. "The sun is shining, the world is lovely, and I have all that heart can wish for."

Still the feeling possessed him. Something was going to happen—something awful. He could not explain it, or give any reason for it, but it was there.

Then suddenly his heart stood still. As the car drew up to his own door he again saw the face of the angel. She was hovering over the entrance just as he had seen her on the day he came to take possession. She seemed to dread something; there was pain almost amounting to agony in the look she gave him.

He had alighted from the car, and he had a dim idea that a man was approaching to take it to the garage, but he paid no attention to him; he stood like one transfixed, looking at the apparition. He was aware that the car had gone, and that he was alone. In a vague way he supposed that the chauffeur, like the lawyer, had seen nothing.

"Who are you? What do you want?"

The words escaped him almost in spite of himself.

But he heard no voice in reply. He thought he saw her lips trying to formulate words, but were not able.

"Tell me," he persisted—"tell me who you are, why you appear to me. What do you want?"

Again the apparition seemed to be trying to become audible, only to fail. Then, although he could hear no distinct voice, her answer seemed to come to him.

"Fight, fight; pray, pray," she seemed to be saying. "Beware of the tempter. Fight, fight; pray, pray. Promise me."

He was not afraid, but it seemed to him that he was face to face with eternal realities. He knew then that there were depths of life and experience of which he was ignorant.

He heard steps in the hall, and then someone opened the door.

There stood, smiling, debonair, sardonic, and—yes—wicked, Count Romanoff.

Chapter VIII
Count Romanoff's Gospel

Count Romanoff!

A weight seemed to settle on Dick Faversham's heart as he saw the sinister face of his visitor. During the excitement of the last few days he had scarcely given him a thought. The dark, saturnine stranger had shrunk away into the background of his life, and no longer seemed of importance to him. It is true he had now and then wondered whether he should ever see him again, but as there seemed no present likelihood of his doing so, he had practically dismissed him from his mind.

His sudden appearance came to him like a shock. Besides, he was nervous, excited at what he had just experienced. Every nerve was tingling, every sense preternaturally awake. What did this apparition mean? Why should the same face and form appear to him again and again?—first in the smoke-room of the ship, then on the island, then as he first put foot into the new inheritance, and now again. What did it mean? Then during that awful struggle in the stormy sea.

"Ha, Faversham. You see, I have taken you at your word."

Dick's thoughts came to earth as the Count's voice reached him.

"I'm glad to see you," he said cordially, and as he led the way to the library he was all that a host should be.

"You see, I was in England, and, having a little spare time, I thought I would look you up. I hope I'm not taking too great a liberty?"

"Liberty, my dear fellow! I should be annoyed beyond words if you had not come to see me. I have hosts of things to discuss with you. Besides," and Dick spoke like one deeply moved, "I cannot help remembering that but for you it is not likely I should be here. I should have been lying somewhere at the bottom of the Indian Ocean."

"Oh, come now; let's have no more of that. Of course, I had the good luck to be of service to you, and jolly glad I am; no decent fellow could have done less than I did."

"All the same, I cannot forget that I owe my life to you," cried Dick fervently. "Do you know, I wondered no end what happened to you; tell me about it."

"Not until I hear about you. Of course, I can guess a great deal. The fact that you are here tells me that the wireless you got on the ship was not only *bona fide* but important. You are master here, eh?"

Dick nodded.

"I've been told that your uncle was a very rich man. Is that so?"

"Yes."

"And you are his heir?"

"Yes."

"I congratulate you. By Jove, it's a lovely place. I didn't know when I've seen anything I like so much. And I've seen a few houses, I can tell you. But really, now, and I hope I'm not impertinent, do you mean to tell me that you have entered into all old Charles Faversham's wealth?"

"I suppose so."

"Shake hands on it. I can think of no one more fitted to own 'big money,' as the Americans say. I'm glad of the privilege of seeing you in possession."

It seemed to Dick that it was a new Romanoff that he saw. He was no longer pessimistic, cynical, saturnine. He looked younger, too, and no one could help admitting that he had that grand air that denotes birth and breeding.

"I only arrived in London last night," went on Romanoff. "I got into Tilbury late in the afternoon, and after I got fixed up at my hotel I began to wonder about you. Presently I called to mind what you told me, and—here I am."

"Of course you'll stay with me a bit?"

"May I?"

"May you? Why, of course you must, if you can. That goes without saying."

"I say, you are awfully good. I should love to stay a bit. This is one of the loveliest corners in the world at the loveliest time of the year. Surrey in May! What can be more attractive!"

"I'll have your room prepared at once, and, by the way, I'll send a man to London for your luggage."

"That is good of you, Faversham. I may as well confess it now. I did bring a suit-case with me in the hope that you could put me up for the night, but of course — —"

"You might have known that I'd want you for a long time," Dick interrupted.

A servant entered, and Dick gave his instructions. "Now tell me," he went on; "what did you do on leaving the island? I know practically nothing about anything. I was very ill, and got no better till the boat landed at Plymouth."

Romanoff hesitated for a few seconds, then he replied:

"Oh, I caught a boat bound for Australia."

"Australia, eh?"

"Yes. Our signals were seen by two vessels, one returning to England, and the other going to Australia, which, as luck would have it, stopped at Bombay for a few hours. So I took that."

"And you didn't stay long in the Antipodes?"

"No, I did not like the country, and I found it necessary to return to England."

"I'm jolly glad."

"Well, here I am anyhow. Isn't life a topsy-turvy business? Who would have thought when we exchanged commonplaces on that boat a short time ago we should forgather like this in a lovely old Surrey house? Facts beat fiction all to bits. Fiction is commonplace, tame, prosy; but facts — real life — are interesting. Now, tell me about your experiences."

"Not yet. It's nearly dinner-time. I suppose you brought no evening clothes?"

Romanoff laughed. "As a matter of fact, I did. Of course, I was not sure you were here; but I thought you might be, so I took the liberty of — —"

"Splendid," interrupted Dick. "There, the dressing-bell is ringing. I'll show you your room. My word, I'm awfully glad you've come. To tell you the truth, I was feeling a bit depressed."

"You depressed! I say! Fancy the heir of all this being depressed."

"But I was. The idea of spending the evening alone dismayed me. You see, a fellow can't be out every night, and — and there you are. But you've come."

"And no one will call to-night?"

"I don't expect so. Young Clavering, who is home on leave, might come over for a game of billiards, but I can't think of anyone else likely to turn up."

"Clavering—Clavering. I don't think I know the name."

"Oh, it is a good name in Surrey, I can assure you. It's a very old family, although I suppose it is frightfully poor. I've only met young Clavering once, but I liked him very much. Most of the young fellows around here are in the Army, and the older men are frightful old fossils. Here's your room. I hope you'll be comfortable."

Romanoff looked around the room with evident pleasure. He walked to the window and gazed steadily at the landscape; then he turned to Dick and gave him a keen, searching glance.

"You are a fortunate man, Faversham. Speaking as a Russian and also as one who has travelled all over the world, I say, commend me to England for comfort. Yes, I'll be all right, my friend."

When Dick had gone Romanoff threw himself in a chair and gazed into vacancy. A change passed over his face. He was no longer cheerful and pleasant; the old sinister, threatening look had come into his eyes, while his mouth was cruel. Once an expression swept over his features which suggested a kind of mocking pity, but it was only for a moment.

During dinner he was in a gay humour. Evidently he had thrown care to the winds, and lived for the pleasure of the moment. Dick found him fascinating. He talked pleasantly—at times brilliantly. His conversation scintillated with sardonic humour. He told stories about many countries. He related anecdotes about the Imperial House of the Romanoffs, and described the influence which Rasputin had on the Tzar and the Tzarina.

"I cannot understand it," remarked Dick after one of these stories.

"Understand what?"

"How a man like the Tzar could allow a dirty charlatan like Rasputin to have such influence. After all, Nicholas was an educated man, and a gentleman."

Romanoff laughed.

"As well Rasputin as the others," he replied.

"What others?"

"The priests of the Holy Orthodox Church. Let me give you a bit of advice, Faversham; keep clear of all this religious rot. It's true that you in England pretend to be more advanced than the poor Russians, but at bottom there's no difference. Wherever religion creeps in, it's the same story. Religion means credulity, and credulity means lies, oppression, cant, corruption."

"Did you meet Rasputin?"

"Oh yes," replied Romanoff, with a sigh of resignation. "On the whole, I admired him."

"I say, that's a bit too thick."

"Anyhow, the fellow was interesting. He had a philosophy of his own. He recognised the fact that the world was populated by fools, and he determined to make the most of his chances. He interpreted religion in a way that would give the greatest possible gratification to his senses. His policy was to suck the orange of the world dry. 'Salvation through sin,' eh?" and Romanoff laughed as he spoke. "Well, it's about the most sensible religion I ever heard of."

"It seems to me devilish and dirty," Dick spoke warmly.

"Nonsense, my dear fellow. Of course, all religion is foolishness—that is, religion as is usually understood. But if there is to be a religion at all, Rasputin got hold of the true one."

"You don't mean that?"

Romanoff looked at Dick steadily for a few seconds. He seemed to be thinking deeply as though he were trying to understand his man.

"Perhaps I don't," he admitted presently. "Sometimes one exaggerates in order to convey what is actually true. Still, there is a substratum of truth in the dirty monk's philosophy, as you'll find out before you are much older. By the way, the evening has turned cold, hasn't it?"

"Do you find it so? The air of a night is often cold in the early summer. Have you finished? Then we'll go into my little den where I always have a fire of an evening."

A few minutes later Romanoff was sprawling in a large easy-chair with his feet close to the fire.

"How long have you been here?" he asked.

"Not quite a month."

"Been well received by your neighbours?"

"On the whole, yes."

Again Romanoff looked steadily at his companion. "Will you forgive me if I ask you a few questions?"

"Certainly. Go ahead."

"First, then, how do you like being a rich man?"

Dick glanced around the room, and then gave a look towards the wide-spreading park-lands.

"How can one help liking it?" he asked.

"Exactly. You do not find money to be the root of all evil, then?"

"Heavens, no!"

"You would not like to be a poor man again?"

"What in the world are you driving at? Of course, the very thought of it is horrible."

"Just so. I am in my way a student of human nature, and I was a bit curious. Now for a second question. Who is she?"

"Oh, I say."

"Of course she exists."

"How do you know?"

"In my way I have the power of divination. When I look at a man I know something, not much perhaps, but something of his hopes. I felt sure before I spoke that you were in love. You've been quick about it, my young friend."

"I don't know that I am in love."

"Of course you are. Who is she?"

"There's no one. At least not yet. I don't suppose she's given me a second's thought."

"But you do. Is she young, beautiful? Is she rich, well connected?"

"Young! beautiful!" laughed Dick.

"Ah, I see. Not a rustic beauty, by any chance?"

"Rustic beauty, eh? There's nothing rustic about Lady Blanche Huntingford."

"Huntingford! That's one of the best known names in England."

"Do you know it?"

"Who doesn't? It's the biggest name in Debrett. But the Huntingfords are as poor as church mice."

"What does that matter?"

"You have enough for both, eh? Of course, that's your hope."

"Why?" and Dick turned rather sharply on his interlocutor.

"Oh, nothing personal, my friend. I'm only speaking from a long experience. The Huntingfords are poor and proud. I do not know of a more unpleasant combination. I've heard of Lady Blanche—she is about twenty-four, a great beauty, and so far has not succeeded in the marriage market. She's had several seasons in London, but the rich aristocrat has not turned up. That's why she may smile on a commoner—a newcomer—providing he's rich enough."

"If you'd seen her, spoken with her, you would not talk like that."

"Shouldn't I? Who knows? But it's nothing to worry about, my dear fellow. All talk about the love of women goes for nothing. It doesn't exist. Of course, there is such a thing as sexual attraction, but nothing else."

"You are a terrible cynic, Romanoff."

"I'm a citizen of the world, and I've gone around the world with my eyes open. But, as I said, you can have an easy mind. The ball is at your feet, my dear fellow. Whatever you want you can have."

"Do be serious." Dick spoke lightly; all the same, he felt uneasy.

"I *am* serious," replied Romanoff. "With wealth like yours, you are master of the world; you can get all the world has to give."

"I wish I could."

"I tell you you can. Money is all-powerful. Just think, if you were poor, not a hope, not an ambition could be realised."

"That won't do. Hosts of poor fellows have——"

"Risen to position and power. Just so; but it's been a terrible struggle, a ghastly grind. In most cases, too, men don't get money until they are too old to enjoy it. But you are young, and the world's at your feet. Do you want titles? You can buy them. Power? fame? Again you can get them. Beautiful women? Love? Yes, even love of a sort you can buy, if you have money. Poverty is hell; but what heaven there is in this world can be bought."

"Then you think the poor can't be happy?"

"Let me be careful in answering that. If a man has no ambitions, if he has no desire for power, then, in a negative way, he may be happy although he's poor. But to you, who are ambitious through and through—you, who see visions and dream dreams—poverty would be hell. That's why I congratulate you on all this. And my advice to you is, make the most of it. Live to enjoy, my dear fellow. Whatever your eyes desire, take it."

Dick realised that Romanoff was talking cheap cynicism, that, to use a journalistic term, it was "piffle" from thread to needle, and yet he was impressed. Again he felt the man's ascendancy over him, knew that he was swayed and moulded by a personality stronger than his own.

Dick did not try to answer him, for at that moment there was a knock at the door and a servant entered.

"Mr. and Miss Stanmore have called, sir."

"I do not think I know them, do I?" asked Dick.

"I don't know, sir. They live not far from the South Park gates. They are old residents, sir."

Whether there was something in the tone of the man's voice, or whether he desired company other than Romanoff's, I cannot tell. Certain it is that, acting on impulse and scarcely realising what he was doing, he said:

"Show them in here, Jenkins, will you?"

Chapter IX
Beatrice Stanmore

"You don't mind, do you?" asked Dick, turning to Romanoff when the man had left the room.

"Not at all, my dear fellow. Why should I?"

Again the servant returned and ushered in an old man and a young girl. The former was a striking-looking figure, and would be noticed in any crowd. Although old, he stood perfectly upright, and was evidently healthy and vigorous. His face was ruddy and almost unlined. His white beard and moustache were allowed to grow long, while his almost massive head was covered with a wealth of wavy white hair. Perhaps, too, his attire helped to make his appearance attractive, and his velvet dinner-jacket suggested the artist or the poet.

"I hope you'll forgive me calling, Mr. Faversham," he said, taking Dick's outstretched hand, "but I'm an old man, as well as a man of moods. I've thought several times of dropping in to see you, but refrained. I was afraid you would have no use for an old buffer such as I. But to-night I felt I must, and here I am. This is my granddaughter, Beatrice."

"It's awfully good of you to call, Mr. Stanmore, and you, too, Miss Stanmore."

Dick looked at the girl full in the face as he spoke, and then all further words were frozen on his lips. The sight of Beatrice Stanmore caused his heart to beat wildly, and made him feel that a new influence had entered the room.

And yet, at first sight, there was nothing remarkable in her presence. Picture a fair-haired, blue-eyed girl of eighteen—a girl with a sweet, winsome, yet mischievous smile, and a perfect complexion; a girl with well-formed features and an evident sense of humour—and you see Beatrice Stanmore. And yet your picture would be incomplete. What I have said suggests a somewhat commonplace girl, such as can be seen by the score in any country town. But she was not commonplace. Her blue eyes were large and haunting; sometimes they were sad, and yet there was a world of mirth and gladness stored in their liquid depths. She was only eighteen or nineteen years of age, and she did not look older than her years; but, if you took a second look at her, you would know that her thoughts were not always a child's thoughts—that she had longings too deep for words.

She was dressed very simply. I cannot describe her apparel, but to Dick it was something light and diaphanous, which set oft a figure which was at once girlish and yet perfect in its proportions. I do not suppose that a connoisseur would call her beautiful, but she suggested health—health of body, of mind, of soul. It would be impossible to associate her with anything impure, rather a flash from her mirth-loving eyes would destroy all thought of such a thing.

"I've seen her before," thought Dick, "but where?"

No, it was only fancy. She was an utter stranger to him, and yet he was haunted with the thought that somewhere, at some time, they had met and known each other, that she had been with him in some crisis.

"Please forgive us, Mr. Faversham," she said, with a laugh; "it's not my fault. I should never have had the courage to beard the lion in his den."

"What lion? What den?" asked Dick, as he looked into the girl's sunny face.

"Of course, you are the lion. You've been the talk of the countryside for weeks; and—and isn't this your den?"

She spoke with all the simplicity and frankness of a child, and seemed to be perfectly unimpressed by the fact that she was talking with one who was spoken of as one of the richest young men in England.

"It's I who am the culprit, Mr. Faversham," broke in the old man. "The impulse came upon me suddenly. I said to Beatrice, 'I am going to call on young Faversham,' and she jumped at the idea of a walk through the park, and that's why she's here with me. Please tell me if we are in the way."

"In the way? I'm just delighted. And—but let me introduce you to Count Romanoff."

Both Hugh Stanmore and his granddaughter looked towards Count Romanoff, who had risen to his feet. The light was shining fully upon his face, and Dick could not help feeling what a striking appearance he had. He half held out his hand to the newcomers and then suddenly withdrew it.

Old Hugh Stanmore looked at the Count steadily for a few seconds, and then bowed in silence. It might seem as though something had frozen his urbanity and cheerfulness. He did not appear to notice the half-outstretched hand, and Dick felt as though there was an instinctive antipathy between them. As for Beatrice, she gave the Count a cold nod, and then, with a perfunctory, "How d'ye do?" turned to Dick again.

"I'm so glad you've come here to live, Mr. Faversham," she said, with girlish enthusiasm.

"You can't be gladder than I," replied Dick; "but, is there a special reason for your gladness?"

"Of course there is. I've wanted for years to see the inside of this house, but I was frightfully afraid of your—your uncle. He always looked so stern, and so—so forbidding that I hadn't the courage to ask him. But you are different."

"Then why haven't you called before?" asked Dick. "I've been here nearly a month, and yet I've never seen you before."

"Of course, you must understand," and it was old Hugh Stanmore who replied, "that we are quite unimportant people. We live in that cottage not far from your South Lodge, and, not knowing you, we felt rather sensitive about calling."

"But your name seems familiar. I'm sure I've heard it somewhere."

"Not among the people around here, I imagine?"

"No, I think not; but I seem to have heard of it, or seen it, years ago."

"I fancy you are mistaken, although what you say is just possible. When I was at Cambridge I had tremendous ambitions, and, like thousands of other callow youths, I made up my mind to win fame. I was something of a linguist, and had a great longing to win renown as an Egyptologist and as an Assyrian scholar. However, I had no money to indulge in such luxuries, so on leaving Cambridge I looked to journalism for a living. I even wrote a novel," and he laughed merrily.

"Splendid!" cried Dick. "What was the title of the novel?"

"I won't tell you that," replied the old man. "I've drawn a very thick curtain over that effort. However, I might have done something if I'd persevered; but, luckily or unluckily for me, I had some money left to me. Not much, but enough to enable me to travel in the East."

"Yes, and then?"

"Oh, I'm afraid I did not shine as an Egyptologist, although I had some wonderful experiences and made some interesting acquaintances. I also contributed to that phase of literature."

"I never saw your name in that connection," Dick confessed.

"I expect not. You see, that was many years ago. Still, although my health would not stand the Eastern climate, I've kept up my interest in my early love. But I've been somewhat of a butterfly. On my return to England I conceived a passion for throwing paint in the eyes of the public, to quote John Ruskin. I even went so far as to get a few pictures hung in the Academy. But, in spite of that, I achieved no fame. Since then I've contributed occasional articles to the reviews, while such papers as *The Spectator* and *The Times* have printed some effusions of mine which I in my vanity have called poetry. Please forgive me for talking about myself in this way. I know it is frightful egotism on my part, but, as I'm one of your nearest neighbours, I'm in a way introducing myself."

"It's awfully good of you," replied Dick. "I hope we shall see a good deal of each other."

"I hope we shall," replied Hugh Stanmore. "I may as well confess it, Mr. Faversham, that although I am an old man, I am a creature of impulses. I do things without being able to give a reason for them. I talk without knowing why. Do you know that I've never spoken so much about myself to anyone in this district as I have to-night, and I've lived here for eighteen years?"

"What—at the cottage you spoke of?"

"Yes, at the cottage. I took up my residence there when my son died. He was an artist who would have won fame if he had lived; but it pleased the good God to take him away. I determined that I would try to bring what comfort I could into the life of his young wife. But I was not with her long. She died at the birth of this little girl here, three months later."

A silence fell upon the little company.

"There, there," laughed Hugh Stanmore, "there's nothing to be sad about. This life is only a beginning. Actual life comes next, as Browning says. Besides, I've been very happy looking after my little maid here. It's rather hard on her, having to see so much of an old man like myself. All the same, we've had a jolly time."

"Old man!" cried Beatrice indignantly. "I assure you, Mr. Faversham, he's the youngest man in Surrey. Sometimes I am quite ashamed of his frivolity. I'm quite a staid, elderly person compared to him."

"Anyhow," said the old man, rising, "we must be going now. But be assured of this, Mr. Faversham: no one wishes you joy in your new home more than I. We give you a glad welcome to the district, and if an old man's prayer and an old man's blessing are worth anything, you have them."

"But please don't go yet," cried Dick. "It's only a little after nine o'clock, and—and I'm so glad to have you here. You see, you've only just come."

"No, no, I know. But we'll be going now. Some other time, when you happen to be alone, I'll be glad to come and smoke a pipe with you—if I may?"

"May! Of course. Besides, Miss Stanmore said she wanted to look over the house. When will you come, Miss Stanmore?"

"I think it must be when you can let Granddad know that you are alone and have nothing to do," was the girl's reply. "I shall look forward to it tremendously."

"So shall I," cried Dick. Then, forgetful of Romanoff, he added, "And I can assure you, you won't have long to wait."

Throughout their conversation, only a part of which I have recorded, Romanoff had not spoken a word. Had Dick been watching him he would have seen that he was not at all pleased at the presence of the visitors. There was a dark, lowering look in his eyes, and almost a scowl on his face. It was evident that a strong feeling of antagonism existed.

"Good-night, Mr. Faversham," said old Hugh Stanmore, holding out his hand; then, bowing gravely to Romanoff, he passed out of the room.

"Oh, but I'll see you to the door, if you *will* go," insisted Dick, as for a moment he held Beatrice Stanmore's hand in his. "Allow me."

He passed through the hall by her side and opened the door. As he did so, he could barely repress an exclamation of wonder and delight, while both the old man and the young girl stood as if spellbound.

It was one of those rare nights which constantly recur to one's remembrance in after days. It was now the end of May, and while the summer had not reached its full glory, the fullness of spring made the earth like a paradise. The sky was cloudless and the silver rays of a nearly full moon lit up the scene with an unearthly beauty. All around giant trees stood, while the flowers, which grew in rich profusion, were plainly to be seen. Away through the leafy trees could be seen the outline of the country. Here and there the birds, which had barely gone to rest, were chirping, while away in the distance a cuckoo proclaimed the advent of summer.

For a few seconds they stood in silence, then Hugh Stanmore said quietly, "One can understand Charles Kingsley's dying words on such a night, Mr. Faversham."

"What did he say?" asked Dick.

"'How beautiful God must be,'" quoted Hugh Stanmore.

Just then a bird burst forth into song—rich-noted, mellow, triumphant.

"A nightingale!" cried the girl. "Look, Granddad, it is over on that tree." She went down the drive under the long avenue of trees as she spoke, leaving Hugh Stanmore and Dick together.

"They can't be far away on such a night as this," murmured the old man.

"Who can't be far away?"

"The angels. The heavens are full of them. Ah, if we could only see!"

"Do you believe in angels?"

"Do I believe in them? How can I help believing? It is nearly nineteen years ago since my boy and his wife died. But they didn't leave me altogether. They come to me."

"Have you seen them?" and Dick's eager question was uttered almost unconsciously.

"No, not with my natural eyes. Why? I wonder. But I have felt them near me. I know they are watching over me. You see, they did not cease to love us when God took them away for some higher service. Naturally, too, they watch over Beatrice. They could not help it."

He spoke quietly, and in an almost matter-of-fact way, yet with a suggestion of reverence in his tones.

"Who knows who is watching over us now?" continued the old man. "Ah, if we could only see! 'Are they not all ministering spirits sent to minister to those who are heirs of Salvation?'"

Dick felt a shiver pass through him. He reflected that on that very spot, only a few hours before, he had seen something, *something*—a luminous figure, a pale, sad face—sad almost to agony!

"Mr. Faversham," asked Hugh Stanmore suddenly, "who is Count Romanoff?"

"I don't know much about him," replied Dick. "He was a fellow-passenger on board the boat on which I was bound for Australia some time ago. Why do you ask?"

"You know nothing else? Excuse me."

"Only that he saved my life."

"Ah!"

"Why do you ask?"

"Nothing. Only he will have a great influence on your life."

"How do you know?" Dick was greatly excited.

"I have no reason to give you. I only know."

"Good or bad?" asked the young man eagerly.

"I don't know. But did you notice that Beatrice didn't like him? And I've never once known her wrong in her estimate of people. There, look at her now, amongst the moon's rays under the trees. Doesn't she look like an angel? Yes, and she *is* an angel—one of God's sweetest and purest and best. But as human as every woman ought to be. Good-night, Mr. Faversham. Yes, my darling, I'm coming," and the old man went down the drive with the activity of a boy.

Dick watched them until they were out of sight. He was influenced more than he knew by their visit. Their presence, after Count Romanoff's cynicism, was like some sweet-scented balm; like a breeze from the mountains after the fetid atmosphere of a cavern.

"Well, what did you think of them?" he asked of Romanoff on his return.

The Count shrugged his shoulders. "There's not much to think, is there?" he asked.

"I think there is a great deal. I found the old man more interesting than almost any caller I have had."

"A dull, prosy, platitudinous old Polonius; as for the girl, she's just a badly behaved, unformed, bread-and-butter miss."

Dick did not speak. The Count's words grated on him.

"By the way," went on Romanoff, "I should like to meet Lady Blanche Huntingford. I think I knew the old Lord."

"I promised to call to-morrow afternoon," replied Dick. "I'll take you over." But he was not so enthusiastic as the Count expected.

After they had retired to their rooms that night, the Count sat long in soliloquy. Of what he was thinking it would be difficult to say. His face was like a mask.

When he rose from his chair, however, there was a look of decision in his eyes.

"The time has come sooner than I thought," he said aloud. "I must bring the matter to a head at once. Otherwise I shall lose him."

And then he laughed in his grim, sardonic way, as if something had made him merry.

Chapter X
Uncertainty

Dick rose early the following morning, and went for a walk in the park. When he returned he found the Count in the breakfast-room.

"Quite a pattern young countryman," he laughed. "I saw you reflecting on the beauties of your own domains. Did you sleep well?"

"Like a healthy dog. And you?"

"I never sleep. I dream sometimes—that's all."

"Still play-acting," laughed Dick.

"No, there's not a more serious man in England than I, as a rule; but I'm not going to be serious to-day while the sun shines. When the sun goes down I shall be tragic. There, Richard is himself again!"

He threw back his shoulders as he spoke, as though he would shift a weight from them. "I am hungry, Faversham," he laughed. "Let us eat. After breakfast I would love a ride. Have you a horse in your stables that you could lend me?"

"Of course I have."

"Good. Then we'll have a gallop till lunch. After that a-wooing we will go. I'm feverish to see the glorious Lady Blanche, the flower of the age, the beauty of the county. I say, Faversham, prepare to be jealous. I can be a most dangerous rival."

"I can't think of you as a marrying man, Count. Domesticity and you are oceans apart."

The Count laughed. "No, a man such as I never marries," he said. "Marriage! What an idiotic arrangement. But such things always follow religion. But for religion, humanity would be natural, happy."

"Come, now. That won't do."

"It is true, my friend. Ever and always the result of religion has been to raise unnatural barriers, to create sin. The man who founds a religion is an enemy to the race. The greatest enemy to the world's happiness was the Founder of Christianity."

"In Heaven's name, why?"

"Because He labelled natural actions as sins, because He was for ever emphasising a distinction between right and wrong. When there is no right, no wrong. The evolution of religion, and of so-called morality, is a crime, because it strikes at the root of human enjoyment. But, there, I'm getting serious, and I won't be serious. This is a day to laugh, to rejoice in, and I've an appetite like a hunter."

Throughout the morning they carried out the programme Romanoff had suggested. Two of the best horses in the stables were saddled, and they rode till noon. During all this time the Count was in high spirits, and seemed to revel in the brightness of the day and the glory of the scenery.

"After all, give me a living thing to deal with," he cried. "This craze for motor-cars is a sign of decadence. 'Enjoyment by machinery' should be the motto of every motorist. But a horse is different. A horse is sentient, intelligent. He feels what his rider feels; he enters into the spirit of whatever is going on."

"But motoring can be jolly good sport," Dick rejoined.

"Of course it can. But a motor is impersonal; it is a thing, not a being. You cannot make it your slave. It is just a matter of steel, and petrol, and oil. It never becomes afraid of you."

"What of that?" asked Dick.

"Without fear there is no real mastery," replied Romanoff.

"But surely the mastery which is obtained through fear is an unsatisfactory sort of thing."

Romanoff looked at Dick as though on the point of replying, but he was silent.

"Anyhow, I love a horse," he ventured presently. "I love to feel his body alive beneath me, love to feel him spurn the ground beneath his feet."

"Yes; I, too, love a horse," replied Dick, "and do you know, although I've only been here a month, this chap loves me. He whines a welcome when I go to the stable, and he kind of cries when I leave."

"And he isn't afraid of you?" asked Romanoff.

"Afraid!" cried Dick. "I hope not. I should hate to feel that a thing I loved was afraid of me."

"Wait till you are married," laughed Romanoff.

"I don't see what that has to do with it."

"But it has everything to do with it. A wife should obey, and no woman obeys unless she fears. The one thing man has to do when he marries is to demand obedience, and until he has mastered the woman he gets none."

"From the little experience I have, a woman is a difficult thing to master."

"Everything can be mastered," replied Romanoff. "It sometimes requires patience, I'll admit, but it can always be done. Besides, a woman never respects her husband until he's mastered her. Find me a man who has not mastered his wife, and I'll show you a man whose wife despises him. Of course, every woman strives for mastery, but in her heart of hearts she's sorry if she gets it. If I ever married——" He ceased speaking.

"Yes; if you married?"

"I'd have obedience, obedience, obedience," and Romanoff repeated the word with increasing emphasis. "As you say, it might be difficult, but it can always be obtained."

"How?"

"Of course, if you go among the lower orders of people, the man obtains his wife's obedience by brute force. If she opposes him he knocks her down, thrashes her. But as you rise in the scale of humanity, the methods are different. The educated, cultured man never loses his temper, seldom utters an angry word. He may be a little sarcastic, perhaps, but nothing more. But he never yields. The wife cries, pleads, protests, goes into hysterics perhaps, threatens, but he never yields. He is polite, cold, cruel if you like, but he never shows a sign of weakness, and in the end he's master. And mastery is one of the great joys of life."

"You think so?"

"I'm sure of it."

Dick felt slightly uncomfortable. "You said you wouldn't be serious to-day, Romanoff," he laughed nervously, "and yet you talk as though something tragic were in the air."

"I can assure you I'm in one of my light moods," replied the Count. "After all, of what account is a woman in a man's life? A diversion if you like—a creature necessary to his pleasure, but nothing more. When a man regards a woman as indispensable to his happiness, he's lost. Always look on a woman, whoever she may be, as a diversion, my friend," and Romanoff laughed quietly.

After lunch, however, Romanoff's mood seemed changed. He spoke of his early days, and of his experiences in St. Petersburg and Moscow.

"People talk about Paris being the great centre of pleasure," he said a little indignantly, "but it is nothing compared with St. Petersburg, or Petrograd, as it is called now. Some day, my friend, I must take you there; I must show you the sights; I must take you behind the scenes. Oh, I envy you!"

"Why should you?" asked Dick.

"Because you are young, because you have the world at your feet."

"And haven't you?"

"Yes, I suppose so. But, then, you go to everything fresh. You will drink the cup of life for the first time; you will drink deep and enjoy. But I can never again drink for the first time—there lies the difference."

"But if the cup of life is good and sweet, why may not one drink it again, and again, and still find enjoyment?"

Romanoff did not reply. He sat for a few seconds in silence, and then started up almost feverishly.

"Let us away, my friend," he cried. "I am longing to see Lady Blanche Huntingford. How did you describe her? Velvety black eyes, rosy lips, hair as black as the raven's wing, tall, stately, shaped like a Juno and a Venus combined—was that it? Please don't let's waste any time. I'm anxious to be off."

"Even although we are going in a motor."

"Motors are useful, my friend. I may not like them, but I use them. For the matter of that, I use everything. I discard nothing."

"Except religion," laughed Dick.

"Oh, I have my religion," replied Romanoff. "Some time I'll tell you about it, but not now. The sunlight is the time for adventure, for love, for happiness. Let us be off."

Evidently the Count was impressed by Lady Blanche. Directly he entered her presence he seemed to forget his cynicism, and to become light-hearted and gay.

"Do you know, Lady Blanche," he said, "that I had an idea I had seen you somewhere. Your name was familiar, and when Faversham spoke of you, I felt I should be renewing an old acquaintance. Of course, I was mistaken."

"Why 'of course'?"

"The true reply would be too obvious, wouldn't it? Besides, it would be as trite and as clumsy as the repartee of an Oxford undergraduate."

"You are beyond me," she sighed.

Romanoff smiled. "Of course, you are laughing at me; all the same, I'll say this: I shall have no doubt from this time on as to whether I've met you. Do you know who I regard as the most favoured man in England?"

She shook her head.

"My friend Faversham, of course," and Romanoff glanced towards Dick, who sat listening and looking with a kind of wonder at the face of the girl.

"Of course, Wendover is just lovely," she replied.

"And only a very short motor-run from here," remarked Romanoff.

The girl pouted as though she were vexed at his words, but it was easy to see she was not. There could be little doubt that she loved flattery, and although she felt slightly uncomfortable under the Count's ardent gaze, she was pleased at his admiration.

She was also bent on being agreeable, and Dick felt that surely no handsomer woman ever lived than this glorious creature with whom he chatted and laughed. More than once he felt his heart beating wildly as her eyes caught his, and while he wished that Romanoff was not there, he felt it to be one of the happiest days of his life.

"If Romanoff were not here I'd ask her to-day," he reflected. "It's true she's almost a stranger to me; but, after all, what does it matter? Love does not depend on a long acquaintance."

For Dick felt sure he was in love. It is true there seemed a kind of barrier between them, a certain something that kept them apart. But that he put down to their different upbringing. She was a patrician, the child of long generations of aristocratic associations, while he, although his father and mother were gentlefolk, was a commoner. All his life, too, he had been poor, while during the last few years he had had to struggle constantly with poverty. It was no wonder, therefore, that there should be a kind of barrier between them. But that would break down. Already he was feeling more as if "he belonged" to his new surroundings, while his neighbours had received him with the utmost kindness. It was only a matter of time before he would feel at one with them all. Meanwhile, Lady Blanche charmed him, fascinated him. She appealed to him as a glorious woman, regal in her carriage, wondrous in her youth and beauty.

Once during the afternoon they were alone together, and he was almost on the point of declaring his love. But something kept him back. What it was he could not tell. She was alluring, gracious, and seemed to offer him opportunities for telling her what was in his heart. And yet he did not speak. Perhaps he was afraid, although he could not have told what he feared.

"When are you going to give me another game of golf?" he asked, as they parted.

"I don't like threesomes," she laughed, looking towards Romanoff.

"I share your antipathy," said Romanoff, "but could you not suggest someone who might bear with me while you and Faversham break the record?"

"Please manage it," pleaded Dick.

"There's a telephone at Wendover, isn't there?"

"Of course there is. You'll ring me up and let me know, won't you?"

"Perhaps."

Her smile was bewildering, and as he felt the warm pressure of her hand he was in Arcadia.

"I congratulate you, Faversham," remarked Romanoff, as they neared Wendover Park. "She's a glorious creature, simply glorious. Cleopatra was plain compared with her. My word, what a mistress for your new home. Such eyes, such hair, such a complexion—and what a magnificent figure. Yes, Faversham, you are a lucky man."

"If I get her," sighed Dick.

"Get her! Of course you'll get her. Unless——"

"Unless what?" asked Dick as the other hesitated.

Romanoff looked at him for some seconds very searchingly; then he sighed.

"Yes, what is it?" persisted Dick, who felt uncomfortable under Romanoff's look.

"I'm wondering."

"Why and at what?"

"If you are a wise man or a fool."

"I'm afraid I don't understand."

"No, but you will presently."

There seemed to be something so ominous in his words that a feeling like fear possessed Dick's heart. He had always felt somewhat uncomfortable in Romanoff's presence, but now the feeling was so intensified that he dreaded what he might mean.

"The sun is still shining," went on the Count, "and I told you that I should be in a festive mood until dark. In another hour the king of day will have disappeared; then I shall have some serious things to say to you."

"Let's have no more play-acting," and Dick laughed nervously.

"I can assure you, there'll be no play-acting. Everything will be real — desperately real. But I'm going to say no more now. After dinner I am going to be serious. But not until. See! Aren't you proud of it all? Don't you revel in it? Was there ever such a lovely old house, standing amidst such gorgeous surroundings? Look at those giant trees, man! See the glorious landscape! Was there ever such a lucky man! What a mistress Lady Blanche will make!"

They were now passing up the long avenue which led to the house. Away in the distance they could see the mansion nestling amidst giant trees centuries old. From the house stretched the gardens, which were glorious in the beauty of early summer. And Dick saw it all, gloried in it all; but fear haunted him, all the same.

"What is the meaning of this strange mood of yours, Romanoff?" he asked.

"After dinner, my friend," laughed the other. "I'll tell you after dinner."

Throughout dinner the Count was apparently light-hearted, almost to flippancy, but directly the servants had left them to their coffee and cigars his mood changed.

"I told you I was going to be serious, didn't I?" he said slowly. "The time for laughter has ceased, Faversham. The next hour will be critical to you — ay, and more than critical; it will be heavy with destiny."

"What in Heaven's name do you mean?"

"Have you ever considered," and Romanoff enunciated every word with peculiar distinctness, "whether you are *really* the owner of all this?"

Chapter XI
The Real Heir

Dick Faversham could not repress a shudder as the other spoke. The Count's words were so ominous, so full of sinister meaning that for the moment he felt like crying out with fear. He mastered himself after a few seconds, however, and his reply was calm.

"I see what you mean," he said quietly. "A few weeks ago I was poor, and without great expectation. Now— —Naturally you wonder whether it is real to me, whether I can believe in my good fortune."

"It goes deeper than that, Faversham," was the Count's rejoinder— "very much deeper than that."

"What do you mean?"

"You believe that you are the owner of all this. You regard yourself as the lawful possessor of the Wendover Park estate, with all its farms, cottages, and villages; you also think of yourself as the owner of mining rights, shipping interests, and a host of other things, added to a very magnificent credit balance at your bankers'. Isn't that so?"

"Of course I do. What have you to say against it?" Dick spoke almost angrily. He was greatly excited, not only by the Count's words, but by his manner of speech.

"On the strength of it you have cast eyes of love on one of the most beautiful women in England; you have dreamed of marrying Lady Blanche Huntingford, who bears one of the oldest names in the land?"

"And if I have, what then?"

"Has it ever occurred to you that your fortune rests on a very slender, a very unsafe, foundation?"

"I say, Count Romanoff— —"

"Don't be angry, my friend, and, above all, look at everything calmly."

"Really, this is a trifle thick, isn't it? I'm afraid I must ask for an explanation of this peculiar manner of speech."

"I deeply regret that I shall have to give an explanation," and there was curious vibration in Romanoff's voice. "But please, *please*, Faversham, don't think unkindly of me because of what I have to tell you. Perhaps I have been very clumsy, but I have been trying all day to prepare you for—for what you will regard as bad news."

"Trying to prepare me? Bad news?"

"Yes, my friend. I told you this morning that I was not going to be serious while the sun shone, but that after the sun went down I was going to be tragically in earnest. The time has come."

"You spoke of my having no right here!" and a gleam of anger shot from Dick's eyes. "Might I suggest, Count, that it is a little out of the common for a guest to tell his host that he has no right to give him hospitality?"

"I was afraid you might take it like that," and Romanoff spoke almost gently. "Doubtless I have been very clumsy, very gauche; all the same, I have come only in kindness."

"Am I to understand, then, that you came here for the purpose of telling me that I am an impostor, an interloper? That, indeed, is interesting."

"I came as a friend, a well-wisher—as one deeply, very deeply, interested in your welfare. I came as one who wants you to enjoy what you believe is your good fortune, and to marry the most beautiful woman in England. If, after you have heard me, you wish me to leave you, I will do so—sadly, I will admit, but I will leave you."

"At least, do not deal in hints, in innuendoes. Tell me exactly what you mean, and perhaps you will also tell me what particular interest you have in the matter, and by what right you—you—talk in this way."

"Faversham, let me first of all admit frankly that I took a great liking to you during the voyage that ended so—tragically. I am no longer a boy, and I do not take to people easily; but I felt an unaccountable interest in you. There were traits in your character that attracted me. I said to myself, 'I should like to know that young fellow, to cultivate his acquaintance.' That must be my reason for taking what interest I have in you. It would have been easy to let you drown, to—to listen to the appeal of the other occupants of the boat, and——"

"Pardon me," interrupted Dick impulsively, "I have behaved like a cad. I forgot that I owed my life to you. But I was excited—angry. You see, the suggestion that I am here under false pretences naturally upsets me. But tell me what you mean. I do not understand you—I am bewildered by your hints."

"Of course, I understand your feelings, and am not in the least offended. I think I know you too well not to take offence easily; besides, my desire, and my only desire, being to help you makes me impervious to ordinary emotions."

"Still," cried Dick, "tell me what you mean. You say my position as owner of my Uncle Faversham's estates rests on a very slender, a very unsafe foundation. That is surely a serious statement to make. How do you know?"

"Your uncle's will—yes, I will admit I went to Somerset House and paid a shilling for the right of reading it—states that he gave his fortune to his sister's sons, and after them to the next-of-kin."

"Exactly."

"Presently it came to pass that only one person stood between you and possession."

"That is so. I did not know it at the time, but such, I am informed, was the case."

"This person's name was Mr. Anthony Riggleton, at that time the only surviving son of your uncle's sister!"

"That is so."

Romanoff lay back in his chair and quietly smoked his cigar.

"But why these questions?" persisted Dick.

"I was only thinking, my friend, on what small issues fortune or poverty may rest."

"But—but really——"

"Here is the case as I understand it. Your lawyer told you that Mr. Anthony Riggleton, the only man who stood between you and all your uncle's possessions, was killed in a drunken brawl in Melbourne, and that on his death you became heir. That was why he sent you that wireless; that was why he summoned you back to England."

"Exactly."

"But what if Mr. Anthony Riggleton is not dead?"

"There is no doubt about that," replied Dick, in tones of relief. "Mr. Bidlake realised the importance of this, and sent to a lawyer in Melbourne to make investigations. Every care was taken, every possible loophole of mistake was investigated. I saw all the documents, all the newspaper reports."

"Has it ever struck you that mistakes might be made about this?"

"Of course. As a consequence I questioned Bidlake closely, and he told me that doubt was impossible."

"Let me understand," and Romanoff continued to speak quietly. "Your position is that Anthony Riggleton, the then heir to all your Uncle Faversham's fortune, was living in Australia; that he was known in Melbourne; that he went to a house near Melbourne with some boon companions; that there was a night of orgy; that afterwards there was a quarrel; and that Mr. Anthony Riggleton was killed."

"Evidently you've worked up the case," and there was a sneer in Dick's voice.

"But I'm right, am I not?"

"As far as you've gone, you are roughly right. Of course, his body was afterwards identified by — —"

"By the cashier of the bank from which he had drawn money, and by others," interrupted Romanoff. "But what if that cashier made a mistake? What if it paid him to make it? What if the others who identified the body were paid to do so? What if Mr. Anthony Riggleton is still alive?"

"What if a hundred things are true?" cried Dick angrily. "One can ask such questions for ever. Of course, if Mr. Anthony Riggleton is still alive, I have no right here. If he is alive, I clear out."

"And does the prospect please you?" and the Count looked at Dick like one anxious.

"Of course, it doesn't please me. If it's true, I'm a pauper, or next door to one. If it's true, I should have to leave everything and go out into the world to begin again."

"And give up all thought of Lady Blanche Huntingford," added the Count.

"I say, Romanoff, if you've anything definite to tell me, tell it. I tell you honestly, I don't enjoy all this."

"Of course you don't. The thought of giving up all this is like thinking of having your eyes pulled out, isn't it?"

"But of course it's all rubbish. Of course you are imagining an ugly bogey man," and Dick laughed nervously.

"I'm imagining nothing, Faversham."

"Then you mean to tell me — —"

"That Mr. Anthony Riggleton is alive? Yes, I do."

Dick gave the Count an angry look, then started to his feet and began to pace the room.

"Of course it's all nonsense," he cried after a few seconds. "Please don't imagine that I'm going to accept a cock-and-bull sort of story like that. Do you think that Bidlake would be deceived? Do you imagine that the man he employed in Melbourne would be duped? No, no, I'm not such a fool as to accept that. Besides, what have you to do with it? Why did you come here in such a fashion, and with such a story? It does not look very friendly, does it?"

"Why I came here, and why I have told you the truth, will leak out presently. You will see then that I came not as an enemy, but as a friend."

"As a friend!" and there was an angry sneer in Dick's voice.

"As a friend," repeated Romanoff. "Of course," he went on quietly, "I expected that you would take it in this way; but you will soon see that my motives are—not unworthy of a friend."

"Tell me then how you came to know of this. Perhaps you will also give me some proofs that Mr. Anthony Riggleton, who was found dead, whose body was identified by responsible witnesses, has so miraculously come to life again. Believe me, this hearsay, this wonderful story does not appeal to me. Do you come to me with this—this farrago of nonsense with the belief that I am going to give up all this?" and he looked out of the window towards the far-spreading parks as he spoke, "without the most absolute and conclusive proof? If Mr. Anthony Riggleton is alive, where is he? Why does he not show himself? Why does he not come here and claim his own?"

"Because I have stopped him from coming," replied Romanoff.

"You have stopped him from coming?" cried Dick excitedly.

"Exactly."

"Then you have seen him?"

"I have seen him."

"But how do you know it was he? Are Mr. Bidlake's inquiries to go for nothing? No, no, it won't do. I can't be deceived like that."

"I know it was he because I have the most absolute proofs—proofs which I am going to submit to you."

"You saw him, you say?"

"I saw him."

"But where?"

"In Australia. I told you, didn't I, that—after leaving you I went to Australia? I told you, too, that I left Australia quickly because I did not like the country. That was false. I came because I wanted to warn you, to help you. You asked me just now why, if Mr. Anthony Riggleton was alive, he did not show himself. I will tell you why. If I had allowed him to do so, if he knew that he was heir to all you now possess, you would be a poor man. And I did not want you to be a poor man. I did not want your life to be ruined, your future sacrificed, your hopes destroyed. That's why, Faversham. That's why I left Australia and came here without wasting an hour. That's why I examined your uncle's will; that's why I came to warn you."

"To warn me?"

"To warn you."

"Against what?"

"Against dangers—against the dangers which might engulf you—ruin you for ever."

"You speak in a tragic tone of voice."

"I speak of tragic things. I told you that this was your hour of destiny. I told you the truth. This night will decide your future. You are a young fellow with your life all before you. You were born for enjoyment, for pleasure, for ease. You, unlike your uncle, who made all the wealth we are thinking of, are not a business genius; you are not a great master personality who can forge your way through difficult circumstances. You are not cast in that mould. But you can enjoy. You have barely felt your feet since you came into possession of great wealth, but already you have dreamt dreams, and seen visions. You have already made plans as to how you can suck the orange of the world dry. And to-night will be the time of decision."

Dick laughed uneasily. "How?" he asked, and his face was pale to the lips.

"Is there a photograph of Mr. Anthony Riggleton in the house?" asked Romanoff.

"Yes, I came across one the other day. Would you like to see it?" He went to a drawer as he spoke and took a packet from it. "Here is the thing," he added.

"Just so," replied Romanoff; "now look at this," and he took a photograph from his pocket. "It's the same face, isn't it? The same man. Well, my friend, that is the photograph of a man I saw in Australia, weeks after you got your wireless from Mr. Bidlake—months after the news came that Mr. Anthony Riggleton was dead. I saw him; I talked with him. He told me a good deal about himself, told me of some of his experiences in this house. There are a number of people in this neighbourhood who knew him, and who could identify him."

"You are sure of this?" gasped Dick.

"Absolutely."

"And does he know—that—that his uncle is dead?"

"Not yet. That's why I hurried here to see you. But he has made up his mind to come to England, and of course he intends coming here."

"He told you this, did he?"

"Yes. I came across him in a little town about five hundred miles from Melbourne, and when I found out who he was I thought of you."

"But how do you explain the news of his death, the inquest, and the other things?"

"I'll come to that presently. It's easily explained. Oh, there's no doubt about it, Faversham. I have seen the real heir to all the wealth you thought your own."

"But what do you mean by saying that you stopped him from coming here?" and Dick's voice was husky.

"I'm going to tell you why I stopped him. I'm going to tell you how you can keep everything, enjoy everything. Yes, and how you can still marry the woman you are dreaming of."

"But if the real heir is alive—I—I can't," stammered Dick.

"I'm here to show you how you can," persisted Romanoff. "Did I not tell you that this was the hour of destiny?"

Chapter XII
The Day of Destiny

Dick Faversham wiped away the beads of perspiration that stood thick upon his forehead. It seemed to him that he was surrounded by peculiar influences, that forces were at work which he could not understand. In one sense he did not at all believe in the story that Count Romanoff had told him. It appeared to him chimerical, unconvincing.

It did not seem at all likely that a man of Mr. Bidlake's experience and mental acumen could have been so deceived. This subtle-minded lawyer, who had lived in London for so many years and had been spoken of as one of the most astute and level-headed men in the profession, would not be likely to communicate news of such great importance to him without being absolutely certain of his ground. He had shown him details of everything, too, and Mr. Bidlake was absolutely certain that Mr. Anthony Riggleton was dead, that he was murdered near Melbourne. The proofs of this were demonstrated in a hundred ways. No, he did not believe in Romanoff's story.

Besides, it was absurd, on the face of it. Who was this Count Romanoff? He knew little or nothing of him. Though he owed his life to him, he knew nothing of his history or antecedents. He was afraid of him, too. He did not like his cynical way of looking at things, nor understand his mockery of current morality. And should he believe the bare word of such a man?

And yet he did believe him. At the back of his mind he felt sure that he had spoken the truth.

It came to him with ghastly force that he was not the owner of this fine old house, and of all the wealth that during the last few weeks he had almost gloated over. There was something in the tones of Romanoff's voice—something in his mocking yet intense way of speaking that convinced him in spite of himself.

And the fact maddened him. To be poor now after these few brief weeks of riches would drive him mad. He had not begun to enjoy yet. He had not carried out the plans which had been born in his mind. He had only just entered into possession, and had been living the life of a pattern young man. But he had meant to enjoy, to drink the cup of pleasure to the very dregs.

His mind swept like lightning over the conversation which had taken place, and every word of it was burnt into his brain. What did the Count mean by telling him that he could retain everything? Why did he persist in urging that he had hurried from Australia to England to save him from losing everything? What did he mean by telling him that this was his hour of destiny—that on his decision would depend the future of his life?

"You mean—to say then, that—that——" he stammered, after a long, painful silence.

"That Anthony Riggleton, the legal heir of old Charles Faversham, is alive," interrupted Romanoff. "I myself have seen him, have talked with him."

"Does he know that he is—is the rightful heir?"

"Not yet," and Romanoff smiled. "I took good care of that."

"You mean——"

"I mean that I did not save your life for nothing. When I had fully convinced myself that he was—who he said he was—I of course reflected on what it meant. I called to mind what you had told me on that island, and I saw how his being alive would affect you."

"How did you know? I did not tell you the terms of the will. I did not know them myself."

"Does it matter how I knew? Anyhow, he—Riggleton—would guess."

"How did he know?"

Romanoff shrugged his shoulders. "How should I know, my dear fellow? But one can easily guess. He knew he was next-of-kin to old Charles Faversham, and would naturally think he would inherit his wealth. But that is not all. Australia, although a long way from England, is not away from the lines of communication. Melbourne is quite a considerable city. It has newspapers, telephones, cablegrams, and a host of other things. But one thing Anthony Riggleton did not know: he did not know that the terms of the will were published in the Melbourne newspapers. He was afraid to go near Melbourne, in fact. He thought it best for the world to think of him as dead. Indeed, he paid a man to personate him in Melbourne, and that man paid the penalty of his deceit by his life."

"It's anything but clear to me."

"Then I'll make it clear. Riggleton had enemies in Melbourne whom it was necessary for him to see, but whom he was personally afraid to meet. He had served them very shabbily, and they had threatened him with unpleasant things. He had as a friend a man who resembled him very closely, and he offered this friend a sum of money if he would go to Melbourne and personate him. This man, ignorant of his danger, accepted the offer—now, do you see?"

After he had asked many questions about this—questions which Romanoff answered freely—Dick looked long and steadily at a picture of old Charles Faversham which hung on the wall. He was trying to co-ordinate the story—trying to understand it.

"And where is Anthony Riggleton now?"

"He is in England."

"In England! Then—then——"

"Exactly," interrupted Romanoff. "You see what I meant when I said that the foundations of your position were very insecure. I do not imagine that Lady Blanche Huntingford would think very seriously about Dick Faversham if she knew the whole truth."

"But—but—in England?"

"Exactly. In England."

"But you say he does not know—the truth?"

"No. He may guess it, though. Who knows?"

"But why did you not tell me this last night? Why wait till now before letting me know?"

Again Romanoff smiled; he might be enjoying himself.

"Because I like you, my friend. Because I wanted to see the state of your mind, and to know whether it was possible to help you."

"To help me?"

"To help you. I saw the kind of man you were. I saw what such wealth as you thought you possessed would mean to you. I saw, too, to what uses you could turn the power that riches would give you. So I made my plans."

"But you say he is in England. If so, he will know—all!"

"No, he does not. I took good care of that."

"But he will find out."

Romanoff laughed. "No, my friend, I have taken care of everything. As I told you, I like you, and I want you to be a great figure in the life of your country. That is why you are safe—for the present."

Again Dick wiped the beads of perspiration from his forehead. It seemed to him as though he were standing on a precipice, while beneath him were yawning depths of darkness. All he had hoped for was mocking him, and he saw himself sinking under the stress of circumstances, just as on that terrible night he felt himself sinking in the deep waters. But there were no arms outstretched to save him, nor friendly help near him. He looked around the room, noble in its proportions, and handsomely appointed, and thought of all it suggested. He remembered his last interview with Mr. Bidlake, when that gentleman gave him an account of his possessions, and told him of the approximate amount of his fortune. And now it would all go to this man who was not even aware of the truth. It was all bewildering, maddening. Before he had properly begun to taste of the sweets of fortune they were being dashed from his lips. He felt as though he were losing his senses, that his brain was giving way under the stress of the news he had heard.

Then his innate manhood began to assert itself. If what Romanoff had said were true, he must bear it. But, of course, he would not yield without a struggle. He would take nothing on the bare word of a man who, after all, was a stranger. Everything should be proved up to the hilt before he relinquished possession.

"Safe for the present!" Dick repeated, and there was a note of angry scorn in his voice. "Of course, if—if you are not mistaken, there is no question of safety."

"No question of safety?"

"Certainly not. If Anthony Riggleton is alive, and if he is the true heir to old Charles Faversham, he must make his claim, as I assume he will."

"Then you will yield without a struggle?" and there was a peculiar intonation in Romanoff's voice.

"No," cried Dick, "I shall not yield without a struggle. I shall place the whole matter in Bidlake's hands, and—and if I'm a pauper, I am—that's all."

"I know a better way than that."

"I don't understand you."

"No, but you will in a minute. Faversham, there's no need for you to fix up anything, no need for anyone to know what only you and I know."

"Look here," and Dick's voice trembled. "Are you sure that this fellow you talk about is Anthony Riggleton—and that he is the lawful heir?"

Romanoff gave Dick a quick, searching glance; then he gave a peculiar laugh. "Am I sure that the man is Anthony Riggleton? Here's the photograph he gave me of himself. I compared the photograph with the man, and I'm not likely to be mistaken. The photograph is the exact representation of the man. You have photographs of Riggleton in this house; compare them. Besides, he's been here repeatedly; he's known, I imagine, to the servants, to the neighbours. If he is allowed to make a claim, it will not be a question of Roger Tichborne and Arthur Orton over again, my friend. He will be able to prove his rights."

"What do you mean by saying, 'if he is allowed to make his claim'?" asked Dick hoarsely. "Of course he'll be allowed."

"Why of course?"

"Naturally he will."

"That depends on you. Did I not tell you that this was your hour of destiny?"

"Then the matter is settled. I will not usurp another man's rights. If he's the lawful owner, he shall have his own. Of course, he will have to prove it."

"You don't mean that?"

"Of course I do. Why not?"

"Because it would be criminal madness—the act of a fool!"

"It is the only attitude for a decent fellow."

Again Romanoff let his piercing eyes fall on Dick's face. He seemed to be studying him afresh, as though he were trying to read his innermost thoughts.

"Listen, my dear fellow," and the Count calmly cut the end of a fresh cigar. "I want to discuss this matter with you calmly, and I want our discussion to be entirely free from sentimental rubbish. To begin with, there is no doubt that the man Anthony Riggleton is alive, and that he is the legal owner of all Charles Faversham's fabulous fortune. Of that I've no doubt. If he came here everyone would recognise him, while there is not a lawyer, not a judge or jury in the land, who would not acclaim him the owner of all which you thought yours. But, as I said, I like you. You were meant to be a rich man; you were meant to enjoy what riches can give you. And of this I am sure, Faversham: poverty after this would mean hell to you. Why, man, think what you can have—titles, position, power, the love of beautiful women, and a thousand things more. If you want to enter public life the door is open to you. With wealth like yours a peerage is only a matter of arrangement. As for Lady Blanche Huntingford— —" and the Count laughed meaningly.

"But what is the use of talking like that if nothing really belongs to me?" cried Dick.

"First of all, Faversham," went on the Count, as though Dick had not spoken, "get rid of all nonsense."

"Nonsense? I don't understand."

"I mean all nonsense about right and wrong, about so-called points of honour and that sort of thing. There is no right, and no wrong in the conventional sense of the word. Right! wrong! Pooh, they are only bogys invented by priests in days of darkness, in order to obtain power. It is always right to do the thing that pays—-the thing that gives you happiness—power. The German philosophy is right there. Do the thing you can do. That's common sense."

"It's devilish!" exclaimed Dick.

"Your mind's unhinged, excited, or you wouldn't say so," replied Romanoff. "Now, look at me," and he fastened Dick's eyes by his intense gaze. "Do I look like a fanatic, a fool? Don't I speak with the knowledge of the world's wisdom in my mind? I've travelled in all the countries in the world, my friend, and I've riddled all their philosophies, and I tell you this: there is no right, no wrong. Life is given to us to enjoy, to drink the cup of pleasure to its depths, to press from the winepress all its sweets, and to be happy."

He spoke in low, earnest tones, and as he did so, Dick felt as though his moral manhood were being sapped. The glitter of the Count's eyes fascinated him, and while under their spell he saw as the Count saw, felt as he felt.

And yet he was afraid. There was something awesome in all this— something unholy.

"Look here!" and Dick started to his feet. "What do you mean by coming to me in this way? Why should you so coolly assert that the moralities of the centuries are nonsense? Who are you? What are you?"

Again the Count laughed.

"Who am I? What am I?" he repeated. "You remember Napoleon Bonaparte's famous words: 'I am not a man. I am a thing. I am a force.

Right and wrong do not exist for me. I make my own laws, my own morals.' Perhaps I could say the same, Faversham."

"Napoleon found out his mistake, though," protested Dick.

"Did he? Who knows? Besides, better taste the sweets of power, if only for a few years, than be a drudge, a nonentity, a poor, struggling worm all your days."

"But what do you want? What have you in your mind?"

"This, Faversham. If you will listen to me you will treat Anthony Riggleton as non-existent— —"

"As non-existent?"

"Yes, you can with safety—absolute safety; and then, if you agree to my proposal, all you hope for, all you dream of, shall be yours. You shall remain here as absolute owner without a shadow of doubt or a shadow of suspicion, and—enjoy. You shall have happiness, my friend—happiness. Did I not tell you that this was your day of destiny?"

Chapter XIII
The Invisible Hand

Again Dick felt as though he were gripped by an irresistible power, and that this power was evil. It was true that the Count sat in the chair near him, faultlessly dressed, urbane, smiling, with all the outward appearance of a polished man of the world; all the same, Dick felt that an evil influence dominated the room. The picture which Romanoff made him see was beautiful beyond words, and he beheld a future of sensuous ease, of satisfied ambition, of indescribable delights. And what he saw seemed to dull his moral sense, to undermine his moral strength. Moreover, the man had by his news undermined the foundations of life, shattered the hopes he had nourished, and thus left him unable to fight.

"Tell me that this is a—a joke on your part," Dick said at length. "Of course it's not true."

"Of course it is true."

"Well, I'll have it proved, anyhow. Everything shall be sifted to the bottom."

"How?"

"I'll go and see Bidlake to-morrow. I'll tell him what you've said."

"You will do no such thing." The Count spoke in the most nonchalant manner.

"Why not? Indeed, I shall."

"You will not. I'll tell you why. First, because it would be criminally insane, and second, because you would be cutting your own throat."

"Please explain."

"Understand," replied Romanoff, "that this is really nothing to me after all. I do not benefit by your riches, or lose by your poverty. Why, I wonder, am I taking an interest in the matter?" And for the moment he seemed to be reflecting. "I suppose it is because I like you—of course that is it. Besides, I saved your life, and naturally one has an interest in the life one has saved. But to explain: accept for the moment the conventional standards of right and wrong, good and evil, and what is the result? Suppose you give up everything to Riggleton—what follows? You give up all this to an unclean beast. You put power in the hands of a man who hasn't an elevated thought or desire. You, now—if you are wise, and retain what you have—can do some good with your money. You can bring comfort to the people on your estates; you can help what you believe worthy causes. You, Faversham, are a gentleman at heart, and would always act like one. Mind, I *don't* accept conventional morality; it is no more to me than so much sawdust. But I do respect the decencies of life. My education has thrown me among people who have a sense of what's fit and proper. Anyhow, judging from your own standards, you would be doing an *immoral* thing by handing this great fortune to Riggleton."

"Tell me about him," and Dick felt a tightening at the throat.

"Tell you about him! An unsavoury subject, my friend. A fellow with the mind of a pig, the tastes of a pig. What are his enjoyments? His true place is in a low-class brothel. If he inherited Wendover Park, he would fill these beautiful rooms with creatures of his own class—men and women."

The Count did not raise his voice, but Dick realised its intensity; and again he felt his influence—felt that he was being dominated by a personality stronger than his own.

"No, no," he continued, and he laughed quietly as he spoke; "copybook morality has no weight with me. But I trust I am a gentleman. If, to use your own term, I sin, I will sin like a gentleman; I will enjoy myself like a gentleman. But this man is dirty. He wallows in filth—wallows in it, and rejoices in it. That is Anthony Riggleton. Morality! I scorn it. But decency, the behaviour of a gentleman, to act as a gentleman under every circumstance—that is a kind of religion with me! Now, then, Faversham, would it not be criminal madness to place all this in the hands of such a loathsome creature when you can so easily prevent it?"

Of course, the argument was commonplace enough. It was a device by which thousands have tried to salve their consciences, and to try to find an excuse for wrong-doing. Had some men spoken the same words, Dick might not have been affected, but uttered by Romanoff they seemed to undermine the foundations of his reasoning power.

"But if he is in England?" he protested weakly.

"He is, but what then?"

"He must know; he must. He is not an idiot, I suppose?"

"No; he is cunning with a low kind of cunning—the cunning of a sensual beast. Some would say he is clever."

"Then he must find out the truth."

"Not if you say he must not."

"What have I to do with it?"

"Everything," and Romanoff's eyes seemed to be searching into Dick's innermost soul.

"But how? I do not understand," and he nervously wiped his moist hands.

"Say so, and he must be got rid of."

"How?"

Romanoff laughed quietly. "These are good cigars, Faversham," he said, like one who was vastly enjoying himself. "Oh, you can do that easily enough," he continued.

"How?" asked Dick. He felt his eyes were hot as he turned them towards the other.

"I said treat him as though he were non-existent. Well, let him *be* non-existent."

"You mean—you mean——" and Dick's voice could scarcely be recognised.

"Why not?" asked the Count carelessly. "The fellow is vermin—just dirty vermin. But he is a danger—a danger to the community, a danger to you. Why, then, if it can be done easily, secretly, and without anyone having the slightest chance of knowing, should you not rid the world of such a creature? Especially when you could save all this," and he looked around the room, "as well as marry that divine creature, and live the life you long to live."

"Never!" cried Dick. "What?—murder! Not for all the wealth ever known. No, no—my God, no!"

"If there are good deeds in the world, that would be a good deed," persisted Romanoff. "You would be a benefactor to your race, your country," and there was a touch of pleading in his voice. "Why, man, think; I have him safe—safe! No one could know, and it would be a praiseworthy deed."

"Then why not do it yourself?" cried Dick. There was a sneer as well as anger in his voice.

"I am not the next heir to the Faversham estates," replied Romanoff. "What does it matter to me who owns all that old Charles Faversham gained during his life?"

"Then why suggest such a thing? Why, it's devilish!"

"Don't—please, don't be melodramatic," the Count drawled. "Would you not kill a rat that ate your corn? Would you not shoot any kind of vermin that infested your house? Well, Riggleton is vermin, human vermin if you like, but still vermin, and he is not fit to live. If I, Romanoff, were in your position, I would have no more hesitation in putting him out of existence than your gamekeeper would have in shooting a dog with rabies. But, then, I am not in your position. I have nothing to gain. I only take a friendly interest in you. I have hurried to you with all speed the moment I knew of your danger, and I have told you how you can rid the world of a coarse, dirty-minded animal, and at the same time save for yourself the thing nearest your heart."

"Did he come in the same vessel with you?"

"Suffice to say that I know he is in England, and in safe keeping."

"Where? How? England has laws to protect everyone."

"That does not matter. I will tell you if you like; but you would be none the wiser."

"Then you have arranged this?"

"If you like—yes."

"But why?"

"Still the same silly question. Have you no sense of proportion, Faversham? Haven't I told you again and again?"

Dick was almost gasping for breath, and as he buried his head in his hands, he tried to understand, to realise. In calmer moments his mind would doubtless have pierced the cheap sophistry of the Count, and discarded it. But, as I have said, he was greatly excited, bewildered. Never as now did he desire wealth. Never as now had the thought of winning Lady Blanche seemed the great thing in life to be hoped for. And he knew the Count was right—knew that without his money she would no more think of marrying him than of marrying the utmost stranger. And yet his heart craved after her. He longed to possess her—to call her his own. He saw her as he had never seen her before, a splendid creature whose beauty outshone that of any woman he had ever seen, as the sun outshone the moon.

And this Anthony Riggleton, whom the Count described as vermin, stood in his way. Because of a quibble on his part this loathsome thing would ruin his future, dash his hopes to the ground, blacken his life.

But the alternative!

"No, of course not!" he cried.

"You refuse?"

"Certainly I do. I'm not a murderer."

"Very well, go your own way. Go to your Mr. Bidlake, see him shrug his shoulders and laugh, and then watch while your cousin—your *cousin!*—turns this glorious old place into a cesspool."

"Yes; rather than stain my hands in——I say, Romanoff," and the words passed his lips almost in spite of himself, "there must be some deep reason why you—you say and do all this. Do you expect to gain anything, in any way, because of my—retaining possession of my uncle's wealth?"

For the first time the Count seemed to lose possession over himself. He rose to his feet, his eyes flashing.

"What!" he cried; "do you mean that I, Romanoff, would profit by your poor little riches? What is all this to me? Why, rich as you thought you were, I could buy up all the Faversham estates—all—all, and then not know that my banking account was affected. I, Romanoff, seek to help a man whom I had thought of as my friend for some paltry gain! Good-night, Mr. Richard Faversham, you may go your own way."

"Stop!" cried Dick, almost carried away by the vehemence of the other; "of course, I did not mean——"

"Enough," and the Count interrupted him by a word and a laugh. "Besides, you do not, cannot, understand. But to rid your mind of all possible doubt I will show you something. Here is my account with your Bank of England. This is for pocket-money, pin-money, petty cash as your business men call it. There was my credit yesterday. In the light of that, do you think that I need to participate in your fortune, huge as you regard it?"

Dick was startled as he saw the amount. There could be no doubt about it. The imprimatur of the Bank of England was plainly to be seen, and the huge figures stood out boldly.

"I'm sure I apologise," stammered Dick. "I only thought that—that—you see——"

"All right," laughed the Count, "let it be forgotten. Besides, have I not told you more than once that I am interested in you? I have shown you my interest, and — —"

"Of course you have," cried Dick. "I owe you my life; but for you I should not be alive to-day."

"Just so. I want to see you happy, Faversham. I want you to enjoy life's sweetness. I want you to be for ever free from the haunting fear that this Anthony Riggleton shall ever cross your path. That is why — —"

He hesitated, as though he did not know what to say next.

"Yes," asked Dick, "why what?"

"That is why I want to serve you further."

"Serve me further? How?"

"Suppose I get rid of Riggleton for you?"

"I do not understand."

"Suppose I offer to get rid of Riggleton for you? Suppose without your having anything to do with him, without knowing where he is, I offer to remove him for ever from your path—would you consent?"

"I consent?"

"Yes; I must have that. Would you give it?"

"You—you—that is, you ask me if I will consent to—to his—his murder?"

"Just that, my friend. That must be—else why should I do it? But—but I love you, Faversham—as if you were my son, and I would do it for your happiness. Of course, it's an unpleasant thing to do, even although I have no moral scruples, but I'll do it for you."

Again Dick felt as though the ground were slipping from under his feet. Never before was he tempted as he was tempted now, never did it seem so easy to consent to wrong. And he would not be responsible. He had suggested nothing, pleaded nothing. His part would be simply to be blindly quiescent. His mind was confused to every issue save one. He had only to consent, and this man Riggleton, the true owner of everything, would be removed for ever.

"And if I do not?" he asked.

"Then nothing more need be said. But look at me, Faversham, and tell me if you will be such a fool. If there is any guilt, I bear it; if there is any danger, I face it; do you refuse, Faversham? I only make the offer for your sake."

Again Dick felt the awful eyes of the Count piercing him; it was as though all his power of judgment, all his volition were ebbing away. At that moment he felt incapable of resistance.

"And if I consent?" he asked weakly.

"Of course you will, you *will*, you will," and the words were repeated with peculiar intensity, while the eyes of the two met. "I only make one stipulation, and I must make it because you need a friend. I must make it binding for your sake."

He took a piece of paper from a desk and scribbled a few words.

"There, read," he said.

Dick read:

"I promise to put myself completely under the guidance of Count Romanoff with regard to the future of my life."

"There, sign that, Faversham," and the Count placed the pen in his hand.

Without will, and almost without knowledge, Dick took the pen.

"What do you want me to do?" asked Dick dully.

"Sign that paper. Just put 'Richard Faversham' and the date. I will do the rest."

"But—but if I do this, I shall be signing away my liberty. I shall make myself a slave to you."

"Nonsense, my dear fellow. Why should I interfere with your liberty?"

"I don't know; but this paper means that." He was still able to think consecutively, although his thoughts were cloudy and but dimly realised.

"Think, Faversham. I am undertaking a dirty piece of work for your sake. Why? I am doing it because I want you to be free from Anthony Riggleton, and I am doing it because I take a deep interest in you."

"But why should I sign this?"

In spite of the Count's influence over him, he had a dull feeling that there was no need for such a thing. Even although he had tacitly consented to Romanoff's proposal he saw no necessity for binding himself.

"I'll tell you why. It's because I know you—because I read your mind like a book. I want to make you my protégé, and I want you to cut a figure in the life of the world. After all, in spite of Charles Faversham's wealth, you are a nobody. You are a commoner all compact. But I can make you really great. I am Romanoff. You asked me once if I were of the great Russian family, and I answered yes. Do you know what that means? It means that no door is closed to me—that I can go where I will, do what I will. It means that if I desire a man's aggrandisement, it is an accomplished fact. Not only are the delights of this country mine for the asking, but my name is an *Open Sesame* in every land. My name and my influence are a key to unlock every door; my hand can draw aside the curtain of every delight. And there are delights in the world that you know nothing of, never dreamt of. As my protégé I want them to be yours. A great name, great power, glorious pleasures, the smile of beautiful women, delights such as the author of *The Arabian Nights* only dimly dreamt of—it is my will that you shall have them all. Charles Faversham's money and my influence shall give you all this and more. But I am not going to have a fretful, puling boy objecting all the time; I am not going to have my plans for your happiness frustrated by conscience and petty quibbles about what is good and evil. That is why I insist on your signing that paper."

Romanoff spoke in low tones, but every word seemed to be laden with meanings hitherto unknown to Dick. He saw pictures of exquisite delights, of earthly paradises, of joys that made life an ecstasy.

And still something kept his hand still. He felt rather than reasoned that something was wrong—that all was wrong. He was in an abnormal state of mind; he knew that the influences by which he was surrounded were blinding him to truth, and giving him distorted fancies about life's values.

"No," he said doggedly; "I won't sign, and I won't consent to this devilish deed."

Again Romanoff laughed. "Look at me, Dick, my boy," he said. "You are not a milksop; you were made to live your whole life. Fancy you being a clerk in an office, a store—a poor little manikin keeping body and soul together in order to do the will of some snivelling tradesman! Think of it! Think of Anthony Riggleton living here, or in London, in Paris, in India—or wherever he pleases—squandering his money, and satiated with pleasure, while you—you——Pooh! I know you. I see you holding Lady Blanche in your arms. I see you basking in the smiles of beautiful women all over the world. I see the name of Faversham world-wide in its power. I see——" and the Count laughed again.

All the while, too, he kept Dick's eyes riveted on his own—eyes which told him of a world of sensuous delights, and which robbed him of his manhood. No, he could not bear to become poor again, and he would not give up the delights he had dreamt of. Right! Wrong! Good! Evil! They were only words. The Count was right. It was his right to enjoy.

"All right, I'll sign," he said.

He dipped the pen into the ink, and prepared to inscribe his name, but the moment he placed his hand on the paper it felt as though it were paralysed.

"There is something here!" he gasped.

"Something here? Nonsense."

"But there is. Look!"

It seemed to him that a ray of light, brighter than that of the electric current that burnt in the room, streamed towards him. Above him, too, he saw the face that was now becoming familiar to him. Strange that he had forgotten it during the long conversation, strange that no memory of the evening before, when over the doorway he had seen an angel's face beaming upon him and warning him, had come to him.

But he remembered now. The night on the heaving sea, the vision on the island, the luminous form over the doorway of the house, all flashed before him, and in a way he could not understand Romanoff's influence over him lessened—weakened.

"Sign—sign there!" urged the Count, pointing towards the paper.

"What is the matter with your eyes?" gasped Dick. "They burn with the light of hell fire."

"You are dreaming, boy. Sign, and let's have a bottle of wine to seal the bargain."

"I must be dreaming," thought Dick. "An angel's face! What mad, idiotic nonsense!"

He still held the pen in his hand, and it seemed to him that strength was again returning to his fingers.

"Where must I sign?" he muttered. "I can't see plainly."

"There—right at the point of your pen," was the Count's reply.

But Dick did not sign, for suddenly he saw a white, shadowy hand appear, which with irresistible strength gripped his wrist.

Chapter XIV
A Scrap of Paper

Suddenly the spell, or whatever had enchained him, was broken. There was a noise of wheels on the gravel outside, and the sound of footsteps in the hall. He heard the Count mutter a savage oath, and a moment later the door opened and he heard a happy, clear, girlish voice:

"Oh, Mr. Faversham, forgive me for coming; but I really couldn't help myself."

It was Beatrice Stanmore who, unheralded and unaccompanied, stood by his side.

He muttered something, he knew not what, although he felt as though a weight had been lifted from his shoulders, and strength came back to his being.

"I really couldn't," the girl went on. "Granddad left me just after a very early dinner, and then I felt awfully miserable and depressed. I didn't know why. It was just ghastly. Nothing had happened, and yet I knew—why, I couldn't tell—that something was terribly wrong. Then something told me that you were in danger, that unless I came to help you, you would be—oh, I can't put it into words! You are not in danger, are you?"

"It was very kind of you to come," muttered Dick. "I'm no end glad to see you."

"But—but I'm afraid!" she said in her childish way. "I don't know what Granddad will say to me. You see, you are a stranger to me, and I had no right to come. But I couldn't help it—I really couldn't. Someone seemed to be saying to me all the time, 'Mr. Faversham is in deadly peril; go to him—go to him quick! quick!' And I couldn't help myself. I kept telling myself that I was very silly, and all that sort of thing, but all the time I heard the voice saying, 'Quick, quick, or you'll be too late!' But I'm afraid it's all wrong. You are all right. You are in no danger, are you?"

"I'm no end glad to see you," he repeated. "And it is awfully good of you to come."

He still seemed to be under strange influences, but he no longer felt as though his strength was gone. His heart was strangely light, too. The presence of the girl by his side gave him comfort.

"You are not angry with me, then? I've not done wrong, have I?"

"Wrong? No! You have done quite right—quite. Thank you very, very much."

"I'm glad of that. When I had left our house I wanted to run to you. Then I thought of the car. I've learnt to drive, and Granddad thinks I'm very clever at it. I simply flew through the park. But I'm glad you are in no danger. I must go now."

She had not once looked at Romanoff; she simply stood gazing at Dick with wide-open, childish-looking eyes, and her words came from her almost pantingly, as though she spoke under the stress of great excitement. Then she looked at the paper before him.

"You are not going to write your name on that, are you?" she asked.

"No," he replied; "I'm not."

"You must not," she said simply. "It would be wrong. When I heard the words telling me to come to you I—I saw—but no, I can't recall it. But you must not sign that. I'll go now. Good-night, and please forgive me for coming."

"Please don't go yet."

"But I must. I could not stay here. There's something wrong, something evil. I'm sure there is."

She glanced nervously towards Romanoff, and shivered. "Good-night," she said, holding out her hand. "I really must go now. I think the danger is over—I feel sure it is; and Granddad will be anxious if he comes back and does not find me."

"I'll see you to the door," said Dick. "I shall never cease to thank you for coming."

Leaving the paper on the table, and without looking at Romanoff, he opened the door to her, and passed into the hall.

"Yes; I shall never cease to thank you," he repeated—"never. You have saved me."

"What from?" and she looked at him with a strangely wistful smile.

"I don't know," he replied—"I don't know."

When they stood together on the gravel outside the door, he gave a deep sigh. It seemed to him as though the pure, sweet air enabled him to lift every weight from himself. He was free—wonderfully, miraculously free.

"Oh, it is heavenly, just heavenly here!" and she laughed gaily. "I think this is the most beautiful place in the world, and this is the most beautiful night that ever was. Isn't the avenue just lovely? The trees are becoming greener and greener every day. It is just as though the angels were here, hanging their festoons. Do you like my car? Isn't it a little beauty?"

"Yes," replied Dick. "May—may I drive you back?"

"Will you? Then you can explain to Granddad. But no, you mustn't. You must go back to your friend."

"He isn't my friend," replied Dick almost involuntarily; "he's just—but perhaps you wouldn't understand."

"He isn't a good man," she cried impulsively. "I don't like him. I know I ought not to say this. Granddad often tells me that I let my tongue run away with me. But he's not a good man, and—and I think he's your enemy."

Dick was silent.

"Is he staying with you long?" she went on.

"No, not long."

"I'm glad of that. He isn't nice. He's—he's—I don't know what. I shall tell Granddad I've been here."

"He won't be angry, will he?"

"No; he's never angry. Besides, I think he'll understand. You'll come and see us soon, won't you?"

"I'm afraid I shall not be able to. I'm going away."

"Going away?"

"Yes; I'm leaving Wendover Park. At least, I expect so."

"You don't mean for always?"

"Yes; for always. To-night has decided it."

She looked at him wistfully, questioningly.

"Has that man anything to do with it? Is he driving you away?"

"No; he wants me to stay."

She again scanned his features in a puzzled, childish way. "Of course, I don't understand," she said.

"No; I hardly understand myself," and he spoke almost involuntarily. "Thank you very much for coming."

She clasped his hand eagerly. "I shall be very sorry if you go," she said, "but please don't do anything that man asks you. Please don't."

"I won't," replied Dick.

He started the car for her, and then watched her while she drove down the avenue. Then he stood for a few seconds looking at the great doorway. He might have been expecting to see there what had been so plainly visible before, but there was nothing.

The grey old mansion was simply bathed in the light of the dying day, while the silvery moon, which was just rising behind the tree-tops, sent its rays through the fast-growing leaves. But as Beatrice Stanmore had said, it was a most wondrous night. All nature was glorying in life, while the light breezes seemed to bring him distant messages. The birds, too, even although the sun had set, perhaps an hour before, sent their messages one to another, and twittered their love-songs as they settled to their rest.

He waited on the steps for perhaps five minutes, then he found his way back to Romanoff. For some seconds neither said anything; each seemed to have a weight upon his lips. Then Romanoff spoke.

"You refuse, then?"

"Yes; I refuse."

"What do you refuse?"

"Everything. I refuse to allow you to do that devilish deed. I refuse to obey you."

Romanoff laughed as his eyes rested on Dick's face.

"You know what this means, of course?"

"Yes, I know."

"Then—then I interfere no further."

"Thank you."

Romanoff waited a few seconds before he spoke again. "Of course, you are very silly, Faversham," he said. "Soon you'll be sorry for this, and some time you'll need my help. Meanwhile I'm tired, and will go to bed."

He passed out of the room as he spoke, and Dick noticed that the scrap of paper was gone.

Chapter XV
Count Romanoff's Departure

The next morning when Dick came downstairs he found Romanoff evidently prepared for a journey. His luggage had been brought into the hall, and he was looking at a time-table.

"Faversham, I am sorry that we part in this way," he said.

"Are you going?" asked Dick.

The Count looked at him steadily, as if trying to divine his state of mind—to know if he had changed his purposes since the previous evening.

"Naturally," he replied.

"You have settled on your train?"

"Yes; I go by the 10.43."

"Then I will see that a car is in readiness."

As may be imagined, Dick had spent a well-nigh sleepless flight, and he was in a nervous condition; but upon one thing he had decided. He would be studiously polite to the Count, and would in no way refer to the happenings of the previous night. Even yet he had not made up his mind about his visitor, except that he agreed with Beatrice Stanmore. The man still fascinated him; but he repelled him also. There was something mysterious, evil, about him; but the evil was alluring; it was made to seem as though it were not evil.

"Should you alter your mind," said the Count on leaving, "this address will find me. After to-night at ten o'clock, it will be useless to try to find me."

Dick looked at the card he had placed in his hand, and found the name of one of the best hotels in London.

When he had gone, the young man felt strangely lonely and fearfully depressed. The air seemed full of foreboding; everything seemed to tell him of calamity. As the morning passed away, too, he, more than once, found himself questioning his wisdom. After all, the Count had asked nothing unreasonable. Why should he not promise to be guided by a man who was so much older and wiser than himself? One, too, who could so greatly help him in the future.

Again and again he wandered around the house, and through the gardens. Again and again he feasted his eyes upon the beauty of the park and the glory of the district. And it was his no longer! Could he not even now— —

No; he could not! If Anthony Riggleton were alive, and was the true heir to old Charles Faversham's wealth, he should have it. The thought of doing what Romanoff had proposed made him shudder.

But he would not give up without a struggle. After all, he was in possession, and he was accepted as the owner of Wendover Park as well as heir to enormous wealth. Why, then, should he give it up? No; he would fight for what he held.

The day passed slowly away. He ate his lonely lunch in silence, and then, taking a two-seater car, ran it in the direction of Lord Huntingford's house. Just as he was passing the gates Lady Blanche appeared, accompanied by a girl of about her own age.

Almost unconsciously he lifted his foot from the accelerator and pressed down the brake.

"Alone, Mr. Faversham?" she asked, with a radiant smile.

"Quite alone, Lady Blanche."

"Your guest is gone, then?"

"He left this morning."

"Then—then please excuse the informality—but then we are neighbours; won't you come to dinner *en famille* on Thursday night? Father will be delighted to see you. And, oh, I want to introduce you to my friend here."

He did not catch the girl's name, but it did not matter. He had only eyes and ears for this glorious woman. Her face was wreathed with smiles, while her eyes shone brightly. Surely such a woman was never known before. In a moment he had forgotten the previous night—forgotten the great crisis in his life.

"Thursday! I shall be delighted!" he cried, lifting his cap.

The two passed on, and he resumed his drive. Why did he not ask them to accompany him? Why? Why?

His mind was in a turmoil. The sight of Lady Blanche had set his nerves tingling, and caused his blood to course madly through his veins. Her smile, her look, her attitude could only mean one thing: she thought kindly of him—she thought more than kindly of him.

Then he remembered. Wendover Park was not his—nothing was his. If Romanoff told him truly, he was a pauper. All—all would have to be sacrificed.

Where he went that afternoon he had no recollection. He only knew that he drove the car at its utmost speed, and that the country through which he was passing was strange to him. He wanted to get away from himself, from his thoughts, from everything that reminded him of the truth.

He returned to Wendover Park in time for dinner, and from eight to ten o'clock he sat alone. On his arrival he had asked whether there had been any callers, any message, and on receiving an answer in the negative, he had heaved a sigh of relief. In the library after dinner, however, the whole ghastly position had to be faced, and for two hours his mind was torn first this way and then that.

But he did nothing. He could not do anything. How could he?

The evening—the night passed, and there was no happening. Everything was orderly, quiet, commonplace. He might never have seen the luminous figure at the doorway, never felt that awesome gripping of his wrist; indeed, the whole experience might have been a dream, so unreal was it.

The next day passed, and still nothing happened. More than once he was on the point of ringing up Mr. Bidlake, but he refrained. What could he say to the keen old lawyer?

He did not leave the house during the whole day. Almost feverishly he listened to every sound. No footstep passed unnoticed, no caller but was anxiously scanned. Every time the telephone bell rang, he rushed to it with fast-beating heart, only to heave a sigh of relief when he discovered that there was no message concerning the things which haunted his mind.

Still another night passed, and still nothing happened. He was beginning to hope that Romanoff had been playing a practical joke on him, and that all his fears were groundless.

Then just before noon the blow came.

The telephone bell tinkled innocently near him, and on putting the instrument to his ear he heard Mr. Bidlake's voice.

"Is that you, Mr. Faversham?"

"Mr. Faversham speaking. You are Mr. Bidlake, aren't you?"

"Yes."

This was followed by a cough; then the lawyer spoke again.

"Will you be home this afternoon?"

"Yes."

"I want to see you very particularly. A strange thing has happened. Grotesque, in fact, and I want you to be prepared for—for anything."

"What?"

"I don't like telling you over the telephone. I'm tremendously upset. I can hardly speak collectedly."

"I think I know. It has to do with Anthony Riggleton and the Faversham estates, hasn't it?"

"How did you know? Yes; it has. It's terribly serious, I'm afraid. I'd better see you at once. Some arrangement, some compromise might be made."

"You mean that Riggleton is not dead? That you've seen him?"

He spoke quite calmly and naturally. Indeed, he was surprised at his command over himself.

"Yes; he's just left me. He's been here for two hours. Of course, I tried at first to take his visit as a joke, but——"

"You are convinced that it *was* Riggleton?"

"I can have no doubt about it—no possible doubt. He's deadly in earnest too, and his case is overwhelming—simply overwhelming. Never, outside the realms of the wildest romance, did I ever come across a case where a lawyer could be so completely mistaken. But I can't help it, and I'm afraid that—that your prospects for the future are materially altered. Of course you might——"

"You are coming down here, you say. There's a good train from Victoria at 1.45. Can you catch it?"

"Ye—s. I think so."

"Then I'll send a car to meet you at this end."

He rang the bell, altered the time of lunch, and then sat down to think. But not for long. Calmly as he had talked to the lawyer, his every nerve was quivering with excitement, every faculty was in tension.

He went to the window and looked out.

All he saw was his no longer. He had no doubt about it, and it seemed to him that an icy hand was placed upon his heart as he realised it.

And he might have retained it!

Was he glad or sorry because of what he had done? Every particle of his being was crying out for the life he longed to live, and yet——As he thought of the price he would have to pay, as he remembered Romanoff's words, he did not repent.

He calmly waited for the lawyer's arrival.

By four o'clock Mr. Bidlake was on his way back to London again, and Dick knew that his own fate was sealed. The lawyer had proved to him that he had no right to be there, and while he advised him to put on a bold face, and in the last extremity to try and compromise with Anthony Riggleton, he held out no hope. Anthony Riggleton was beyond doubt the true heir of old Charles Faversham, and he had undisputable proofs of the fact.

"I am more upset than I can say, Faversham," said the lawyer, when he had described Riggleton's visit, "but we can't help ourselves. He is perfectly sure of his ground, and he has reason to be."

"He convinced you entirely, then?"

"Absolutely—absolutely."

Dick was still calm. Perhaps the experiences of the last few days left him almost incapable of feeling.

"What sort of fellow is he?"

The lawyer puckered up his face, and shook his head dismally. "He will not be a Society favourite," was all he said.

"But he has no doubts as to his plans?"

"He says he's going to take possession immediately. If you offer any opposition, he will apply for an injunction."

"Has he any money?"

"He appeared to be quite well off. His clothes are quite new," added the lawyer, "and he sported some very flashy jewellery. I was impressed by the thought that he had someone behind him."

"Did he say so?"

"No, not definitely, but I formed that impression. Anyhow, you can be certain of this. He will lose no time in making his claim. Indeed, I should not be at all surprised if the papers don't contain some notice of his advent and his claims to-morrow morning."

"You said something about a compromise."

"Yes, you see" — and the lawyer coughed almost nervously — "this will be very awkward for you. You've no right here; you've been spending money which has not been your own. Still, your case is not without its good points. You are in possession, you have been accepted as the owner of — all this, and even although he has the prior claim, you would have great sympathy from a jury — should it come to that. I told him so. I don't promise anything, but it might be that he might be disposed to — do something considerable to persuade you to leave him in possession quietly."

"As a kind of salve for my disappointment?" and there was an angry light in Dick's eyes.

"If you like to put it that way, yes. But, bless my soul, it is close on four o'clock, and I must be going. I can't say how sorry I am, and — and if I can do anything — —"

"Is the fellow married?" interrupted Dick.

"No — nothing of that sort. After all, no one but he stands in the way of possession."

"What shall I do?" Dick asked himself. "I'm worse off than I was before. At any rate I was in the way of earning a few hundred pounds when that wireless came. But now everything is altered, and I don't know where to turn. Still — —" and there was a grim, hard look in his eyes.

Slowly he walked down the avenue towards the lodge gates. Away in the distance, as though coming towards him, he saw a young girl. It was Beatrice Stanmore. He took a few steps towards her, and then turned back. Something forbade his speaking to her; somehow she seemed closely connected with the black calamity which had fallen on him.

He had barely returned to the house when he heard the tooting of a motor horn, and, looking out, he saw a large, powerful motor-car coming rapidly up the avenue. A minute later he heard voices in the hall — voices which suggested recognition. Then the door opened.

"Mr. Anthony Riggleton!" said the servant excitedly.

Chapter XVI
Riggleton's Homecoming

A young fellow about twenty-eight years of age entered the room. He was a round-faced, thickly built man, and he carried himself with a swagger. Evidently it had been his desire to get himself up for the occasion. His clothes were new, and shouted aloud of his tastes. They suggested a bookmaker. He smoked a large cigar, and wore an aggressive buttonhole. He did not take off his hat on entering, but, having advanced a couple of steps, took a survey of the room.

"Yes," he said, and his voice was somewhat thick; "I remember the old place well. It's as natural as life." Then, coming up to where Dick was, he continued, "Of course you know who I am?"

Dick, who had difficulty in repressing his excitement, mentioned something about never having seen him before.

"Oh, stow that!" said the newcomer. "I'm Tony Riggleton, I am. You know that well enough."

"I don't see why I should," and Dick's voice was a little angry. He instinctively disliked Tony Riggleton.

"I do, though. Why, Bidlake hasn't been gone half an hour. Hopper has just told me."

Dick was silent. He did not see at the moment what there was for him to say.

"You guess why I'm here?" he went on.

"I'm not good at guessing." Dick felt that Riggleton had the whip hand of him, and while he did not intend to make any concessions to his whilom cousin, he felt sure what the upshot of their meeting would be.

"Oh, I say, Faversham," and Riggleton moved farther into the room, "it's no use taking the high hand with me. Of course I don't blame you, and naturally you're cut up. Anyone would be in your place. But there's nothing green about me. All this show belongs to me, and I mean to finger the coin. That's straight. Mind, I've come down here in a friendly way, and I don't want to be unreasonable. See? I'm old Faversham's heir. Old Bidlake was obliged to own it, although he wriggled like a ferret in a hole. I can see, too, that you're a bit of a swell, and would suit his book better than I can; but I can make the money go. Don't you make any mistake."

He laughed as he spoke, and made a pretence of re-lighting his cigar.

"Come now," he went on, "let's have a bottle of champagne, and then we can talk over things quietly."

"There's nothing to talk over as far as I can see," interposed Dick.

"What do you mean by that?" In spite of his assertive attitude, he did not appear at ease, and was constantly casting furtive and suspicious glances towards Dick.

"I mean," replied Dick, "that if you are old Charles Faversham's heir, and if you can prove it, there's nothing more to be said."

"You mean that you'll clear out quietly?"

There was evident astonishment in his voice. Apparently he had expected bluster, and perhaps a scene.

"Of course I shall clear out quietly. Naturally there are formalities with which you'll have to comply; but, if you are the true owner, you are, and there's no more to be said."

Riggleton looked at him with open-mouthed wonder, evidently staggered that Faversham was taking the matter so calmly.

Dick was silent. The fellow was getting on his nerves, and he had difficulty in keeping calm.

"Then you don't mean to fight it out?" he continued.

"Why should I?" asked Dick quietly. "You have placed your papers in Mr. Bidlake's hands, and left everything for his examination. Your identity will have to be proved, and all that sort of thing; but I hope I've too much self-respect to try to hold anything that isn't mine."

"Put it there!" cried Anthony Riggleton, holding out his hand. "That's what I call acting like a gentleman, that is. I sort of thought you'd get your monkey up, and—but there. It's all right. There's nothing fishy about me. I don't pretend to be a saint, I don't. In fact, I don't believe old Uncle Charlie ever meant me to come in for all his wad. S'welp me bob, I don't. I was never his sort, and I don't mind telling you that he as good as kicked me out from here. You see, I was always fond of a bit of life, and I've gone the whole hog in my time. But that's all over now."

"You mean that you're going to reform?"

"Reform! Not 'alf. No, Faversham; I'm going to have the time of my life. I'm going to—but—I say, have you been here ever since you thought you came in for the old man's whack?"

"Yes; why?"

"You *are* a plaster saint. By gosh, you are! But you don't see me burying myself in this hole. Of course it's very grand, and all that sort of thing; but, no, thank you! Tony Riggleton is going the whole hog. What's the use of money else? Of course I shall use the place now and then. When I feel my feet a bit I shall get some music-hall people down here for week-ends, and all that sort of thing. But, as for living here like Bidlake says you have!—no, thank you. London's my mark! I tell you, I mean to paint the town red. And then, if I can get passports and that sort of tommy-rot, I'll do Paris and Madrid and Rome. You don't catch me burying myself like a hermit. Not a little bit. Now I've got the money, I mean to make it fly. I *should* be a fool if I didn't!"

The man was revealing himself by every word he spoke. His tastes and desires were manifested by his sensual lips, his small, dull eyes and throaty voice.

"Now, look here, Faversham," he went on, "I'll admit you are different from what I expected you to be. I was prepared for a bit of a shindy, and that's straight. But you've taken a knock-down blow in a sporting way, and I want to do the thing handsome. Of course I own this show just as I own all the rest of the old man's estates; but there's nothing mean about me. Live and let live is my motto. You can stay on here for a week or a fortnight if you like. I don't want to be hard. For that matter, although I'm going back to town to-night, I'll come back on Saturday and bring some bits of fluff from the Friv, and we'll make a week-end of it. I expect you've plenty of fizz in the house, haven't you?"

Dick was silent. The conversation, only a part of which I have recorded, so disgusted him that, although he was not a Puritan by nature, he felt almost polluted by the man's presence. It seemed like sacrilege, too, that this fellow should turn Wendover Park into a sty, as he evidently meant to do, and he found himself wondering whether, after all, he would not have been justified in accepting Romanoff's offer.

"Come, what do you say?" went on Riggleton. "I tell you— —" and then he went on to give details of his programme. "There's no need for you to be so down in the mouth," he concluded. "There's plenty of money, as you know, and I'll not be hard on you."

The fellow was so coarsely patronising that Dick with difficulty kept himself from starting up and rushing from the room. At that moment, however, a servant entered and brought him a telegram, and a moment later his brain seemed on fire as he read:

"Riggleton's claim undoubtedly valid, but can still save situation if you accept my terms.—Romanoff, Hotel Cosmopolitan."

The words burnt into his brain; he felt as he had felt a few nights before when Romanoff had placed the paper before him to sign.

"Any answer, sir?"

He looked towards a pen which lay on the table before him. Why should he not send back an acceptance?

"I say," said Riggleton, "is that about the estate? Because if it is, I demand to see it."

His tone was loud and arrogant. The sight of the telegram had evidently aroused his suspicions and his desire to assert his mastery.

"Oh, I mean it," he went on. "I'm an easy chap to get on with, but I'm master here. I tell you that straight."

Dick felt as though his nerves were raw; the man's presence was maddening. And he had to give up everything to him!

"It's a purely personal telegram," he replied. "I'm only considering how I shall answer it."

He seized a telegraph form, and dipped a pen into an inkstand, but he did not write a word. His mind again flew back to the night when Romanoff tempted him, and when he had felt a hand grip his wrist.

"Let's get out," he said, cramming the telegram into his pocket.

"Yes; let's," assented Riggleton; "but let's have a drink before we go. I say, my man," and he turned to the servant, who still waited, "bring a bottle of fizz. Yes; do as you're told. I'm your new master. Everything belongs to me. See?"

The servant turned to Dick. Doubtless there had been a great deal of excited conversation in the servants' quarters, and he awaited confirmation of what he had heard.

"Do as he tells you," assented Dick, and then he left the room.

But he could not help hearing what took place between Riggleton and the servant.

"What do you mean by looking to him?" asked Riggleton angrily. "Any of your nonsense and it'll be right about face with you. I'm master here and no error. It was all a mistake about Faversham. Everything belongs to me. See? And look here, there's going to be a change here. I ain't no milksop, I can tell you, and the whole lot of you'll have to get a move on, or out you go. It isn't much time that I shall spend in this gloomy hole, but when I am here there'll be something doing. I shall get the place full of a jolly lot of girls, and Wendover Park won't be no mouldy church, nor no bloomin' nunnery. You can bet your life on that. There'll be plenty of booze, and plenty of fun. Now then, get that fizz, and be quick about it."

The man's raucous, throaty voice reached him plainly, and every word seemed to scrape his bare nerves. He left the hall, and went out on the lawn where the sun shone, and where the pure spring air came to him like some healing balm.

This, then, was his cousin! This was the man who was the heir of old Charles Faversham's great wealth!

The whole situation mocked him. He believed he had done the thing that was right, and this was the result of it.

Like lightning his mind swept over his experiences, and again he wondered at all that had taken place. He tried to understand his strange experiences, but he could not. His thoughts were too confused; his brain refused to grasp and to co-ordinate what he could not help feeling were wonderful events.

He looked towards the great doorway, where, on the day of his coming to Wendover Park, he had seen that luminous figure which had so startled him. But there was nothing to be seen now. He wondered, as he had wondered a hundred times since, whether it was an objective reality, or only the result of a disordered imagination. There, in the bright sunlight, with Anthony Riggleton's raucous voice still grating on his ears, he could not believe it was the former. But if it were pure imagination, why—why—— And again his mind fastened on the things which in spite of everything were beginning to revolutionise his life.

Then a thought startled him. He realised that a change had come over him. If he had met Tony Riggleton a few months before, neither the man's presence nor his language would have so disgusted him. He had writhed with anger when Riggleton had unfolded his plans to him, and yet a little while before he himself had contemplated a future which was not, in essence, so far removed from what his cousin had so coarsely expressed. Yes; he could not blind himself to the fact that since—since——But no, nothing was clear to him.

"I say, Faversham."

He turned and saw that Riggleton had joined him.

"Show me around a bit, will you? You see, the old man wouldn't have me here much, and—I should like to talk things over."

"I think, when Mr. Bidlake has got everything in order——"

"Oh, hang Bidlake! Besides, it's no use your talking about Bidlake. I've settled with him. You don't feel like talking, eh? Very well, let's go for a walk."

Almost instinctively Dick turned down the drive which led to the cottage where Beatrice Stanmore lived.

"Yes," reflected Riggleton, after they had walked some time in silence; "I suppose this kind of thing appeals to a poetical bloke like you seem to be. But it doesn't do for Tony R. I love a bit of life, I do. I always did. Did you ever hear that I ran away from school, and went off on my own when I was fifteen? Went to sea, I did, and knocked about the world. I had a rough time, too; that's why I've no polish now. But I know the value of money, I do, and you may bet your bottom dollar that I'll make things hum. Ah, here we are at the lodge gates."

Dick looked across a meadow, and saw old Hugh Stanmore's cottage. Even although it was some little distance away he could see the gaily coloured flowers in the garden and the pleasant quaintness of the cottage. But it was no longer his. In future it would belong to this clown by his side, and——

His thoughts were interrupted by the sound of a motor, and a few seconds later he caught sight of Lady Blanche Huntingford in her two-seater car. His heart gave a leap as he saw her put her foot on the clutch, while the car slowed down by his side.

The girl smiled into his face. "You've not forgotten your promise for to-morrow night, Mr. Faversham?" she said, and then, stopping the engine, she stepped lightly into the lane.

Chapter XVII
Faversham's Resolution

It seemed to Dick that nothing could have happened more unfortunately. Painfully aware as he was that Anthony Riggleton was standing by his side, and devouring every detail of the girl's appearance, he felt ashamed that she should see him. He wanted to run away, longed to disown all knowledge of the vulgar creature who accompanied him.

"No, I've not forgotten, Lady Blanche," he managed to say.

"And we may expect you?" There was eagerness in her voice, expectancy in the gladness of her bright eyes.

"I—I'm afraid not," he stammered.

The girl flashed a quick look upon him—a look partly of questioning, partly of disappointment. "Really, Mr. Faversham——" she protested, and then stopped. Perhaps she felt that something untoward had taken place.

"You see," he went on confusedly, "while I'd just love to come, things have happened since I saw you. I did not know——" and almost unconsciously he glanced towards Riggleton.

"I say, Faversham," and Riggleton put on his most fascinating smile, "introduce me to your lady friend, won't you? I don't think, when I've been in the neighbourhood before, that I've had the pleasure of meeting the young lady."

But Dick was silent. He simply could not speak of the fellow as his cousin. Evidently, too, Riggleton felt something of what was passing in Dick's mind; perhaps, too, he noticed the haughty glance which the girl gave him, for an angry flush mounted his cheeks, and his small eyes burnt with anger.

"Oh, you don't feel like it!" he exclaimed aloud. "And no wonder. Well, miss, I'll tell you who I am. I'm the owner of this place, that's what I am. My name's Anthony Riggleton, and I'm what the lawyers call next-of-kin to old Charles Faversham. That's why I'm boss here. There's been a big mistake, that's what there's been, and Dick Faversham got here, not under false pretences—I don't say that—but because people thought I was dead. But I ain't dead by a long chalk. I'm jolly well alive, and I'm the heir. That's the situation, miss. I thought I'd tell you straight, seeing we may be neighbours. As for Dick here, of course he's jolly well disappointed. Not that I mayn't do the handsome thing by him, seeing he means to be reasonable. I may make him my steward, or I might make him an allowance. See?"

The girl made no response whatever. She listened in deadly silence to Riggleton, although the flush on her cheek showed that the man's words had excited her. Also she looked at Dick questioningly. She seemed to be demanding from him either an affirmation or a denial of what the man said. But Dick remained silent. Somehow he felt he could not speak.

"You don't seem to take me, miss," went on Riggleton, who might have been under the influence of the champagne he had been drinking, "but what I'm telling you is gospel truth. And it may interest you to know that I mean to paint this part of the country red. Oh, I'll shake things up, never fear. Might you be fond of hunting, and that kind of thing, miss? Because after the war I mean to go in for it strong."

Still Lady Blanche did not speak to him. The only reply she made was to get into her car and turn on the engine. "Good afternoon, Mr. Faversham," she said. "Then must I tell my father that you'll not be able to come tomorrow?"

"Perhaps you'd better," replied Dick, "but—I'll explain later."

Almost unconsciously he lifted his hat, while the car passed out of sight.

"By gosh!" exclaimed Riggleton, "she's a stunner, she is!—a regular stunner. Who is she?"

But Dick turned and hurried up the drive towards the house. He felt that he could no longer bear to be near the creature who had robbed him of everything worth living for.

"I say, you needn't be so huffy," cried Riggleton, who again joined him. "Why didn't you introduce me? I don't know when I've seen such a stunning bit of fluff. She looks regular top-hole stuff too! And hasn't she got a figure? And I say, Faversham, seeing that I said I was prepared to do the handsome by you, you might have done the correct thing. What! Oh, I suppose you were riled because I told her how things are. But the truth was bound to come out, man! Do you think I would be such a ninny as not to let her know I was the bloomin' owner of this show? Tell me, who is she?"

"Lady Blanche Huntingford."

He uttered the name curtly, savagely. He was angry with himself for having spoken at all.

"Whew! She's Lord Huntingford's daughter, is she?" and he gave a hoarse laugh. "Well, she's a beauty, she is—just a beauty!"

He laughed again in high good-humour, indeed, he seemed to be enjoying himself vastly.

"You are a deep one, Faversham, you are," he shouted, as he slapped Dick on the back. "Here was I calling you a fool for staying in this hole instead of going to London and gay Paree. But I see the reason now. Dining with her to-morrow night, were you? And it seems that I've spoilt your little game. Well, she's a bit of all right, that's what she is. A regular bit of all right. I don't know but after all I shall do the country squire touch, and make up to her. What are you looking like that for?"

For Dick's face was crimson with rage. The fellow's coarse vulgarity was driving him mad.

"Are you in love with her?" persisted Riggleton. "Is that it?"

Still Dick did not speak. He was walking rapidly towards the house—so rapidly that Riggleton had difficulty in keeping up with him.

"I say, don't be huffy," went on Tony. "I'm sorry if I didn't do the correct thing. I didn't mean anything wrong, and I'm not up to the ways of the swells. As I told you, I ran away from school, and got in with a rough set. That was why, when I came back here, Uncle Charlie cleared me out. But I don't believe in grudges, I don't, and I'm sorry if I've put your nose out. I can't say fairer than that, can I?"

Dick felt slightly ashamed of himself. He was beginning to understand Riggleton better now, and to appreciate his coarse kindness.

"It's all right, Riggleton," he said, "and no doubt you've done the natural thing. But—but I don't feel like talking."

"Of course you don't," said Tony, "and of course my coming is a regular knock-out blow to you. If it was me, I'd have—well, I don't know what I wouldn't have done. But I'm not such a bad chap after all. And look here, I meant what I said, and I'm prepared to do the handsome thing. You play fair with me, and I'll play fair with you. See? I shall make an unholy mess of things if I'm left alone, and if you like I'll keep you on here. You shall be my steward, and I'll make you a good allowance. Then you can stay here, and I'll give you my word of honour that I'll not try to cut you out with Lady Blanche, although she takes the fancy of yours truly more than any bit of fluff I've seen for years."

"For Heaven's sake, drop it!" cried Dick, exasperated.

"All right," laughed Tony. "I don't mind. There's plenty of girls to be had. Besides, she's not my sort. She's too high and mighty for me. Besides," and he laughed raucously, "it all comes back to me now. Once when I was here before, I nearly got into trouble with her. I was trespassing on her father's grounds, and she came along and saw me. She told me to clear out or she'd set the dogs on me. Good Lord! I'd forgotten all about it, and I never thought I'd see her again. So if you're gone on her, I'll give you a clear field, my boy. I can't say fairer than that, now can I?"

They had reached the house, and Dick again, almost unconsciously, looked at the great doorway. He dreaded, yet he almost longed to see the great haunting eyes of the figure which, whether imaginary or real, had become such a factor in his existence.

But there was nothing. No suggestion of the luminous form appeared.

Of course it was all a mad fancy—all the result of exciting and disturbing experiences.

"Riggleton," he said, when they had reached the library, "I want to be quiet; I want to think. You don't mind, do you? I'll explain presently."

"As you like, my boy. Think as much as you bloomin' well want to. I see the servant hasn't taken away the fizz, so I'll have another drink."

Dick threw himself on a chair and covered his face with his hands. He tried to think, tried to co-ordinate events, tried to understand the true bearings of the situation. But he could not. His mind was either a blank or it was filled with mad, confusing thoughts.

What should he do?

He thought he had decided on his course of action before Riggleton's advent, but now everything was a wild chaos; he seemed to be in a maelstrom. Should he accept Riggleton's offer? The fellow was a fool; there could be no doubt about that—a coarse-minded, vulgar, gullible fool. With careful treatment, he, Dick, could still remain master of Wendover Park; he could have all the money he wanted; he could—and a vista of probabilities opened up before him. He was sure he could play with his cousin as a cat plays with a mouse. He could get him in his power, and then he could do what he liked with him.

And why not?

Perhaps, perhaps——He turned towards Riggleton, who was pouring out a glass of champagne and humming a popular music-hall song. Yes; he could mould the fellow like clay; he could make him do anything—*anything*!

He was on the point of speaking, of starting a conversation which would naturally lead to the thing he had in his mind, but no words passed his lips. It seemed to him as though two distinct, two antagonistic forces were in the room. Almost unconsciously he took Romanoff's telegram from his pocket, and as he did so, he felt as though the sender was by his side; but even while he thought of the man he remembered something else. He remembered the night when he had unfolded his plans to him, and when he had pointed to the paper which he had prepared for him.

Again he felt the grip of the hand upon his wrist, again he felt a presence which he could not explain—a presence which forbade him to sign away his liberty—his soul.

He thought, too, how immediately afterwards that guileless child Beatrice Stanmore had rushed into the room, and had told him that she had been impelled to come to him.

Suddenly a prayer came to his lips: "O God, help me! For Christ's sake, help me!"

It was strange, bewildering. He was not a praying man. He had not prayed for years, and yet the prayer, unbidden, almost unthought of, had come into his heart.

"Well, have you made up your mind?"

It was Tony Riggleton's voice, and he felt like a man wakened out of a trance.

"Yes."

"Good. You take me on, eh? We'll be pals, and you'll stay on here as my steward?"

"No."

"What are you going to do, then?"

"I'm going to London."

"To London, eh? But when?"

"To-night."

"To-night! Well, I'm——But—but, all right. I'll drive you there in my car, and we'll make a night of it."

"No, thank you. Look here, Riggleton, I'm very much obliged to you, and I appreciate all you have said; but our paths must lie apart."

"Lie apart?" Tony's mind was a little confused. "You mean to say that you don't accept the allowance I'm willing to make you?"

"I mean that. I thank you very much, but I don't accept."

"But—but what are you going to do?"

"I don't know."

"Have you any money?"

"No. Yes, I have, though. I've a few pounds which I saved before I thought I—I was——"

"Old Uncle Charlie's heir," concluded Tony as Dick hesitated. "But what about the estate?"

"The lawyer must settle all that. I'm sorry I'm intruding here. I'll go and pack my things right away. Some day I'll repay you for the money I've spent while I've been here."

"Look here," and Tony came to Dick's side, "don't you be a fool. You just take things sensibly. Pay me money! Money, be blowed! You just——"

"No, thank you. I'll go now if you don't mind."

He left the room as he spoke, and a few minutes later he had packed a small suit-case. He returned to the room where Tony still remained.

"Good-bye, Riggleton; I'm off."

"But you—you're mad."

"I think I am. Good-bye."

"But where are you going?"

"To the station. If I make haste I shall catch the next train to London."

Riggleton looked at him in open-mouthed wonder. "Well, you *are* a fool!" he gasped.

Dick rushed out of the house without a word to the servants. He felt as though he dared not speak to them. Something in his heart—something which he could not explain—was telling him to fly, and to fly quickly.

When he reached the doorway he turned and looked. He wanted to see if—if——But there was nothing. The westering sun shed its bright rays not only on the house, but on the flowers which bloomed in glorious profusion; but there was no suggestion of anything beyond the ordinary to be seen.

"Of course I *am* a fool," he reflected; "perhaps I am mad," and then he again tried to understand the experiences which had so bewildered him. But he could not. All was confusion.

He hurried along the drive which led to the lodge near which Beatrice Stanmore lived. He had a strange longing to see once more the home of the child who had come to him in the hour of his dire temptation.

When he had gone some distance he turned to have a last look at the house. Never had it seemed so fair; never as now did he realise what he was leaving. What a future he was giving up! What a life he was discarding! Yes; he had been a fool—an egregious fool! Oh, the folly of his actions!—the mad folly!

"Holloa, Mr. Faversham!"

He turned and saw Beatrice Stanmore.

"You are going away?"

"Yes; I'm going to London."

"And walking to the station? Why?"

"Because I've no conveyance."

The girl looked at him wonderingly. Questions seemed to hang upon her lips—questions which she dared not ask.

"I'm going away," he went on, "because nothing is mine. There's been a great mistake—and so I'm going away. Do you understand?"

She looked at him with childlike wonder. In years she was nearly a woman, but she was only a child in spirit.

"But surely you need not go and leave everything?" she queried.

"No; I need not go." He hardly knew what he was saying. He seemed like a man under a spell.

"Then what makes you go?"

"You," he replied. "Don't you remember? Good-bye."

He hurried on without another word. He felt he was going mad, even if he were not mad already. And yet he had a kind of consciousness that he was doing right.

"But I will come back some day," he said between his set teeth. "I'll not be beaten! Somehow—somehow I'll make my way. I'll conquer—yes, I'll conquer! At all hazards, I'll conquer!"

There was a grim determination in his heart as he set his face towards the unknown.

PART II
THE SECOND TEMPTATION

Chapter XVIII
Mr. Brown's Prophecy

"Yes, Mr. Faversham; I see such a future before you as was never possible to any other Englishman."

The speaker was a man about fifty years of age, short, stout, well fed, seemingly prosperous. A smile played around his lips—a smile which to a casual observer suggested a kindly, almost a childlike, innocence. He might have been interested in orphan schools, charity organisations, or any other philanthropic movement. His voice, too, was sympathetic and somewhat caressing, and his whole appearance spoke of a nature full of the milk of human kindness.

The two men were sitting in the corner of a smoking-room in a London club. A most respectable club it was, whose members were in the main comprised of financiers, prosperous merchants, and men of the upper middle classes. Money was writ large everywhere, while comfort, solid comfort, was proclaimed by the huge, softly cushioned chairs, the thickly piled carpets, and the glowing fires. Any stranger entering the club would have said that its members were composed of men who, having plenty of this world's goods, meant to enjoy the comforts which their gains justly entitled them to.

Dick Faversham, to whom the words were spoken, smiled, and the smile was not without incredulity and a sense of wonder.

"Yes," went on the speaker, "you smile; you say in your heart that I am a bad example of my theories; but one mustn't be deceived by appearances. You think, because I am fat and prosperous, that I take no interest in my fellow-creatures, that I do not dream dreams, see visions, eh? Is not that so?"

"Not at all," replied Dick; "but your views are so out of accord with all this," and he looked around the room as he spoke, "that I am naturally a bit puzzled."

"It is because I have accustomed myself to this, because I have seen inside the minds of rich men, and thus understand their prejudices and points of view, that I also see the other things. You have seen me in places different from this, my friend."

"Yes," replied Dick; "I have."

"Little as you have realised it," went on the other, "I have watched you for years. I have followed you in your career; I have seen your sympathies expand; I have been thrilled with your passion too. You did not suspect, my friend, three years ago, that you would be where you are to-day, eh?"

"No," assented Dick; "I didn't."

"You have thought much, learnt much, suffered much, seen much."

"Yes; I suppose so," and a wistful look came into his eyes, while his face suggested pain.

"It is said," went on the stout man, "that there is no missioner so ardent, so enthusiastic, as the new convert; but, as I have told you, you do not go far enough."

Dick was silent.

"You are spoken of by many as a man with advanced ideas, as one who has an intense passion for justice, as one, too, who has advanced daring plans for the world's betterment; but I, the fat old Englishman, the respectable millionaire, the man whom Governments have to consider—mark that—the man whom Governments have to consider and consult, tell you that your scheme, your plans are mere palliatives, mere surface things, mere sticking-plasters on the great, gaping sores of our times. That if all your ideas were carried out—yes, carried out to the full—you would not advance the cause of humanity one iota. In a few months the old anachronisms, the old abuses, would again prevail, while you would be a back number, a byword, a fellow who played at reform because you neither had the vision to see the world's real needs nor the courage to attempt real reform. A back number, my dear sir, and a mere play-actor to boot."

The fat man watched the flush on Dick's face as he spoke, and was apparently gratified.

"You see," he went on, still watching Dick's face closely, "I am getting on in life, and I have shed my illusions. I have my own philosophy of life, too. I do not believe that the reformer, that the man who lives to relieve the woes of others must of necessity be a monk, a Peter the Hermit, a Francis of Assisi. The labourer is worthy his hire; the great worker should have a great reward. Why should honour, riches, fall into the lap of kings who do nothing, of an aristocracy which is no aristocracy? Youth is ambitious as well as altruistic. Thus ambitions should be ministered unto, realised. Shakespeare was only a shallow parrot, when he wrote the words, 'Cromwell, I charge thee, fling away ambition.' The man who flings away ambition becomes a pulpy reed. He lacks driving force, lacks elemental passions. If one opposes primitive instincts, one is doomed to failure."

"Pardon me if I fail to see what you are driving at," interposed Dick.

"You'll see in a minute," asserted the other. "What I urge is this: the man who sets up a new kingdom should be a king. It is his right. The man who sees a new earth, a more glorious earth, an earth where justice and right abound, and where neither poverty nor discontent is known—I say the man who sees that new earth and brings it to pass should rule over it as king. He should have, not the pomp and empty pageantry of a paltry hereditary king, but the honour, the power, the riches of the true king."

The man paused as if he expected Dick to reply, but no reply was forthcoming. Still, the stout man was evidently satisfied by his survey of Dick's face, and he noted the flash of his eyes.

"That is why, to come back to where we were a few minutes ago," he went on, "I see such a future for you as was never possible to any other Englishman. I see you, not only as the man who will revolutionise the life of this starved and corrupt country, not only as the man who will bring in a new era of prosperity and happiness for all who are citizens of the British Empire, but as the man who can enjoy such a position, such honours, such riches as no man ever enjoyed before. Do you follow me? The people who are redeemed will make haste to heap glory and honour upon their redeemer."

"History does not bear that out," was Dick's reply.

"No, and why, my friend? I will tell you. It is because the men who have aimed to be saviours have been fools. It is because they have been blind to the elemental facts of life. The first business of the saviour is not self-interest—I do not say that—but to regard his own welfare as essential to the welfare of others. The man who allows himself to be crucified is no true saviour, because by allowing it he renders himself powerless to save. No, no, I see you, not only as one who can be a great reformer, and as one who can strike death-blows at the hoary head of abuse, but as one who can lift himself into such fame and power as was never known before. The plaudits of the multitudes, the most glorious gifts of the world, the love of the loveliest women—all, all, and a thousand times more, can be yours. That is your future as I see it, my friend."

"Do you know what I think of you?" asked Dick, with a nervous laugh.

"It would be interesting to know," was the reply.

"That your imaginative gifts are greater than your logical powers."

The stout man laughed heartily. "I suppose I puzzle you," he replied. "You think it strange that I, the financier, the millionaire if you like, who eats well, drinks good wine, smokes good cigars, and who is a member of the most expensive clubs in London, should talk like this, eh? You think it strange that I, who two hours hence will be hobnobbing with financiers and Cabinet ministers, should be talking what some would call rank treason with an advanced labour leader, eh? But do not judge by outward appearances, my friend; do not be misled by the world's opinions. It is not always the ascetic who feels most acutely or sympathises most intensely.

"As I told you, I have watched you for months—years. For a long time I did not trust you; I did not believe you were the man who could do what I saw needed doing. Even when I heard you talking to the masses of the people—yes, carrying them away with the passion of your words—I did not altogether believe in you. But at length I have come to see that you are the man for my money, and for the money of others."

Again he looked at Dick keenly.

"Ah, I astonish you, don't I? You have looked upon such as I as enemies to the race. You have not realised that there are dozens of millionaires in this city of millionaires who almost hate the money they have made, because they see no means whereby it can be used for the uplifting and salvation of the oppressed and downtrodden. They do not talk about it, yet so it is. I tell you frankly, I would at this moment give half—two-thirds—of all I possess if thereby I could carry out the dream of my life!"

The man spoke with passion and evident conviction. There was a tremor in his voice, and his form became almost rigid. His eyes, too, flashed with a strange light—a light that spoke almost of fanaticism.

"You already have in your mind what burns in mine like a raging furnace," he went on. "You see from afar what has become a fixed, settled conviction with me. You behold as a hazy vision what I have contemplated for a long time, until it is clearly outlined, thoroughly thought out. I will tell you what it is directly. And if that great heart of yours, if that fine quick mind of yours does not grasp it, assimilate it, and translate it into actuality, it will be one of the greatest disappointments of my life. I shall for evermore put myself down as a blind fool, and my faith in human nature will be lost for ever."

"Tell me what it is," and Dick's voice was tense with eagerness.

Months, years had passed since Dick had left Wendover Park, and both his life and thoughts had become revolutionised. Perhaps this was not altogether strange. His manner of life had been altered, his outlook altogether new.

Even now as he looked back over those fateful days he could not understand them. They seemed to him rather as some wild fantastic series of dreams than as sane and sober realities. Yet realities they were, even although they were a mystery to him. Often in his quiet hours he caught himself thinking of the figure of the woman in the smoke-room of the outward-bound ship, which no one but himself could see, while again and again he almost shivered as he felt himself sinking in the black, turbulent sea, while conflicting powers seemed to be struggling to possess him. Indeed, the wonder of that night never left him. The light which shone in the darkness, the luminous form above him, the great, yearning, pitying eyes which shone into his, and the arms outstretched to save.

Sometimes it was all visionary and unreal—so visionary was it that he could not believe in its reality, but at other times he could not doubt. It was all real—tremendously real. Especially was it so as he thought of those after days when he had fought the greatest battles of his life. Again and again he had seen himself in the library at Wendover while Romanoff stood beside him and told him of his plans; again and again had he recalled the moment when he took the pen in his hand to sign the paper, and had felt the grip on his wrist which had paralysed his hand.

Was it real, or was it imaginary?

"Suppose I had signed it?" he had often asked himself; "where should I be now? I should be a rich man—the owner of old Charles Faversham's huge fortune. Possibly I should have married Lady Blanche Huntingford and acted the part of the rich squire. But what would Romanoff have exacted of me? What would be my thoughts about Tony Riggleton?"

Yes; those were wonderful days, whether they were a dream or a reality, and sometimes he called himself a fool for not following the Count's advice, while at others he shuddered to think of the dangers from which he had escaped.

He had never seen nor heard of Lady Blanche since. On his arrival in London he had written an explanatory letter, and had expressed the hope that she would not lose interest in him. But he had received no reply.

Evidently she regarded him as a kind of an impostor, with whom she could no further associate herself.

Neither had he ever seen or heard of Romanoff. This dark, sinister man had passed away into the shadows, and only remained a strange memory, a peculiar influence in his life.

Of Tony Riggleton he had heard various stories, all of which were of the same nature. Tony had been true to the programme he had marked out. He had filled Wendover Park with a motley crowd of men and women, and the orgies there were the talk of the neighbourhood. He had also a flat in London where he had indulged in his peculiar tastes.

It was on hearing these stories that Dick had felt that he had acted the fool. He had become cynical, too, and laughed at the idea that virtue and honour were wise.

"If I had followed Romanoff's advice," he had said to himself, "I might have——" And repeatedly he had recounted what he might have done with the wealth which he had thought was his.

For many months Dick had a hard struggle to live. His few weeks of riches had unfitted him for the battle of life. Society was shaken to its foundations; the world was a maddening maze. Again and again he had offered himself for the Army—only to be rejected. He was conscious of no illness, but the doctors persistently turned him down.

Presently he drifted towards the industrial North of England and became employed in a huge factory where thousands of people worked. It was here that Dick's life underwent a great change. For the first time he found himself the daily, hourly companion of grimy-handed toilers.

This gave him a new vision of life; it placed new meanings on great problems; he was made to look at life from new angles. For the first time he felt the squalor, the ugliness of life. He lived in a grimy street, amidst grimy surroundings. He saw things as the working classes saw them, saw them with all their grey unloveliness, their numbing monotony.

Still ambitious, still determined to carve out a career, he felt oppressed by the ghastly atmosphere in which he found himself. He was now fast approaching thirty, and he found himself unable to adapt himself to his new conditions. He thought of all he had hoped to do and be, and now by some sport of fate he had become engulfed in this maelstrom of life.

Little by little the inwardness of it all appealed to him. He had to do with men and women who were drunken, foul-mouthed, depraved. What wonder that he himself was becoming coarsened every day! Things at which he would once have shuddered he now passed by with a shrug of his shoulders. How could the working classes be refined, how could they have exalted ideas amidst such surroundings?

He noticed the tremendous disparity between the moneyed and the working classes. The former were deliberately exploiting the great world convulsion, and the peculiar conditions caused thereby, to make huge profits. It was all wrong—utterly wrong. What was the worker, on whose labour everything depended? Mere means for swelling the capitalists' profits. Who cared about them? Politicians talked glibly about what they meant to do; but they did nothing.

Newspapers shrieked, and capitalists talked about the disloyalty of the working classes. How could men go on strike while the very existence of empire, civilisation, humanity hung in the balance? they asked. But what of their own disloyalty? What of those who held a pistol at the head of the Government, and threatened to disorganise the trade of the country and paralyse output, if they could not stuff their money-bags still fuller?

And so on, and on. His new environment changed him—changed his sympathies, his thoughts, his outlook. He thought of Tony Riggleton spending the money these people were making for him in wild orgies among loose men and women, and he became angry and bitter.

Little by little his superior education asserted itself. He found, too, that he had a remarkable aptitude for public speech. He discovered that he could sway huge multitudes by the burning fervour of his words. He was able to put into language what the people felt, and before long became a popular hero.

The world was in a state of flux; old ideas, old conceptions were swept aside as worn-out fallacies. What ten years before were regarded as madmen's dreams no longer appeared either unreasonable or quixotic. The forces of life had become fluid, and it was the toiler of the nation who was to decide into what channels the new movements were to flow.

And Dick became a doctrinaire, as well as a dreamer of a new heaven and a new earth. He became an ardent reader, too. He was surprised at the ease with which his mind grasped theories hitherto unknown to him, how he absorbed the spirit of unrest, and how he flung himself into the world's great fray.

"Faversham's our man," people said on every side. "He's got eddication, he's got a fair grip on things, and he can knock the masters to smithereens when it comes to argument and the gilt o' th' gab."

"But who is he?" asked others. "He's noan our sort. He was noan brought up a workin' man."

"Nay, but he's a workin' man naa. He's worked side by side with the best on us, and he knows how to put things. I tell thee, he mun go into Parlyment. He'll mak 'em sit up. He mun be our member."

This feeling became so strong that Dick was on two occasions selected to be one of deputations to the Prime Minister, and more than that, he was chosen to be the chief spokesman to state the workers' claims.

In all this, not only were his sympathies aroused, but his vanity was appealed to. It was very pleasant to feel himself emerging from obscurity; the roar of cheering which the mention of his name elicited became as sweet as the nectar of the gods to him.

Again he saw visions, and dreamt dreams. They were different from those of the old days, but they did a great deal to satisfy him. They told him of position, of power, of a place among the great ones of the world. Sometimes he was almost glad that Tony Riggleton inherited Charles Faversham's huge fortune. If he had retained it, and gained high position, that position would have been through the toil and brain of another. Now he would do everything by himself — unaided and alone.

More than once during the many stormy and excited meetings Dick had attended, he had seen a kindly, benevolent-looking man, whose face suggested the milk of human kindness. Dick rather wondered how he came there, and on asking his name was told that he was called John Brown, and that, although he did not directly belong to the working classes, he was in deep sympathy with them, and had more than once subscribed to their funds. Presently Dick became acquainted with Mr. Brown, and something like intimacy sprang up between them.

He found that Mr. Brown was a great admirer of his speeches, and more than once that gentleman had hinted that if he found any money difficulty in entering Parliament, he, John Brown, would see that the difficulty should be removed.

"I am almost ashamed of being something of a capitalist," he confided to Dick, "but, at any rate, I can use what money I have for the advance of the cause which is so dear to me."

Just before Dick was going to London the next time, he received a letter from Mr. Brown asking him to meet him at a well-known club. "I have certain things to say to you," he said, "certain propositions to make which I think will be worthy of your consideration."

On Dick's arrival in London he made certain inquiries about Mr. Brown, which, however, did not help him much. He was by no means a prominent character, he learnt, but he was believed by many to be a man of enormous wealth. He was told, moreover, that he was somewhat eccentric, and loved doing good by stealth.

It was therefore with aroused curiosity that Dick made his way to the club in question. He was not yet quite sure of his man, and so he determined to listen carefully to what Mr. Brown had to say without committing himself. Before long he found himself deeply interested. The stout, benevolent-looking man was revealing himself in a new light, and Dick found himself listening with fast-beating heart.

"Yes; I will tell you what it is," said Mr. Brown. "I will make plain to you what I meant when I said that I see such a future before you as was never possible to any other Englishman."

Chapter XIX
An Amazing Proposal

Dick unconsciously drew his chair nearer the fire, while every nerve in his body became tense. He felt that the millionaire had not brought him here for mere pastime.

"Tell me," said Mr. Brown, "what your plans for the future are."

"Too hazy to outline," was Dick's reply.

"That's truer than you think, my friend—far truer than you think; that's why your position is so absurd. And yet you answer me falsely."

Dick gave the other a look that was almost angry.

"No, no, my friend," went on Mr. Brown; "do not mistake me. I do not accuse you of falsehood. You think you are speaking the truth. But you are not. In a way, your plans are defined. You mean to be Member of Parliament for Eastroyd. You mean to be the first Labour Member for that great working-class constituency. Already you have been approached by the various unions of the town, and you have been assured that you will be returned by a triumphant majority. And you've practically accepted, although you have persuaded yourself that you've not yet made up your mind. So far so good—or bad; but you are unsettled. There is something at the back of your mind that you can't explain. It doesn't satisfy you. Am I not speaking the truth?"

"Perhaps," assented Dick.

"And naturally, too. Oh, my young friend, I know—I know. I have been through it all. What is a Labour Member after all? Just one of a few others, who is submerged by the great so-called Liberal and Conservative Parties. What can he do? Speak now and then when he's allowed to, beat the air, be listened to by a handful of his own supporters, and then forgotten. Consider the history of the Labour Party. What influence has it really had on the life of the nation? My friend, the government of the country is still in the hands of the upper and middle classes in spite of all you do and say."

"Pardon me," interrupted Dick, "but what are you driving at? What you say may be partly true, but at least the hope of the working classes, politically speaking, lies in the Labour Party."

"Moonshine, my friend—mere moonshine. The atmosphere of the British House of Commons stifles the aspiration of the Labour Members. One by one they are absorbed into the old orthodox parties, and nothing is done. You know it, too. That's why the thought of becoming a Labour Member is unsatisfying to you. You would never be a real power, and you would always be regarded as an outsider, and you would never touch the helm of affairs."

Dick was silent. After all, he was not a working man. He had social ambitions. He desired not only to be a prominent figure among the working classes; he wanted to be an equal of, a peer amongst the dominant forces of the world. He still remembered Lady Blanche Huntingford—as a Labour Member he would be outside her sphere.

"You see it, don't you?" persisted Mr. Brown.

"And if I do? What then?"

"Everything then, my friend. Your present plans would end in nothing. Not only would you fail to do anything real for the people, but you yourself would be stultified. A Labour Member! What is he?—a man who, socially, is patronised; who is recognised only on sufferance; who, if he marries, must marry a commoner, a woman of the people, with all her limitations. Oh, I know, I know. And meanwhile the working people still continue to be trodden underfoot, and who toil for what they can squeeze out of their employers—their social superiors. Yes, yes, you are impatient with me. You say I am a long time in getting to my point. But be patient, my friend; I will get there. I only want you to realise the truth."

"Then please get to your point," urged Dick a little impatiently.

"I will," replied Mr. John Brown, and he placed his chubby hand on Dick's knee. "Here is the fact, my friend: we live in a time when nothing is impossible. The world is in travail, in wild convulsions. The new channels of life are not made. All the forces of life are in a state of flux. Now is the time for the real leader, the strong man. The great proletariat is waiting for that leader, longing for him. The people are tired of the old worn pathways; they are waiting for the new kingdom, the new deliverer."

"You are still in the clouds," cried Dick. "Come down to the solid earth."

"I will, my friend. England is ripe for real reform, ripe for the new order. The open sores of the country cannot be healed by sticking-plasters. They must be cauterised; the cancers must be cut out. In one word—Revolution!"

Dick started to his feet, and took a hasty glance around the room. For a wonder, it was empty. They were alone.

"You are mad!" he cried.

"Of course I am," laughed Mr. Brown. "Every man is called mad who sees a new heaven and a new earth. But, my friend, I speak as an Englishman, as one who loves his country. I am a patriot, and I want to see a greater, grander England. I want to see a Britain that shall be happy, prosperous, contented. I want to destroy poverty, to smash up the old order of things—an order which has dragged squalor, misery, poverty, injustice, inequality at its heels. I am tired—*tired* of seeing criminal wealth and mad luxury and waste on the one hand, and abject grinding poverty on the other. And to cure it all you must go to the roots of things; there must be great upheavals, revolutions. The land must be the people's, the mineral must be the people's, the water, the food, the wealth, the Army, the Navy, the *everything* must belong to the people."

"Bolshevism!" The word came from him abruptly—angrily.

"Yes, Bolshevism," replied the other; "and what then?"

"Russia!" and there was a sneer in Dick's voice as he uttered the word.

"Yes, Russia if you like. And still, what then? Would you have Russia go on century by century as it had been going? Would you have scores upon scores of millions of men and women go on existing as they were existing? You know the history of Russia for ten centuries past. What has it been?—a criminal, bloated, corrupt, cruel, overbearing, persecuting aristocracy and bureaucracy on the one hand, and a welter of poor, suffering, starving, outraged, diseased, dying people on the other. That was Russia. And desperate diseases need desperate remedies, my friend. Of course, the very name of Russia is being shuddered at just now. But think, my friend. Birth is always a matter of travail, and Russia is being re-born. But wait. In ten years Russia will be regarded as the pioneer of civilisation—as the herald of a new age. Russia is taking the only step possible that will lead to justice, and to peace, and prosperity for all."

"You don't mean that!" Dick scarcely knew that he spoke.

"I am as certain of it as that I sit here. I swear it by whatever gods there be!"

Plain, stout Mr. John Brown was changed. Dick forgot his fat, chubby hands, his round, benevolent, kindly, but commonplace face. It was a new Mr. John Brown that he saw. A new light shone in his eyes, a new tone had come to his voice, a seemingly new spirit inspired him.

"I go further," cried Mr. Brown, "and I say this: England—the British Isles need the same remedy. All that you have been thinking about are sticking-plasters—palliatives, and not cures. What England needs is a Revolution. All the old corrupt, crushing forces must be destroyed, the old gods overthrown, and a new evangelist must proclaim a new gospel."

"A madman's dream," protested Dick. "Let's talk of something else."

"Not yet," replied Mr. John Brown. "Tell me this, you who long for a new heaven and a new earth—you who plead for justice, for fraternity, for brotherhood: do you believe that the programme—I mean the organised programme—of the Labour Party or the Socialist Party will ever bring about what you desire?"

Dick was silent.

"Ah, you are honest. You know it will not. In your heart of hearts you know, too, that nothing but a thorough upheaval, a complete Revolution of the bad old order of things can bring about what you desire. Patching up an old building whose walls are cracked, whose drains are corrupt, whose foundations are insecure, is waste of time and energy. If you want a new sanitary house the old place has to be demolished and the rubbish *cleared away*! That's it, my friend. That's what's needed in this country. The rubbish must be cleared away. That's what the people want. For the moment they are crying out for something, they hardly know what, but they will have a Revolution, and they are longing for a leader to lead them, a prophet to interpret their needs."

"But for England to become another Russia!" Dick's response was that of a man who had not yet grasped all that was in the other's mind.

"There is no need of that. Because England has not sunk to the depths of Russia, her revolution would be less violent. There would be no need for excesses, for violence. But here is the fact, my friend: three-fourths of our population belong to the wage-earning classes; they are the toilers and the moilers; let the true gospel be preached to them, let the true prophet and leader appear, and they would follow him."

"And who is to be the prophet, the leader?"

"You, my friend."

"I!" gasped Dick.

"You. Richard Faversham. You who have tasted the sweets of wealth. You who have toiled and sweated with the workers. You who have eyes to see, ears to hear. You who have the power to interpret the people's longings. You who have the qualities of the leader, who can take them to the Promised Land. You!"

"Madness!"

"You say that now. You will not say it in a few hours from now. You can understand now what I meant when I startled you an hour ago by saying that I see such a future before you as was never possible to any Englishman. You are young; you are ambitious. It is right you should be. No man who is not ambitious is worth a rotten stick to his age. Here is such a career as was never known before. Never, I say! Man, it's glorious! You can become the greatest man of the age—of all the ages!"

Mr. Brown looked at Dick intently for a few seconds, and then went on, speaking every word distinctly.

"A Labour Member, indeed! A voting machine at four hundred a year! The hack of his party organisation! Is that a career for a man like you? Heavens, such a thought is sacrilege! But this, my friend, is the opportunity of a life—of all time."

"Stop!" cried Dick. "I want to grasp it—to think!"

Chapter XX
"The Country for the People"

"But you *are* mad," said the young man at length. "Even if you are right in your diagnosis of the disease from which the country is suffering, if the remedy you suggest is the only one, I am not the man you need. And even if I were, the remedy is impossible. England is not where France was a hundred years ago; she is not where Russia is to-day."

"And you are not a Lenin, a Trotsky, eh?" and Mr. John Brown laughed like a man who had made a joke.

"No, thank Heaven, I am not," and Dick spoke quickly. "I do not believe in the nationalisation of women, neither do I believe in the destruction of the most sacred institutions of life."

"Of course you don't," replied Mr. John Brown, "and I am glad of it. Russia has gone to many excesses which we must avoid. But what can you expect, my friend? After centuries of oppression and persecution, is it any wonder that there has been a swing of the pendulum? The same thing was true of France a hundred years ago. France went wild, France lost her head, and neither Danton nor Robespierre checked the extravagances of the people. But, answer me this. Is not France a thousand times better to-day than when under the Bourbons and the Church? Is not such a Republic as France has, infinitely better than the reign of a corrupt throne, a rotten aristocracy, and a rottener Church? Besides, did not a great part of those who were guillotined deserve their doom?"

"Perhaps they did; but—but the thing is impossible, all the same."

"Why impossible?"

"For one thing, Lenin and Trotsky are in a country without order and law. They murdered the Tzar and his family, and they seized the money of the Government and of the banks. Such a thing as you suggest would need millions, and you could not get any body of Englishmen to follow on the Russian lines. Besides—no, the thing is impossible!"

"Money!" repeated Mr. John Brown, like a man reflecting. "I myself would place in your hands all the money you need for organisation and propaganda."

"In *my* hands!"

"In your hands, my friend. Yes, in your hands. But we have talked enough now. You want time to think over what has been said. But will you do something, my friend?"

"I don't know. I suspect not."

"I think you will. To-night I want you to accompany me to a place where your eyes will be opened. I want you to see how deep are the feelings of millions, how strong is the longing for a leader, a guide. You, who have felt the pulses of the millions who live and act in the open, have no idea of what is felt by the millions who act in the dark."

"I do not understand."

"Of course you don't. You and other so-called Labour leaders, because you mingle with a class which you call the people, think you know everything. You believe you know the thought, the spirit of the age. Come with me to-night and I will show you a phase of life hitherto unknown to you. You will come? Yes?"

"Oh yes, I will come," replied Dick, with a laugh. The conversation had excited him beyond measure, and he was eager for adventure.

"Good. Be at the entrance to the Blackfriars Underground Station to-night at eleven o'clock."

"At eleven; all right."

Mr. John Brown looked at his watch, and then gave a hasty glance round the room. He saw two portly looking men coming in their direction.

"I am sure you will excuse me, Mr. Faversham. It is later than I thought, and I find I have appointments. But it has been very interesting to know your point of view. Good evening. Ah, Sir Felix, I thought you might drop in to-night," and leaving Dick as though their talk had been of the most commonplace nature, he shook hands with the newcomers.

Dick, feeling himself dismissed, left the club, and a minute later found himself in the thronging crowd of Piccadilly. Taxicabs, buses, richly upholstered motor-cars were passing, but he did not heed them. People jostled him as he made his way towards Hyde Park gates, but he was unaware of it. His head was in a whirl; he was living in a maze of conflicting thoughts.

Of course old John Brown was a madman! Nothing but a madman would advance such a quixotic programme! He pictured the club he had just left—quiet, orderly, circumspect—the natural rendezvous for City and West End magnates, the very genius of social order and moneyed respectability. How, then, could a respected member of such a place advance such a mad-brained scheme?

But he had.

Not that he—Dick Faversham—could regard it seriously. Of course he had during the last two years been drawn into a new world, and had been led to accept socialistic ideas. Some, even among the Socialists, called them advanced. But this!

Of course it was impossible.

All the same, there was a great deal in what John Brown had said. A Labour Member. A paid voting machine at £400 a year! The words rankled in his mind.

And this scheme was alluring. The country for the people!...

He made his way along the causeway, thinking of it.

A Revolution! The old bad, mad order of things ended by one mighty upheaval! A new England, with a new outlook, a new Government!... A mighty movement which might grip the world. A new earth....

And he—Dick Faversham?

Here was scope for new enterprises! Here was a career! On the one hand, a paid working man member at £400 a year, regarded with a supercilious smile by the class to which he really belonged; and, on the other, a force which shook Society to its foundations—a leader whose name would be on all lips....

Of course it was all nonsense, and he would drive it from his mind.

And he would not meet Mr. John Brown that night. What a madcap idea to go to some midnight gathering—where, Heaven only knew! And for what?

He had reached Park Lane, and almost unconsciously he turned eastward.

He could not remember a single thing that had happened during his walk from Park Lane to Piccadilly Circus. The great tide of human life surged to and fro, but he was oblivious of the fact.

He was thinking—wildly thinking.

Then suddenly he gave a start. Just as he reached the Circus he saw a face which set his heart beating wildly.

"Ah, Faversham, is that you?"

"Count Romanoff!" Dick almost gasped.

"Yes; who would have thought of seeing you? Still, the world is small."

The Count was not changed. He still carried himself proudly, and was dressed to perfection. Also, he still seemed to regard others with a degree of indifference. He was the same contemptuous, cynical man of the world.

"What are you doing, eh? Still living at Wendover Park?"

"No. You know I am not."

"No? Ah, I remember now. I have been knocking around the world ever since, and had almost forgotten. But your quondam cousin entered possession, didn't he? But you, what did you do?"

"Oh, I—I drifted."

"Drifted—where?—to what? You look changed. Things are not going well with you, eh?"

"Yes—quite well, thank you."

"Yes? You married Lady Blanche? But no, I should have heard of it."

"No; I did not marry. I am living in Eastroyd."

"Eastroyd! Where's that?"

"Don't you know?"

"Never heard of it before. Is it in England?"

Dick was growing angry; there was a sneer in every tone of the man's voice. He felt a mad desire to make the Count see that he had become a man of importance.

"Yes; it's in the North," he replied. "It's a huge town of a quarter of a million people. A great industrial centre."

"And what are you doing there?"

"I'm contemplating an invitation to become a Member of Parliament for the town. I'm assured that, if I accept, my return to the House of Commons is certain."

"Ah, that's interesting. And which side will you take—Conservative or Liberal? Conservative, I suppose?"

"No; I should stand as a Labour candidate."

"As a——Surely I didn't hear you aright?"

"Quite right. My sympathies have come to lie in that direction."

"But—but—a Labour Member! I thought you had some pretensions to be a gentleman."

Dick felt as though he had received the lash of a whip. He wanted to lash back, to make Romanoff feel what he felt. But no words came.

"You have no sympathy with the working classes?" he asked feebly.

"Sympathy! What gentleman could? See what they've done in my own country. I had little sympathy with Nicky; but great heavens, think! Of course I'm angry. I had estates in Russia; they had been in the families for centuries—and now! But the thing is a nightmare! Working classes, eh! I'd take every mal-content in Europe and shoot him. What are the working classes but lazy, drunken swine that should be bludgeoned into obedience?"

"I don't think you understand the British working classes," was Dick's response.

"No? I'm sure I don't want to. I prefer my own class. But pray don't let me keep you from them. Good evening."

Without another word, without holding out his hand, the Count turned on his heel and walked away.

The incident affected Dick in two ways. First of all, it made his experiences three years before in the Wendover Park very shadowy and unreal. In spite of everything, he had not been able to think of the Count save as an evil influence in his life, as one who desired to get him into his power for his own undoing. He had had a vague belief that in some way unknown to him, Romanoff desired to hold him in his grip for sinister purposes, and that he had been saved by an opposing power. Had he been asked to assert this he would have hesitated, and perhaps been silent. Still, at the back of his doubt the feeling existed. But now, with the memory of the Count's contemptuous words and looks in his mind, it all appeared as groundless and as unreal as the fabric of a dream. If he had been right, he would not have treated him in such a fashion.

The other way in which the incident affected him was to arouse an angry determination to win a position equal to and superior to that which would be his as Charles Faversham's heir. He would by his own endeavours rise to such heights that even the Count's own position would pale into insignificance. After all, what were kings and princes? Their day was over. Soon, soon thrones all over the world would topple like ninepins; soon the power of the world would be in new hands.

A Labour Member, indeed! Working people swine, were they? Soon the working people of the world would be masters! Then woe be to a useless, corrupt aristocracy! As for the leaders of the toilers...

"I'll meet Mr. John Brown again to-night," he reflected. "I'll go to this, this!... I wonder what he has in his mind?"

Meanwhile Count Romanoff wandered along Piccadilly till he came to St. James's Street. He was smiling as though something pleasant had happened to him. His eyes, too, shone with a strange light, and he walked like a victor.

He walked past the Devonshire Club, and then turned into a street almost opposite St. James's Square. Here he looked at his watch and walked more slowly. Evidently he knew his way well, for he took several turnings without the slightest hesitation, till at length he reached a house at the corner of a street. He selected a key from a bunch, opened the door of the house, and entered. For a moment he stood still and listened; then, walking noiselessly along a thick carpet, he opened the door of a room and entered.

"Sitting in the dark, eh? Reflecting on the destiny of nations, I suppose?"

The Count's manner was light and pleasant. He was in a good humour. He switched on the light and saw Mr. John Brown. It would seem that they had met by appointment.

"Yes," replied Mr. Brown; "I was reflecting on the destiny of nations—reflecting, too, on the fact that the greatest victories of the world are won not by armies who fight in the open, but by brains that act in the dark."

"You have seen him. I know that."

"How do you know?"

"I know everything, my friend. You met him about an hour ago. You had a long talk with him. You have baited your hook, and thrown it. Before you could tell whether the fish would rise, you thought it better to wait. You decided to make further preparations."

"Romanoff, I believe you are the devil."

"Many a true word is spoken in jest, my friend. But, devil or not, am I not right?"

"You have seen him? He has told you?"

"He has told me nothing. Yes, he has, though. He has told me he had ambitions to be a Labour Member of Parliament."

"But nothing more?"

"Nothing more. I was passing along the street and spoke to him." The two were looking at each other eagerly, questioningly. Mr. John Brown's face had become flabby; the flesh around his eyes was baggy. The eyes had a furtive look, as though he stood in awe of his companion. Romanoff, too, in spite of his claim to omniscience, might be a little anxious.

"The fellow's career is a miracle," remarked Mr. John Brown at length. "A millionaire one day, a pauper the next. And then to settle down as a toiler among toilers—to become the popular hero, the socialist leader, the rebel, the seer of visions, the daring reformer! A miracle, I say! But with proper guidance, he is the man we need. He can do much!"

Count Romanoff laughed like one amused.

"Germany is in a bad way, eh? Poor Wilhelm, what a fool! Oh, what a fool!"

"Be quiet!" cried the other hoarsely. "Even here the walls may have ears, and if it were suspected that——"

"Exactly, my friend," sneered the Count. "But tell me how you stand."

For some time they talked quietly, earnestly, the Count asking questions and raising objections, while Mr. John Brown explained what he had in his mind.

"Germany is never beaten," he said—"never. When arms fail, brains come in. Russia has become what Russia is, not by force of arms, but by brains. Whose? And Germany will triumph. This fellow is only one of many who are being used. A network of agencies are constantly at work."

"And to-night you are going to introduce him to Olga?" and the Count laughed.

"The most fascinating woman in Europe, my friend. Yes; to-night I am going to open his eyes. To-night he will fall in love. To-night will be the beginning of the end of Britain's greatness!"

Chapter XXI
The Midnight Meeting

Dick Faversham stood at the entrance of the underground station at Blackfriars Bridge. It was now five minutes before eleven, and the traffic along the Embankment was beginning to thin. New Bridge Street was almost deserted, for the tide of theatre-goers did not go that way. Dick was keenly on the look out for Mr. John Brown, and wondered what kind of a place he was going to visit that night.

He felt a slight touch upon his shoulder, and, turning, he saw Mr. Brown go to the ticket office.

"Third single for Mark Lane," he said, carelessly throwing down two coppers, yet so clearly that Dick could not help hearing him.

Without hesitation Dick also went to the office and booked for the same place. Mr. Brown took no apparent notice of him, and when the train came in squeezed himself into a third-class compartment. Having secured a seat, he lit a cheap black cigar.

Dick noticed that he wore a somewhat shabby over-coat and a hat to match. Apparently Mr. Brown had not a thought in his mind beyond that of smoking his cigar and reading a soiled copy of an evening paper.

Arrived at Mark Lane, Mr. Brown alighted and, still without taking notice of Dick, found his way to the street. For some time he walked eastward, and then, having reached a dark alley, turned suddenly and waited for Dick to come up.

"Keep me in sight for the next half-mile," he said quickly. "When I stop next, you will come close to me, and I will give you necessary instructions."

They were now in a part of London which was wholly strange to the young man. There were only few passers-by. It was now nearly midnight, and that part of London was going to sleep. Now and then a belated traveller shuffled furtively along as though anxious not to be seen. They were in a neighbourhood where dark things happen.

Evidently Mr. John Brown knew his way well. He threaded narrow streets and dark alleys without the slightest hesitation; neither did he seem to have any apprehension of danger. When stragglers stopped and gave him suspicious glances, he went straight on, unheeding.

Dick on the other hand, was far from happy. He did not like his midnight journey; he did not like the grim, forbidding neighbourhood through which they were passing. He reflected that he was utterly ignorant where he was, and, but for a hazy idea that he was somewhere near the river, would not know which way to turn if by any chance he missed his guide.

Presently, however, Mr. Brown stopped and gave a hasty look around. Everywhere were dark, forbidding-looking buildings which looked like warehouses. Not a ray of light was to be seen anywhere. Even although vast hordes of people were all around the spot where he stood, the very genius of loneliness reigned.

He beckoned Dick to him, and spoke in low tones.

"Be surprised at nothing you see or hear," he advised in a whisper. "There is no danger for either you or me. This is London, eh? And yet those who love England, and are thinking and working for her welfare, are obliged to meet in secret."

"Still, I'd like to know where we are going," protested Dick. "I don't like this."

"Wait, my young friend. Wait just five minutes. Now, follow me in silence."

Had not the spirit of adventure been strong upon the young fellow, he would have refused. There was something sinister in the adventure. He could not at all reconcile Mr. John Brown's membership of the club he had visited that afternoon with this Egyptian darkness in a London slum.

"Follow without remark, and without noise," commanded the older man, and then, having led the way a few yards farther, he flashed a light upon some narrow stone steps.

Dick was sure he heard the movement of a large body of water. He was more than ever convinced that they were close to the Thames.

Mr. Brown descended the steps, while Dick followed. His heart was beating rapidly, but he had no fear. A sense of curiosity had mastered every other feeling. At the bottom of the steps Mr. Brown stopped and listened, but although Dick strained his powers of hearing, he could detect no sound. The place might have been exactly what it appeared in the darkness—a deserted warehouse.

"Now, then," whispered Mr. Brown, and there was excitement in his voice.

A second later he tapped with his stick on what appeared to be the door of the warehouse. Dick, whose senses were keenly alert, counted the taps. Three soft, two loud, and again two soft ones.

The door opened as if by magic. There was no noise, and Dick would not have known it was opened save for the dim light which was revealed. A second later he had entered, and the door closed.

In the dim light Dick saw that he was following two dark forms. Evidently the person who had opened the door was leading the way. But he could discern nothing clearly; he thought they were passing through some kind of lumber room, but he could have sworn to nothing. After that there was a passage of some sort, and again they descended some more steps, at the bottom of which Dick heard what seemed the confused murmur of voices....

Dick found himself standing in a kind of vestibule, and there was a sudden glare of light. Both he and Mr. John Brown were in a well-lit room, in which some two hundred people had gathered.

When Dick's eyes had become accustomed to the light, he saw that he was in the midst of one of the most curious crowds he had ever seen. The people seemed of many nationalities, and the sexes appeared equally divided. Very few old people were present. In the main they were well dressed, and might have been comfortably situated. Nevertheless, it was a motley crowd—motley not so much because of any peculiarity in their attire as because of their personalities. What impressed Dick more than anything else was the look of fierce intelligence on their faces, and the nervous eagerness which characterised their every movement. Every look, every action spoke of intensity, and as Dick swept a hasty glance around the room, he felt that he was breathing an atmosphere which was altogether new to him—an atmosphere which was electric.

The room was evidently arranged for a meeting. At one end was a platform on which was placed a table and half a dozen chairs, while the people who formed the audience were waiting for the speakers to appear.

Then Dick realised that all eyes were turned towards himself and that a sudden silence prevailed. This was followed by what Dick judged to be a question of some sort, although he could not tell what it was, as it was asked in a language unknown to him.

"It is all right. I, John Brown, vouch for everything."

"But who is he?" This time the question was in English, and Dick understood that it referred to himself.

"It is all right, I repeat," replied Mr. Brown. "My companion is a comrade, a friend, whom you will be glad to hear. Who is he? He is a Labour leader, and is chosen by the working people of Eastroyd to represent them in the British Parliament."

A great deal of scornful laughter followed this. It might have been that Mr. Brown were trying to play a practical joke upon them.

"Listen," said Mr. Brown. "I am not unknown to you, and I think I have proved to you more than once that I am in sympathy with your aims. Let me ask you this: have I ever introduced anyone who was not worthy and whose help you have not gladly welcomed?"

There was some slight cheering at this, and Mr. Brown went on:

"I need not assure you that I have taken every precaution—*every* precaution—or tell you that, if good does not come of my being here, harm will surely not come of it. This, my friends, is Mr. Richard Faversham of Eastroyd, whose fiery zeal on behalf of the world's toilers cannot be unknown to you."

Again there was some cheering, and Dick noted that the glances cast towards him were less hostile, less suspicious.

Mr. Brown seemed on the point of speaking further, but did not. At that moment a curtain at the back of the platform was drawn aside, and three men accompanied by two women appeared. It would seem that the time for the commencement of the meeting had come.

Dick had some remembrance afterwards that one of the men addressed the meeting, and that he spoke about the opportunities which the times offered to the struggling millions who had been crushed through the centuries, but nothing distinct remained in his mind. Every faculty he possessed was devoted to one of the two women who sat on the platform. He did not know who she was; he had never seen her before, and yet his eyes never left her face.

Never before had he seen such a woman; never had he dreamed that there could be anyone like her.

Years before he had seen, and fancied himself in love with, Lady Blanche Huntingford. He had been captivated by her glorious young womanhood, her abundant vitality, her queenly beauty. But, compared with the woman on the platform, Blanche Huntingford was as firelight to sunlight.

Even as he sat there he compared them—contrasted them. He remembered what he had thought of the proud Surrey beauty; how he had raved about her eyes, her hair, her figure; but here was a beauty of another and a higher order. Even in his most enthusiastic moments, Lady Blanche's intellectuality, her spirituality, had never appealed to him. But this woman's beauty was glorified by eyes that spoke of exalted thoughts, passionate longings, lofty emotions.

Her face, too, was constantly changing. Poetry, humour, passion, pity, tenderness, scorn were expressed on her features as she looked at the speaker. This woman was poetry incarnate! She was pity incarnate! She was passion incarnate!

Dick forgot where he was. He was altogether unconscious of the fact that he was in a meeting somewhere in the East End of London, and that things were being said which, if known to the police, would place the speaker, and perhaps the listeners, in prison. All that seemed as nothing; he was chained, fascinated by the almost unearthly beauty of the woman who sat on the little shabby-looking platform.

Then slowly the incongruity of the situation came to him. The audience, although warmly dressed and apparently comfortably conditioned, belonged in the main to the working classes. They were toilers. Most of them were malcontents—people who under almost any conditions would be opposed to law and order. But this woman was an aristocrat of aristocrats. No one could doubt it any more than he could doubt the sunlight. Her dress, too, was rich and beautiful. On her fingers costly rings sparkled; around her neck diamonds hung. And yet she was here in a cellar warehouse, in a district where squalor abounded.

The speaker finished; evidently he was the chairman of the meeting, and after having finished his harangue turned to the others on the platform.

Dick heard the word "Olga," and immediately after the room was full of deafening cheers.

The woman he had been watching rose to her feet and waited while the people continued to cheer. Fascinated, he gazed at her as her eyes swept over the gathering. Then his heart stood still. She looked towards him, and their eyes met. There might have been recognition, so brightly did her eyes flash, and so tender was the smile which came to her lips. She seemed to be saying to him, "Wait, we shall have much to say to each other presently." The air of mystery, which seemed to envelop her, enveloped him also. The hard barriers of materialism seemed to melt away, and he had somehow entered the realm of romance and wonder.

Then her voice rang out over the audience—a voice that was rich in music. He did not understand a word she said, for she spoke in a language unknown to him. And yet her message reached him. Indeed, she seemed to be speaking only to him, only for him. And her every word thrilled him. As she spoke, he saw oppressed peoples. He saw men in chains, women crushed, trodden on, little children diseased, neglected, cursed. The picture of gay throngs, revelling in all the world could give them in pleasure, in music, in song, and wine, passed before his mind side by side with harrowing, numbing want and misery.

Then she struck a new note—vibrant and triumphant. It thrilled him, made his heart beat madly, caused a riot of blood in his veins.

Suddenly he realised that she was speaking in English, that she was calling to him in his own language. She was telling of a new age, a new era. She described how old things had passed away, and that all things had become new; that old barriers had been broken down; that old precedents, old prejudices which for centuries had crushed the world, were no longer potent. New thoughts had entered men's minds; new hopes stirred the world's heart. In the great cataclysm through which we had passed, nations had been re-born, and the old bad, mad world had passed away in the convulsions of the world's upheaval.

"And now," she concluded, "what wait we for? We await the prophet, the leader, the Messiah. Who is he? How shall he come? Is he here? Is the man who is able to do what the world needs brave enough, great enough to say, like the old Hebrew prophet, 'Here am I, send me'?"

And even as she spoke Dick felt that her eyes were fastened upon him, even as her words thrilled his heart. Something, he knew not what it was, formed a link between them—gave this woman power over him.

There was no applause as she sat down. The feeling of the people was too intense, the magnetic charm of the speaker too great.

Still with her eyes fixed upon Dick, she made her way towards him. He saw her coming towards him, saw her dark, flashing eyes, her white, gleaming teeth, felt the increasing charm of her wondrous face.

Then there was a change in the atmosphere—a change indefinable, indescribable. Just above the woman's head Dick saw in dim outline what years before had become such a potent factor in his life. It was the face of the angel he had seen when he was sinking in the deep waters, and which appeared to him at Wendover Park.

"Mr. Richard Faversham," said the woman who had so thrilled him that night, "I have long been waiting for this hour."

Chapter XXII
"You and I Together"

For some time Dick Faversham was oblivious to the fact that the woman who had so fascinated him a few minutes before stood near him with hands outstretched and a smile of gladness in her eyes. Again he was under the spell of what, in his heart of hearts, he called "The Angel." Even yet he had no definite idea as to who or what this angel was, but there was a dim consciousness at the back of his mind that she had again visited him for an important reason. He was certain that her purposes towards him were beneficent, that in some way she had crossed the pathway of his life to help him and to save him.

Like lightning the memory of that fearful night when he was sinking in the stormy sea came surging back into his mind. He remembered how he had felt his strength leaving him, while the cold, black waters were dragging him into their horrible depths. Then he had seen a ray of light streaming to him across the raging sea; he had seen the shadowy figure above him with outstretched arms, and even while he had felt himself up-borne by some power other than his own, the words had come to him—"Underneath are the Everlasting Arms."

It was all shadowy and unreal—so much so that in later days he had doubted its objective reality, and yet there had been times when it had been the most potent force in his life. It had become such a great and glorious fact that everything else had sunk into insignificance.

Then there was that scene in the library at Wendover. He had been on the point of signing the paper which Count Romanoff had prepared for him. Under this man's influence, right and wrong had appeared to him but a chimera of the imagination. The alternative which had appeared before him stood out in ghastly clearness. He had only to sign the paper, and all the riches which he thought were his would remain in his possession. But he had not signed it. Again that luminous form had appeared, while a hand, light as a feather, but irresistible in its power, had been laid upon his wrist, and the pen had dropped from his fingers.

And now the angel had come to him again. Even as he looked, he could see her plainly, while the same yearning eyes looked into his.

"Mr. Faversham!"

He started, like a man suddenly wakened from a dream, and again he saw the woman who had been spoken of as Olga, and who had thrilled him by her presence and by the magic of her voice, standing by his side.

"Forgive me," he said, "but tell me, do you see anyone on the platform?"

The girl, for she appeared to be only two or three and twenty, looked at him in a puzzled kind of way.

"No," she replied, casting her eyes in that direction; "I see no one. There is no one there."

"Not a beautiful woman? She is rather shadowy, but she has wonderful eyes."

"No," she replied wonderingly.

"Then I suppose I was mistaken. You are Olga, aren't you?"

"Yes; I am Olga."

"And you made that wonderful speech?"

"Was it wonderful?" and she laughed half sadly, half gaily.

Suddenly the spell, or whatever it was, left him. He was Dick Faversham again—keen, alert, critical. He realised where he was, too. He had accompanied Mr. John Brown to this place, and he had listened to words which were revolutionary. If they were translated into action, all law and order as he now understood them would cease to be.

Around him, too, chattering incessantly, was a number of long-haired, wild-eyed men. They were discussing the speech to which they had just listened; they were debating the new opportunities which the times had created.

"Ah, you two have met!" It was Mr. John Brown who spoke. "I am glad of that. This is Olga. She is a Princess in Russia, but because she loved the poor, and sought to help them, she was seized by the Russian officials and sent to Siberia. That was two years ago. She escaped and came to England. Since then she has lived and worked for a new Russia, for a new and better life in the world. You heard her speak to-night. Did you understand her?"

"Only in part," replied Dick. "She spoke in a language that was strange to me."

"Yes, yes, I know. But, as you see, she speaks English perfectly. We must get away from here. We must go to a place where we can talk quietly, and where, you two can compare ideas. But meanwhile I want you to understand, Mr. Faversham, that the people you see here are typical of millions all over Europe who are hoping and praying for the dawn of a new day. Of course there are only a few thousands here in London, but they represent ideas that are seething in the minds of hundreds of millions."

"Mr. Brown has told me about you," said Olga. "I recognised you from his description the moment I saw you. I felt instinctively what you had thought, what you had suffered, what you had seen in visions, and what you had dreamed. I knew then that you were the prophet—the leader that we needed."

Dick gave her a quick glance, and again felt the spell of her beauty. She was like no woman he had ever seen before. Her eyes shone like stars, and they told him that this was a woman in a million. The quickly changing expressions on her face, the wondrous quality of her presence, fascinated him.

"I shall be delighted to discuss matters with you," replied Dick. "That part of your speech which I understood made me realise that we are one in aim and sympathy. If you will come to my hotel to-morrow, we can speak freely."

Olga laughed merrily. "I am afraid you do not understand, Mr. Faversham," she said. "I am a suspect; I am proscribed by your Government. A price has been placed on my head."

Dick looked at her questioningly.

"No; I am afraid I don't understand," was his reply.

"Don't you see?" and again she laughed merrily. "I am looked upon as a dangerous person. News has come to your authorities that I am a menace to society, that I am a creator of strife. First of all, I am an alien, and as an alien I am supposed to subscribe to certain regulations and laws. But I do not subscribe to them. As a consequence I am wanted by the police. If you did your duty, you would try to hand me over to the authorities; you would place me under arrest."

"Are—are you a spy, then?" Dick asked.

"Of a sort, yes."

"A German?"

A look of mad passion swept over her face.

"A German!" she cried. "Heaven forbid. No, no. I hate Germany. I hate the accursed war that Germany caused. And yet, no. The war was a necessity. The destruction of the old bad past was a necessity. And we must use the mad chaos the war has created to build a new heaven and create a new earth. What are nationalities, peoples, country boundaries, man-made laws, but the instruments of the devil to perpetuate crime, brutality, misery, devilry?"

Dick shook his head. "You go beyond me," he said. "What you say has no appeal for me."

"Ah, but it has," she cried; "that is why I want to talk with you. That is why I hail you as a comrade—yes, and more than a comrade. I have followed your career; I have read your speeches. Ah, you did not think, did you, when you spoke to the people in the grimy north of this country about better laws, better conditions—ay, and when you made them feel that all the people of *every* country should be one vast brotherhood—that your words were followed, eagerly followed, by a Russian girl whose heart thrilled as she read, and who longed to meet you face to face?"

"You read my speeches? You longed to see me?" gasped Dick.

"Every word I read, Mr. Faversham; but I saw, too, that you were chained by cruel tradition, that you were afraid of the natural and logical outcome of your own words. But see, we cannot talk here!" and she glanced towards the people who had come up to them, and were listening eagerly.

"Come, my friend," whispered Mr. Brown, "you are honoured beyond all other men. I never knew her speak to any man as she speaks to you. Let us go to a place where I will take you, where we can be alone. Is she not a magnificent creature, eh? Did you ever see such a divine woman?"

"I'm perfectly willing," was Dick's reply, as he watched Olga move towards the man who had acted as chairman. Truly he had never seen such a woman. Hitherto he had been struck by her intellectual powers, and by what had seemed to him the spiritual qualities of her presence. But now he felt the charm of her womanhood. She was shaped like a goddess, and carried herself with queenly grace. Every curve of her body was perfect; her every movement was instinct with a glowing, abundant life. Her complexion, too, was simply dazzling, and every feature was perfect. A sculptor would have raved about her; an artist would have given years of his life to paint her. Her eyes, too, shone like stars, and her smile was bewildering.

A few minutes later they were in the street, Dick almost like a man in a dream, Mr. John Brown plodding stolidly and steadily along, while Olga, her face almost covered, moved by his side. Dick was too excited to heed whither they were going; neither did he notice that they were being followed.

They had just turned into a narrow alley when there was a quick step behind them, and a man in a police officer's uniform laid his hand on Olga's arm and said:

"You go with me, please, miss."

The girl turned towards him with flashing eyes.

"Take your hand from me," she said; "I have nothing to do with you."

"But I have something to do with you. Come, now, it's no use putting on airs. You come with me. I've been on the look out for you for a long while."

"Help her! Get rid of the man!" whispered Mr. Brown to Dick. "For God's sake do something. I've a weak heart and can do nothing."

"Now, then," persisted the policeman. "It's no use resisting, you know. If you won't come quiet, I may have to be a bit rough. And I *can* be rough, I can assure you!"

"Help! help!" she said hoarsely.

She did not speak aloud, but the word appealed to Dick strongly. It was sacrilege for the police officer to place his hands on her; he remembered what she had told him, and dreaded the idea of her being arrested and thrown into prison.

"You won't, eh?" grumbled the policeman. "We'll soon settle that."

Dick saw him put his whistle to his lips, but before a sound was made, the young fellow rushed forward and instantly there was a hand-to-hand struggle. A minute later the police constable lay on the pavement, evidently stunned and unconscious, while Dick stood over him.

"Now is our chance! Come!" cried Mr. Brown, and with a speed of which Dick thought him incapable, he led the way through a network of narrow streets and alleys, while he and the girl followed. A little later they had entered a house by a back way, and the door closed behind them.

"Thank you, Faversham," panted Mr. Brown. "That was a narrow squeak, eh?"

He switched on a light as he spoke, and Dick, as soon as his eyes had become accustomed to the light, found himself in a handsomely, even luxuriously, appointed room.

"Sit down, won't you?" said Olga. "Oh, you need not fear. You are safe here. I will defy all the police officers in London to trace me now. Ah! thank you, Mr. Faversham! But for you I might have been in an awkward position. It would have been horrible to have been arrested — more horrible still to be tried in one of your law courts."

"That was nothing," protested Dick. "Of course I could not stand by and see the fellow — —"

"Ah, but don't you see?" she interrupted merrily. "You have placed yourself in opposition to the law? I am afraid you would be found equally guilty with me, if we were tried together. Did I not tell you? There is a price on my head. I am spoken of as the most dangerous person in London. And you have helped me to escape; you have defeated the ends of justice."

"But that is nothing," cried Mr. John Brown. "Of course, Mr. Faversham is with us now. It could not be otherwise."

Every event of the night had been somewhat unreal to Dick, but the reality of his position was by no means obscure at that moment. He, Dick Faversham, who, when he had advocated his most advanced theories, had still prided himself on being guided by constitutional methods, knew that he had placed himself in a most awkward position by what he had done. Doubtless, efforts would be made to find him, and if he were discovered and recognised, he would have a very lame defence. In spite of the honeyed way in which Mr. Brown had spoken, too, he felt there was something like a threat in his words.

But he cast everything like fear from his mind, and turned to the young girl, who had thrown off her cloak, and stood there in the brilliant light like the very incarnation of splendid beauty.

"I would risk more than that for this opportunity of talking with you," he could not help saying.

"Would you?" and her glorious eyes flashed into his. "I am so glad of that. Do you know why? Directly I saw you to-night, I felt that we should be together in the greatest cause the world has ever known. Do you think you will like me as a co-worker? Do you believe our hearts will beat in unison?"

Again she had cast a spell upon him. He felt that with such a woman he could do anything—dare anything.

Still, he kept a cool head. His experiences of the last few years had made him wary, critical, suspicious.

"I am going to be frank," she went on. "I am going to lay bare my heart to you. The cause I have at heart is the world's redemption; that, too, is the cause I believe you, too, have at heart. I want to destroy poverty, crime, misery; I want a new earth. So do you. But the way is dangerous, stormy, and hard. There will be bleeding footsteps all along the track. But you and I together!—ah, don't you see?"

"I am afraid I don't," replied Dick. "Tell me, will you?"

She drew her chair closer to him. "Yes; I will tell you," she said in a whisper.

Chapter XXIII
The So-called Dead

"Don't be frightened at a word," she laughed. "I shall explain that word in a few minutes. But it will not need much explanation. At heart you and I are one."

Dick waited in silence.

"You do not help me," and her laugh was almost nervous. "And yet—oh, I mean so much. But I am afraid to put it into a word, because that word has been so misunderstood, so maligned. It is the greatest word in the world. It sweeps down unnatural barriers, petty creeds, distinctions, man-made laws, criminal usages. It is the dawn of a new day. It is the sunrise. It is universal liberty, universal right. It is the divine right of the People!"

Still Dick was silent, and as she watched him she started to her feet.

"Who have held the destinies of the great unnumbered millions in the hollow of their hands?" she cried passionately. "The few. The Emperors, the Kings, the Bureaucrats. And they have sucked the life blood of these dumb, suffering millions. They have crushed them, persecuted them, made them hewers of wood and drawers of water. Why have the poor lived? That they might minister to the rich. Just that and nothing more. Whether the millions have been called slaves, serfs, working classes—whatever you like—the result has been the same. They have existed that the few might have what they desired. But at last the world has revolted. The Great War has made everything possible. The world is fluid, and the events of life will be turned into new channels. Now is the opportunity of the People. Whatever God there is, He made the world and all that is in it for the People. In the past it has been robbed from them, but now it is going to be theirs! Don't you see?"

Dick nodded his head slowly. This, making allowance for the extravagance of her words, was what he had been feeling for a long time.

"Yes," he said presently; "but how are they to get it?"

"Ah!" she laughed. "I brought you here to-night to tell you. You are going to give it them, my friend. With me to help you, perhaps, if you will have me. Will you? Look into my eyes and tell me that you see—that you understand?"

Her eyes were as the eyes of a siren, but still Dick did not lose his head.

"I see no other way of giving the people justice than by working on the lines I have been trying to work for years," he said.

"Yes, you do," she cried triumphantly. "You are a Labour man—a Socialist if you like. You have a vision of better conditions for the working classes in England—the British Isles. But what is that? What does it all amount to? Sticking-plasters, *mon ami*—sticking-plasters."

"Still, I do not understand," replied Dick.

"But you do," she persisted, still with her great, lustrous eyes laughing into his, in spite of a certain seriousness shining from them. "Think a minute. Here we are at a crisis in the world's history. Unless a mighty effort is made now, power, property, everything will drift back to the old ruling classes, and that will mean what it has always meant. Still the same accursed anomalies; still the same blinding, numbing, crushing poverty on the one hand; still the same pampered luxury and criminal waste on the other. All things must be new, my friend—new!"

"But how?"

"In one word—Bolshevism. No; don't be startled. Not the miserable caricature, the horrible nightmare which has frightened the dull-minded British but a glorious thing! Justice for humanity, the world for the people! That's what it means. Not for one country, but for all the countries—for the wide world. Don't you see? The world must become one, because humanity is one. It must be. Disease in any part of the organism hurts the whole body. If wrong is done in Russia, England has to pay; therefore, all reform must be world wide; right must be done everywhere."

"Words, words, words," quoted Dick.

"And more than words, my friend. The most glorious ideal the world has ever known. And every ideal is an unborn event."

"Beautiful as a dream, but, still, words," persisted Dick.

"And why, my friend?"

"Because power cannot be wrested from the hands in which it is now vested——"

"That is where you are mistaken. Think of Russia."

"Yes; think of Russia," replied Dick—"a nightmare, a ghastly crime, hell upon earth."

"And I reply in your own language, 'Words, words, words.' My friend, you cannot wash away abuses hoary with age with rose water. Stern work needs stern methods. Our Russian comrades are taking the only way which will lead to the Promised Land. Do not judge Russia by what it seems to-day, but by what it will be when you and I are old. Already there are patches of blue in the sky. In a few years from now things will have settled down, and Russia, with all its wealth and all its possibilities, will belong to the people—the great people of Russia. That is what must be true of every nation. You talk of the great wealth of European countries, and of America. Who holds that wealth? Just a few thousands—whereas it should be in the hands of all—all."

"And how will you do this mighty thing?" laughed Dick.

"By the people not simply demanding, but taking their rights—taking it, my friend."

"By force?"

"Certainly by force. It is their right."

"But how?"

"Think, my friend. Do you believe the people will ever get their rights by what is called constitutional means? Do you think the landed proprietors will give up their lands? That the Capitalists will disgorge their millions? That the bourgeoisie will let go what they have squeezed from the sweat and toil of the millions? You know they will not. There is but one way all over the world. It is for the people everywhere to claim, to *force*, their rights."

"Revolution!"

"Yes, Revolution. Do not be afraid of the word."

"Crime, anarchy, blood, ruin, the abolition of all law and order!"

"What is called crime and anarchy to-day will be hailed a few years hence as the gospel which has saved the world."

Dick could not help being influenced by her words. There was an intellectual quality in her presence which broke down his prejudices, a spiritual dynamic in her beauty and her earnestness which half convinced him.

"Admitting what you say," he replied presently, "you only proclaim a will-o'-the-wisp. Before such a movement could be set on foot, you must have the whole people with you. You must have a great consensus of opinion. To do this you must educate the people. Then you must have a tremendous organisation. You would have to arm the people. And you would need leaders."

She laughed gaily. "Now we are getting near it," she cried. "You've seen the vision. You've been seeing it, proclaiming it, unknowingly, for years, but you've not dared to be obedient to your vision. But you will, my friend. You will."

She placed her hand on his arm, and looked half beseechingly, half coyly, into his face.

"Do you not see with me?" she cried. "Could you not join with me in a great crusade for the salvation of the world? For I can be a faithful comrade—faithful to death. Look into my eyes and tell me."

Again he looked into her eyes, and he saw as she saw, felt as she felt. His past life, his past work, seemed but as a mockery, while the vision she caused him to see was like a glimpse of Paradise. Even yet, however, a kind of hard, Saxon, common sense remained with him; and she appeared to realise it, for, still keeping her hand upon his arm, she continued her appeal. She told him what she had seen and heard, and tried to prove to him how impossible it was for the poor to have their rights save by rising in their millions, seizing the helm of power, and claiming, taking, their own. Still he was not altogether convinced.

"You describe a beautiful dream," he said, "but, like all beautiful dreams, it vanishes when brought into contact with hard realities. What you speak of is only mob rule, and mob rule is chaos. To achieve anything you must have leaders, and when you get your leaders, you simply replace one set of rulers by another."

"Of course we do," was her answer. "But with this difference. The present leaders are the result of an old bad system of selfish greed. They think and act for themselves instead of for the good of the people. But, with you as a leader, we should have a man who thinks only of leading the children of the world into Light."

"I?—I?" stammered Dick.

"Of course, you, my friend. Else why should I long to see you, speak with you, know you?"

"Of course it's madness," he protested.

"All great enterprises are madness," was her reply; "but it is Divine madness. You were born from the foundation of the world for this work. You have vision, you have daring, you have the essential qualities of the leader, for you have the master mind."

It is easy for a young man to be flattered by a beautiful woman, especially when that woman is endowed with all charms, physical, intellectual, personal. Her hand was still on his arm; her eyes were still burning into his.

"Of course it is impossible," he still persisted.

"Why?" she asked.

"A huge organisation which is international requires the most careful arrangement—secret but potent."

"The organisation exists in outline."

"Propaganda work."

"It has been going on for years. Even such work as you have been doing has been preparing the way for greater things."

"Money—millions of money!" he cried. "Don't you see? It's easy to talk of leading the people, but difficult to accomplish—impossible, in fact, in a highly organised country like this."

"Give me your consent—tell me you will consent to lead us, and I will show you that this is already done. Even now a million British soldiers are ready—ready with arms and accoutrements!"

Again she pleaded, again she fired his imagination! Fact after fact she related of what had been done, and of what could be done. It needed, she said, but the strong man to appear, and the poor, the suffering from every byway, would flock to his standard.

"But don't you see?" cried Dick, half bewildered and altogether dazzled by the witchery of her words. "If I were to respond to your call, you would be placing not only an awful responsibility upon me, but a terrible power in my hands?"

"Yes, I do see!" she cried; "and I glory in the thought. Look here, my friend, I have been pleading with you not for your own sake, but for the sake of others—for the redemption of the world. But all along I have thought of you—*you*. It is right that you should think of yourself. Every man should be anxious about his own career. This is right. We cannot go against the elementary truths of life. There must be the leaders as well as the led. And leadership means power, fame! Every strong man longs for power, fame, position. You do, my friend. For years you have been craving after it, and it is your right, your eternal right. And here is the other ground of my appeal, my friend. Such a position, such fame, such power is offered you as was never offered to any man before. To be a leader of the world! To focus, to make real the visions, longings, hopes of unnumbered millions. To make vocal, to translate into reality all the world has been sighing for—striving after. Great God! What a career! What a position!"

"Ah—h!" and Mr. John Brown, who had been silent during the whole conversation, almost sobbed out the exclamation, "that is it! that is it! What a career! What a position to struggle after, to fight for! Power! Power! The Kings and Emperors of the world become as nothing compared with what you may be, my friend."

Dick's heart gave a wild leap. Power! place! greatness! Yes; this was what he had always longed for. As the thought gripped him, mastered him, impossibilities became easy, difficulties but as thistledown.

And yet he was afraid. Something, he knew not what, rose up and forbade him to do things he longed to do. He felt that every weakness of his life had been appealed to—his vanity, his selfishness, his desire for greatness, as well as his natural longing for the betterment of the world. And all the time the beautiful woman kept her hand on his arm. And her touch was caressing, alluring, bewildering. Her eyes, wondrous in their brilliance, fascinating, suggesting all the heart of man could long for, were burning into his.

He rose to his feet. "I must go," he said. "I will consider what you have said."

The woman rose too. She was nearly as tall as he, and she stood by his side, a queen among women.

"And you will think kindly, won't you?" she pleaded. "You will remember that it is the dearest hope of my life to stand by your side, to share your greatness."

Dick was silent as he made his way through the dark and silent streets with Mr. Brown by his side. He was still under the influences of the night through which he had passed; his mind was still bewildered.

Just before he reached his hotel, he and Mr. Brown parted—the latter to turn down Piccadilly, Dick to make his way towards Bloomsbury. When Mr. Brown had gone, Dick stood and watched him. Was he mistaken, or did he see the figure of a man like Count Romanoff move from the doorstep of a large building and join him? Was it Count Romanoff's voice he heard? He was not sure.

The night porter of his hotel spoke to him sleepily as he entered.

"No Zepps to-night, sir," he said.

"No; I think not. I fancy the Huns have given up that game."

"Think so, sir? Well, there's no devilish thing they won't think of. I hear they're going to try a new dodge on us."

"Oh, what?"

"I don't know. But if it isn't one thing it's another. Nothing's too dirty for 'em. Good night—or, rather, good morning, sir."

"Good morning."

Dick went to bed, but not to sleep. Again and again his mind rehearsed the scenes through which he had passed. It all seemed like a dream, a phantasmagoria, and yet it was very wonderful.

When daylight came he plunged into a bath, and as he felt the sting of the cold water on his body, he felt his own man again. His mind was clear; his senses were alert.

After breakfast he went for a walk towards Hyde Park. The air was clear and exhilarating; the great tide of human life stirred his pulses and caused his blood to course freely through his veins. His mind was saner, more composed. He turned into the Park at the Marble Arch, and he watched the crowds of gaily dressed women and swiftly moving motor-cars.

Presently his heart gave a wild leap. Coming towards him he saw Lady Blanche Huntingford. He thought he saw her smile at his approach, and with eager footsteps he moved towards her. He held out his hand. "This is indeed a pleasure, Lady Blanche," he said.

She gave him a quick, haughty stare, and passed on. He was sure she recognised him, but she acted as though he did not exist. She had cut him dead; she had refused to know him. The woman's action maddened him. Yet why should she not refuse to recognise him? He was a nobody, whom she remembered as a kind of Roger Tichborne—an impostor.

But she should know him! Again the memory of his recent experiences came surging back into his mind. He could reach a position where such as she would be as nothing, and like lightning his mind fastened upon Olga's proposal.

Yes; he would accept. He would throw himself heart and soul into this great work. He would become great—yes, the greatest man in England—in the world! He would go back to his hotel and write to her.

A little later he sat at a table in the writing-room of the hotel, but just as he commenced to write the pen dropped from his hand. Again he thought he felt that light yet irresistible hand upon his wrist—the same hand that he had felt in the library at Wendover Park.

He gave a quick, searching glance around the room, and he saw that he was alone.

"Who are you? What do you want?" he asked aloud.

Again he looked around him. Did he see that luminous form, those yearning, searching eyes, the memory of which had been haunting him for years? He was not sure. But of this he was sure. The place seemed filled with a holy influence, and he thought he heard the words, "Watch and pray, that ye enter not into temptation."

"Speak, speak, tell me who you are," he again spoke aloud. But no further answer came to him.

Bewildered, wondering, he rose to his feet and sauntered around the room. His attention was drawn to a number of papers that were scattered on a table. A minute later he was reading an article entitled

"Do the So-called Dead speak to Us?"

The paper containing the article was a periodical which existed for the purpose of advocating spiritualism. It announced that a renowned medium would take part in a séance that very afternoon in a building not far away, and that all earnest and reverent seekers after truth were invited to be present.

"I'll go," determined Dick as he read.

Chapter XXIV
Visions of Another World

After Dick had decided to attend the séance he read the article more carefully. It purported to be written by a man who had given up all faith in religion and all forms of spiritual life. He had tried to find satisfaction in the pleasures and occupations of his daily existence, and had treated everything else as a played-out fallacy. Then two of his sons had been killed in the war, and life had become a painful, hollow mockery. By and by he became impressed by the thought that his sons were alive and wanted to speak to him. Sometimes, too, he had felt as though presences were near him, but who they were or what they meant he could not tell. After this he had by pure accident heard two people talking about their experiences at a séance, and one had distinctly stated that he had seen and spoken to a dear dead friend. This caused the writer to turn his attention to spiritualism. The result was that he remained no longer a materialist, but was an ardent believer in the spiritual world. He distinctly stated that he had had irrefutable assurance that his sons were alive, that they had spoken to him, and had brought him messages from the spirit world. Things which before had been bewildering and cruel now became plain and full of comfort. Life was larger, grander, and full of a great hope.

Dick's heart warmed as he read. Surely here was light. Surely, too, he would be able to find an explanation to what for years had been a mystery to him.

He thought of the conversations he had heard in Eastroyd, in relation to this, to which he had paid but little attention because his mind had been too full of other matters, but which were now full of significance. His mind again reverted to the discussion on the Angels at Mons. If there were no truth in the stories, how could so many have believed in them? How could there be such clear and definite testimonies from men who had actually seen?

And had not he, Dick Faversham, both seen and heard? What was the meaning of the repeated appearances of that beautiful, luminous figure with great, yearning eyes and arms outstretched to save?

Yes; he would go to this séance. He would inquire, and he would learn.

He felt he had need of guidance. He knew he had come to another crisis in his life. The proposal which had been made to him was alluring; it appealed to the very depths of his being.

Power, position, fame! That was what it meant. To take a leading part in the great drama of life, to be a principal factor in the emancipation of the world! But there was another side. If this movement was spreading with such gigantic strides—were to spread to England and dominate the thoughts and actions of the toiling millions of the country—what might it not mean?

He was sure of nothing. He could not grasp the issues clearly; he could not see his way to the end. But it was grand; it was stupendous! Besides, to come into daily, hourly, contact with that sublime woman—to constantly feel the magnetic charm of her presence! The thought stirred his pulses, fired his imagination! How great she was, too. How she had swept aside the world's conventions and man-made moralities. She seemed like a warm breath from the lands of sunshine and song. And yet he was not sure.

For hours he sat thinking, weighing pros and cons, trying to mark out the course of his life. Yes; he had done well. Since he had left Wendover Park he had become an influence in the industrial life of the North; he had become proclaimed a leader among the working classes; in all probability he would soon be able to voice their cause in the Mother of Parliaments.

But what did it all amount to after all? A Labour Member of Parliament! The tool of the unwashed, uneducated masses! A voting machine at £400 a year! Besides, what could he do? What could the Labour Party do? When their programme was realised, if ever it was realised, what did it all amount to? The wealth, the power, would still be in the hands of the ruling, educated classes, while he would be a mere nobody.

"Sticking-plasters."

The term stuck to him—mocked him. He was only playing at reform. But the dream of Olga—the emancipation of the race! the dethronement of the parasites—the bloodsuckers of the world!—a new heaven and a new earth!—while he, Dick Faversham, would be hailed as the prophet, the leader of this mighty movement, with infinite wealth at his command and power unlimited. Power!

Men professed to sneer at Trotsky; they called him a criminal, an outrage to humanity. But what a position he held! He was more feared, more discussed, than any man in the world—he who a few months before was unknown, unheard of. And he defied kings and potentates, for kings and potentates were powerless before him. While behind him was a new Russia, a new world.

To be such a man in England! To make vocal and real the longings of the greatest Democracy in the world, and to lead it. That would mean the premier place in the world, and — —

So he weighed the position, so he thought of this call which had come to him.

During the afternoon he left his hotel and made his way towards the house where the spiritualistic séance was to be held. In spite of all his dreams of social reforms, and the appeal made to his own ambitions, his mind constantly reverted to the vision which had again come to him — to the influences he could not understand.

He found the house, and was admitted without difficulty. It was in a commonplace, shabby-looking street not far from Tottenham Court Road. On his arrival he was admitted into a room, where an absurd attempt had been made to give it an Oriental appearance. An old woman occupied the only arm-chair in the room. She looked up at his entrance, stared at him for a few seconds, and then muttered indistinctly. He was followed by half a dozen others who might have been habitués of the place.

Presently a man entered, who glanced inquiringly around the room. He appeared to be about fifty years of age, and had light watery-looking eyes. He made his way to Dick.

"You desire to be present at the séance?" he asked of Dick.

"If I may?" was Dick's reply.

"You come as a sincere, earnest, reverent inquirer?"

"I hope so."

"Is there any friend you have lost, any message you want to receive?" and he scrutinised Dick closely.

"At a time like this, we have all lost friends," Dick replied.

"Ah, then you come as an inquirer?"

"That is true. I have come to learn."

"Certainly. But of course there are certain expenses. Would it be convenient for you to give me ten shillings?"

Dick gave him a ten-shilling note, whereupon the man turned to another visitor.

"A great medium, but keen on business," Dick heard someone say.

"Yes, but why not? Mediums must live the same as other people."

Another man entered. He was much younger than the other. He looked very unhealthy, and his hands twitched nervously.

"The room is ready," he said, and his voice was toneless. "Perhaps you would like to see it and examine it before the light is excluded, so that you may be sure there is no deception."

Dick with two others accepted the man's invitation. The room into which he was led was carpetless and completely unfurnished save for a number of uncushioned chairs and a plain deal table. Nothing else was visible. There was not a picture on the walls, not a sign of decoration. Dick and the others professed satisfaction with what they had seen.

A few minutes later the others joined them, accompanied by the man who had been spoken of as a "great medium," also the man with the nervous, twitching hands, who Dick afterwards learned was the leader of the two mediums.

"My friends," he said, "will you seat yourselves around the table? We promise you nothing. The spirits may come, and they may not. I, personally, am a medium of the old order. I do not pretend to tell you what spirits say; I make no claim to be a clairvoyant. If the spirits come they will speak for themselves—if they wish to speak. If there are persons here who desire a message from the spirit world they will, if they receive such a message at all, receive it direct from the spirits. I pretend to explain nothing, just as I promise nothing. But in the past spirits have come to such gatherings as this, and many comforting messages have been given. That is all."

The party then sat down at the table, placed their hands upon it in such a way that the fingers of one person joined those of the persons sitting next, and thus formed a circle. All light was excluded.

For three minutes there was silence. No sound was heard; no light was seen. All was darkness and silence.

Then suddenly there was a faint voice—a child's voice. It sounded as though it came from the ceiling.

"I am come," wailed the voice.

"Yes, and I am come." This time the voice seemed to come from the direction of the window. It was hoarse, and coarse.

"Who are you?

"I am Jim Barkum. I was killed at Mons."

"Anything to tell us?"

"No; nothin' except I'm all right. I come fro' Sheffield. If you could tell my mother, Emily Barkum, that I'm very happy I'd be very thankful."

"What's your mother's address?"

"Number 14 Tinkers Street."

After this a number of other spirits purported to come, one of whom said he was the son of a sitter in the circle, and that he had been killed in the war.

"Will you reveal yourself?" said the medium.

Some phosphorous light shone in the darkness, in the radiance of which was the outline of a face.

"Do you recognise it?" asked the medium.

"It might be Jack," Dick heard a voice say.

After this there seemed to be a quarrel among the spirits. There was a good deal of confused talk and a certain amount of anger expressed. Also a number of feeble jokes were passed and far-away laughter heard. Evidently the spirits were in a frolicsome humour.

Dick, whose purpose in coming to the séance was not to take part in a fiasco, grew impatient. In his state of mind he felt he had wasted both money and time. It was true he had seen and heard what he could not explain, but it amounted to nothing. Everything seemed silly beyond words. There was nothing convincing in anything, and it was all artificial.

"I should like to ask a question," he ventured at length.

"Go ahead," said a voice, which seemed to come from the ceiling.

"I should like to ask this: why is it that you, who have solved the great secret of death, should, now you are permitted to come back and speak to those of us who haven't, talk such horrible drivel?"

"Hear! hear!" assented a member of the circle.

"Oh, it's this way," answered the spirit: "every one of you sitting here have your attendant spirits. If you are intellectual, intellectual spirits attend you and come to talk to you, but as you are not they just crack silly jokes."

There was laughter at this, not only from the sitters, but among the spirits, of which the room, by this time, seemed to be full.

"That's not bad," replied Dick. "One might think you'd said that before, but as it happens we are not all fools, and I personally would like something more sensible. This is a time when thousands of hearts are breaking," he added.

"What would you like to know?"

It was another voice that spoke now—a sweeter and more refined voice, and might have belonged to a woman.

"I would like to know if it is true that each of us have attendant spirits, as one of you said just now?"

"Yes; that is true."

"You mean guardian angels?"

"Yes; if you like to call them that. But they are not all guardian angels. There are spirits who try to do harm, as well as those who try to guard and to save."

"Are they here now?"

"Yes; they are here now. I can see one behind you at this moment."

The atmosphere of the room had suddenly changed. It seemed as though something solemn and elevating had entered and driven away the frivolous, chattering presences which had filled the room. A hush had fallen upon the sitters too, and all ears seemed to be listening eagerly.

"You say you can see a spirit behind me now?"

"Yes."

"Tell me, is it a good spirit or a bad one?"

"I do not know. The face is hidden."

"But surely you can cause the face to be seen. I am anxious to learn—to know."

"I think I can tell directly. Wait."

There was a silence for perhaps ten seconds; then the voice spoke again.

"The spirit will not show its face," it said, "but it is always with you. It never leaves you night nor day."

"Why does it not leave me?"

"I cannot tell; I do not know."

"Tell me," persisted Dick, "you do not seem like the other spirits who have been here—if they are spirits," he added in an undertone. "Can you not find out if I am watched over for any particular purpose?"

"Yes, yes, I can. I can see now. It is a guardian angel, and she loves you."

"She loves me—why does she love me?"

"When she was alive she loved you. I think you were engaged. But she died, and you never married her. But she is always watching over you—trying to help you. Were you ever engaged to anyone who died?"

"That is surely a leading question," was Dick's retort. "Is that all you can tell me?"

"That is all, except that you have enemies, one in particular, who is trying to do you harm, and your guardian angel is always near you, seeking to protect you. Have you an enemy?"

"Possibly—I don't know. Is that enemy a man or a woman?"

"I cannot tell. Everything is becoming hazy and dim. I am not a spirit of the highest order. There, everything is blank to me now."

After this the séance continued for some time, but as far as Dick was concerned, it had but little definite interest. Many things took place which he could not explain, but to him they meant nothing. They might have been caused by spirits, but then again they might have been the result of trickery. Nothing was clear to him except the one outstanding fact that no light had been thrown on the problem of his life. He wanted some explanation of the wonderful apparition which had so affected his life, and he found none. For that matter, although the spirit world had been demonstrated to him, he had no more conviction about the spirit world after the séance than he had before. All the same, he could not help believing, not because of the séance, but almost in spite of it, that a presence was constantly near him, and that this presence had a beneficent purpose in his life.

"You were not convinced?" asked a man of him as presently he left the house.

Dick was silent.

"Sometimes I think I am, and sometimes I think I am not," went on the man. "It's all a mystery. But I know one thing."

"What?" asked Dick.

"My old mother, who held fast to the old simple faith in Christ, had no doubts nor fears," was the man's reply. "I was with her when she was dying, and she told me that angels were beckoning to her. She said she saw the face of her Lord, and that He was waiting to welcome her on the other side. I wish I could see as she saw."

"Did she believe in angels?" asked Dick.

"She had no doubt," replied the man. "She said that God sent His angels to guard those they loved, and that those angels helped them to fight evil spirits."

"Accepting the idea of a spirit world, it seems reasonable," and Dick spoke like one thinking aloud rather than to be answering the man.

"Did not angels minister to Christ after He was tempted of the Devil?" persisted the man. "Did not angels help the Apostles? I don't think I'll bother about spiritualism any more. There may be truth in it; there may not; but I'd rather get hold of the faith my mother had."

"I wonder?" mused Dick, as he went away alone. "I wonder? But I'll have to send an answer to Olga. My word, what a glorious woman, and what a career! But I don't see my way clear."

He made his way back to his hotel, thinking and wondering. He felt he had come to a crisis in his life, but his way was not plain, and he did not know where to look for light.

Chapter XXV
Romanoff's Philosophy

Count Romanoff sat in a handsomely furnished room. It formed a part of a suite he had taken in a fashionable London hotel. He was smoking a cigar, while at his side was a tray with several decanters containing spirits.

He seemed to be puzzled, and often there was an angry gleam in his eyes, a cruel smile on his lips.

"I am not sure of him," he muttered, "and so far I've failed altogether. More than once I was certain that I had him—certain that he was bound to me hand and foot, and then——"

He started to his feet and strode impatiently across the room. He appeared angry. Looking out of the window, he could see the tide of human beings which swept hither and thither in the London street.

"Good and evil," he said aloud—"good and evil. Those people are all the time tempted, and yet—and yet——But I'll have him. It's only a matter of time now."

He heard a knock at the door, and started violently. For a self-contained, strong man, he seemed at times to be peculiarly apprehensive.

"Yes; come in. Ah, it's you, is it? I was expecting you."

"Count Romanoff, are you ever surprised?" It was Mr. John Brown who spoke, and who quietly came into the room.

"Rarely," replied the Count. "Why should I? After all, the events of life are a matter of calculation. Certain forces, certain powers of resistance—and there you are."

"It takes a clever man to calculate the forces or the powers of resistance," replied Mr. Brown.

"Just so. Well, I am clever."

Mr. Brown looked at him curiously, and there was an expression almost of fear in his eyes.

"Count Romanoff," he said, "I wonder sometimes if you are not the Devil—if there is a devil," he added as if in afterthought.

"Why, do you doubt it?"

"I don't know. It would be difficult to explain some things and some people unless you postulate a devil."

The Count laughed almost merrily. "Then why not accept the fact?" he asked.

"Do you?" asked Mr. Brown.

"I have no doubt of it. I—but wait. You must clear the ground. The existence of a devil presupposes evil—and good. If what the world calls evil is evil—there is a devil."

"You speak like one who knows."

"I do know."

"How do you know?"

"Because——But look here, my friend, you did not come here to discuss *that* problem."

"No; I did not. I came because I wanted to discuss——"

"A young man called Richard Faversham. Very well, let's discuss him," and the Count took a fresh cigar and lit it.

"I've been thinking a good deal since I saw you last," said Mr. Brown—"thinking pretty deeply."

The Count for reply looked at Mr. Brown steadily, but spoke no word.

"I have been wondering at your interest in him," said Mr. Brown. "He's not your sort."

"Perhaps that's a reason," he suggested.

"Still I do not understand you."

"But I understand you. I know you through and through. You, although you are a member of the best London clubs, although you pass as a Britisher of Britishers, and although you bear a good old commonplace English name, hate Britain, and especially do you hate England. Shall I tell you why?"

"Not aloud, my friend—not aloud; there may be servants outside—people listening," and Mr. Brown spoke in a whisper.

"I *shall* speak aloud," replied the Count, "and there is no one listening. I feel in a communicative, garrulous mood to-night, and it's no use mincing words. You hate England, because you are German at heart, and a German by birth, although no one knows it—but me. I also hate England."

"Why?" asked Mr. Brown.

"Because it stands for those things I abominate. Because, in spite of its so-called materialism, it still holds fast to the old standards of religion, and all that religion means. It stands for what the world calls progress, for civilisation, and Democracy. And I hate Democracy."

"You are a Russian," commented Mr. Brown—"a Russian aristocrat, therefore you would naturally hate Democracy."

"Am I?" and the Count laughed. "Well, call me that if you like."

"You told me so when we first met."

"Did I? I know you came to me in a sad way. You began to doubt your country, and your country's victory. You saw that it would never gain what it desired and hoped on the battlefield. You realised that this England—this Britain that you had scorned—was mightier than you thought. You saw that John Bull, whom I hate as much as you, was practically invincible."

"Yes; I could not help realising that. I admitted it to you, and you told me to— —"

"Take special note of Faversham. I told you his story."

"Yes, you did, and I accepted your advice. I went to Eastroyd; I made his acquaintance."

"And were impressed by the power he had obtained over the working classes, the Democracy, that we hear so much about. As you told me, he had taken up their cause, and that he had developed the gift of public oratory so assiduously that his power over working-class audiences was almost magnetic."

"But look here, Count, I— —"

"Pardon me a moment. I had studied Faversham for years. For reasons of my own, I wanted him to do certain things."

Mr. Brown sat quietly, watching the Count, who ceased speaking suddenly, and seemed to be staring into vacancy.

"Did you ever read a book by a man named John Bunyan, called *The Holy War*?" he asked, with seeming irrelevance.

Mr. Brown laughed. "Years ago, when I was a boy," he replied.

"A wonderful book, my friend. I have read it many times."

"*You* read it many times! Why, what interest could such a book have for you?"

"A very deep interest," and there was a curious intonation in his voice.

"What interest?" asked Mr. Brown.

The Count rose to his feet and knocked some ash from the end of his cigar. "Corpo di Bacco!" he cried. "Did not the man get deep? The city of Mansoul! And the Devil wanted to get it. So he studied the fortifications. Eyegate, nosegate, touchgate, eargate he saw, he understood!"

"What on earth are you talking about?" asked Mr. Brown in astonishment.

"There is one passage which goes deep," went on the Count as though Mr. Brown had not spoken. "It contained some of the deepest philosophy of life; it went to the roots of the whole situation. I had it in my mind when I advised you to make Faversham's acquaintance."

"What passage?" asked Mr. Brown, still failing to catch the drift of the other's words.

"It is this," and the Count spoke very quietly. "*For here lay the excellent wisdom of Him who built Mansoul, that the walls could never be broken down, nor hurt by the most mighty adverse potentate, unless the townsmen gave consent thereto.*"

Mr. Brown looked puzzled. "I don't follow you," he said.

"Don't you? Bunyan wrote in parable, but his meaning is plain. He said that Diabolus could never conquer Mansoul except by the consent of Mansoul. Well, I saw this: England—Britain—could never be conquered except by the consent of the people of England. United, Britain is unconquerable."

"Well?"

"Therefore, I made you see that if your country, which stands for force, and militarism, and barbarism, was to conquer England you must get England divided; you must get her own forces in a state of disunity. A country at war with itself is powerless. Set class against class, interest against interest, party against party, and you produce chaos. That is the only hope of your country, my friend. The thing was to get a man who could do this for you."

"And you thought of Faversham?"

"I told you to make his acquaintance."

"Which I have done. The results you know."

"Are you satisfied with the results?"

Mr. John Brown was silent a few seconds. Evidently he was thinking deeply.

"He is no Bolshevist at heart," he said.

"Are you?"

"I? Great heavens, no! I hate it, except for my enemies. But it has served our purpose so far. Russia is in a state of chaos; it is powerless—bleeding at our feet. If Russia had remained united, we, the Germans, would have been crushed, beaten, ruined. As it is— —"

"I love the condition of Russia," and Romanoff spoke almost exultantly. "I love it! It is what I hoped for, strove for, prayed for!"

"You—a Russian—say that! And *you* pray?"

"Yes; I pray. What then?"

"But you did not pray to God?" and there was a note of fear in Mr. Brown's voice.

"I prayed to my own god," replied Romanoff, "who is a very good counterpart of the god of your Kaiser. The good old German god, eh?" and he laughed ruthlessly. "And what is he, my friend? A god of force, a god of cruelty. Ruthlessness, mercilessness, anything to win. That's the German god. I prayed to that."

Mr. Brown almost shuddered.

"Yes; the condition of Russia is one of the great joys of my life. It means victory—victory for me, for you—if we can only get England to follow Russia's example."

"If we only could," assented Mr. Brown.

"And there are elements at work which, properly used, will bring this about," went on the Count. "I, Romanoff, tell you so. And Faversham is your man."

"He is no Bolshevist," again urged Mr. Brown. "At heart he knows what it means. That's why I am nearly hopeless about him. Give him time to think, and he will see that it will mean chaos—ruin to the things he has been taught to love."

"Before Adam ate the forbidden fruit two things happened," remarked Romanoff.

"What?"

"First the serpent worked. Then the woman."

"The woman! Yes; the woman!"

"Human nature is a curious business," went on the Count. "There are several points at which it is vulnerable. I have made a special point of studying human nature, and this I have seen."

"I don't quite follow you."

"I don't speak in riddles, my friend. Take a strong character like Faversham, and consider it. What is likely to appeal to it? As I understand the case, there are three main channels of appeal. First, money, and all that money means. Next there is ambition, greed for power, place, position, dominance. Then there is the eternal thing—the Senses. Drink, gluttony, drugs, women. Generally any one of these things will master a man, but bring them altogether and it is certain he will succumb."

"Yes, yes, I see."

"Money, and all that money brings, is not enough in Faversham's case. That I know. But he is intensely ambitious—and—and he is young."

"That is why you told me to introduce him to Olga?"

"A woman can make a man do what, under ordinary circumstances, he would scorn to do. If you advocated Bolshevism to him, even although you convinced him that he could be Lenin and Trotsky rolled into one, and that he could carry the Democracy of Britain with him, he would laugh at you. I saw that yesterday after your conversation with him. He was attracted for an hour, but I saw that he laughed at your proposals. That was why I told you to let him see and hear Olga. Now, tell me of their meeting."

Mr. Brown described in correct detail Dick's experiences in the East of London.

"Never did I believe a woman could be such a siren," Mr. Brown concluded. "She charmed, she magnetised, she fascinated."

"Is he in love with her?" asked the Count.

"If he is not he must be a stone," said Mr. Brown.

"Yes, but is he? I told you to watch him—to report to me."

"I do not know. He did not consent readily; he must have time to think, he said. But, man, he cannot resist her!"

"I do not know."

"But have you ever heard of any man who could resist her blandishments? Has she not been called a sorceress?"

"Yes, yes, I know—but he promised her nothing?"

"He said he would let her know later."

"Then he has resisted. My friend, I do not understand him. But—but—let me think."

"He was greatly impressed not only by her, but by her arguments," went on Mr. Brown presently. "I tell you, the woman is a sibyl, a witch. She was wonderful—wonderful. While I listened, I—even I—almost believed in her description of Bolshevism. A new heaven, and a new earth! I tell you, I almost believed in it. She pictured a paradise, an El Dorado, an Elysium, and she made Faversham see, understand. I tell you, he cannot resist her, and if he promises her, as he will, I can see England in a state of chaos in six months. Then—then——"

But the Count did not seem to be listening. His eyes were turned towards the streets, but he saw nothing.

"He went to a spiritualistic séance this afternoon," he said presently.

"What?—Faversham?"

"Yes, Faversham. What do you think it means?"

"I cannot think. He has never struck me as that sort of fellow."

"Look here, Brown, have you had many intimate talks with him?"

"Intimate? Yes, I think so."

"What have you talked about?"

"Always about the condition of the people, politics, and things of that nature."

"Have you ever discussed religion with him?"

"I don't believe he has any religion."

"I wonder?"

"What do you wonder?"

"I say, during your conversations with him—during your visits to Eastroyd—have you ever heard, have you ever discovered, that he is in love with anyone?"

"Never. He has taken no notice of women since I have known him. He seems to have been engrossed in his socialistic work. Mind, I doubt whether, at heart, he is even a socialist, much less a Bolshevist."

"That does not matter if we can get him to enlist in Olga's crusade. He has enough influence among, not only the working classes of the country, but among the leaders of the working classes all over the land, to create disturbances. He can inspire strikes; he can cause anarchy among the people. He can imbue them with Bolshevist ideals; he can make great promises. That done, the British Army is powerless. Without coals, and without the means of transport—don't you see?"

"Of course I see. That's what I've had in my mind from the first. If that can be done, Germany will be master of the world!"

"And more than that," and the Count spoke exultantly, "I shall have him, body and soul."

"But we must be very careful. If our plans leak out, my life will not be worth a row of pins."

Again the Count paced the room. He did not seem to be heeding Mr. Brown. His face worked convulsively, his eyes burned red, his hands clenched and unclenched themselves.

"I vowed I'd have him," he reflected—"vowed he should be mine. Left by himself he will do great things for what is called the good of the world. He will work for sobriety, purity, British national life. The man has powers, qualities which mean great things for what pietists call the world's betterment. But he is an aristocrat at heart; he loves money, and, more, he loves position, fame. He is as ambitious as Napoleon. He longs for power. But he has a conscience; he has a strong sense of what he calls right and wrong. I thought I had him down at Wendover. But I failed. Why, I wonder? But I will not fail this time. Olga will dull his conscience. She has charmed, fascinated him. She will make him her slave. Then—then——"

"Yes, yes," broke in Mr. Brown, who had only half understood the Count's monologue; "then he will cause a revolution here in England, and Britain as a fighting power will be paralysed. But I am not sure of him. He loves his country, and unless Olga gets hold of him, and that soon, he will see what our plans mean, and he will refuse to move hand or foot. You see, we've got no hold on him."

"We've every hold on him," almost snapped the Count. "We've appealed to his every weakness, and Olga will do the rest. I select my tools carefully, my friend."

A knock was heard at the door, and the Count impatiently opened it. "I am engaged; I cannot be disturbed," he said.

"The lady said she must see you," protested the servant, "so I—I thought I'd better come."

The Count looked beyond the man, and saw a woman closely veiled.

"Show the lady in," and a few seconds later she threw off her wraps and revealed her face.

"Olga?" cried both men together.

"Yes; I thought I'd better brave all danger. I've heard from him."

"From Faversham?"

"Yes; a long telegram."

"What does he say?" gasped Mr. Brown.

"I have it here," replied Olga breathlessly.

Chapter XXVI
A Voice from Another World

Dick Faversham walked along Oxford Street thinking deeply. Although he had been by no means convinced by what he had seen and heard, he could not help being impressed. The whole of the proceedings might be accounted for by jugglery and clever trickery, or, on the other hand, influences might have been at work which he could not understand—influences which came from the unseen world. But nothing satisfied him. Everything he had experienced lacked dignity. It was poor; it was sordid. He could not help comparing the outstanding features of the séance with the events which had so affected him. The face of the woman in the smoking-room of the steamer, the sublime figure which had upheld him when he was sinking in the wild, stormy sea, was utterly removed from the so-called spirits who had obeyed the summons of the mediums, and acted through them. How tawdry, too, were the so-called messages compared with the sublime words which had come to him almost like a whisper, and yet so plainly that he could hear it above the roar of the ocean:

"The Eternal God is thy Refuge, and underneath are the Everlasting Arms."

This was sublime—sublime in the great comfort it gave him, sublimer still in what it signified to the life of the world.

"It's true, too!" he exclaimed aloud, as he threaded his way along the crowded thoroughfare. "True!"

He stopped as the meaning of the words came to him:

"The Eternal God is thy Refuge, and underneath are the Everlasting Arms."

And because that was true, everything was possible!

As he thought of it, his materialism melted like snow in a tropical sun, and he realised how superficial and how silly his past scepticism had been.

God was behind all, underneath all, in all, through all. And if that was true, He had a thousand agents working to do His will, an infinite variety of means whereby His purposes were carried out. He, Dick Faversham, could not understand them; but what of that? God was greater than the thoughts of the creatures He had made.

But what of his own immediate actions? He had promised Olga that he would that very day send her a telegram where and when he could meet her, and that this telegram would signify his intention to fall in with her plans. She had given him directions where this telegram was to be sent, and he had to confess that he had looked forward to meeting her again with no ordinary pleasure.

The memory of their strange conversation on the previous night, and the picture of her glorious womanhood came to him with a strange vividness. Well, why should he not send the telegram?

He passed a post office just then, and turned as though he would enter. But he did not pass through the doorway. Something, he could not tell what, seemed to hold him back. He thought little of it, however, and still made his way along Oxford Street, towards High Holborn.

Again the problem of the future faced him, and he wondered what to do. Somehow, he could not tell why, but the thought of meeting the beautiful Russian did not seem to be in accord with the sublime words which were surging through his brain:

"The Eternal God is thy Refuge."

He found himself thinking of the wondrous face which had appeared to him as he stood at the door of Wendover Park, and he remembered the words that came to him.

"Pray, pray!" the voice had said. "Watch and pray!"

"God help me!" he cried almost involuntarily. "Great God help me!"

He still threaded his way through the crowd in the great thoroughfare, almost unconscious of what he did. He was scarcely aware that he had uttered a cry to Heaven for help. He passed the end of Chancery Lane and then came to the old timbered houses which stand opposite Gray's Inn Road. But this ancient part of London did not appeal to him. He did not notice that the houses were different from others. He was almost like a man in a dream.

Then suddenly he found himself in Staple Inn. How he had come there he did not know. He had no remembrance of passing through the old doorway, but he was there, and the change from the roar of the great thoroughfare outside and the silence of this little sequestered nook impressed him.

There was not a soul visible in the little square. As all Londoners know, Staple Inn is one of the smallest and quietest in the metropolis. The houses which form it are mostly occupied by professional men, and there is scarcely ever anything like traffic there. But this afternoon there was no one to be seen, and the change from the crowded highway was pleasant.

"What in the world am I doing here?" he asked himself.

But before he had time to answer the question he had propounded he realised a strange sensation. Although he could see nothing, he felt that some presence was near him.

"Listen."

The word was scarcely above a whisper, but he heard it plainly. He looked around him, his senses alert, but nothing was to be seen.

"Can you hear me?"

"Yes." He spoke the word almost involuntarily, and his voice seemed strange to his own ears.

"Do you know Drury Lane?"

"Yes," and he looked around wonderingly, trying to locate the voice.

"To-night, at nine o'clock, you must go to Drury Lane. You must walk westward until you come to Blot Street. Turn up at Blot Street, and keep along the right side. You must turn at the third street. You are sure you are following my instructions?"

"Yes, yes," he answered excitedly. "Who are you? Where are you?"

"You must walk along the third street for about twenty steps, stopping at the door marked 13a. You will knock five times in quick succession. You will wait five seconds, then you will give two more knocks louder than the first. The door will be opened, and you will be asked your business. Your reply will be two words, 'Victory,' 'Dominion.' You will be admitted without further questions. After that use your own judgment."

Suddenly there was a change as if in the whole atmosphere. He had, as it seemed to him, been in a kind of trance, but now he was more than ordinarily awake. And he was alone. Whatever had been near him was gone. The voice had ceased speaking. [1]

For some time Dick Faversham stood alone in the square without moving hand or foot. He was in a state of astonishment which was beyond the power of words to describe. But he had no doubt that he had heard the voice; he was as certain that some presence which he could not see had been near him as that he was certain he stood there at that moment.

Outside the square in Holborn the tide of traffic rolled on. Conveyances filled with human life rushed eastward and westward; men and women, oblivious to the fact of any world save their own, made their way to their destinations; but inside the square a man felt he had been in touch with mystery, eternity.

He moved into High Holborn like a man in a dream, and stood for a few seconds watching the faces of the passers-by.

"And not one of them seems to realise that the spirit world is all around them," he reflected.

He never thought of disobeying the commands he had received. The voice had come to him with a note of authority; the message was one which must be obeyed.

Slowly he made his way westward again, and presently came to a post office. He entered without hesitation, wrote a telegram, gave it to the clerk, and, having paid for its dispatch, again made his way along the street.

"There, that's done with," he said, with a sigh of relief.

At nine o'clock that night he found himself in Drury Lane following the instructions he had received. He was quite calm, although his heart throbbed with expectancy. He had little or no thought of what he was going to see or hear; enough for him that he was obeying instructions, that he was acting upon the commands which had come to him for his good. For he had no doubt that these commands were somehow for his benefit. Almost unconsciously he associated the presence near him with the one who had hovered over him with arms outstretched when he had been sinking in the stormy sea.

He had no difficulty in finding Blot Street, and quickly found himself at the third turning of that shabby-looking thoroughfare.

"Chainley Alley," he read in the dim light of the darkened street lamp at the corner.

The place was very quiet. He was now away from the traffic of the broad streets, and ordinary business had ceased for the day. There was nothing to mark Chainley Alley from a hundred others which may still be found in the centre of London. It was simply a dark, grimy little opening which, to the ordinary passer-by, presented no interest whatever. A minute later he stood at 13a. All was dark here, and it was with difficulty that he discerned the number. He listened intently, but heard no sound, and then, with a fast-beating heart, he knocked five times in quick succession. Then, waiting five seconds, he knocked again according to instructions.

The door opened as if by magic. It might seem that he was expected. But the passage into which he looked was as black as ink; neither could he hear anything.

Then suddenly the silence was broken. "Who are you? What do you want?" asked someone unseen.

"'Victory,' 'Dominion,'" he whispered.

A dim light shone, and he saw what looked like a woman of the caretaker order. Evidently the house was bigger than he imagined, for the woman led him down a long corridor which suggested that it was a way to another and a larger block of buildings in the rear.

She opened a door and told him to go in. "You will wait there till I call you," she whispered, and then closed the door behind him.

There was a thick rug on the floor, which muffled the sound of his footsteps, but there was no furniture in the room save a deal table and one straight-backed chair. A tiny gas-jet burnt on the wall, which, however, was extinguished a few seconds after the door had closed.

"This is darkness with a vengeance," reflected Dick, but the fact did not trouble him so much because he had brought a small electric lamp with him. He switched on this light and saw that the room had no outlet at all, save the door. There was neither window nor fireplace, and, in fact, was little more than a large cupboard.

Before he had time to realise what this might mean, he heard the sound of footsteps, which seemed to be close by; this was followed by murmuring voices. Then there were more footsteps, and the voices became clearer.

"Is he come?" he heard one man say.

"Not yet. But he'll soon be here. He did not promise to get here till half-past nine."

From that time there was a general hum of conversation, which was intermingled by the clinking of glasses. It might be that he was close to a kind of club-room, and that the members were arriving and ordering refreshments. The conversation continued, now indistinct, and again more clear. Dick caught snatches of it, but it was not connected, and conveyed but little meaning to him.

Suddenly he heard everything plainly, and a sentence struck him. "I hope he'll be careful," he heard someone say. "The whole lot of us would swing if we were found here together." The man spoke in German, and Dick's interest became tense.

"More likely be shot," someone retorted, with a laugh.

"But we're safe enough. This is the first time we've been here, and every care has been taken."

"I know," said someone, who appeared doubtful, "but if the British Secret Service people have been fools in the past, they are sharp enough now. Schleswig thought he was as safe as houses, but he was cleverly nabbed, and now he's cold meat."

"Never mind," said another voice, "our turn is coming. Gott in Himmel, won't we let them know when we are masters of London! Even now the English don't know that their country is a powder magazine. They little think that, in spite of their Alien Acts and the rest of it, the country is still riddled with friends of the Fatherland. Hark, he's coming!"

This was followed by a general shuffling of feet, and Dick instinctively felt that something of importance was about to happen. He wondered at the ease with which he could now hear. Evidently the partition which hid him from the room in which the conspirators had met (for evidently they were conspirators) was thin, or else there must have been some secret channel by which the sounds reached him. He realised, too, that these people had not entered by way of Chainley Alley, but that their room must have an outlet somewhere else. Possibly, probably too, as they had used this meeting-place for the first time that night, these people would be ignorant of the closet where he was hidden.

Dick heard a new voice, and he detected in a moment that it was a voice of authority. I will not attempt to relate all he heard, or attempt to give a detailed description of all that took place. I will only briefly indicate what took place.

The newcomer, who was evidently the person for whom the others had waited, seemed to regard those to whom he spoke as his subordinates. He was apparently the leader of a movement, who reported to his workers what progress had been made, and who gave them instructions as to the future.

He began by telling them that things were not going altogether well for the Fatherland, although he had no doubt of final victory.

But England—Great Britain—was their great enemy, and, unless she were conquered, Germany could never again attempt to be master of the world. But this could never be done altogether by force of arms.

"Russia is conquered!" he declared; "it lies bleeding, helpless, at our feet, but it was not conquered on the battlefield. By means of a thousand secret agencies, by careful and skilful propaganda, by huge bribes, and by playing on the ignorance of the foolish, we set the Bolshevist movement on foot, and it has done our work. Of course it has meant hell in Russia, but what of that? It was necessary for the Fatherland, and we did our work.

What, although the ghastliest outrages are committed, and millions killed, if Germany gains her ends!"

What was done in Russia was also being done in Great Britain, he assured them. Of course, our task was harder because the people had, on the whole, been well conditioned and had the justest Government in the world. But he had not been dismayed. Thousands of agencies existed, and even among the English the Germans had many friends. The seeds which had been sown were bringing forth their harvest.

They had fermented strikes, and the English people hadn't known that they had done it. If some of the key industries, such as coal and transport, could be captured, England was doomed. This could be done by Bolshevism; and it was being done.

"But what real progress has been made?" someone dared to ask presently.

"We have workers, agents in all these industries," replied the man, "and I'm glad to tell you that we have won a new recruit, who, although he is a patriotic Englishman, will help our cause mightily. Our trusted friend, Mr. John Brown, has got hold of a man who has a tremendous influence among not only the working-class people in various unions, but among the leaders of those unions, and who will be of vast help in our cause, and of making Great Britain another Russia; that done, victory is ours."

"Who is he?"

"A young man named Faversham. John Brown has had him in hand for months, and has now fairly made him his tool. Even to-night, comrades, we shall get him into our net."

"Tell us more about him," cried someone; but before the speaker could reply, some sort of signal was evidently given, for there was a general stampede, and in an incredibly short time silence reigned.

Almost unconsciously Dick switched on his electric lamp and looked at his watch. It was eleven o'clock. Although he had not realised it, he had been in the little cupboard of a room more than an hour and a half, while these men had been plotting the ruin and the destruction of the country he loved.

For some time he could not grasp all he had heard, but the meaning of it was presently clear to him. The thought almost overwhelmed him. He had unwittingly been again and again playing into the hands of the enemy.

"I must get out of this," he reflected after a few seconds. "I must get back to the hotel and think it all out."

"You can go now." It was the woman who showed him there who spoke.

A few seconds later he was in the open air, making his way towards Drury Lane.

"Thank God!"

The words passed his lips involuntarily. It seemed the natural expression of his heart.

Almost unconsciously he found his way back to his hotel. He had no remembrance afterwards of the streets he had traversed, or of the turnings he had taken. His mind was too full of the thought that but for his wonderful experience in Staple Inn the facts he had learnt that night would not have been made known to him.

On reaching his hotel he made his way to his sitting-room, and on opening the door he saw a letter lying on the table, which on examination he found to be signed "Olga."

Chapter XXVII
Olga makes Love

In order to relate this story in a connected manner it is necessary to return to Count Romanoff's rooms, where, a few hours earlier, both the Count and Mr. John Brown were startled by the sudden entrance of Olga.

"Let me see the telegram," the Count said, holding out his hand. His voice was somewhat hoarse, and his eyes had a peculiar glitter in them.

The girl handed it to him without a word.

"*Impossible for me to come. Am leaving London almost immediately.*—Faversham."

"What time did you get this?" he asked.

"I scarcely know. Almost directly I got it I came to you. I thought it best. Do you think it is true? Do you believe he will leave London?"

The Count was silent for a few seconds. "It would seem so, wouldn't it?" he answered grimly. "But he must *not* leave London. At all hazards, he must be kept here."

"But it means that Olga has failed," cried Mr. John Brown. "It means that we have lost him!"

"We have not lost him. I'll see to that," and there was a snarl in Romanoff's voice. "Olga Petrovic, all now depends on you. At your peril you must keep him here; you must win him over. If you fail, so much the worse for you."

Evidently the girl was angered. "Do you threaten me?" she said, with flashing eyes.

"And if I do, what then?"

"Simply that I will not be threatened. If you speak to me in that fashion, I refuse to move another finger."

"I am not in the habit of having my plans destroyed by the whims of a petulant woman," said the Count very quietly. "I tell you that if you fail to keep him in London, and if you fail to make him your slave, ready to obey your every bidding, you pay the penalty."

"What penalty?"

"What penalty?" and the Count laughed. "Need you ask that? You are in my power, Countess Olga Petrovic. I know every detail of your history—every detail, mind you—from the time you were waiting-maid to the Czarina. Yours is a curious history, Countess. How much would your life be worth if it were known to the British authorities that you were in London? What would our German friends do to you if they knew the part you played at Warsaw?"

"You know of that?" she gasped.

"I know everything, Countess. But I wish you no harm. All I demand is that you gain and keep Faversham in your power."

"Why are you so anxious for him to be in my power?"

"Because then he will be in my power."

"Your power? Why do you wish him in your power? Do you want to do him harm?"

"Harm!" Then Romanoff laughed. "And if I do, what then?"

"That I refuse to serve you. Carry out your threats; tell the British authorities who I am. Tell the Germans what I did at Warsaw. I do not care. I defy you. Unless you promise me that you will not do Faversham harm, I will do nothing."

"Why are you interested as to whether I will do Faversham harm?"

"I am—that's all."

The Count was silent for a few seconds. Evidently his mind was working rapidly. "Look at me!" he cried suddenly, and, as if by some power she could not resist, she raised her eyes to his.

The Count laughed like one amused.

"You have fallen in love with him, eh?"

The girl was silent, but a flush mounted her cheeks.

"This is interesting," he sneered. "I did not think that Olga Petrovic, who has regarded men as so many dogs of the fetch-and-carry order, and who has scorned the thought of love, should have fallen a victim to the malady. And to a thick-headed Englishman, too! Surely it is very sudden."

"You sneer," she cried, "but if I want to be a good woman; what then?"

The Count waved his hand airily. "Set's the wind in that quarter, eh? Well, well. But it is very interesting. I see; you love him—you, Olga Petrovic."

"And if I do," she cried defiantly, "what then?"

"Only that you will obey me the more implicitly."

"I will not obey you," she cried passionately. "And remember this, I am not a woman to be played with. There have been many who have tried to get the better of Olga Petrovic, and—and you know the result."

"La, la!" laughed the Count, "and so my lady threatens, does she? And do you know, if I were susceptible to a woman's beauty, I should rejoice to see you angry. Anger makes you even more beautiful than ever. For you are beautiful, Olga."

"Leave my beauty alone," she said sullenly. "It is not for you anyhow."

"I see, I see. Now listen to me. If you do not obey me in everything, I go to Richard Faversham, and I tell him who and what you are. I give him your history for the last ten years. Yes, for the last ten years. You began your career at eighteen and now you are twenty-eight. Yes, you look a young girl of twenty-two, and pride yourself upon it. Now then, Countess, which is it to be? Am I to help you to win the love of Faversham—yes and I can promise you that you shall win his love if you obey my bidding—or am I to go to him and tell him who Olga Petrovic really is?"

The girl looked at him angrily, yet piteously. For the first time she seemed afraid of him. Her eyes burnt with fury, and yet were full of pleading at the same time. Haughty defiance was on her face, while her lips trembled.

"But if you tell him, you destroy my plans. You cannot do that, Count!" It was Mr. John Brown who spoke, and there was a note of terror in his voice.

"*Your* plans! What do I care for your plans?" cried the Count. "It is of my own plans I am thinking."

"But I thought, and as you know we agreed——"

"It is not for you to think, or to question my thoughts," interrupted the Count. "I allow no man to interpret my plans, or to criticise the way in which I work them out. But rest contented, my dear friend, John Brown," he added banteringly, "the success of your plans rests upon the success of my own."

While they were speaking Olga Petrovic gazed towards the window with unseeing eyes. She looked quite her age now: all suggestion of the young girl had gone, she was a stern, hard-featured woman. Beautiful she was, it is true, but with a beauty marked by bitter experience, and not the beauty of blushing girlhood.

"Well, Countess Olga, which is it to be?" asked Romanoff, who had been watching her while he had been speaking to Mr. Brown.

"What do you want me to do?"

"Do! Keep him in London. Enlist his sympathies. Make him your slave as you have made other men your slaves. Bind him to you hand and foot. Make him love you."

A strange light burned in the girl's eyes, for at the Count's last words she had seemingly thrown off years of her life. She had become young and eager again.

"Swear to me that you mean him no harm, and I will do it," was her reply. "If I can," she added, as an afterthought.

"Do you doubt it?" asked Romanoff. "Have you ever failed when you have made up your mind?"

"No, but I do not feel certain of him. He is not like those others. Besides, I failed last night. In his heart he has refused me already. He said he was leaving London almost immediately, which means that he does not intend to see me again."

"And you want to see him again?"

"Yes," she replied defiantly; "I do."

"Good." He seized a telephone receiver as he spoke and asked for a certain number. Shortly after he was connected with Dick's hotel.

"Mr. Richard Faversham of Eastroyd is staying with you, isn't he?"

"Mr. Richard Faversham? Yes, sir."

"Is he in?"

"No, sir, he went out a few minutes ago."

"Did he say when he was likely to return?"

"No, sir, he said nothing."

"But you expect him back to-night?"

"As far as I know, sir."

"Thank you. Either I, or a lady friend, will call to see him to-morrow morning at ten o'clock on a very important matter. Tell him that, will you?"

"Certainly, sir. What name?"

But the Count did not reply. He hung up the telephone receiver instead.

"Why did you say that?" asked Olga. "How dare I go to his hotel in broad daylight?"

"You dare do anything, Countess," replied the Count. "Besides, you need not fear. Although you are wanted by the British authorities, you are so clever at disguise that no detective in Scotland Yard would be able to see through it." He hesitated a moment, and then went on: "If we were in Paris I would insist on your going to see him to-night, but Mrs. Grundy is so much in evidence in England that we must not risk it."

"But if they fail to give him your message?" she asked. "Suppose he leaves to-morrow morning before I can get there?" Evidently she was eager to carry out this part of his plans.

"He will not leave," replied Romanoff; "still, we must be on the safe side. You must write and tell him you are coming. There is ink and paper on yonder desk."

"What shall I write?" she asked.

"Fancy Olga Petrovic asking such a question," laughed the Count. "Word your letter as only you can word it, and he will spend a sleepless night in anticipation of the joy of seeing you."

She hesitated for a few seconds, and then rushing to the desk began to write rapidly.

"And now," said Romanoff, when she had finished, "to avoid all danger we must send this by a special messenger."

Thus it was, when Dick Faversham returned from Chainley Alley that night that he found the letter signed "Olga" awaiting him.

It was no ordinary letter that he read. A stranger on perusing it would have said that it was simply a request for an interview, but to Dick it was couched in such a fashion that it was impossible for him to leave London before seeing her. For this is what he had intended to do. When he had sent the telegram a few hours earlier his mind was fully made up never to see her again. Why he could not tell, but the effect of his strange experience in Staple Inn was to make him believe that it would be best for him to wipe this fascinating woman from the book of his life. Her influence over him was so great that he felt afraid. While in her presence, even while she fascinated him, he could not help thinking of the fateful hours in Wendover Park, when Romanoff stood by his side, and paralysed his manhood.

But as he read her letter, he felt he could do no other than remain. Indeed he found himself anticipating the hour of her arrival, and wondering why she wished to see him.

He had come to London ostensibly on business connected with his probable candidature in Eastroyd, and as he had to see many people, he had engaged a private sitting-room in the hotel. To this room he hurried eagerly after breakfast the following morning, and although he made pretensions of reading the morning newspaper, scarcely a line of news fixed itself on his memory. On every page he saw the glorious face of this woman, and as he saw, he almost forgot what he had determined as he left Chainley Alley.

Precisely at ten o'clock she was shown into the room, and Dick almost gave a gasp as he saw her. She was like no woman he had ever seen before. If he had thought her beautiful amidst the sordid surroundings of the warehouse in the East End of London, she seemed ten-fold more so now, as slightly flushed with exercise, and arrayed in such a fashion that her glorious figure was set off to perfection, she appeared before him. She was different too. Then she was, in spite of her pleading tones, somewhat masterful, and assertive. Now she seemed timid and shrinking, as though she would throw herself on his protection.

"Are you sure you are safe in coming here?" he asked awkwardly. "You remember what you told me?"

"You care then?" she flashed back. Then she added quickly, "Yes, I do not think anyone here will recognise me. Besides, I had to take the risk."

"Why?" he questioned.

"Because your telegram frightened me."

"Frightened you? How?"

"Because—oh, you will not fail me, will you? I have been building on you—and you said you were leaving London. Surely that does not mean that all my hopes are dashed to the ground? Tell me they are not."

Her great dark eyes flashed dangerously into his as she spoke, while her presence almost intoxicated him. But he mastered himself. What he had heard the previous night came surging back to his memory.

"If your hopes in any way depend on me, I am afraid you had better forget them," he said.

"No, no, I can never forget them. Did you not inspire them? When I saw you did I not feel that you were the leader we needed? Ah no, you cannot fail me."

"I cannot do what you ask."

"But why? Only the night before last you were convinced. You saw the vision, and you had made up your mind to be faithful to it. And oh, you could become so great, so glorious!"

He felt the woman's magnetic power over him; but he shook his head stubbornly.

"But why?" she pleaded.

"Because I have learned what your proposal really means," he replied, steeling himself against her. "I was carried away by your pleading, but I have since seen that by doing what you ask I should be playing into the hands of the enemies of my country, the enemies of everything worth living for."

"You mean the Germans; but I hate Germany. I want to destroy all militarism, all force. I want the world to live in peace, in prosperity, and love."

"I cannot argue with you," replied Dick; "but my determination is fixed. I have learnt that Mr. John Brown is a German, and that he wants to do in England what has been done in Russia, so that Germany may rule the world."

"Mr. John Brown a German!" she cried like one horror-stricken. "You cannot mean that?"

"Did you not know it?"

"I? Oh no, no, no! you cannot mean it! It would be terrible!"

She spoke with such passion that he could not doubt her, but he still persisted in his refusal.

"I have seen that what you dream of doing would turn Europe, the world, into a hell. If I were to try to persuade the people of this country to follow in the lines of Russia, I should be acting the part of a criminal madman. Not that I could have a tithe of the influence you suggested, but even to use what influence I have towards such a purpose would be to sell my soul, and to curse thousands of people."

She protested against his statement, declaring that her purposes were only beneficent. She was shocked at the idea that Mr. John Brown was a German, but if it were true, then it only showed how evil men would pervert the noblest things to the basest uses. She pleaded for poor humanity; she begged him to reconsider his position, and to remember what he could do for the betterment of the life of the world. But although she fascinated him by the magic of her words, and the witchery of her presence, Dick was obdurate. What she advocated he declared meant the destruction of law and order, and the destruction of law and order meant the end of everything sacred and holy.

Then she changed her ground. She was no longer a reformer, pleading for the good of humanity, but a weak woman seeking his strength and guidance, yet glorious in her matchless beauty.

"If I am wrong," she pleaded, "stay with me, and teach me. I am lonely too, so lonely in this strange land, and I do so need a friend like you, strong, and brave, and wise. And oh, I will be such an obedient pupil! Ah, you will not leave London, will you? Say you will not—not yet."

Again she almost mastered him, but still he remained obdurate.

"I must return to my work, Miss——You did not tell me your name." And she thought she detected weakness in his tones.

"My name is Olga Petrovic," she replied. "In my own country, when I had a country, I was Countess Olga Petrovic, and I suppose that I have still large estates there; but please do not call me by your cold English term 'Miss.' Let me be Olga to you, and you will be Dick to me, won't you?"

"I—I don't understand," he stammered.

"But you do, surely you do. Can you look into my eyes, and say you do not? There, look at me. Yes, let me tell you I believe in the sacredness of love, the sacredness of marriage. Now you understand, don't you? You will stay in London, won't you, and will teach a poor, ignorant girl wherein she is in error."

He understood her now. Understood that she was making love to him, asking him to marry her, but still he shook his head. "I must return to my work," he said.

"But not yet—tell me not yet. Forgive me if I do not understand English ways and customs. When I love, and I never loved before, I cannot help declaring it. Now promise me."

A knock came to the door, and a servant came bearing cards on a tray.

"Mr. Hugh Edgeware," "Miss Beatrice Edgeware," he read. He held the cards in his hands for a second, then turned to the woman, "I must ask you to excuse me," he said. "I have friends who have come to see me."

Olga Petrovic gave him a look which he could not understand, then without a word left the room, while he stood still like a man bewildered.

"Show them up," he said to the servant.

PART III
THE THIRD TEMPTATION

Chapter XXVIII
The Count's Confederate

Count Romanoff sat alone in his room. On one side the window of his room faced Piccadilly with its great seething tide of human traffic, from another St. James's Park was visible. But the Count was not looking at either; he was evidently deep in his own thoughts, and it would appear that those thoughts were not agreeable.

He was not a pleasant-looking man as he sat there that day. He was carefully dressed, and had the appearance of a polished man of the world. No stranger would have passed him by without being impressed by his personality—a dark and sinister personality possibly, but still striking, and distinguished. No one doubted his claim to the title of Count, no one imagined him to be other than a great personage. But he was not pleasant to look at. His eyes burnt with a savage glare, his mouth, his whole expression, was cruel. It might seem as though he had been balked in his desire, as though some cruel disappointment had made him angry.

More than once his hands clenched and unclenched themselves as he muttered angrily, savagely, while again and again a laugh of vindictive triumph passed his lips. And yet even in his laugh of triumph there was something of doubt. He was perturbed, he was furious.

"But he shall be mine," he said at length, "mine! and then——"

But his tone lacked certainty; his eyes burnt with anger because he had not been able to accomplish his designs.

"It might be that he was especially watched over," he reflected, as though some beneficent Providence were fighting for him. "Providence! Providence! As though——!"

He started to his feet and began to pace the room. His stride was angry, his whole appearance suggested defeat—a defeat which he had determined to transform to triumph.

"Good! Evil!" he cried. "Yes, that is it. Good! Evil! And I have given myself over to evil, and I have sworn that evil could be made stronger than good! I have sworn to exemplify it, in the case of that young fool, Dick Faversham. I thought I should have accomplished it long ago but I have so far failed, failed!"

He still continued to pace the room, although apparently he was unconscious of the fact. There was a far-off look in his eyes, a look that almost suggested despair.

"Does it mean after all that right is stronger than wrong, that right is more eternally established in the world than wrong? That in the sweep of events the power of right is slowly but surely conquering and crushing the evil, that the story of what is called evolution is the story of the angel in man overcoming the beast?"

Again he laughed, and the laugh had a cruel ring in it.

"No, no; evil is triumphant. Nearly two thousand years have passed since the Man of Nazareth was crucified, and yet for years the devil has been triumphant. Europe has been deluged in blood, world hatreds have been created, murder has been the order of the day, and the earth has been soaked in blood. No, no; evil is triumphant. The Cross has been a failure, and Him who died on it defeated!"

He paused in his angry march around the room, and again he looked doubtful.

"No, no," he cried; "cruelty, lies, treason, have not triumphed. Germany is beaten; her doctrine that might was right—a doctrine born in hell—has been made false. After all this sword-clanging, all the vauntings about an invincible army, materialism, devilry, have failed. Germany is being humbled to the dust, and her militarism defeated and disgraced."

The thought was evidently wormwood to him, for his features worked convulsively, his eyes were bloodshot. It might seem that the triumph of right filled him with torture.

Presently he shrugged his shoulders impatiently, and lifted his hands above his head as though he would throw a burden from him.

"But that is not my affair," he cried. "It was for me to conquer that man, to make him my slave. I swore to do it. I had every chance, and I thought that he, young, ambitious, and subject to all human passions, would be an easy victim. He was no dreamer, he had none of the makings of an ascetic, much less a saint, and yet so far he has beaten me. He still lives what is called the clean, healthy life. He still mocks me. It might be that he is specially guarded, that some angel of good were constantly fighting against me, constantly defeating me."

The thought seemed to disconcert Romanoff. A look almost like fear swept over his features, and again something like despair came into his eyes.

"But no, I have other weapons in my armoury yet," he reflected. "He is no religious fanatic, no pious prig with ideals, he is still ambitious, still craves for all the things that humanity longs for."

A clock on the mantelpiece chimed the hour of six.

"He should soon be here," he reflected. "I told him not to waste a second."

At that moment there was a knock at the door, and a second later a man entered who gave the appearance of having come from a distance.

He was a mild, placid-looking creature whose very walk suggested that he was constantly making an apology for his existence. A creature not of highways, but of byways, a humble Uriah Heep sort of fellow who could act like a whipped cur in his desire to curry favour, but who in his hour of triumph would show his fangs, and rend his victim without mercy.

"You are back to time, Slyme. Well, what news?"

By this time Romanoff was the great gentleman again—haughty, patronising, calm, and collected.

"Of course your honour has heard that he's in? I wired the moment I knew."

"Yes, I knew that before I got your wire. A servant in the hotel here told me the moment it was ticked off on the tape. Of course I expected that. Naturally it was uncertain, as all such things are. One can calculate on the actions of the few; but not on those of the many. Human nature is a funny business."

"Isn't it, your Excellency? It's a remark I've often dared to make; one can never tell what'll happen. But he's in; he's the Member for Eastroyd."

"With over a thousand majority."

"I've discovered that he's coming up to town by the midnight train from Eastroyd."

"Ah!" The Count's eyes flashed with interest.

"Yes, he seemed very much delighted at his victory, and is coming up I suppose to consult with other Members of his party."

"Of course he's delighted with his victory. For heaven's sake refrain from remarking on the obvious. Tell me about the election."

"What does your honour, that is, your lordship, want to hear about? What phase of the election, I mean?"

"You had your instructions. Report on them."

"Well, if I may say so," remarked Slyme apologetically, "although he has over a thousand majority, he has very much disappointed the people."

"Why? In what way?"

"He isn't so much of a firebrand as he was. The people complain that he is too mealy-mouthed."

"Less of a people's man, do you mean?"

"I don't say that quite. But he's more moderate. He talks like a man trying to see all sides of a question."

The Count reflected a few seconds, and then snapped his fingers.

"And his private life?" the Count questioned.

"As far as I could find out, blameless."

"Have the wealthier classes taken up with him at all?"

"No, not actively. But they are far less bitter towards him. They are saying that he's an honest man. I do not say that for myself. I'm only quoting," added the little man.

Romanoff asked many questions on this head, which the little man answered apologetically, as if with a desire to know his employer's views before making direct statements.

"There are generally a lot of scandals at a political election," went on the Count. "I suppose that of Eastroyd was no exception?" He said this meaningly, as though there were an understanding between them.

Little Polonius Slyme laughed in a sniggering way. "Polonius" was the name by which he was known among his friends, and more than once the Count used it when addressing him.

"I made many inquiries in that direction," he replied; "I even went so far as to insinuate certain things," he added with a covert look towards the Count. "I had some success, but not much."

But the Count's face was like a mask. Polonius Slyme could tell nothing of his thoughts.

"I did not think your lordship would be offended?" he queried with a cunning look in his eyes.

"Go on."

"I had some success, but not much."

"What were your insinuations about? Drink, drug-taking, debt, unfaithfulness to his class?—what?"

"Oh, there was no possibility of doing anything on those lines, although, as I said, there was some disappointment on the last head. But that's nothing. I reflected that he was a young man, and a bachelor—a good-looking bachelor." He added the last words with a suggestive giggle.

"I see. Well?"

"Of course he is a great favourite with the fair sex. By dint of very careful but persistent investigation I discovered that two ladies are deeply in love with him."

Romanoff waited in silence.

"One is the daughter of a wealthy manufacturer, quite the belle of the town among the moneyed classes. I inquired about her. There is no doubt that she's greatly interested in him."

"And he?"

"He's been seen in her company."

"What do you mean by that?"

"Oh, nothing. She would be a good match for him, that's all. There was a rumour that she had visited his lodgings late at night."

"Which rumour you started?"

"I thought it might be useful some day. As for the other woman, she's a mill girl. A girl who could be made very useful, I should think."

"Yes, how?"

"She's undoubtedly very much in love with him—after her own fashion. She possesses a kind of gipsy beauty, has boundless ambitions, is of a jealous disposition, and would stop at nothing to gain her desires."

"And is Faversham friendly with her?"

"Just friendly enough for one to start a scandal in case of necessity. And the girl, as you may say, not being overburdened with conscientious scruples, could be made very useful."

Romanoff reflected for some time, then he turned to Slyme again.

"Slyme," he said, "I don't think you need go any further in that direction. Faversham is scarcely the man to deal with in the way you suggest. Still you can keep them in mind. One never knows what may happen."

Polonius Slyme was evidently puzzled. He looked cautiously, suspiciously, at the face of the other, as if trying to understand him.

"I have tried to do your lordship's will," he ventured.

"Yes, and on the whole I'm satisfied with what you've done. Yes, what is it?"

"If your lordship would deign to trust me," he said.

"Trust you? In what way?"

"If you would tell me what is in your mind, I could serve you better," he asserted, with a nervous laugh. "All the time I have been acting in the dark. I don't understand your lordship."

The Count smiled as though he were pleased.

"What do you want to know?" he asked.

"I am very bold, I know, and doubtless I am not worthy to have the confidence of one so great and so wise as your lordship. But I have tried to be worthy, I have worked night and day for you—not for the wages, liberal though they are, but solely for the purpose of being useful to you. And I could, I am sure, be more useful if I knew your mind, if I knew exactly what you wanted. I am sure of this: if I knew your purposes in relation to Faversham, if I knew what you wanted to do with him, I could serve you better."

The Count looked at Slyme steadily for some seconds.

"I allow no man to understand my mind, my purposes," the Count answered.

"Certainly, your lordship," assented the little man meekly; "only your lordship doubtless sees that—that I am handicapped. I don't think I'm a fool," he added; "I am as faithful as a dog, and as secret as the grave."

"You want to know more than that," replied Romanoff harshly.

Polonius Slyme was silent.

"You want to know who I am," continued the Count. "You have been puzzled because I, who am known as a Russian, should interest myself in this man Faversham, and up to now you, in spite of the fact that you've hunted like a ferret, have found out nothing. More than that, you cannot think why I fastened on you to help me, and, cunning little vermin that you are, you stopped at nothing to discover it."

"But only in your interest," assented the little man eagerly; "only because I wanted to deserve the honour you have bestowed upon me."

"I am disposed to be communicative," went on the Count; "disposed to make something of a confidante of you. Of my secret mind, you, nor no man, shall know anything, but I will let you know something."

Polonius Slyme drew nearer his master and listened like a fox. "Yes, your lordship," he whispered.

"Look here, Polonius, you have just told me that you are a man of brains: suppose that you wanted to get a strong man in your power, to make him your slave, body and soul, what would you do? Suppose also that you had great, but still limited power, that your knowledge was wide, but with marked boundaries, how would you set to work?"

"Every man has his weaknesses," replied Polonius. "I should discover them, fasten upon them, and make my plans accordingly."

"Yes, that's right. Now we'll suppose that Faversham is the man, what would you regard as his weaknesses?"

"Pride, ambition, a love, almost amounting to a passion, for power," answered the little man quickly. "That would mean a longing for wealth, a craving for fame."

"And conscience?" queried the Count.

"He has a conscience," replied the little man; "a conscience which may be called healthily normal."

"Just so. Now I'll tell you something. I've placed wealth in his way, and he has rejected it for conscience sake. I've tempted him with power and fame, almost unlimited power and fame, and although he's seen the bait, he has not risen to it."

Polonius was silent for some time. Evidently he was thinking deeply; evidently, too, he saw something of what lay behind the Count's words, for he nodded his head sagely, and into his cunning eyes came a look of understanding.

"Of course you do not care to tell me why you want to make him your slave, body and soul?" he whispered.

"No!" the Count almost snarled. "No man may know that."

"You ask what I would do next?"

"Yes, I ask that."

"No man is invulnerable," said the little man, as though he were talking to himself. "No man ever was, no man ever will be. Every man has his price, and if one can pay it——"

"There is no question of price," said the Count eagerly; "nothing need stand in the way, any price can be paid."

"I see, I see," and the little man's foxy eyes flashed. "You want to work the man's moral downfall," he added. "You want to make him a slave to your will—*not* to make him a saint?"

The Count was silent.

"If I wanted to make such a man a slave to my will, and I had such means as you suggest, I should find a woman to help me. A woman beautiful, fascinating, unscrupulous. I would instruct her to be an angel of light. I would make her be the medium whereby he could obtain all that such as he desires, and I would make him believe that in getting her he would find the greatest and best gift in life, a gift whereby all that was highest and best in this life, and in the life to come, could be got. At the same time she must be a *woman*, a woman that should appeal to his desires, and make his pulses throb at the thought of possessing her."

For some time they spoke eagerly together, the Count raising point after point, which the little man was not slow to answer.

"Polonius, did I not know otherwise, I should say you were the devil," laughed Romanoff.

"I know you are," replied the little man in great glee.

"What do you mean?" and there was a kind of fear in the Russian's voice.

"Only that your cleverness is beyond that of ordinary mankind. You have thought of all this long before you asked me."

"Have I? Perhaps I have; but I wanted your opinion."

"The difficulty is to find the woman."

"In two minutes she will be here. Go into the next room and watch, and listen. After she has gone, you shall tell me what you think of her."

A minute later the door opened, and Olga Petrovic entered the room.

Chapter XXIX
In Quest of a Soul

"Good evening, Countess. Thank you for coming so promptly. Be seated, won't you?"

Olga Petrovic looked at the Count eagerly, and accepted the chair he indicated. She looked older than when she left Dick Faversham after the interview I have described, and there were indications on her face that she had suffered anxious thoughts, and perhaps keen disappointment. But she was a strikingly beautiful woman still. Tall, magnificently proportioned; and almost regal in her carriage. She was fast approaching thirty, but to a casual observer she appeared only two- or three-and-twenty. She had the air of a grand lady, too, proud and haughty, but a woman still. A woman in a million, somewhat captivating, seductive; a woman to turn the head of any ordinary man, and make him her slave. One felt instinctively that she could play on a man's heart and senses as a skilful musician plays on an instrument.

But not a good woman. She had a world of experience in her eyes. She suggested mystery, mystery which would appear to the unwary as Romance. Because of this she could impress youth and inexperience by her loveliness, she could appear as an angel of light.

She was magnificently dressed, too. Every detail of her glorious figure was set off to the full by her *costumier*, and her attire spoke of wealth, even while this fact was not ostentatious or even intended. In short, her *costumier* was an artist who knew her business.

Evidently, if ever she had been in danger by appearing in public, that danger was over. There was no suggestion of fear or apprehension in her demeanour.

"Why do you wish to see me?" she asked abruptly.

"I am quite aware," said Romanoff, without taking any apparent notice of her question, "that I took a liberty in asking you to come here. I should have asked you when it would have been convenient for you to graciously receive me at your flat. For this I must crave your pardon."

There was something mocking in his voice, a subtle insinuation of power which the woman was not slow to see.

"You asked me to come here because you wanted me, and because you knew I should come," she replied. "You knew, too, that I could not afford to disobey you."

"We will let that drop," replied the Count suavely. "I count myself honoured by your visit. How could it be otherwise?" and he cast an admiring glance towards her.

The woman watched him closely. It seemed as though, in spite of their acquaintance, she did not understand him.

"You see," went on Romanoff, "our Bolshevism is a thing of the past. The proletariat of England will have none of it. A few malcontents may have a hankering after it; but as a class the people of England see through it. They see what it has done for Russia, and they know that under a Bolshevist régime all liberty, all safety, all prosperity would be gone for ever."

The woman nodded.

"Besides," went on the Count, "you are in a far more becoming position as the Countess Petrovic, with estates in Russia and elsewhere, than as Olga, the high priestess of a wild and irresponsible set of fanatics."

"You have changed your views about those same fanatics," responded the woman rather sullenly.

"Have I? Who knows?" was the Count's smiling and enigmatical reply. "But I did think they might have served my purpose."

"What purpose?"

"Dear lady, even to you I cannot disclose that. Besides, what does it matter?"

"Because I would like to know. Because—because——" There she broke off suddenly.

"Because through it the man Faversham crossed your path, eh?" and the smile did not leave his face.

"You knew that Bolshevism would fail in England," cried the woman. "You knew that the whole genius of the race was against it. Why then did you try to drag—Faversham into it? Why did you tell me to dazzle him with its possibilities, to get him involved in it to such a degree that he would be compromised?"

"Ah, why?"

"But he would have none of it," retorted the woman. "He saw through it all, saw that it was an impossible dream, because in reality it was, and is, a wild delusion and a nightmare."

"Perhaps that was your fault," replied Romanoff. "Perhaps your powers of fascination were not as great as I thought. Anyhow——"

"Have you seen him lately?" she interrupted. "You know where he is? What he is doing?"

Her voice vibrated with eagerness; she looked towards Romanoff with a flash of pleading in her great lustrous eyes.

"Don't you read the newspapers?"

"Not the English. Why should I? What is there in them for me? Of course I get the Polish and the Russian news."

"If you read the English newspapers you would have no need to ask where he is," replied Romanoff.

"Why, has he become famous?"

As if in answer to her question there was a knock at the door, and a servant entered bringing three London evening papers.

"There," said the Count, pointing to some bold headlines—"there is the answer to your question."

"Great Labour Victory in Eastroyd," she read. "Triumphant Return of Mr. Richard Faversham."

Her eyes were riveted on the paper, and almost unheeding the Count's presence she read an article devoted to the election. Especially was her attention drawn to the Career of the Successful Candidate.

"Although Mr. Faversham, because of his deep sympathy with the aims of the working classes, has been returned to Parliament by them," she read, "he is not a typical Labour Member. As the son of a scholar, and the product of one of our best public schools, he has naturally been associated with a class different from that which has just given him its confidence. Years ago he was regarded as the heir of one of our great commercial magnates, and for some time was in possession of a great country house. His association with the middle classes, however, has not lessened his passionate interest in the welfare of the poor, and although he has of late become less advanced in his views, there can be no doubt that he will be a strong tower to the party with which he has identified himself."

"He will be in London to-morrow," remarked Romanoff, when presently the woman lifted her head.

"In London? To-morrow!"

The Count noted the eagerness with which she spoke.

"Yes," he said; "to-morrow."

"And he will be a great man?"

"Not necessarily so," answered Romanoff. "He will be a Labour Member at four hundred pounds a year. He will have to be obedient to the orders of his party."

"He never will! He is not a man of that sort!"

Her voice was almost passionate. Evidently her interest in him was deep.

"Won't he? We shall see. But he will find it hard to live in London on four hundred pounds a year. London is not a cheap city in these days. You see he has all the instincts of his class."

"Will he be one of the working men? Will he live as they live? Will he be of their order?" asked Olga.

"You seem greatly interested, Countess."

"Naturally. I—I— —"

"Yes, I remember your last interview."

The woman's eyes flashed with anger. She suggested the "woman scorned."

"You made love to him, didn't you, Countess? And he—he politely declined your advances?" Romanoff laughed as he spoke.

The woman started to her feet. "Did you get me here to taunt me with that?" she cried. "Besides, did I not obey your bidding? Was it not at your command that I— —"

"Yes, but not against your will, Countess. You had what our French neighbours call the *grand passion* for Faversham, eh?"

"Why do you taunt me with that?"

"Because the game is not played out. I do not break my promise, and I promised you that he should be yours—yours. Well, the time has come when my promise may be fulfilled."

"What do you mean?"

"Countess, are you still in love with Faversham?"

"I don't know. Sometimes I think I hate him. Tell me, why have you brought me here to-day?"

"To give you your opportunity. To tell you how, if you still love Faversham, you can win him; and how, if you hate him, you can have your revenge. Surely, Olga Petrovic, you are not the kind of woman who sits down meekly to a snub. To offer your love to a man, and then accept a cold rebuff. I thought I knew you better."

Deeply as his words wounded her, she did not forget her caution.

"What interest have you in him?" she asked. "I have never been able to understand you."

"No, I am not easily understood, and I do not make my motives public property. But Faversham will in future live in London. He, although he is a Labour Member, will have but little sympathy, little in common with his confrères. He will be lonely; he will long for the society of women, especially for those who are educated, fascinating, beautiful. Olga, are you the woman to be beaten? Listen, he with his tastes, will need money. You can give it to him. He will be lonely; he will need companionship. You have a beautiful flat in Mayfair, and you can be as fascinating as an angel."

She listened to every word he said, but her mind might be far away.

"Why do I care for him?" she cried passionately. "What is he to me? A middle-class Englishman, with an Englishman's tastes and desires, an Englishman with the morality of his class. Just a plain, stupid, uninteresting bourgeois, a specimen of the self-satisfied Puritan."

"You found him vastly interesting though."

"Yes, but why should I? Why do I care what becomes of him? He is nothing to me."

"He can be something to you though, Countess; you are a beautiful, fascinating woman. You can appeal to every man's weaknesses, no matter what they are. With time and opportunity no man can resist you. Say the word, and I will give you these opportunities."

"You mean——?"

"That I want him to be yours. You want him, and I owe you at least this."

"You have some other purpose."

"And if I have, what then? He will be yours, body and soul. Tell me, are you still in love with him?"

The woman walked to the window, and looked out on the tide of human traffic in Piccadilly. For some time she seemed to be lost in thought, then she burst out passionately.

"I am angry whenever I think of him. He was as cold as an icicle; I was like a woman pleading with a stone. Something seemed to stand between us—something—I don't know what."

"What, you?" and there was a taunt in the Count's voice. "You, Olga Petrovic, said to be the most beautiful, the most dangerous woman in Europe, you whom no man has been able to resist, but who have fascinated them as serpents fascinate birds? Are you going to be beaten by this middle-class Englishman, this Labour Member of Parliament with £400 a year? Will you have him boast that Countess Olga Petrovic threw herself at him, and that he declined her without thanks?"

"Has he boasted that?" she cried hoarsely.

"What do you think?" laughed the Count. "Is he not that kind of man?"

"No," the word came from her involuntarily. "Only— —"

"Only he is much in favour with the ladies at Eastroyd. I have just been told that."

"I hate him!" she said, and her voice was hoarse.

"I wonder?" queried the Count mockingly.

"Do you know, have you found out who his visitors were that day, that morning when I saw him last?"

"An old man and a chit of a girl."

"Yes, I know that; I saw them as I left the room. The man might have been a poet, an artist, and the girl was an unformed, commonplace miss. But he did not regard them as commonplace. His eyes burnt with a new light as he read their cards. I saw it. I believe I should have had him but for that. I had conquered him; he was ready to fall at my feet; but when he read their names, I knew I had lost. Who were they?"

"I have not discovered. They could have been only casual acquaintances. I have had him watched ever since he left London that day, and he has never seen them since. Of course he may be in love with her. It may be that he prefers an English wayside flower to such a tropical plant as yourself. That he would rather have youth and innocence than a woman twenty-eight years of age, who—who has had a past."

"He never shall! Never!"

Her eyes flashed dangerously. She had evidently decided on her course.

"You may have to play a bold, daring game," insinuated the Count.

"I will play any game. I'll not be beaten."

"You love him still—you who never loved any man for more than a month! And Faversham——"

"You must find out where he lives, you must let me know."

"And then?"

"You may leave everything to me."

"Mind, Olga, you may have to appear an Angel of Light in order to win him. In fact I think that will have to be your plan. He has all the old-fashioned morality of the middle-classes."

"We shall see!" cried the woman triumphantly.

"I may trust you then?"

"Tell me why you wish this? Suppose I—I love him really, suppose I am willing to become his slave? Suppose I want to settle down to—to quiet domestic happiness, to loving motherhood? Suppose I want to be good—and to pray?"

The Count's eyes burnt red with anger as she spoke, while his features were contorted as if with pain.

"Stop that," he almost snarled. "I know you, Olga Petrovic, I know too much about you. Besides, the Bolshevists have taken your estates, and—but why argue? You love luxury, don't you? Love beautiful dresses, love your life of ease, love what money can buy, money that you can't get without me?"

"You must tell me all I need to know," she answered with sullen submissiveness.

"Yes."

"Then I will go."

"And you will not fail?"

"No, I will not fail."

She left the room without another word, while Romanoff returned to his chair, and sat for some time immovable. His face was like a mask. His deep impenetrable eyes were fixed on vacancy.

"Yes, Polonius, you can come in. I can see that you are almost tired of watching me. But my face tells you nothing, my little man."

Polonius Slyme slinked into the room like a whipped cur.

"Look here, little man," went on the Count, "I pay you to watch others, not me. The moment you begin to spy on me, that moment you cease to be my servant. Do you understand?"

"But, indeed, your lordship——"

"Do not try to deny. I know everything. I forgive you for this once; but never again. Obey me blindly, unquestioningly, and all will be well with you, but try to spy upon me, to discover anything about me, and the lost souls in hell may pity you. Ah, I see yow understand."

"Forgive me, my lord. I will obey you like a slave."

"What do you think of her?"

"She is magnificent, glorious! She can turn any man's brain. She is a Circe, a Sybil, a Venus—no man with blood in his veins can resist her!"

"That is your opinion, eh?"

"I never saw such a creature before. And—and she has no conscience!"

The Count laughed. "Now, Slyme, I have some more work for you."

"To watch her!" he cried eagerly, rubbing his hands.

"No, not yet. That may be necessary some time, but not now. I have other work for you."

"Yes, my lord."

"To-morrow morning you will go to Surrey. I will give you all particulars about the trains and the stations presently. You will go to a place known as Wendover Park. Near one of the lodge gates of this house is a pretty cottage. It was occupied, and probably still is, by a man called Hugh Stanmore and his granddaughter. You must find out whether he is still there, and learn all you can about them. Report all to me. You understand?"

"Perfectly, your Highness," replied Polonius, whose terminology in relation to the Count was uncertain.

"You will report to me."

"Yes, certainly, my lord, everything."

"Very well, now go."

The night came on, and the room grew dark, but Count Romanoff did not switch on the light. He sat alone in the dark thinking, thinking.

"I have him now," he muttered presently. "Master, you shall have Richard Faversham's soul."

Chapter XXX
Voices in the Night

Dick Faversham was on his way to London. He was going there as the Member for Eastroyd, and he was somewhat excited. He was excited for several reasons. Naturally he was elated at being a Member of Parliament, and he looked forward with pleasant anticipation to his political life in the Metropolis, and to his experiences in the House of Commons. But that was not all. This was his first visit to London since he had experienced those strange happenings which we described some time ago. As the train rushed on through the night he became oblivious to the presence of his fellow-passengers in the recollection of the events which were a mystery to him then, even as they were a mystery now.

Especially did his mind revert to that wonderful experience in Staple Inn. He had heard a voice although he saw nothing, and that voice had meant a great deal to him. More than once he had wondered if he had done right in being silent about what had taken place afterwards. Ought he not to have gone to the police and told them what he had heard? But he had not been able to make up his mind to do this. Somehow everything had been associated with what had come to him in Staple Inn, and of that he could not speak. It would be sacrilege to do so. Besides, it might not have been necessary. From the fact that the traitors had left the house so suddenly, he concluded that the police were cognizant of their existence.

But his eyes had been opened. That was why, when Olga Petrovic visited him, he was unresponsive. And yet he was not sure.

Should he ever see this beautiful woman again, he wondered?

He was afraid of her even while he longed to see her. Even then he recalled the tones of her voice, and the look in her eyes as she had pleaded with him. He had felt himself yielding to her pleading, all the barriers of his being seemed to be breaking down before the power of her glorious womanhood.

Then there was the coming of Hugh Stanmore and his granddaughter. They were the last persons he had expected to see, and yet the sight of their names seemed to break the spell which Olga Petrovic had cast over him.

There seemed no reason why they should come, and their interview, considering the circumstances under which he had seen them last was of a very prosy nature. Hugh Stanmore had happened to meet with a man who was a Government official, and who had told him of one Richard Faversham who was one of a deputation to his department, and who had pleaded passionately for certain things which the working-classes desired. This led to his learning the name of his hotel, and to the visit which had followed.

Hugh Stanmore had scarcely referred to his life at Wendover, and seemed to be in ignorance of Tony Riggleton's whereabouts. Dick wondered at this after the interview, and reproached himself with not asking many questions. At the time, however, he seemed to be indifferent.

To Beatrice he spoke only a few words. She appeared to be shy and diffident. If the truth must be told, she seemed ill at ease, and not at all pleased that her grandfather had brought her there. She was far less a child than when he had seen her at Wendover, and he had reflected that she was neither so interesting nor so good-looking as she had been two or three years before. Still, he was glad to see her, and he remembered the pleasant smile she had given him when she had left the room. His conversation with Hugh Stanmore had been almost entirely about his life at Eastroyd, and the conditions which obtained there.

He realised, too, that a subtle change had come over his opinions on his return to Eastroyd. Not that he had less interest in the class whose cause he had espoused; but he knew that he had been led to take larger views.

That was why some discontent had been felt among his most ardent supporters. Even those who had worked hardest for him during the election felt it incumbent upon them to raise a note of warning as they accompanied him to the station that night.

"It's all very well, Dick, lad," said one advanced Socialist, "but we mun make a bold front. I don't hold with Bolshevism, or owt of that sort; but the Capitalist is the enemy of the working man, and we mun put those money-bags in their right place."

It was a cold, dark, wintry morning when he arrived in London. The station and the streets were almost empty, the vehicles were few, and he felt cold and lonely. He had made no arrangements for his stay in the Metropolis, but he felt sure that the manager of the hotel where he had previously made his home would find him temporary accommodation. As it was impossible to get a taxi, he left his luggage at the station, and determined to walk. He knew the way well, and as the distance was only about a mile, he started with comparative cheerfulness.

As I have said, the streets were well-nigh deserted, and not a single soul passed him as he made his way up Euston Road. Nevertheless he had the feeling that he was being followed. More than once he looked around, but could see no one. Several times, too, he felt sure he heard following footsteps, but when he stopped there was silence.

When he turned at St. Pancras Church he looked up and down the street, but nothing suspicious met his gaze. A milkman's cart, a drayman's waggon, and that was all. The street lamps threw a sickly light on the cold wet road, and the houses were dark. London looked asleep.

For some time after he had passed St. Pancras Church he heard nothing; but, as he neared Woburn Square, he again heard footsteps. It seemed to him, too, that he was surrounded by dark influences. Something sinister and evil seemed to be surrounding him. He was not afraid, and his nerves were steady, but his brain was filled with strange fancies.

Almost unconsciously his mind reverted to Count Romanoff. He had seen him only once since he had left Wendover Park, and the man was still an enigma to him. He had a thousand times reflected on the strange happening in the library there, but although he felt he had been saved from something terrible, he had not definitely associated the Count with anything supernatural. For Dick was not cast in a superstitious mould.

The footsteps drew nearer, and again he looked around. Was it a fact, or was it fancy that he saw a dark form which hurriedly passed from his sight?

He was aware a few seconds later that he was walking more rapidly, and that something like fear was in his heart.

"Listen."

He heard the word plainly, and stopped. All was silent here. He saw that he was in one of the several squares which exist in the neighbourhood, but he was not sure which. He did not think it was Woburn Square, but it might be Taviton Square. He was not intimately acquainted with that part of London.

"Yes, what is it? Who are you?"

He spoke aloud, spoke almost unconsciously, but there were no answering words. He was the only person there. He moved to a lamp and looked at his watch; he had a vague idea that he wanted to know the time. The watch pointed to half-past one. Evidently he had forgotten to wind it, for he knew his train was due to arrive something after three, and that it was late.

He was about to start again when he thought he heard the words:

"Go to Wendover."

But there was nothing distinct. No voice reached him, and no one was in sight. At that moment the wind wailed across the open space, and moaned as it passed through the leafless branches of the trees. The wind seemed to formulate the same words.

"Go to Wendover."

"Of course it's all fancy," he reflected. "I expect my nerves are playing me tricks. I never knew I had any nerves; but I've been through an exciting time. I've been making speeches, meeting committees, and replying to deputations for the last fortnight, and I expect I'm about done up. After all, fighting an election is no make-believe."

A shiver passed through him. To say the least of it, even although it might be pure fancy, there was something uncanny about it all, and he could not help reflecting on his past experience.

He did not move, but stood like one spellbound, listening to the wind as it soughed its way through the shrubs and trees which grew in the centre of the Square.

"Who are you?" he asked again. "What do you want?"

He was sure there was a voice this time. It rose above the wailing wind, but he could see no one.

"You are in danger—great danger!"

"What danger? Who are you?"

"'Watch and pray, that ye enter not into temptation.'"

He recognised the words. They were spoken by One Whose Name he always held in reverence, spoken to His disciples in a far back age, before the knowledge of science and critical investigation had emerged from its swaddling clothes. But they were spoken in a woman's voice, spoken in almost wailing accents.

His whole being was filled with a great awe. The voice, the words coming to him, at such a time and in such a way, filled him with a great wonder, solemnised him to the centre of his being.

"If it were not a woman's voice, I might think it was He Himself who spoke," he said in a hoarse whisper.

Then he thought of the footsteps, thought of the ominous, sinister influences which had surrounded him a few minutes before.

"Lord, Lord Jesus Christ, help me!"

He said the words involuntarily. They had passed his lips before he knew he had spoken.

Was there any answer to his prayer? He only knew that he did not feel any fear, that a great peace came into his heart. He felt as he had never felt before, that God was a great reality. Perhaps that was why he was no longer lonely. There in the heart of the greatest city of the world, there in the darkness of a winter night, he was filled with a kind of consciousness that God was, that God cared, that he was not an orphan for whom no one cared, but a child of the Universal Father.

He looked up and saw the clouds swept across the sky. Here and there was a break through which a star shone. Eyes of heaven, they seemed to him. Yes, the spirit world was very near to him. Perhaps, perhaps—who knew?—there were messengers of the Unseen all around him.

"Earth is crammed with heaven, And every common bush afire with God."

Where had he heard those words? Ah yes, was it not Elizabeth Barrett Browning who wrote them, wrote them while in Italy, where she sojourned with her husband, the greatest poet of his time?

Again he looked around him, but nothing could be seen by his natural eyes. The houses, the trees, the gardens all lay wrapped in the gloom of the cold and darkness of that wintry morning, there in the heart of London. All the same it seemed that something had been born within him, something which he could not define, and again he seemed to hear, as he had heard years before, the glorious words which turned to naught the ribald and trifling scepticism of men:

"The Eternal God is thy Refuge, and underneath are the Everlasting Arms."

The sublimity of the message appealed to him. Surely no greater words were ever spoken. They peopled the dark wintry heavens with angels, they made everything possible.

"Lord, tell me what to do."

The prayer came naturally to his lips. It seemed to him that there was nothing else for him to say. But there were no answering words. All was silent, save for the soughing of the wind across the square. And yet I am wrong. He did hear words; they might be born of his own consciousness, and have no objective reality whatever, but again the wind seemed to speak to him.

"Go to Wendover."

Why should he go to Wendover? He had no right to be there, and from the rumours that he had heard, Tony Riggleton had turned the old house into a scene of drunken and sensual orgies. But in answer to his question the wailing wind seemed to reiterate, as if in a kind of dreary monotony, the same words, "Go to Wendover, go to Wendover."

Then suddenly everything became mundane.

"Good-night, or good morning rather."

It was a policeman who spoke, and who looked rather suspiciously at the lonely looking young man.

"Good morning," replied Dick; "it's not long to daylight is it?"

"Another hour or two yet. Lost your way?"

"I've come from King's Cross. I travelled by the midnight train, and there were no conveyances to be got."

"Ah, petrol's a bit scarce yet; but I hear we shall have more soon. Anywhere you want to get?"

"Yes, I'm going to Jones' Hotel."

"That's close to the British Museum; and only a few minutes away. I suppose your room's booked all right. The hotels are very crowded in London just now."

"That'll be all right. Good morning, and thank you!"

"That's all right, sir. Go to the end of the square, turn to the right, then take the second street to the left and you are there."

A few minutes later Dick was at the hotel. The night porter knew him well, and showed him into the smoke-room, where there was a good fire, and comfortable arm-chairs.

"You'll be all right here till breakfast, sir, won't you? After that you can see the manager."

Five minutes later Dick was asleep.

A few hours later he met some of his political confrères, two of whom begged him to lodge with them.

It was not much of a place they assured him, but the best their money would run to. "Four hundred a year's very little in London, and that you'll find out before long," one of them assured him.

"Every penny has to be looked after, and by living two or three together we can do things cheaper."

After seeing their lodgings, however, Dick determined to look around for himself. He did not relish the idea of sharing apartments with others. He wanted privacy, and he felt, although, like himself, these men were "Labour Members," that he had little in common with them.

"I thought of trying to get a small, cheap flat," he said.

"Not to be thought of with our pay," was the laughing response. "Of course you being a bachelor may have saved up a bit, or it may be that you think you'll be able to make a few pounds by journalism."

"Some do it, don't they?" he asked.

"They all want to do it, that's why there's so little chance. But I hear you are a bit of a swell, been to a public school and all that kind of thing, so you may have friends at court. Done anything that way?"

Dick shook his head. "Never," he replied; "but no one knows what he can do till he tries."

After considerable difficulty Dick happened upon a service flat which, although it cost more than he had calculated upon, was so convenient, and appealed to him so strongly, that he took it there and then.

Indeed he felt a pleasant sense of proprietorship, as he sat alone in his new home that night. The room was very small, but it was cosy. A cheerful fire burnt in the grate, and the reading-lamp threw a grateful light upon the paper he held in his hand.

"I must get a writing-desk and some book-cases, and I shall be as right as rain," he reflected. "This is princely as a sitting-room, and although the bedroom is only a box, it's quite big enough for me."

He closed his eyes with lazy contentment, and then began to dream of his future. Yes, ambition was still strong within him, and the longing to make a material, yes, an international, reputation was never so insistent as now. He wondered if he could do it, wondered whether being a Labour Member would ever lead to anything.

"A voting machine at four hundred a year."

He started up as though something had strung him. He remembered who had said those words to him, remembered how they had wounded him at the time they were spoken. Was that all he was after his hopes and dreams? He had been a big man at Eastroyd. People had stopped in the streets to point him out; but in London he was nobody.

"A voting machine at four hundred a year!"

The Everlasting Arms

Yes, but he would be more. He had proved that he had brains, and that he could appeal to the multitude. He had his feet on the ladder now, and — —

His mind suddenly switched off. He was no longer in his newly acquired flat, he was walking from King's Cross to Jones' Hotel, he was passing through a lonely square.

"Go to Wendover."

How the words haunted him. Every time the wind blew he had heard them, and — —

He started to his feet. "Well, why not? I have nothing to do to-morrow, and I can get there in a couple of hours."

The next morning he eagerly made his way to Victoria Station.

Chapter XXXI
Dick hears Strange News

"Good mornin', sir."

The porter touched his cap and looked at Dick curiously.

"Good morning, Wheelright. You are here still?"

"Yes, sir. They took the other chap, and left no one in his place, so to speak. So me and the stationmaster have had to do everything. I was sort of superannuated, so to speak, when you was 'ere, so I had to take on my old job when Ritter went. However, I'd 'ear that he'll soon be back."

"Yes, the boys are coming home now."

"And a good job, too. Not but what me and the stationmaster have carried on, so to speak, and I'm as good a man as ever I was."

Dick remembered old Wheelright well. He did odd jobs at the station during his short stay at Wendover Park, and was known among the people in the neighbourhood as "Old So-to-speak." He was also noted as an inveterate gossip.

"Comin' down to live 'ere again, so to speak?" he queried, looking at Dick curiously.

"No," replied Dick. "Just paying a short visit. I shall be returning by the 4.20 at the latest."

Wheelright shuffled on at Dick's side. He was much tempted to ask him further questions, but seemed afraid.

"You don't know where—where Squire Riggleton is, I suppose, sir?"

"Why do you ask that?"

"I was wondering, that's all. There's been a good deal of talk about him, so to speak. Some say he was took for the army just the same as if he hadn't sixpence. I have heard he was took prisoner by the Germans, too. But some people *will* talk. Have you heard 'bout his being killed, sir?"

"No, I never heard that."

"Ah." He looked at Dick questioningly, and then ventured further. "He didn't do hisself much credit as a squire," he added.

"Indeed."

"No, there was nice carryings on, so I've heard. But then some people will talk. However, there's no doubt that Mrs. Lawson, who had her two daughters as servants there in your day, took them both away. It was no place for respectable Christians to live, she said."

Dick made no reply. He had just come by train, and was the only passenger who alighted. Old Wheelright immediately recognised him. He did not feel altogether at ease in listening to him while he discussed his cousin, but was so interested that he let him go on talking. The truth was that Dick did not know why he was there, except that he had obeyed the command he had heard when walking from King's Cross. As he stood there that day he was not sure whether he had heard a voice or whether it was only an impression. But the words haunted him, and he felt he could do no other than obey. Now he was here, however, he did not know where to go, or what to do. He felt sensitive about going to the house which he had thought was his, and asking for admission. The action would call up too many painful memories. And yet he did not like going back without once again seeing the home that had meant so much to him.

"You know that people have talked a lot about *you*, sir?"

"I dare say."

"And everybody was sorry when you left. It was all so funny. Young Riggleton he came to the Hare and Hounds, and told the landlord all about it."

"Indeed."

"Yes. I did hear that the London lawyers called him over the coals for talking so much, so to speak. But some people will talk. However, as I'd say, 'twasn't the lawyer's business. If Riggleton liked to talk, that's his business. Still I s'pose he had a drop of drink in him, or p'r'aps he mightn't a' done it. He told the landlord that he'd offered you a good job if you'd stay, but as the landlord said, 'How could you expect a gentleman like Mr. Faversham to stay as a servant where he'd been master?' I suppose he did make the offer, sir?"

"Is the same housekeeper at Wendover?" asked Dick, not noticing Wheelright's questions.

"Oh yes, bless you, sir, yes. I've been told she gave notice to leave like the other servants; but Riggleton went away instead. He said he couldn't stand living in a cemetery. That's what he called Wendover, sir. He came back a few times, but only for a day or two. From what I hear he hasn't showed his face there for years. All the same, it's kept in good repair. I suppose the London lawyer do see to that."

The old man went on retailing the gossip of the neighbourhood, but beyond what I have recorded he said little that interested Dick. After all, why should he care about stories concerning Anthony Riggleton, or pay attention to the scandalous tales which had been afloat? He had no doubt but that Mr. Bidlake would have given him all information about his cousin, if he had called and asked him; but he had not gone.

He made his way along the country lanes, scarcely seeing a single soul. He was angry with himself for coming, and yet he knew that he had not been able to help himself. He was there because he had been drawn there by an irresistible impulse, or because he was under the power of something, or someone whom he dared not disobey.

The day was dark and cloudy, and the air was dank and cold. The trees were leafless, not a flower appeared, and the whole countryside, which had once appeared to him so glorious, now seemed grim and depressing.

"Of course, I'm a fool," he muttered savagely, but still he trudged along until he came to the lodge gates. How proud he had been when he had first seen them! How his heart had thrilled at the thought that all he saw was his own, his very own! But now he had no right there. He might have been the veriest stranger.

He had carefully avoided the entrance near which old Hugh Stanmore lived. He did not want the old man to know of his visit.

He was altogether unnoticed by the people who lived in the lodge, and a few seconds later was hurrying up the drive. Yes, in spite of the winter, in spite of the leafless trees, the place was very beautiful. The noble avenue under which he was walking was very imposing, the rhododendron, and a dozen other kinds of shrubs relieved the wintry aspect. Besides, the woods were so restful, the fine park lands were the finest he had ever seen.

And he had thought they were all his. He for a short time had been master of everything!

Suddenly the house burst on his view, and with a cry, almost like a cry of pain, he stood still, and looked long and yearningly. No wonder he had loved it. It was all a country home should be.

And it might have been his! If he had obeyed Romanoff; but no; even then he felt thankful that he had not yielded to the man who tempted him.

For a moment he thought of turning back. It would be too painful to go and ask for permission to go in. But he did not turn back. As if urged on by some unseen power he made his way towards the entrance.

He had an eerie feeling in his heart as he approached the steps. He called to mind his first visit there, when he had asked the lawyer if he saw anything. For a moment he fancied he saw the outline of a shadowy form as he saw it then. But there was nothing. The grey stone walls, half hidden by ivy, stood before him as they stood then, but that wondrous face, with pitiful pleading eyes, was not to be seen.

He felt half disappointed at this. He could understand nothing, but he had a feeling that it was the form of someone who loved him, someone sent to protect him.

At first he had fought the idea. He had told himself that he was too matter-of-fact, that he had too much common sense to think of an optical illusion as something supernatural; but as event after event took place he could not help being possessed by the thought that he was under the guardianship of something, someone who watched over him, helped him. He never spoke about it to anyone; it was too sacred for discussion.

But there was nothing. He heard no voice, saw no form, and a feeling like disappointment crept into his heart. Dick Faversham was not a morbid fellow, and he had a feeling of dislike for anything like occultism. As for spiritualism, in the ordinary sense of the word, it made no appeal to him. But this was different. Somehow he had a kind of consciousness that the spirit world was all around him, and that the Almighty Beneficence used the inhabitants of that spirit world to help His children.

No, there was nothing. His visit had been purposeless and vain, and he would find his way back to the station. Then suddenly the door opened, and the old housekeeper appeared.

"It is, it *is* Mr. Faversham!"

But he did not speak. A weight seemed on his lips.

"Come in, sir, come in."

Before he realised what had taken place he stood in the entrance hall, and the door closed behind him.

"Are you come for good?"

The housekeeper's voice was tremulous with excitement, and her eyes were eagerly fastened on his face.

Dick shook his head. "No, I'm only here for a few minutes."

"But he's dead."

"Who's dead?"

"That man. The man Riggleton. Haven't you heard about it?"

"No, I've not heard."

"But there were rumours, and I thought you'd come to tell me they were true. Oh, I am sorry, so sorry. I should love to have you here as master again. It was such a joy to serve you. And that man, he nearly drove me mad. He brought bad people here. He filled the house with a lot of low men and women. And there were such goings on. I stood it as long as I could, and then I told him I must leave the house at once. So did several of the servants. He begged me to stop, he offered to double my wages, but I told him I must go, that I was a respectable woman, and had served only gentry who knew how to behave themselves. Then he said he would leave himself, and he persuaded me to stay on. Didn't you hear, sir?"

"No, I did not hear. I went away to the North of England."

"Oh, there were such stories. I suppose he threw away a fortune in London."

"Is he there now?" asked Dick.

"I don't know. I asked Mr. Bidlake, but he would tell me nothing. The last I heard was that he was forced into the army, and was killed."

"How long was that ago?"

"Several months now."

"And you've heard nothing since?"

"No, sir; nothing."

"Well, I will go now."

"But you'll stay for lunch? I'm not stinted in any way, and Mr. Bidlake sends me a liberal allowance for the expenses of the house. I can easily manage lunch, sir, and it would be such a joy to me."

"You are very kind, and I appreciate it very much; but I really couldn't—after what took place. I'll go to the Hare and Hounds and have some bread and cheese."

"Couldn't you, sir? I'm so sorry, and it's a long way to Lord Huntingford's."

"Yes, of course, that's out of the question."

"But you must have lunch somewhere, and you couldn't go to the Hare and Hounds."

"Oh yes, I could. I dare say Blacketter would give me some bread and cheese. That will be all I shall need."

The housekeeper began to rub her eyes. "It's just awful," she sobbed. "To think that you who were master here, and whom we all liked so much, should have to go to a place like that. But I know. Mr. Stanmore is at home; he'll be glad to welcome you there."

"Mr. Stanmore is at home, is he?"

"Yes, sir. He called here yesterday, and Miss Beatrice is at home too. They were both here. Mr. Stanmore brought Sir George Weston over to see the house."

"Sir George Weston?" and Dick felt a strange sinking at his heart as he heard the words. "I don't seem to remember the name."

"He's from the west, sir, from Devonshire, I think. It has been said that he came to see Miss Beatrice," and the housekeeper smiled significantly.

"You mean——"

"I don't know anything, sir; it may be only servants' gossip. He's said to be a very rich man, and has been serving in Egypt. Some say that he came to discuss something about Egypt with Mr. Stanmore; but it was noticed that he was very attentive to Miss Beatrice."

"He's been staying at the cottage, then?"

"For nearly a week, sir."

"Is he there now?"

"I don't know, sir. All I know is that he was here with them yesterday. Mr. Stanmore brought a letter from Mr. Bidlake authorising me to show them over the house."

"Is Sir George a young man? You said he was in the army, didn't you?" Dick could not understand why his heart was so heavy.

"About thirty, I should think, sir. Yes, I believe he had a high command in our Egyptian army. He's a great scholar too, and Mr. Stanmore said that this house was the finest specimen of an Elizabethan house that he knew of. A very pleasant gentleman too. It's not my business, but he'd be a good match for Miss Beatrice, wouldn't he? Of course Mr. Stanmore belongs to a very good family, but I suppose he's very poor, and Miss Beatrice has hardly a chance of meeting anyone. You remember her, sir, don't you? She was little more than a child when you were here, but she's a very beautiful young lady now."

The housekeeper was fairly launched now, and was prepared to discuss the Stanmores at length, but Dick hurried away. He would have loved to have gone over the house, but he dared not; besides, in a way he could not understand, he longed to get into the open air, longed to be alone.

"I hope, oh, I do hope that something'll happen," said the housekeeper as he left the house; but what she did not tell him.

A little later Dick found himself on the drive leading to Hugh Stanmore's cottage. He had not intended to take this road, but when he realised that he was in it, he did not turn back. Rather he hurried on with almost feverish footsteps.

Sir George Weston had been spending a week at the cottage, had he? Why? Was it because he was an Egyptologist, and interested in Hugh Stanmore's previous researches, or was he there because of Beatrice, as the servants' gossip said? It was nothing to him, but he had an overwhelming desire to know. Was Beatrice Stanmore a beautiful girl? She had not appealed to him in this light when her grandfather brought her to see him months before; but girls often blossomed into beauty suddenly. Still, wasn't it strange that Weston should stay at the cottage a week?

Of course he would not call. He was simply taking the longer road to the station. Yes, he could plainly see the house through the trees, and——

"Is that Mr. Faversham? Well, this is a surprise; but I *am* glad to see you."

It was old Hugh Stanmore who spoke, while Dick in a strangely nervous way took the proffered hand.

"Come to look at your old house, eh? I see you've come from that direction."

"Yes, I have been—talking with my old housekeeper," he stammered.

"And you've never been here before since—you left?"

Dick shook his head.

"Well, well, life's a strange business, isn't it? But come in, my dear fellow. You're just in time for lunch."

Dick began to make excuses, but the other refused to listen, and they entered the cottage together.

"I'm afraid I couldn't presume upon your kindness so far."

"Kindness! Nonsense. Of course you must. Besides, I see that you are a Member of Parliament, and a Labour Member too. I must talk with you about it. Lunch will be on the table in five minutes."

"You are sure I shouldn't be bothering you?" He had an overwhelming desire to stay.

"Bother! What bother can there be? I'm only too delighted to see you. Come in."

They entered the cottage together.

"Oh, by the way," went on Hugh Stanmore, as they entered a cosy sitting-room, "let me introduce you to Sir George Weston."

A strikingly handsome man of about thirty rose from an arm-chair and held out his hand. He was in mufti; but it was impossible to mistake him for anything but a soldier. Head erect, shoulders squared, and a military bearing proclaimed him to be what he was.

"Glad to see you, Mr. Faversham," said Sir George heartily "I suppose you've come down to see— —" He stopped abruptly. He felt he had made a *faux pas*.

"It's all right," said Dick with a laugh. He felt perfectly at ease now. "Yes, I came to see the old place which years ago I thought was mine. You've heard all about it, I've no doubt?"

"Jolly hard luck," sympathised Sir George. "But anyhow you— —"

"Ah, here's Beatrice," broke in Hugh Stanmore. "Beatrice, my dear, here's an old friend dropped in to lunch with us. You remember Mr. Faversham, don't you?"

The eyes of the two met, and then as their hands met Dick's friendly feeling towards Sir George Weston left him. He could not tell why.

Chapter XXXII
Beatrice Confesses

Dick Faversham saw at a glance that Beatrice Stanmore had ceased being a child. She was barely twenty. She was girlish in appearance, and her grandfather seemed to still regard her as a child. But her childhood had gone, and her womanhood had come. Rather tall, and with a lissom form, she had all a girl's movements, all a girl's sweetness, but the flash of her eyes, the compression of her lips, the tones of her voice, all told that she had left her childhood behind. But the first blush of her womanhood still remained. She retained her child's naturalness and winsomeness, even while she looked at the world through the eyes of a woman.

Dick was struck by her beauty too. When years before she had rushed into the library at Wendover, almost breathless in her excitement, she had something of the angularity, almost awkwardness, of half-development. That had all gone. Every movement was graceful, natural. Perfect health, health of body, health of mind had stamped itself upon her. She had no suggestion of the cigarette-smoking, slang-talking miss who boasts of her freedom from old-time conventions. You could not think of Beatrice Stanmore sitting with men, smoking, sipping liqueurs, and laughing at their jokes. She retained the virginal simplicity of childlikeness. All the same she was a woman. But not a woman old beyond her years. Not a woman who makes men give up their thoughts of the sacredness of womanhood.

No one could any more think of Beatrice Stanmore being advanced, or "fast," than one could think of a rosebud just opening its petals to the sun being "fast."

She had none of the ripe beauty of Lady Blanche Huntingford, much less the bold splendour of Olga Petrovic. She was too much the child of nature for that. She was too sensitive, too maidenly in her thoughts and actions. And yet she was a woman, with all a woman's charm.

Here lay her power. She was neither insipid nor a prude. She dared to think for herself, she loved beautiful dresses, she enjoyed pleasure and gaiety; but all without losing the essential quality of womanhood—purity and modesty. She reminded one of Russell Lowell's lines:

"A dog rose blushing to a brook
Ain't modester, nor sweeter."

That was why no man, however blasé, however cynical about women, could ever associate her with anything loud or vulgar. She was not neurotic; her healthy mind revolted against prurient suggestion either in conversation or in novels. She was not the kind of girl who ogled men, or practised unwomanly arts to attract their attention. No man, however bold, would dream of taking liberties with her. But she was as gay as a lark, her laughter was infectious, the flash of her eyes suggested all kinds of innocent mischief and fun. She could hold her own at golf, was one of the best tennis players in the district, and could ride with gracefulness and fearlessness.

Does someone say I am describing an impossible prodigy? No, I am trying to describe a sweet, healthy, natural girl. I am trying to tell of her as she appeared to me when I saw her first, a woman such as I believe God intended all women to be, womanly, pure, modest.

She was fair to look on too; fair with health and youth and purity. A girl with laughing eyes, light brown hair, inclined to curl. A sweet face she had, a face which glowed with health, and was unspoilt by cosmetics. A tender, sensitive mouth, but which told of character, of resolution and daring. A chin firm and determined, and yet delicate in outline. This was Beatrice Stanmore, who, reared among the sweet Surrey hills and valleys, was unsmirched by the world's traffic, and who recoiled from the pollution of life which she knew existed. A girl modern in many respects, but not too modern to love old-fashioned courtesies, not too modern to keep holy the Sabbath Day, and love God with simple faith. A religious girl, who never paraded religion, and whose religion never made her monkish and unlovely, but was the joy and inspiration of her life.

"I'm so glad to see you, Mr. Faversham," she said. "I've often wondered why you never came to Wendover."

"In a way it was very hard to keep away," was Dick's reply. "On the other hand, I had a kind of dread of seeing it again. You see, I had learnt to love it."

"I don't wonder. It's the dearest old house in the world. I should have gone mad, I think, if I'd been in your place. It was just splendid of you to take your reverse so bravely."

"I had only one course before me, hadn't I?"

"Hadn't you? I've often wondered." She gave him a quick, searching glance as she spoke. "Are you staying here long?"

"No, only a few hours. I return to London this afternoon. I came down to-day just on impulse. I had no reason for coming."

"Hadn't you? I'm glad you came."

"So am I."

There was a strange intensity in his tones, but he did not know why he spoke with so much feeling.

"Of course Granddad and I have often talked of you," she went on. "Do you know when we called on you that day in London, I was disappointed in you. I don't know why. You had altered so much. You did not seem at all like you were when we saw you down here. I told Granddad so. But I'm so glad you are Member of Parliament for Eastroyd, and so glad you've called. There, the lunch is ready. Please remember, Mr. Faversham, that I'm housekeeper, and am responsible for lunch. If you don't like it, I shall be offended."

She spoke with all the freedom and frankness of a child, but Dick was not slow to recognise the fact that the child who had come to Wendover when Romanoff was weaving a web of temptation around him, had become a woman who could no longer be treated as a child.

"Are you hungry, Sir George?" she went on, turning to her other visitor. "Do you know, Mr. Faversham, that these two men have neglected me shamefully? They have been so interested in rubbings of ancient inscriptions, and writings on the tombs of Egyptian kings, that they've forgotten that I've had to cudgel my poor little brains about what they should eat. Housekeeping's no easy matter in these days."

"That's not fair," replied Sir George. "It was Mr. Stanmore here, who was so interested that he forgot all about meal-times."

The soldier was so earnest that he angered Dick. "Why couldn't the fool take what she said in the spirit of raillery?" he asked himself.

"Adam over again," laughed Beatrice. "'The woman tempted me and I did eat.' It's always somebody else's fault. Now then, Granddad, serve the fish."

It was a merry little party that sat down to lunch, even although Dick did not seem inclined for much talk. Old Hugh Stanmore was in great good-humour, while Beatrice had all the high spirits of a happy, healthy girl.

"You must stay a few hours now you are here, Mr. Faversham," urged the old man presently. "There's not the slightest reason why you should go back to town by that four something train. It's true, Sir George and I are going over to Pitlock Rectory for a couple of hours, but we shall be back for tea, and you and Beatrice can get on all right while we are away."

Sir George did not look at all delighted at the suggestion, but Beatrice was warm in her support of it.

"You really must, Mr. Faversham," she said. "I shall be alone all the afternoon otherwise, for really I can't bear the idea of listening to Mr. Stanhope, the Rector of Pitlock, prose about mummies and fossils and inscriptions."

"You know I offered to stay here," pleaded Sir George.

"As though I would have kept you and Granddad away from your fossils," she laughed. "Mr. Stanhope is a great scholar, a great Egyptologist, and a great antiquary, and you said it would be your only chance of seeing him, as you had to go to the War Office to-morrow. So you see, Mr. Faversham, that you'll be doing a real act of charity by staying with me. Besides, there's something I want to talk with you about. There is really."

Sir George did not look at all happy as, after coffee, he took his seat beside old Hugh Stanmore, in the little motor-car, but Dick Faversham's every nerve tingled with pleasure at the thought of spending two or three hours alone with Beatrice. Her transparent frankness and naturalness charmed him, the whole atmosphere of the cottage was so different from that to which for years he had been accustomed.

"Mr. Faversham," she said, when they had gone, "I want you to walk with me to the great house, will you?"

"Certainly," he said, wondering all the time why she wanted to go there.

"You don't mind, do you? I know it must be painful to you, but—but I want you to."

"Of course I will. It's no longer mine—it never was mine, but it attracts me like a magnet."

Five minutes later they were walking up the drive together. Dick was supremely happy, yet not knowing why he was happy. Everything he saw was laden with poignant memories, while the thought of returning to the house cut him like a knife. Yet he longed to go. For some little distance they walked in silence, then she burst out suddenly.

"Mr. Faversham, do you believe in premonitions?"

"Yes."

"So do I. It is that I wanted to talk with you about."

He did not reply, but his mind flashed back to the night when he had sat alone with Count Romanoff, and Beatrice Stanmore had suddenly and without warning rushed into the room.

"Do you believe in angels?" she went on.

"I—I think so."

"I do. Granddad is not sure about it. That is, he isn't sure that they appear. Sir George is altogether sceptical. He pooh-poohs the whole idea. He says there was a mistake about the Angels at Mons. He says it was imagination, and all that sort of thing; but he isn't a bit convincing. But I believe."

"Yes." He spoke almost unconsciously. He had never uttered a word about his own experiences to anyone, and he wondered if he should tell her what he had seen and heard.

"It was a kind of premonition which made me go to see you years ago," she said quietly. "Do you remember?"

"I shall never forget, and I'm very glad."

"Why are you very glad?"

"Because—because I'm sure your coming helped me!"

"How did it help you?"

"It helped me to see, to feel; I—I can't quite explain."

"That man—Count Romanoff—is evil," and she shuddered as she spoke.

"Why do you say so?"

"I felt it. I feel it now. He was your enemy. Have you seen him since?"

"Only once. I was walking through Oxford Circus. I only spoke a few words to him; I have not seen him since."

"Mr. Faversham, did anything important happen that night?"

"Yes, that night—and the next."

"Did that man, Count Romanoff, want you to do something which—which was wrong? Forgive me for asking, won't you? But I have felt ever since that it was so."

"Yes." He said the word slowly, doubtfully. At that moment the old house burst upon his view, and he longed with a great longing to possess it. He felt hard and bitter that a man like Tony Riggleton should first have made it a scene of obscene debauchery and then have left it. It seemed like sacrilege that such a man should be associated with it. At that moment, too, it seemed such a little thing that Romanoff had asked him to do.

"If I had done what he asked me, I might have been the owner of Wendover Park now," he added.

"But how could that be, if that man Riggleton was the true heir?" she asked.

"At that time there seemed—doubt. He made me feel that Riggleton had no right to be there, and if I had promised the Count something, I might have kept it."

"And that something was wrong?"

"Yes, it was wrong. Of course I am speaking to you in absolute confidence," he added. "When you came you made me see things as they really were."

"I was sent," she said simply.

"By whom?"

"I don't know. And do you remember when I came the second time?"

"Yes, I remember. I shall never forget."

"I never felt like it before or since. Something seemed to compel me to hasten to you. I got out the car in a few seconds, and I simply flew to you. I have thought since that you must have been angry, that you must have looked upon me as a mad girl to rush in on you the way I did. But I could not help myself. That evil man, Romanoff, was angry with me too; he would have killed me if he had dared. Do you remember that we talked about angels afterwards?"

"I remember."

"They were all around us. I felt sure of it. I seemed to see them. Afterwards, while I was sorry for you, I felt glad you had left Wendover, glad that you were no longer its owner. I had a kind of impression that while you were losing the world, you were saving your soul."

She spoke with all a child's simplicity, yet with a woman's earnestness. She asked no questions as to what Romanoff had asked him to do in order to keep his wealth; that did not seem to come within her scope of things. Her thought was that Romanoff was evil, and she felt glad that Dick had resisted the evil.

"Do you believe in angels?" she asked again.

"Sometimes," replied Dick. "Do you?"

"I have no doubt about them. I know my mother often came to me."

"How? I don't quite understand. You never saw her—in this world I mean—did you?"

"No. But she has come to me. For years I saw her in dreams. More than once, years ago, when I woke up in the night, I saw her hovering over me."

"That must have been fancy."

"No, it was not." She spoke with calm assurance, and with no suggestion of morbidness or fear. "Why should I not see her?" she went on. "I am her child, and if she had lived she would have cared for me, fended for me, because she loved me. Why should what we call death keep her from doing that still, only in a different way?"

Dick was silent a few seconds. It did not seem at all strange.

"No; there seems no real reason why, always assuming that there are angels, and that they have the power to speak to us. But there is something I would like to ask you. You said just now, 'I know that my mother often came to me.' Has she ceased coming?"

Beatrice Stanmore's eyes seemed filled with a great wonder, but she still spoke in the same calm assured tones.

"I have not seen her for three years," she said; "not since the day after you left Wendover. She told me then that she was going farther away for a time, and would not be able to speak to me, although she would allow no harm to happen to me. Since that time I have never seen her. But I know she loves me still. It may be that I shall not see her again in this life, but sometime, in God's own good time, we shall meet."

"Are you a Spiritualist?" asked Dick, and even as he spoke he felt that he had struck a false note.

She shook her head decidedly. "No, I should hate the thought of using mediums and that sort of thing to talk to my mother. There may be truth in it, or there may not; but to me it seems tawdry, sordid. But I've no doubt about the angels. I think there are angels watching over you. It's a beautiful thought, isn't it?"

"Isn't it rather morbid?" asked Dick.

"Why should it be morbid? Is the thought that God is all around us morbid? Why then should it be morbid to think of the spirits of those He has called home being near to help us, to watch over us?"

"No," replied Dick; "but if there are good angels why may there not be evil ones?"

"I believe there are," replied the girl. "I am very ignorant and simple, but I believe there are. Did not Satan tempt our Lord in the wilderness? And after the temptation was over, did not angels minister to Him?"

"So the New Testament says."

"Do you not believe it to be true?"

Chapter XXXIII
Sir George's Love Affair

The great house stood out boldly against the wintry sky, and Dick Faversham could plainly see the window of the room where, years before, he had taken the pen to sign the paper which would have placed him in Count Romanoff's power. Like lightning his mind flashed back to the fateful hour. He saw himself holding the pen, saw the words which Romanoff had written standing clearly out on the white surface, saw himself trying to trace the letters of his name, and then he felt the hand on his wrist. It was only a light touch, but he no longer had the power to write.

Was it a moral impulse which had come to him, or was it some force which paralysed his senses, and made him incapable of holding the pen? It seemed to be both. He remembered having a loathing for the thing Romanoff wanted him to do. Even then he felt like shuddering at the dark influences which sapped his will-power, and made wrong seem like right. But there was more than that. Some force *outside* himself kept him from writing.

And he was glad. True, he was a poor man, and instead of owning the stately mansion before him, he would presently return to his tiny flat, where he would have to calculate about every sixpence he spent. But he was free; he was master of his soul. He was a man of some importance too. He was the Labour Member for Eastroyd; he had secured the confidence of many thousands of working people, and his voice was listened to with much respect by Labour leaders, and in Labour conferences.

But he was not quite satisfied. He did not want to be the representative of one class only, but of all classes. He remembered that he had been lately spoken of as being "too mealy-mouthed," and as "having too much sympathy with the employers."

"A voting machine at four hundred a year!"

Romanoff's words still stung him, wounded him. He longed for a larger life, longed to speak for all classes, longed to mingle with those of his own upbringing and education.

"What are you thinking of?"

For the moment he had forgotten the girl at his side, almost forgotten the subject they had been discussing.

"Of many things," he replied.

"You were thinking of that man, Count Romanoff."

"Was I? Yes, I suppose I was. How did you know?"

"Telepathy," she replied. "Shall we go back?"

"If you will. Did you not say you wanted to go to the house?"

"I don't think I do now. I'm afraid it would be painful to you. But, Mr. Faversham, I'm glad I helped you; glad you do not own Wendover Park."

"So am I," he replied; "the price would have been too terrible."

She looked at him questioningly. She did not quite understand his words.

"I wonder if you would think it an impertinence if I asked you to promise me something," she said.

"Nothing you could ask would be an impertinence," he responded eagerly; "nothing."

"That Count Romanoff is evil," she said, "evil; I am sure he is. I know nothing about him, but I am sure of what I say. Will you promise to have nothing to do with him? I think you will meet him again. I don't know why, but I have a feeling that you will. That is why I wanted to say this, and I wanted to say it in sight of the house which you love."

"I promise," replied Dick. "It is very good of you to have so much interest in me."

"In a way, I don't know that I have very much interest," she said simply; "and I'm afraid I'm acting on impulse. Granddad says that that is my weakness."

"I don't think it is a weakness. I'm not likely to see Count Romanoff again; but I promise, gladly promise, that if I do I'll yield to him in nothing. Is that what you mean?"

"Yes, that's what I mean."

Her humour suddenly changed. She seemed to have no further interest in Wendover Park, or its possessor, whoever it might be, and their conversation became of the most commonplace nature. They chatted about the possibilities of peace, the future of Germany, and the tremendous problems Britain would have to face, but all interest in the question which had engrossed her mind seemed to have left her. Dick was to her only an ordinary acquaintance who had casually crossed the pathway of her life, and who might never do so again. Indeed, as presently they reached the highroad, he thought she became cold and reserved, it might seem, too, that he somewhat bored her.

Presently they heard the sound of horses' hoofs coming toward them, and they saw a lady on horseback.

"That's Lady Blanche Huntingford," she said; "do you know her?"

"I did know her slightly," replied Dick, who felt no excitement whatever on seeing her.

"Oh yes, of course you did. She's a great beauty, isn't she?"

"I suppose so." Dick remembered how, in London months before, she had refused to recognise him.

For a moment Lady Blanche seemed surprised at seeing Dick. She scrutinised him closely, as if she was not quite sure it was he. Then her colour heightened somewhat, and with a nod which might have embraced them both, she passed on.

"We must get back to the house," Beatrice said; "Granddad and Sir George will have returned by this time, and they will want their tea."

"Sir George is leaving you to-morrow, isn't he?" asked Dick.

"Yes," she replied, and Dick's heart grew heavy as he saw the look in her eyes. He did not know why.

"He's a great soldier, I suppose? I think I've been told so."

"The greatest and bravest man in the army," she replied eagerly. "He's simply splendid. It's not often that a soldier is a scholar, but Granddad says there are few men alive who are greater authorities on Egyptian questions."

A feeling of antagonism rose in Dick's heart against Sir George Weston, he felt angry that Beatrice should think so highly of him.

"He's a Devonshire man, isn't he?" he asked.

"Yes; he has a lovely old place down there. The house is built of grey granite. It is very, very old, and it looks as though it would last for hundreds and hundreds of years. It is situated on a wooded hillside, and at the back, above the woods, is a vast stretch of moorland. In front is a lovely park studded with old oaks."

"You describe the place with great enthusiasm." There was envy in his tones, and something more than envy.

"Do I? I love Devonshire. Love its granite tors, its glorious hills and valleys. No wonder it is called 'Glorious Devon.'"

By the time they reached the cottage Sir George Weston and Hugh Stanmore had returned, and tea was on the table. Sir George seemed somewhat excited, while old Hugh Stanmore was anything but talkative. It might seem as though, during the afternoon, the two had talked on matters of greater interest than the tombs of Egyptian kings.

When the time came for Dick to depart, Hugh Stanmore said he would walk a little way with him. For a happy, and singularly contented man, he appeared much disturbed.

"I am so glad you came, Mr. Faversham," said Beatrice as she bade him good-bye. "We had a lovely walk, hadn't we?"

"Wonderful," replied Dick. "I shall never forget it."

"And you'll not forget your promise, will you?"

"No, I shall not forget it."

"You will let us know, won't you, when you are going to speak in the House of Commons? I shall insist on Granddad taking me to hear you."

Sir George Weston looked from one to the other suspiciously. He could not understand her interest in him.

"What do you think of Weston?" asked Hugh Stanmore, when they had walked some distance together.

"I suppose he's a very fine soldier," evaded Dick.

"Oh yes, there's no doubt about that. But how did he strike you—personally?"

"I'm afraid I didn't pay much attention to him. He seemed a pleasant kind of man." Dick felt very non-committal. "Do you know him well?"

"Yes; fairly well. I met him before the war. He and I were interested in the same subjects. He has travelled a great deal in the East. Of course I've known of his family all my life. A very old family which has lived in the same house for generations. I think he is the eighth baronet. But I was not thinking of that. I was thinking of him as a man. You'll forgive my asking you, won't you, but do you think he could make my little girl happy?"

Dick felt a strange weight on his heart. He felt bitter too.

"I am afraid my opinion would be of little value," he replied. "You see I know nothing of him, neither for that matter am I well acquainted with Miss Stanmore."

"No, I suppose that's true, and perhaps I ought not to have asked you. I often scold Beatrice for acting so much on impulse, while I am constantly guilty of the same offence. But I don't look on you as a stranger. Somehow I seem to know you well, and I wanted your opinion. I can speak freely to you, can't I?"

"Certainly."

"He has asked me this afternoon if I'll consent to Beatrice becoming his wife."

Dick was silent. He felt he could not speak.

"Of course, from a worldly standpoint it would be a good match," went on Hugh Stanmore. "Sir George is a rich man, and has a fine reputation, not only as a scholar and a soldier, but as a man. There has never been a blemish on his reputation. He stands high in the county, and could give my little girl a fine position."

"Doubtless," and Dick hardly knew that he spoke.

"I don't think I am a snob," went on the old man; "but such things must weigh somewhat. I am not a pauper, but, as wealth is counted to-day, I am a poor man. I am also old, and in the course of nature can't be here long. That is why I am naturally anxious about my little Beatrice's future. And yet I am in doubt."

"About what?"

"Whether he could make her happy. And that is everything as far as I am concerned. Beatrice, as you must have seen, is just a happy child of nature, and is as sensitive as a lily. To be wedded to a man who is not—how shall I put it?—her affinity, her soul comrade, would be lifelong misery to her. And unless I were sure that Sir George is that, I would not think of giving my consent."

"Aren't you forgetful of a very important factor?" asked Dick.

"What is that?"

"Miss Stanmore herself. In these days girls seem to take such matters largely into their own hands. The consent of relations is regarded as a very formal thing."

"I don't think you understand, Faversham. Beatrice is not like the common run of girls, and she and I are so much to each other that I don't think for a moment that she would marry any man if I did not give my sanction. In fact, I'm sure she wouldn't. She's only my granddaughter, but she's all the world to me, while—yes, I am everything to her. No father loved a child more than I love her. I've had her since she was a little mite, and I've been father, mother, and grandfather all combined. And I'd do anything, everything in my power for her welfare. I know her—know her, Faversham; she's as pure and unsullied as a flower."

"But, of course, Sir George Weston has spoken to her?"

"No, he hasn't. For one thing, he has very strict ideas about old-fashioned courtesies, and, for another, he knows our relations to each other."

"Do you know her mind?—know whether she cares for him—in that way?" asked Dick.

"No, I don't. I do know that, a week ago, she had no thought of love for any man. But, of course, I couldn't help seeing that during the past week he has paid her marked attention. Whether she's been aware of it, I haven't troubled to ascertain."

In some ways this old man was almost as much a child as his granddaughter, in spite of his long life, and Dick could hardly help smiling at his simplicity.

"Of course, I imagine she'll marry sometime," and Dick's voice was a trifle hoarse as he spoke.

"Yes," replied Hugh Stanmore. "That is natural and right. God intended men and women to marry, I know that. But if they do not find their true mate, then it's either sacrilege or hell—especially to the woman. Marriage is a ghastly thing unless it's a sacrament—unless the man and the woman feel that their unity is of God. Marriage ceremonies, and the blessing of the Church, or whatever it is called, is so much mockery unless they feel that their souls are as one. Don't you agree with me?"

"Yes, I do. I suppose," he added, "you stipulate that whoever marries her—shall—shall be a man of wealth?"

"No, I shouldn't, except in this way. No man should marry a woman unless he has the wherewithal to keep her. He would be a mean sort of fellow who would drag a woman into want and poverty. But, of course, that does not obtain in this case."

"I'm afraid I can't help, or advise you," said Dick. "I'm afraid I'm a bit of an outsider," and he spoke bitterly. "Neither do I think you will need advice. Miss Stanmore has such a fine intuition that——"

"Ah, you feel that!" broke in Hugh Stanmore almost excitedly. "Yes, yes, you are right! I can trust her judgment rather than my own. Young as she is, she'll choose right. Yes, she'll choose right! I think I'll go back now. Yes, I'll go back at once. Our conversation has done me good, and cleared my way, although I've done most of the talking. Good-night, Faversham. I wish you well. I think you can do big things as a politician; but I don't agree with you."

"Don't agree with me? Why?"

"I don't believe in these party labels. You are a party man, a Labour man. I have the deepest sympathy with the toilers of the world. I have been working for them for fifty years. Perhaps, too, the Labour Party is the outcome of the injustice of the past. But all such parties have a tendency to put class against class, to see things in a one-sided way, to foster bitterness and strife. Take my advice and give up being a politician."

"Give up being a politician! I don't understand."

"A politician in the ordinary sense is a party man; too often a party hack, a party voting machine. Be more than a politician, be a statesman. All classes of society are interdependent. We can none of us do without the other. Capital and labour, the employer and the employee, all depend on each other. All men should be brothers and work for the common interest. Don't seek to represent a class, or to legislate for a class, Faversham. Work for all the classes, work for the community as a whole. And remember that Utopia is not created in a day. Good-night. Come and see us again soon."

Hugh Stanmore turned back, and left Dick alone. The young man felt strangely depressed, strangely lonely. He pictured Hugh Stanmore going back to the brightness and refinement of his little house, to be met with the bright smiles and loving words of his grandchild, while he plodded his way through the darkness. He thought, too, of Sir George Weston, who, even then, was with Beatrice Stanmore. Perhaps, most likely too, he was telling her that he loved her.

He stopped suddenly in the road, his brain on fire, his heart beating madly. A thousand wild fancies flashed through his brain, a thousand undefinable hopes filled his heart.

"No, it's impossible, blankly impossible!" he cried at length. "A will-o'-the-wisp, the dream of a madman—a madman! Why, even now she may be in his arms!"

The thought was agony to him. Even yet he did not know the whole secret of his heart, but he knew that he hated Sir George Weston, that he wished he had urged upon old Hugh Stanmore the utter unfitness of the great soldier as a husband for his grandchild.

But how could he? What right had he? Besides, according to all common-sense standards nothing could be more suitable. She was his equal in social status, and every way fitted to be his wife, while he would be regarded as the most eligible suitor possible.

"A voting machine at four hundred a year!"

Again those stinging words of Count Romanoff. And old Hugh Stanmore had spoken in the same vein. "A party hack, a party voting machine!"

And he could not help himself. He was dependent on that four hundred a year. He dared ask no woman to be his wife. He had no right. He would only drag her into poverty and want.

All the way back to town his mind was filled with the hopelessness of his situation. The fact that he had won a great victory at Eastroyd and was a newly returned Member of Parliament brought him no pleasure. He was a party hack, and he saw no brightness in the future.

Presently Parliament assembled, and Dick threw himself with eagerness into the excitement which followed. Every day brought new experiences, every day brought new interests.

But he felt himself hampered. If he only had a few hundreds a year of his own. If only he could be free to live his own life, think his own thoughts. Not that he did not agree with many of the ideas of his party. He did. But he wanted a broader world, a greater freedom. He wanted to love, and to be loved.

Then a change came. On returning to his flat late one night he found a letter awaiting him. On the envelope was a coroneted crest, and on opening it he saw the name of Olga Petrovic.

Chapter XXXIV
The Dawn of Love

The letter from Olga ran as follows:

"Dear Mr. Faversham,—I have just discovered your address, and I am writing to congratulate you on the fine position you have won. It must be glorious to be a Member of the Mother of Parliaments, to be a legislator in this great free country. I rejoice, too, that you have espoused the cause of the toilers, the poor. It is just what I hoped and expected of you. You will become great, my friend; my heart tells me so. Your country will be proud of you.

"I wonder whether, if in spite of your many interests and duties, you will have time to visit a lonely woman? There are so many things I would like to discuss with you. Do come if you can. I shall be home to-morrow afternoon, and again on Friday. Will you not have pity on me?—Yours,

Olga Petrovic."

Dick saw that her address was a fashionable street in Mayfair, and almost unconsciously he pictured her in her new surroundings. She was no longer among a wild-eyed, long-haired crew in the East End, but in the centre of fashion and wealth. He wondered what it meant. He read the letter a second time, and in a way he could not understand, he was fascinated. There was subtle flattery in every line, a kind of clinging tenderness in every sentence.

No mention was made of their last meeting, but Dick remembered. She had come to him after that wonderful experience in Staple Inn—on the morning after his eyes had been opened to the facts about what a number of Bolshevists wanted to do in England. His mind had been bewildered, and he was altogether unsettled. He was afraid he had acted rudely to her. He had thought of her as being associated with these people. If he had yielded to her entreaties, and thrown himself into the plans she had made, might he not have become an enemy to his country, to humanity?

But what a glorious creature she was! What eyes, what hair, what a complexion! He had never seen any woman so physically perfect. And, added to all this, she possessed a kind of charm that held him, fascinated him, made him think of her whether he would or not.

And yet her letter did not bring him unmixed pleasure. In a way he could not understand he was slightly afraid of her, afraid of the influence she had over him. He could not mistake the meaning of her words at their last meeting. She had made love to him, she had asked him to marry her. It is true he had acted as though he misunderstood her, but what would have happened if old Hugh Stanmore and Beatrice had not come? The very mystery which surrounded her added to her charm. Who *was* she? Why did she go to the East End to live, and how did she possess the means to live in Mayfair?

He walked around his little room, thinking hard. For the last few days his parliamentary duties had excited him, kept him from brooding; but now in the quietness of the night he felt his loneliness, realised his longing for society. His position as a Labour Member was perfectly plain. His confrères were good fellows. Most of them were hard-headed, thoughtful men who took a real interest in their work. But socially they were not of his class. They had few interests in common, and he realised it, even as they did. That was why they looked on him with a certain amount of suspicion. What was to be his future then? A social gulf was fixed between him and others whose equal he was, and whatever he did he would be outside the circle of men and women whose tastes were similar to his own.

No, that was not altogether true. Hugh Stanmore and Beatrice treated him as a friend. Beatrice!

The very thought of her conjured up all sorts of fancies. He had not heard from her, or of her since his visit to Wendover. Was she engaged to Sir George Weston, he wondered?

He knew now that he had never loved Lady Blanche Huntingford. He had been attracted to her simply because of her looks, and her social position. At the time she had appealed to him strongly, but that was because he had regarded her as a means whereby he could attain to his social ambitions. But a change had come over him since then—a subtle, almost indescribable change. The strange events of his life had led him to see deeper. And he knew he had no love for this patrician woman. When he had seen her last she had not caused one heart-throb, he was almost indifferent to her.

But Beatrice! Why did the thought of her haunt him? Why was he angry with Sir George Weston, and bitter at the idea of his marrying this simple country girl? As for himself he could never marry.

The following morning he wrote to Countess Olga Petrovic. It was a courteous note saying that at present he was too engaged to call on her, but he hoped that later he might have that pleasure. Then he plunged into his work again.

About a fortnight after his visit to Hugh Stanmore, a letter came to him from the housekeeper at Wendover. He had told her his London address, and she had taken advantage of her knowledge by writing.

"There are all sorts of rumours here about Mr. Anthony Riggleton," she wrote; "and we have all been greatly excited. Some soldiers have been in the neighbourhood who declare that they know of a certainty that he is dead. I thought it my duty to tell you this, sir, and that is my excuse for the liberty I take in writing.

"Perhaps, sir, you may also be interested to learn that Sir George Weston and Miss Beatrice Stanmore are engaged to be married. As you may remember, I told you when you were here that I thought they would make a match of it. Of course she has done very well, for although the Stanmores are a great family, Mr. Stanmore is a poor man, and Miss Beatrice has nothing but what he can give her. It is said that the wedding will take place in June."

The letter made him angry. Of course he understood the old lady's purpose in writing. She thought that if Anthony Riggleton died, the estate might again revert to him, and she hoped he would find out and let her know. She had grown very fond of him during his short sojourn there, and longed to see him there as master again. But the letter made him angry nevertheless. Then as he read it a second time he knew that his anger was not caused by her interest in his future, but because of her news about Beatrice Stanmore. The knowledge that she had accepted this Devonshire squire made his heart sink like lead. It seemed to him that the sky of his life had suddenly become black.

Then he knew his secret; knew that he loved this simple country girl with a consuming but hopeless love. He realised, too, that no one save she had ever really touched his heart. That this was why Lady Blanche Huntingford had passed out of his life without leaving even a ripple of disappointment or sorrow.

Oh, if he had only known before! For he had loved her as he had walked by her side through Wendover Park; loved her when he had almost calmly discussed her possible marriage with Sir George Weston. Even then he had hated the thought of it, now he knew why His own heart was aching for her all the time.

But what would have been the use even if he had known? He was a homeless, penniless man. He could have done nothing. He was not in a position to ask any woman to be his wife.

His mood became reckless, desperate. What mattered whatever he did? Were not all his dreams and hopes so much madness? Had he not been altogether silly about questions of right and wrong? Had he not been Quixotic in not fighting for Wendover? Supposing he had signed that paper, what could Romanoff have done? He almost wished—no, he didn't; but after all, who could pass a final judgment as to what was right and wrong?

While he was in this state of mind another letter came from Olga Petrovic.

"Why have you not visited me, my friend?" she wrote. "I have been expecting you. Surely you could have found time to drop in for half an hour. Besides, I think I could help you. Lord Knerdon was here yesterday with one or two other Members of the Government. He expressed great interest in you, and said he would like to meet you. Has he not great influence? I shall be here between half-past three and six to-morrow, and some people are calling whom I think you would like to know."

Lord Knerdon, eh? Lord Knerdon was one of the most respected peers in the country, and a man of far-reaching power. He would never call at the house of an adventuress. Yes, he would go.

The street in which Olga Petrovic had taken up her abode was made up of great houses. Only a person of considerable wealth could live there. This he saw at a glance. Also three handsome motor-cars stood at her door. He almost felt nervous as his finger touched the bell.

She received him with a smile of welcome, and yet there was a suggestion of aloofness in her demeanour. She was not the woman he had seen at Jones' Hotel long months before, when she had almost knelt suppliant at his feet.

"Ah, Mr. Faversham," she cried, and there was a suggestion of a foreign accent in her tones, "I am pleased to see you. It is good of such a busy man to spare a few minutes."

A little later she had introduced him to her other visitors—men and women about whose position there could not be a suggestion of doubt. At least, such was his impression. She made a perfect hostess, too, and seemed to be a part of her surroundings. She was a great lady, who met on equal terms some of the best-known people in London. And she was queen of them all. Even as she reigned over the motley crew in that queer gathering in the East of London, so she reigned here in the fashionable West.

In a few minutes he found himself talking with people of whom he had hitherto known nothing except their names, while Olga Petrovic watched him curiously. Her demeanour to him was perfectly friendly, and yet he had the feeling that she regarded him as a social inferior. He was there, not because he stood on the same footing as these people, but on sufferance. After all, he was a Labour Member. Socially he was an outsider, while she was the grand lady.

People condoled with her because her Russian estates had been stolen from her by the Bolshevists, but she was still the Countess Olga Petrovic, bearing one of the greatest names in Europe. She was still rich enough to maintain her position in the wealthiest city in the world. She was still a mystery.

Dick remained for more than an hour. Although he would not admit it to himself, he hoped that he might be able to have a few minutes alone with her. But as some visitors went, others came. She still remained kind to him; indeed, he thought she conveyed an interest in him which she did not show to others. But he was not sure. There was a suggestion of reserve in her friendliness; sometimes, indeed, he thought she was cold and aloof. There were people there who were a hundred times more important than he—people with historic names; and he was a nobody. Perhaps that was why a barrier stood between them.

And yet there were times when she dazzled him by a smile, or the turn of a sentence. In spite of himself, she made him feel that it was a privilege of no ordinary nature to be the friend of the Countess Olga Petrovic.

When at length he rose to go she made not the slightest effort to detain him. She was courteously polite, and that was all. He might have been the most casual stranger, to whom she used the most commonplace forms of speech. Any onlooker must have felt that this Polish or Russian Countess, whatever she might be, had simply a passing interest in this Labour Member, that she had invited him to tea out of pure whim or fancy, and that she would forget him directly he had passed the doorstep. And yet there was a subtle something in her manner as she held out her hand to him. Her words said nothing, but her eyes told him to come again.

"Must you go, Mr. Faversham? So pleased you were able to call. I am nearly always home on Thursdays."

That was all she said. But the pressure of her hand, the pleading of her eyes, the smile that made her face radiant—these somehow atoned for the coldness of her words.

"Well, I've called," thought Dick as he left the house, "and I don't intend to call again. I don't understand her; she's out of my world, and we have nothing in common."

But these were only his surface thoughts. At the back of his mind was the conviction that Olga Petrovic had an interest in him beyond the ordinary, that she thought of him as she thought of no other man. Else why that confession months before? Why did she ask him to call?

She was a wonderful creature, too. How tame and uninteresting the other women were compared with her! Her personality dominated everything, made everyone else seem commonplace.

She captivated him and fascinated him even while something told him that it was best for him that he should see nothing more of her. The mystery that surrounded her had a twofold effect on him: it made him long to know more about her even while he felt that such knowledge could bring him no joy.

But this she did. She kept him from brooding about Beatrice Stanmore, for the vision of this unsophisticated English girl was constantly haunting him, and the knowledge that his love for her was hopeless made him almost desperate. He was a young man, only just over thirty, with life all before him. Must he for ever and ever be denied of love, and the joys it might bring to his life? If she had not promised herself to Sir George Weston, all might be different. Yes, with her to help him and inspire him, he would make a position for her; he would earn enough to make a home for her. But she was not for him. She would soon be the wife of another. Why, then, should he not crush all thoughts of her, and think of this glorious woman, compared with whom Beatrice Stanmore was only as a June rosebud to a tropical flower?

A few days later he called on Olga Petrovic again. This time he spent a few minutes alone with her. Only the most commonplace things were said, and yet she puzzled him, bewildered him. One minute she was all smiles and full of subtle charm, another he felt that an unfathomable gulf lay between them.

In their conversation, while he did not speak in so many words of the time she had visited him at his hotel, he let her know that he remembered it, and he quickly realised that the passionate woman who had pleaded with him then was not the stately lady who spoke to him now.

"Every woman is foolish at times," she said. "In hours of loneliness and memory we are the creatures of passing fancies; but they are only passing. I have always to remember that, in spite of the tragic condition of my country, I have my duty to my race and my position."

Later she said: "I wonder if I shall ever wed? Wonder whether duty will clash with my heart to such a degree that I shall go back to my own sphere, or stay here and only remember that I am a woman?"

He wondered what she meant, wondered whether she wished to convey to him that it might be possible for her to forsake all for love.

But something, he could not tell what, made him keep a strong hold upon himself. It had become a settled thought in his mind by this time that at all hazards he must fight against his love for Beatrice Stanmore. To love her would be disloyal to her; it would be wrong. He had no right to think thoughts of love about one who had promised to be the wife of another man.

Yet his heart ached for her. All that was best in him longed for her. Whenever his love for her was strongest, he longed only for the highest in life, even while his conscience condemned him for thinking of her.

Dick paid Olga Petrovic several visits. Nearly always others were there, but he generally managed to be alone with her for a few minutes, and at every visit he knew that she was filling a larger place in his life.

His fear of her was passing away, too, for she was not long in showing an interest in things that lay dear to his heart. She evidenced a great desire to help him in his work; she spoke sympathetically about the conditions under which the toilers of the world laboured. She revealed fine intuitions, too.

"Oh yes," she said on one occasion, "I love your country. It is home— home! I am mad, too, when I think of my insane fancies of a year ago. I can see that I was wrong, wrong, all wrong! Lawlessness, force, anarchy can never bring in the new day of life and love. That can only come by mutual forbearance, by just order, and by righteous discipline. I was mad for a time, I think; but I was mad with a desire to help. Do you know who opened my eyes, Mr. Faversham?"

"Your own heart—your own keen mind," replied Dick.

"No, my friend—no. It was you. You did not say much, but you made me see. I believe in telepathy, and I saw with your eyes, thought with your mind. Your eyes pierced the darkness, you saw the foolishness of my dreams. And yet I would give my last penny to help the poor."

"I'm sure you would," assented Dick.

"Still, we must be governed by reason. And that makes me think, my friend. Do you ever contemplate your own future?"

"Naturally."

"And are you always going to remain what you are now?"

"I do not follow you."

"I have thought much about you, and I have been puzzled. You are a man with great ambitions—high, holy ambitions—but if you are not careful, your life will be fruitless."

Dick was silent.

"Don't mistake me. I only mean fruitless comparatively. But you are handicapped, my friend."

"Sadly handicapped," confessed Dick.

"Ah, you feel it. You are like a bird with one wing trying to fly. Forgive me, but the best houses in London are closed to you; you are a paid Labour Member of Parliament, and thus you represent only a class—the least influential class. You are shut out from many of the delights of life. Channels of usefulness and power are closed to you. Oh, I know it is great to be a Labour Member, but it is greater to be independent of all classes—to live for your ideals, to have enough money to be independent of the world, to hold up your head as an equal among the greatest and highest."

"You diagnose a disease," said Dick sadly, "but you do not tell me the remedy."

"Don't I?" and Dick felt the glamour of her presence. "Doesn't your own heart tell you that, my friend?"

Dick felt a wild beating of his heart, but he did not reply. There was a weight upon his tongue.

A minute later she was the great lady again—far removed from him.

He left the house dazzled, almost in love with her in spite of Beatrice Stanmore, and largely under her influence. He had been gone only a few minutes when a servant brought a card.

"Count Romanoff," she read. "Show him here," she added, and there was a look in her eyes that was difficult to understand.

Chapter XXXV
The Eternal Struggle

Count Romanoff was faultlessly dressed, and looked calm and smiling.

"Ah, Countess," he said, "I am fortunate in finding you alone. But you have had visitors, or, to be more exact, a visitor."

"Yes; I have had visitors. I often have of an afternoon."

"But he has been here."

"Well, and what then?"

The Count gazed at her steadily, and his eyes had a sinister gleam in them.

"I have come to have a quiet chat with you," he said—"come to know how matters stand."

"You want to know more than I can tell you."

Again the Count scrutinised her closely. He seemed to be trying to read her mind.

"Olga," he said, "you don't mean to say that you have failed? He has been in London some time now, and as I happen to know, he has been here often. Has not the fish leaped to the bait? If not, what is amiss? What?—Olga Petrovic, who has turned the heads of men in half the capitals of Europe, and who has never failed to make them her slaves, fail to captivate this yokel! I can't believe it."

There was sullen anger in her eyes, and at that moment years seemed to have been added to her life.

"Beaten!" went on the Count, with a laugh—"Olga Petrovic beaten! That is news indeed."

"I don't understand," said the woman. "Something always seems to stand between us. He seems to fear me—seems to be fighting against me."

"And you have tried all your wiles?"

"Listen, Count Romanoff, or whatever your name may be," and Olga Petrovic's voice was hoarse. "Tell me what you want me to do with that man."

"Do? Make him your slave. Make him grovel at your feet as you have made others. Make him willing to sell his soul to possess you. Weave your net around him. Glamour him with your fiendish beauty. Play upon his hopes and desires until he is yours."

"Why should I?"

"Because it is my will—because I command you."

"And what if I have done all that and failed?"

"You fail! I can't believe it. You have not tried. You have not practised all your arts."

"You do not understand," replied the woman. "You think you understand that man; you don't."

The Count laughed. "There was never a man yet, but who had his price," he said. "With some it is one thing, with some it is another, but all—all can be bought. There is no man but whose soul is for sale; that I know."

"And you have tried to buy Faversham's soul, and failed."

"Because I mistook the thing he wanted most."

"You thought he could be bought by wealth, position, and you arranged your plans. But he was not to be bought. Why? You dangled riches, position, and a beautiful woman before his eyes; but he would not pay the price."

"I chose the wrong woman," said the Count, looking steadily at Olga, "and I did not reckon sufficiently on his old-fashioned ideas of morality. Besides, I had no control over the woman."

"And you think you have control over me, eh? Well, let that pass. I have asked you to tell me why you wish to get this man in your power, and you will not tell me. But let me tell you this: there is a strange power overshadowing him. You say I must practise my arts. What if I tell you that I can't?"

"I should say you lie," replied the Count coolly.

"I don't understand," she said, as if talking to herself. "All the time when he is with me, I seem to be dealing with unseen forces—forces which make me afraid, which sap my power."

The Count looked thoughtful.

"I thought I had captivated him when that German man brought him to the East End of London," she went on. "I saw that I bewildered him—dazzled him. He seemed fascinated by my picture of what he could become. His imagination was on fire, and I could see that he was almost held in thrall by the thought that he could be a kind of uncrowned king, while I would be his queen. He promised to come to me again, but he didn't. Then I went to see him at his hotel, and if ever a woman tempted a man, I tempted him. I know I am beautiful—know that men are willing to become slaves to me. And I pleaded with him. I offered to be his wife, and I almost got him. I saw him yielding to me. Then suddenly he turned from me. A servant brought him a card, and he almost told me to go."

"You saw who these visitors were?"

"Yes; an old man and a slip of a girl. I do not know who they were. Since he has been living in London, I have watched my opportunities, and he has been here. I have flattered him; I have piqued his curiosity. I have been coy and reserved, and I have tried to dazzle him by smiles, by hand pressures, and by shy suggestions of love. But I cannot pierce his armour."

"And you will give up? You will confess defeat?"

The woman's eyes flashed with a new light. "You little know me if you think that," she cried angrily. "At one time I—yes, I, Olga Petrovic—thought I loved him. I confessed it to you, but now—now——"

"Yes, now?" questioned the Count eagerly.

"Now that thought is not to be considered. I will conquer him; I will make him my slave. He shall be willing to sacrifice name, position, future, anything, everything for me—*everything*."

"Only, up to now, you've failed."

"Because, because—oh, Romanoff, I don't understand. What is he? Only just a commonplace sort of man—a man vulnerable at a hundred points—and yet I cannot reach him."

"Shall I tell you why?" asked the Count.

"Tell me, tell me!" she cried. "Oh, I've thought, and thought. I've tried in a hundred ways. I've been the grand lady with a great position. I've been an angel of light who cares only for the beautiful and the pure. I've appealed to his ambition—to his love for beautiful things. I've tried to make him jealous, and I've nearly succeeded; but never altogether. Yes; he is just a clever man, and very little more; but I can't reach him. He baffles me. He does not drink, and so I cannot appeal to that weakness. Neither is he the fast man about town that can be caught in my toils. He honours, almost venerates, pure womanhood, and——"

"Tah!" interrupted the Count scornfully.

"You do not believe it?"

"Woman is always man's weak point—always!"

"But not his—not in the way you think. I tell you, he venerates ideal womanhood. He scorns the loud-talking, free-spoken women. He told me his thought of woman was like what Wordsworth painted. At heart I think he is a religious man."

"Listen," said the Count, "I want to tell you something before I go. Sit here; that's it," and he drew a chair close to his side.

He spoke to her half earnestly, half cynically, watching her steadily all the time. He noted the heaving of her bosom, the tremor of her lips, the almost haunted look in her eyes, the smile of satisfied desire on her face.

"That is your plan of action," he concluded. "Remember, you play for great stakes, and you must play boldly. You must play to win. There are times when right and wrong are nothing to a man, and you must be willing to risk everything. As for the rest, I will do it."

Her face was suffused half with the flush of shame, half with excited determination.

"Very well," she said; "you shall be obeyed."

"And I will keep my compact," said the Count.

He left her without another word, and no sign of friendship passed between them.

When he reached the street, however, there was a look of doubt in his eyes. He might have been afraid, for there was a kind of baffled rage on his face.

He stopped a passing taxi, and drove straight to his hotel.

"Is he here?" he asked his valet as he entered his own room.

"He is waiting, my lord."

A minute later the little man who had visited him on the day after Dick Faversham's return to Parliament appeared.

"What report, Polonius?" asked Romanoff.

"Nothing of great importance, I am afraid, my lord, but something."

"Yes, what?"

"He went to Wendover on the day I was unable to account for his whereabouts."

"Ah, you have discovered that, have you?"

"Yes; I regret I missed him that day, but I trust I have gained your lordship's confidence again."

The Count reflected a few seconds. "Tell me what you know," he said peremptorily.

"He went down early, and had a talk with an old man at the station. Then he walked to the house, and had a conversation with his old housekeeper."

"Do you know what was said?"

"There was not much said. She told him there were rumours that Anthony Riggleton was dead."

The Count started as though a new thought had entered his mind; then he turned towards his spy again.

"He did not pay much attention to it," added Polonius, "neither did he pay much attention to what she told him about Riggleton's doings at Wendover."

"Did he go through the house?"

"No; he only stayed a few minutes, but he was seen looking very hard at the front door, as though something attracted him. Then he returned by another route, and had lunch with that old man who has a cottage near one of the lodge gates."

"Hugh Stanmore—yes, I remember."

"After lunch he went through the park with the old man's granddaughter. They were talking very earnestly."

The Count leapt to his feet.

"You saw this girl?" he asked.

"Yes. A girl about twenty, I should think. Very pretty in a simple, countrified way. She is very much loved among the cottage people. I should say she's a very religious girl. I'm told that she has since become engaged to be married to a Sir George Weston, who was a soldier in Egypt."

"Sir George Weston. Let me think. Yes; I remember. Ah, she is engaged to be married to him, is she?"

"That is the rumour. Sir George was staying at Stanmore's cottage at the time of Faversham's visit. He left the day after."

"And Faversham has not been there since?"

"No, my lord."

"Well, go on."

"That is all I know."

"Then you can go; you know my instructions. Remember, they must be obeyed to the very letter."

"They shall be—to the very letter."

The Count entered another room, and opened a safe. From it he took some papers, and read carefully. Then he sat thinking for a long time. Presently he looked at his watch.

Daylight had now gone, early as it was, for winter still gripped the land. Some days there were suggestions of spring in the air, but they were very few. The night was cold.

The Count went to the window, and looked out over St. James's Park. Great, black ominous-looking clouds rolled across the sky, but here and there were patches of blue where stars could plainly be seen. He had evidently made up his mind about something.

His servant knocked at the door.

"What time will your lordship dine?"

"I shall not dine."

"Very good, my lord."

Count Romanoff passed into the street. For some time he walked, and then, hailing a taxi-cab, drove to London Bridge. He did not drive across the bridge, but stopped at the Cannon Street end. Having paid the driver, he walked slowly towards the southern bank of the river. Once he stood for more than a minute watching while the dark waters rolled towards the sea.

"What secrets the old river could tell if it could speak," he muttered; "but all dark secrets—all dark."

He found his way to the station, and mingled with the crowd there.

Hours later he was nearly twenty miles from London, and he was alone on a wide heath. Here and there dotted around the outskirts of the heath he saw lights twinkling.

The sky was brighter here; the clouds did not hang so heavily as in the city, while between them he occasionally saw the pale crescent of a waxing moon. All around him was the heath.

He paid no heed to the biting cold, but walked rapidly along one of the straight-cut roads through the heather and bushes. It was now getting late, and no one was to be seen. There were only a few houses in the district, and the inhabitants of these were doubtless ensconced before cosy fires or playing games with their families. It was not a night to be out.

"What a mockery, what a miserable, dirty little mockery life is!" he said aloud as he tramped along. "And what pigmies men are; what paltry, useless things make up their lives! This is Walton Heath, and here I suppose the legislators of the British Empire come to find their amusement in knocking a golf-ball around. And men are applauded because they can knock that ball a little straighter and a little farther than someone else. But—but—and there comes the rub—these same men can think—think right and wrong, do right and wrong. That fellow Faversham—yes; what is it that makes him beat me?"

Mile after mile he tramped, sometimes stopping to look at the sullen, angry-looking clouds that swept across the sky, and again looking around the heath as if trying to locate some object in which he was interested.

Presently he reached a spot where the road cut through some woodland. Dark pine trees waved their branches to the skies. In the near distance the heath stretched away for miles, and although it was piercingly cold, the scene was almost attractive. But here it was dark, gloomy, forbidding. For some time he stood looking at the waving pine trees; it might have been that he saw more than was plainly visible.

"What fools, what blind fools men are!" he said aloud. "Their lives are bounded by what they see, and they laugh at the spiritual world; they scorn the suggestion that belting the earth are untold millions of spirits of the dead. Here they are all around me. I can see them. I can see them!"

His eyes burnt red; his features were contorted as if by pain.

"An eternal struggle," he cried—"just an eternal struggle between right and wrong, good and evil—yes, good and evil!

"And the good is slowly gaining the victory! Out of all the wild, mad convulsions of the world, right is slowly emerging triumphant, the savage is being subdued, and the human, the Divine, is triumphing."

He lifted his right hand, and shook his fist to the heavens as if defiantly.

"I had great hopes of the War," he went on. "I saw hell let loose; I saw the world mad for blood. Everywhere was the lust for blood; everywhere men cried, 'Kill! kill!' And now it is over, and wrong is being defeated—defeated!"

He seemed to be in a mad frenzy, his voice shook with rage.

"Dark spirits of hell!" he cried. "You have been beaten, beaten! Why, even in this ghastly war, the Cross has been triumphant! Those thousands, those millions of men who went out from this land, went out for an ideal. They did not understand it, but it was so. They felt dimly and indistinctly that they were fighting, dying, that others might live! And some of the most heroic deeds ever known in the history of the world were done. Men died for others, died for comradeship, died for duty, died for country. Everywhere the Cross was seen!

"And those fellows are not dead! They are alive! they have entered into a greater life!

"Why, even the ghastly tragedy of Russia, on which we built so much, will only be the birth-pains which precede a new life!

"Everywhere, everywhere the right, the good, is emerging triumphant!"

He laughed aloud, a laugh of almost insane mockery.

"But men are blind, blind! They do not realise the world of spirits that is all around them, struggling, struggling. But through the ages the spirits of the good are prevailing!

"That is my punishment, my punishment spirits of hell, my punishment! Day by day I see the final destruction of evil!"

His voice was hoarse with agony. He might have been mad—mad with the torture of despair.

"All around me, all around me they live," he went on. "But I am not powerless. I can still work my will. And Faversham shall be mine. I swore it on the day he was born, swore it when his mother passed into the world of spirits, swore it when his father joined her. What though all creation is moving upwards, I can still drag him down, down into hell! Yes, and she shall see him going down, she shall know, and then she shall suffer as I have suffered. Her very heaven shall be made hell to her, because she shall see her son become even what I have become!"

He left the main road, and followed a disused drive through the wood. Before long he came to a lonely house, almost hidden by the trees. A dark gloomy place it was, dilapidated and desolate. Years before it had perchance been the dwelling-place of some inoffensive respectable householder who loved the quietness of the country. For years it was for sale, and then it was bought by a stranger who never lived in it, but let it fall into decay.

Romanoff found his way to the main entrance of the house, and entered. He ascended a stairway, and at length found his way to a room which was furnished. Here he lit a curiously-shaped lamp. In half an hour the place was warm, and suggested comfort. Romanoff sat like one deep in thought.

Presently he began to pace the room, uttering strange words as he walked. He might have been repeating incantations, or weaving some mystic charms. Then he turned out the lamp, and only the fire threw a flickering light around the room.

"My vital forces seem to fail me," he muttered; "even here it seems as though there is good."

Perspiration oozed from his forehead, and his face was as pale as death.

Again he uttered wild cries; he might have been summoning unseen powers to his aid.

"They are here!" he shouted, and there was an evil joy in his face. Then there was a change, fear came into his eyes. Looking across the room, he saw two streaks of light in the form of a cross, while out of the silence a voice came.

"Cease!" said the Voice.

Chapter XXXVI
His Guardian Angel

Romanoff ceased speaking, and his eyes were fixed on the two streaks of light.

"Who are you? What do you want?" he asked.

"I am here to bid you desist."

"And who are you?"

Slowly, between him and the light, a shadowy figure emerged. Second after second its shape became more clearly outlined, until the form of a woman appeared. But the face was obscure; it was dim and shadowy.

Romanoff's eyes were fixed on the figure; but he uttered no sound. His tongue was dry, and cleaved to the roof of his mouth. His lips were parched.

The face became plainer. Its lineaments were more clearly outlined. He could see waves of light brown hair, eyes that were large and yearning with a great tenderness and pity, yet lit up with joy and holy resolve. A mouth tender as that of a child, but with all the firmness of mature years. A haunting face it was, haunting because of its spiritual beauty, its tenderness, its ineffable joy; and yet it was stern and strong.

It was the face of the woman whom Dick Faversham had seen in the smoke-room of the outward-bound vessel years before, the face that had appeared to him at the doorway of the great house at Wendover.

"You, you!" cried Romanoff at length. "You! Madaline?"

"Yes!"

"Why are you here?"

"To plead with you, to beseech you to let my son alone."

A change came over Romanoff's face as he heard the words. A new strength seemed to have come to him. Confidence shone in his eyes, his every feature spoke of triumph.

"Your son! His son!" he cried harshly. "The son of the man for whom you cast me into the outer darkness. But for him you might have been the mother of *my* son, and I—I should not have been what I am."

"You are what you are because you have always yielded to the promptings of evil," replied the woman. "That was why I never loved you—never could love you."

"But you looked at me with eyes of love until he came."

"As you know, I was but a child, and when you came with your great name, your great riches, you for a time fascinated me; but I never loved you. I told you so before he came."

"But I loved you," said Romanoff hoarsely. "You, the simple country girl, fascinated me, the Russian noble. And I would have withheld nothing from you. Houses, lands, position, a great name, all—all were yours if you would have been my wife. But you rejected me."

"I did not love you. I felt you were evil. I told you so."

"What of that? I loved you. I swore I would win you. But you—you—a simple country girl, poor, ignorant of the world's ways, resisted me, me—Romanoff. And you married that insipid scholar fellow, leaving me scorned, rejected. And I swore I would be revenged, living or dead. Then your child was born and you died. I could not harm you, you were beyond me, but your son lived. And I swore again. If I could not harm you, I could harm him, I could destroy him. I gave myself over to evil for that. I, too, have passed through the doorway which the world calls death; but powers have been given me, powers to carry out my oath. While his father was alive, I could do nothing, but since then my work has been going forward. And I shall conquer, I shall triumph."

"And I have come here to-night to plead with you on my son's behalf. He has resisted wrong for a long time. Leave him in peace."

"Never," cried Romanoff. "You passed into heaven, but your heaven shall be hell, for your son shall go there. He shall become even as I am. His joy shall be in evil."

"Have you no pity, no mercy?"

"None," replied Romanoff. "Neither pity nor mercy have a place in me. You drove me to hell, and it is my punishment that the only joy which may be mine is the joy of what you call evil."

"Then have pity, have mercy on yourself."

"Pity on myself? Mercy on myself? You talk in black ignorance."

"No, I speak in light. Every evil you do only sinks you deeper in mire, deeper in hell."

"I cannot help that. It is my doom."

"It is not your doom if you repent. If you turn your face, your spirit to the light."

"I cannot repent. I am of those who love evil. I hate mercy. I despise pity."

"Then I must seek to save him in spite of you."

"You cannot," and a laugh of savage triumph accompanied his words. "I have made my plans. Nothing which you can do will save him. He has been given to me."

For a few seconds there was tense unnatural silence. The room was full of strange influences, as though conflicting forces were in opposition, as though light and darkness, good and evil, were struggling together.

"No, no, Madaline," went on Romanoff. "Now is my hour of triumph. The son you love shall be mine."

"Love is stronger than hate, good is stronger than evil," she replied. "You are fighting against the Eternal Spirit of Good; you are fighting against the Supreme Manifestation of that Goodness, which was seen two thousand years ago on the Cross of Calvary."

"The Cross of Calvary!" replied Romanoff, and his voice was hoarse; "it is the symbol of defeat, of degradation, of despair. For two thousand years it has been uplifted, but always to fail."

"Always to conquer," was the calm reply. "Slowly but surely, age after age, it has been subduing kingdoms, working righteousness, lifting man up to the Eternal Goodness. It has through all the ages been overcoming evil with good, and bringing the harmonies of holiness out of the discord of sin."

"Think of this war!" snarled Romanoff. "Think of Germany, think of Russia! What is the world but a mad hell?"

"Out of it all will Goodness shine. I cannot understand all, for full understanding only belongs to the Supreme Father of Lights. But I am sure of the end. Already the morning is breaking, already light is shining out of the darkness. Men's eyes are being opened, they are seeing visions and dreaming dreams. They are seeing the end of war, and talking of Leagues of Nations, of the Brotherhood of the world."

"But that does not do away with the millions who have died in battle. It does not atone for blighted and ruined homes, and the darkness of the world."

"Not one of those who fell in battle is dead. They are all alive. I have seen them, spoken to them. And the Eternal Goodness is ever with them, ever bearing them up. They have done what they knew to be their duty, and they have entered into their reward."

"What, the Evil and the Good together?" sneered Romanoff. "That were strange justice surely."

"Shall not the Judge of all the Earth do Right? They are all in His care, and His pity and His love are Infinite. That is why I plead with you."

"What, to spare your son? If what you say is true I am powerless. But I am not. Wrong is stronger than right. I defy you."

"Then is it to be a fight between us?"

"If you will. He must be mine."

"And what then?" There was ineffable sorrow in the woman's voice. "Would you drag him into æons of pain and anguish to satisfy your revenge?"

"I would, and I will. What if right is stronger than wrong, as you say? What if in the end right shall drag him through hell to heaven? I shall still know that he has lived in hell, and thus shall I have my revenge."

"And I, who am his mother, am also his ministering angel, and it is my work to save him from you."

"And you are powerless—powerless, I tell you?"

"All power is not given to us, but God has given His angels power to help and save."

"If you have such power, why am I not vanquished?"

"Have you not been vanquished many times?"

"Not once!" cried Romanoff. "Little by little I have been enveloping him in my toils."

"Think," replied the other. "When he was tossing on the angry sea, whose arms bore him up? Think again, why was it when you and he were in the library together at Wendover, and you tempted him to sell his soul for gain;—whose hand was placed on his, and stopped him from signing the paper which would have made him your slave?"

"Was it you?" gasped Romanoff.

"Think again. When the woman you selected sought to dazzle him with wild dreams of power and ambition, and who almost blinded him to the truth, what led him to discard the picture that came to him as inventions of evil? Who helped to open his eyes?"

"Then you—you," gasped Romanoff—"you have been fighting against me all the time! It was you, was it?"

"I was his mother, I am his mother; and I, who never intentionally did you harm, plead with you again. I love him, even as all true mothers, whether on earth or in the land of spirits, love their children. And I am allowed to watch over him, to protect him, to help him. It is my joy to be his guardian angel, and I plead with you to let him be free from your designs."

"And if I will—what reward will you give me?"

"I will seek to help you from your doom—the doom which must be the lot of those who persist in evil."

"That is not enough. No, I will carry out my plans; I will drag him to hell."

"And I, if need be, will descend into hell to save him."

"You cannot, you cannot!" and triumph rang in his voice. "I swore to drag him to hell, swore that his soul should be given over to evil."

The woman's face seemed to be drawn with pain, her eyes were filled with infinite yearning and tenderness. She moved her lips as if in speech, but Romanoff could distinguish no words. Then her form grew dimmer and dimmer until there was only a shadowy outline of what had been clear and distinct.

"What do you say? I cannot hear!" and his voice was mocking.

The man continued to look at the place where he had seen her, but, as her form disappeared, the two shafts of light grew more and more luminous. He saw the bright shining Cross distinctly outlined, and his eyes burnt with a great terror. Then out of the silence, out of the wide spaces which surrounded the house, out of the broad expanse of the heavens, words came to him:

"Underneath, *underneath*, Underneath are the Everlasting Arms."

Fascinated, Romanoff gazed, seeing nothing but the shining outline of the Cross, while the air seemed to pulsate with the great words I have set down.

Then slowly the Cross became more and more dim, until at length it became invisible. The corner of the room which had been illumined by its radiance became full of dark shadows. Silence became profound.

"What does it mean?" he gasped. "She left me foiled, defeated, in despair. But the Cross shone. The words filled everything."

For more than a minute he stood like one transfixed, thinking, thinking.

"It means this," he said presently, and the words came from him in hoarse gasps, "it means that I am to have my way; it means that I shall conquer him—drag him to hell; but that underneath hell are the Everlasting Arms. Well, let it be so. I shall have had my revenge. The son shall suffer what the mother made me suffer, and she shall suffer hell, too, because she shall see her son in hell."

He turned and placed more wood on the fire, then throwing himself in an arm-chair he sat for hours, brooding, thinking.

"Yes, Olga will do it," he concluded after a long silence. "The story of the Garden of Eden is an eternal principle. 'The woman tempted me and I did eat,' is the story of the world's sin. He is a man, with all a man's passions, and she is a Venus, a Circe—a woman—and all men fall when a woman tempts."

All through the night he kept his dark vigils; there in the dark house, with only flickering lights from the fire, he worked out his plans, and schemed for the destruction of a man's soul.

In the grey dawn of the wintry morning he was back in London again; but although the servants looked at him questioningly when he entered his hotel, as if wondering where he had been, he told no man of his doings. All his experiences were secret to himself.

During the next few days the little man Polonius seemed exceptionally busy; three times he went to Wendover, where there seemed to be many matters that interested him. Several times he made his way to the War Office, where he appeared to have acquaintances, and where he asked many questions. He also found his way to the block of buildings where Dick Faversham's flat was situated, and although Dick never saw him, he appeared to be greatly interested in the young man's goings out and his comings in. He also went to the House of Commons, and made the acquaintance of many Labour Members. Altogether Polonius's time was much engaged. He went to Count Romanoff's hotel, too, but always late at night, and he had several interviews with that personage, whom he evidently held in great awe.

More than a week after Romanoff's experiences at Walton Heath, Olga Petrovic received a letter which made her very thoughtful. There was a look of fear in her eyes as she read, as though it contained disturbing news.

And yet it appeared commonplace and innocent enough, and it contained only a few lines. Perhaps it was the signature which caused her cheeks to blanch, and her lips to quiver.

This was how it ran:

> "Dear Olga,—You must get F. to take you to dinner on Friday night next. You must go to the Moscow Restaurant, and be there by 7.45 prompt. Please look your handsomest, and spare no pains to be agreeable. When the waiter brings you liqueurs be especially fascinating. Act on the Berlin plan. This is very important, as a danger has arisen which I had not calculated upon. The time for action has now come, and I need not remind you how much success means to you.
>
> "Romanoff.
>
> "P.S.—Destroy this as you have destroyed all other correspondence from me. I shall know whether this is done.—R."

This was the note which had caused Olga Petrovic's cheeks to pale. After reading it again, she sat thinking for a long time, while more than once her face was drawn as if by spasms of pain.

Presently she went to her desk, and taking some scented notepaper, she wrote a letter. She was evidently very particular about the wording, for she tore up several sheets before she had satisfied herself. There was the look of an evil woman in her eyes as she sealed it, but there was something else, too; there was an expression of indescribable longing.

The next afternoon Dick Faversham came to her flat and found Olga Petrovic alone. He had come in answer to her letter.

"Have I done anything to offend you, Mr. Faversham?" she asked, as she poured out tea.

"Offend me, Countess? I never thought of such a thing. Why do you ask?"

"You were so cold, so distant when you were here last—and that was several days ago."

"I have been very busy," replied Dick.

"While I have been very lonely."

"Lonely! You lonely, Countess?"

"Yes, very lonely. How little men know women. Because a number of silly, chattering people have been here when you have called, you have imagined that my life has been full of pleasure, that I have been content. But I haven't a friend in the world, unless— —" She lifted her great languishing eyes to his for a moment, and sighed.

"Unless what?" asked Dick.

"Nothing, nothing. Why should you care about the loneliness of a woman?"

"I care a great deal," replied Dick. "You have been very kind to me—a lonely man."

From that moment she became very charming. His words gave her the opening she sought, and a few minutes later she had led him to the channel of conversation which she desired.

"You do not mind?" she said presently. "I know you are the kind of man who finds it a bore to take a woman out to dinner. But there will be a wonderful band at The Moscow, and I love music."

"It will be a pleasure, a very great pleasure," replied Dick.

"And you will not miss being away from the House of Commons for a few hours, will you? I will try to be very nice."

"As though you needed to try," cried Dick. "As though you could be anything else."

She looked half coyly, half boldly into his eyes.

"To-morrow night then?" she said.

"Yes, to-morrow night. At half-past seven I will be here."

Chapter XXXVII
At the Café Moscow

During the few days which had preceded Dick's visit to the Countess Olga's house, he had been very depressed. The excitement which he had at first felt in going to the House of Commons as the Member for Eastroyd had gone. He found, too, that the "Mother of Parliaments" was different from what he had expected.

The thing that impressed him most was the difficulty in getting anything done. The atmosphere of the place was in the main lethargic. Men came there for the first time, enthusiastic and buoyant, determined to do great things; but weeks, months, years passed by, and they had done nothing. In their constituencies crowds flocked to hear them, and applauded them to the echo; but in the House of Commons they had to speak to empty benches, and the few who remained to hear them, yawned while they were speaking, and only waited because they wanted to catch the Speaker's eye.

Dick had felt all this, and much more. It seemed to him that as a legislator he was a failure, and that the House of Commons was the most disappointing place in the world. Added to this he was heart-sore and despondent. His love for Beatrice Stanmore was hopeless. News of her engagement to Sir George Weston had been confirmed, and thus joy had gone out of his life.

Why it was, Dick did not know; but he knew now that he had loved Beatrice Stanmore from the first time he had seen her. He was constantly recalling the hour when she first came into his life. She and her grandfather had come to Wendover when he was sitting talking, with Romanoff, and he remembered how the atmosphere of the room changed the moment she entered. His will-power was being sapped, his sense of right and wrong was dulled; yet no sooner did she appear than his will-power came back, his moral perceptions became keen.

It was the same at her second visit. He had been like a man under a spell; he had become almost paralysed by Romanoff's philosophy of life, helpless to withstand the picture he held before his eyes; yet on the sudden coming of this bright-eyed girl everything had changed. She made him live in a new world. He remembered going outside with her, and they had talked about angels.

How vivid it all was to him! Everything was sweeter, brighter, purer, because of her. Her simple, childish faith, her keen intuition had made his materialism seem so much foolishness. Her eyes pierced the dark clouds; she was an angel of God, pointing upward.

He knew the meaning of it now. His soul had found a kindred soul, even although he had not known it; he had loved her then, although he was unaware of the fact. But ever since he had learnt the secret of his heart he had understood.

But it was too late. He was helpless, hopeless. She had given her heart to this soldier, this man of riches and position. Oh, what a mockery life was! He had seen the gates of heaven, he had caught a glimpse of what lay beyond, but he could not enter, and in his disappointment and hopelessness, despair gnawed at his heart like a canker.

Thus Dick Faversham was in a dangerous mood. That was why the siren-like presence of Olga Petrovic acted upon his senses like an evil charm. Oh, if he had only known!

At half-past seven on the Friday night he called at her flat, and he had barely entered the room before she came to him. Evidently she regarded it as a great occasion, for she was resplendently attired. Yet not too much so. Either she, or her maid, instinctively knew what exactly suited her kind of beauty; for not even the most critical could have found fault with her.

What a glorious creature she was! Shaped like a goddess, her clothes accentuated her charms. Evidently, too, she was intent on pleasing him. Her face was wreathed in smiles, her eyes shone with dangerous brightness. There was witchery, allurement in her presence—she was a siren.

Dick almost gave a gasp as he saw her. A girl in appearance, a girl with all the winsomeness and attractiveness of youth, yet a woman with all a woman's knowledge of man's weakness—a woman bent on being captivating.

"Do I please your Majesty?" and her eyes flashed as the words passed her lips.

"Please me!" he gasped. "You are wonderful, simply wonderful."

"I want you to be pleased," she whispered, and Dick thought he saw her blush.

They entered the motor-car together, and as she sat by his side he felt as though he were in dreamland. A delicate perfume filled the air, and the knowledge that he was going to dine with her, amidst brightness and gaiety, made him forgetful of all else.

They were not long in reaching The Moscow, one of the most popular and fashionable restaurants in London. He saw at a glance, as he looked around him, that the wealth, the beauty, the fashion of London were there. The waiter led them to a table from which they could command practically the whole room, and where they could be seen by all. But he took no notice of this. He was almost intoxicated by the brilliance of the scene, by the fascination of the woman who sat near him.

"For once," she said, "let us forget dull care, let us be happy."

He laughed gaily. "Why not?" he cried. "All the same, I wonder what my constituents at Eastroyd would say if they saw me here?"

She gave a slight shrug, and threw off the light gossamer shawl which had somewhat hidden her neck and shoulders. Her jewels flashed back the light which shone overhead, her eyes sparkled like stars.

"Let us forget Eastroyd," she cried; "let us forget everything sordid and sorrowing. Surely there are times when one should live only for gladness, for joy. Is not the music divine? There, listen! Did I not tell you that some of the most wonderful artists in London play here? Do you know what it makes me think of?"

"I would love to know," he responded, yielding to her humour.

"But I must not tell you—I dare not. I am going to ask a favour of you, my friend. Will you grant it, without asking me what it is?"

"Of course I will grant it."

"Oh, it is little, nothing after all. Only let me choose the wine to-night."

"Why not? I am no wine drinker, and am no judge of vintages."

"Ah, but you must drink with me to-night. To-night I am queen, and you are——"

"Yes, what am I?" asked Dick with a laugh, as she stopped.

"You are willing to obey your queen, aren't you?"

"Who would not be willing to obey such a queen?" was his reply.

The waiter hovered around them, attending to their slightest wants. Not only was the restaurant noted as being a rendezvous for the beauty and fashion of London, but it boasted the best *chef* in England. Every dish was more exquisite than the last, and everything was served in a way to please the most captious.

The dinner proceeded. Course followed course, while sweet music was discoursed, and Dick felt in a land of enchantment. For once he gave himself over to enjoyment—he banished all saddening thoughts. He was in a world of brightness and song; every sight, every sound drove away dull care. To-morrow he would have to go back to the grim realities of life; but now he allowed himself to be swept along by the tide of laughter and gaiety.

"You seem happy, my friend," said the woman presently. "Never before did I see you so free from dull care, never did I see you so full of the joy of life. Well, why not? Life was given to us to be happy. Yes, yes, I know. You have your work to do; but not now. I should feel miserable for days if I thought I could not charm away sadness from you—especially to-night."

"Why to-night?"

"Because it is the first time we have ever dined together. I should pay you a poor compliment, shouldn't I, if when you took me to a place where laughter abounded I did not bring laughter to your lips and joy to your heart. Let us hope that this is the first of the many times we may dine together. Yes; what are you thinking about?"

"That you are a witch, a wonder, a miracle of beauty and of charm. There, I know I speak too freely."

He ceased speaking suddenly.

"I love to hear you speak so. I would rather—but what is the matter?"

Dick did not reply. His eyes were riveted on another part of the room, and he had forgotten that she was speaking. Seated at a table not far away were three people, two men and a woman. The men were Sir George Weston and Hugh Stanmore. The woman was Beatrice Stanmore. Evidently the lover had brought his fiancée and her grandfather there that night. It seemed to Dick that Weston had an air of proprietorship, as he acted the part of host. He watched while the baronet smiled on her and spoke to her. It would seem, too, that he said something pleasant, for the girl laughed gaily, and her eyes sparkled with delight.

"You see someone you know?" and Olga Petrovic's eyes followed his gaze. "Ah, you are looking at the table where that pretty but rather countrified girl is sitting with the old man with the white hair, and the other who looks like a soldier. Ah yes, you know them, my friend?"

"I have seen them—met them," he stammered.

"Ah, then you know who they are? I do not know them, they are strangers to me; but I can tell you about them. Shall I?"

"Yes." His eyes were still riveted on them, and he did not know he had spoken.

"The girl is the younger man's fiancée. They have lately become engaged. Don't you see how he smiles on her? And look how she smiles back. She is deeply in love with him, that is plain. There, don't you see—she has a ring on her engagement finger. They are very happy. I think the man has brought the girl and the old man here as a kind of celebration dinner. Presently they will go to some place of amusement. She seems a poor simpering thing; but they are evidently deeply in love with each other. Tell me, am I not right?"

Dick did not reply. What he had seen stung him into a kind of madness. He was filled with reckless despair. What matter what he did, what happened to him? Of course he knew of the engagement, but the sight of them together unhinged his mind, kept him from thinking coherently.

"You seem much interested in them, my friend; do you know them well? Ah, they have finished dinner, I think. There, they are looking at us; the girl is asking who we are, or, perhaps, she has recognised you."

For a moment Dick felt his heart stop beating; yes, she was coming his way. She must pass his table in order to get out.

With a kind of despairing recklessness he seized the wineglass by his side and drained it. He was hardly master of himself; he talked rapidly, loudly.

The waiter appeared with liqueurs.

"Yes," cried the Countess, with a laugh; "I chose the wine—I must choose the liqueurs also. It is my privilege."

The waiter poured out the spirits with a deft hand, while the woman laughed. Her eyes sparkled more brightly then ever; her face had a look of set purpose.

"This is the only place in London where one can get this liqueur," she cried. "What is it? I don't know. But I am told it is exquisite. There! I drink to you!"

She lifted the tiny glass to her lips, while her eyes, large, black, bold, seductive, dangerous, flashed into his.

"Drink, my friend," she said, and her voice reached some distance around her; "it is the drink of love, of *love*, the only thing worth living for. Drain it to the bottom, and let us be happy."

He lifted the glass, but ere it reached his lips he saw that Beatrice Stanmore and her companions were close to him, and that she must have heard what Olga Petrovic had said. In spite of the fact that he had drunk of rich, strong wine, and that it tingled through his veins like some fabled elixir, he felt his heart grow cold. He saw a look on the girl's face which startled him—frightened him. But she was not looking at him; her eyes were fixed on his companion.

And he saw the expression of terror, of loathing, of horror. It made him think of an angel gazing into the pit of hell. But Olga Petrovic seemed unconscious of her presence. Her eyes were fixed on Dick's face. She seemed to be pleading with him, fascinating him, compelling him to think only of her.

Meanwhile Hugh Stanmore and Sir George Weston hesitated, as if doubtful whether they should speak.

Dick half rose. He wanted to speak to Beatrice. To tell her—what, he did not know. But he was not master of himself. He was dizzy and bewildered. Perhaps it was because he was unaccustomed to drink wine, and the rich vintage had flown to his head—perhaps because of influences which he could not understand.

"Beatrice—Miss Stanmore," he stammered in a hoarse, unnatural voice, so hoarse and unnatural that the words were scarcely articulated, "this—this *is* a surprise."

He felt how inane he was. He might have been intoxicated. What must Beatrice think of him?

But still she did not look at him. Her eyes were still fixed on Olga's face. She seemed to be trying to read her, to pierce her very soul. Then suddenly she turned towards Dick, who had dropped into his chair again, and was still holding the tiny glass in his hand.

"You do not drink, Dick," said Olga Petrovic, and her voice, though low and caressing, was plainly to be heard. "You must drink, because I chose it, and it is the drink of love—the only thing worth living for," and all the time her eyes were fixed on his face.

Almost unconsciously he turned towards her, and his blood seemed turned to fire. Madness possessed him; he felt a slave to the charms of this bewitching woman, even while the maiden for whom his heart longed with an unutterable longing was only two or three yards from him. He lifted the glass again, and the fiery liquid passed his lips.

Again he looked at Beatrice, and it seemed to him that he saw horror and disgust in her face. Something terrible had happened; it seemed to him that he was enveloped in some form of black magic from which he could not escape.

Then rage filled his heart. The party passed on without further notice of him, and he saw Beatrice speak to Sir George Weston. What she said to him he did not know, but he caught a part of his reply. "I heard of her in Vienna. She had a curious reputation. Her *salon* was the centre of attraction to a peculiar class of men. Magnificent, but— —"

That was all he heard. He was not sure he heard even that. There was a hum of voices, and the sound of laughter everywhere, and so it was difficult for him to be sure of what any particular person said. Neither might the words apply to the woman at his side.

Bewildered, he turned towards Olga again, caught the flash of her eyes' wild fire, and was again fascinated by the bewildering seductiveness of her charms. What was the matter with him? He did not seem master of himself. Everything was strange—bewildering.

Perhaps it was because of the wine he had drunk, perhaps because that fiery liquid had inflamed his imagination; but it seemed to him that nothing mattered. Right! Wrong! What were they? Mere abstractions, the fancies of a diseased mind. Wild recklessness filled his heart. He had seen Beatrice Stanmore smile on Sir George Weston, and he had heard the woman at his side say that she, Beatrice, wore this Devonshire squire's ring.

Well, what then? Why should he care?

And all the time Olga Petrovic was by his side. She had seemed unconscious of Beatrice's presence; she had not noticed the look of horror and loathing in the girl's eyes. She was only casting a spell on him—a spell he could not understand.

Then he had a peculiar sensation. This mysterious woman was bewitching him. She was sapping his will even as Romanoff had sapped it years before. Why did he connect them?

"Countess," he said, "do you know Count Romanoff?"

The woman hesitated a second before replying.

"Dick," she said, "you must not call me Countess. You know my name, don't you? Count Romanoff? No, I never heard of him."

"Let us get away from here," he cried. "I feel as though I can't breathe."

"I'm so sorry. Let us go back home and spend the evening quietly. Oh, I forgot. Sir Felix and Lady Fordham are calling at ten o'clock. You don't mind, do you?"

"No, no. I shall be glad to meet them."

A few minutes later they were moving rapidly towards Olga Petrovic's flat, Dick still excited, and almost irresponsible, the woman with a look of exultant triumph on her face.

Chapter XXXVIII
The Shadow of a Great Terror

"Sit down, my friend. Sir Felix and Lady Fordham have not come; but what matter? There, take this chair. Ah, you look like yourself again. Has it ever struck you that you are a handsome man? No; I do not flatter. I looked around The Moscow to-night, and there was not a man in the room to compare with you—not one who looked so distinguished, so much—a man. I felt so glad—so proud."

He felt himself sink in the luxuriously upholstered chair, while she sat at his feet and looked up into his face.

"Now, then, you are king; you are seated on your throne, while I, your slave, am at your feet, ready to obey your will. Is not that the story of man and woman?"

He did not answer He was struggling, struggling and fighting, and yet he did not know against what he was fighting. Besides, he had no heart in the battle. His will-power was gone; his vitality was lowered; he felt as though some powerful narcotic were in his blood, deadening his manhood, dulling all moral purpose. He was intoxicated by the influences of the hour, careless as to what might happen to him, and yet by some strange contradiction he was afraid. The shadow of a great terror rested on him.

And Olga Petrovic seemed to know—to understand.

She started to her feet. "You have never heard me sing, have you? Ah no, of course you have not. And has it not ever been in song and story that the slave of her lord's will discoursed sweet music to him? Is there not some old story about a shepherd boy who charmed away the evil spirits of the king by music?"

She sat at a piano, and began to play soft, dreamy music. Her fingers scarcely touched the keys, and yet the room was filled with peculiar harmonies.

"You understand French, do you not, my friend? Yes; I know you do."

She began to sing. What the words were he never remembered afterwards, but he knew they possessed a strange power over him. They dulled his fears; they charmed his senses; they seemed to open up long vistas of beauty and delight. He seemed to be in a kind of Mohammedan Paradise, where all was sunshine and song.

How long she sung he could not tell; what she said to him he hardly knew. He only knew that he sat in a luxuriously appointed room, while this wonder of womanhood charmed him.

Presently he knew that she was making love to him, and that he was listening with eager ears. Not only did he seem to have no power to resist her—he had no desire to do so. He did not ask whether she was good or evil; he ceased to care what the future might bring forth. And yet he had a kind of feeling that something was wrong, hellish—only it did not matter to him. This woman loved him, while all other love was impossible to him.

Beatrice! Ah, but Beatrice had looked at him with horror; all her smiles were given to another man—the man to whom she had promised to give herself as his wife. What mattered, then?

But there was a new influence in the room! It seemed to him as if a breath of sweet mountain air had been wafted to him—air full of the strength of life, sweet, pure life. The scales fell from his eyes and he saw.

The woman again sat at his feet, looking up at him with love-compelling eyes, and he saw her plainly. But he saw more: the wrappings were torn from her soul, and he beheld her naked spirit.

He shuddered. What he saw was evil—evil. Instead of the glorious face of Olga Petrovic, he saw a grinning skull; instead of the dulcet tones of her siren-like voice, he heard the hiss of snakes, the croaking of a raven.

He was standing on the brink of a horrible precipice, while beneath him was black, unfathomable darkness, filled with strange, noisome sounds.

What did it mean? He still beheld the beauty—the somewhat Oriental beauty of the room; he was still aware of the delicate odours that pervaded it, while this woman, glorious in her queenly splendour, was at his feet, charming him with words of love, with promises of delight; but it seemed to him that other eyes, other powers of vision, were given to him, and he saw beyond.

Was that Romanoff's cynical, evil face? Were not his eyes watching them with devilish expectancy? Was he not even then gloating over the loss of his manhood, the pollution of his soul?

"Hark, what is that?"

"What, my friend? Nothing, nothing."

"But I heard something—something far away."

She laughed with apparent gaiety, yet there was uneasiness in her voice.

"You heard nothing but my foolish confession, Dick. I love you, love you! Do you hear? I love you. I tried to kill it—in vain. But what matter? Love is everything—there is nothing else to live for. And you and I are all the world. Your love is mine. Tell me, is it not so? And I am yours, my beloved, yours for ever."

But he only half heard her; forces were at work in his life which he could not comprehend. A new longing came to him—the longing for a strong, clean manhood.

"Do you believe in angels?" he asked suddenly.

Why the question passed his lips he did not know, but it sprung to his lips without thought or effort on his part. Then he remembered. Beatrice Stanmore had asked him that question weeks before down at Wendover Park.

Angels! His mind became preternaturally awake; his memory flashed back across the chasm of years.

"Are they not all ministering spirits, sent forth to minister for them who shall be heirs of salvation?"

Yes; he remembered the words. The old clergyman had repeated them years before, when he had seen the face of the woman which no other man could see.

Like lightning his mind swept down the years, and he remembered the wonderful experiences which had had such a marked influence on his life.

"Angels!" laughed the woman. "There are no angels save those on earth, my friend. There is no life other than this, so let us be happy."

"Look, look!" he cried, pointing to a part of the room which was only dimly lit. "She is there, there! Don't you see? Her hand is pointing upward!"

Slowly the vision faded, and he saw nothing.

Then came the great temptation of Dick Faversham's life. His will-power, his manhood, had come back to him again, but he felt that he had to fight his battle alone. His eyes were open, but because at his heart was a gnawing despair, he believed there was nothing to live for save what his temptress promised.

She pleaded as only a woman jealous for her love, determined to triumph, can plead. And she was beautiful, passionate, dangerous. Again he felt his strength leaving him, his will-power being sapped, his horror of wrong dulled.

Still something struggled within him—something holy urged him to fight on. His manhood was precious; the spark of the Divine fire which still burnt refused to be extinguished.

"Lord, have mercy upon me! Christ, have mercy upon me!"

It was a part of the service he had so often repeated in the old school chapel, and it came back to him like the memory of a dream.

"Countess," he said, "I must go."

"No, no, Dick," cried the woman, with a laugh. "Why, it is scarcely ten o'clock."

"I must go," he repeated weakly.

"Not for another half an hour. I am so lonely."

He was hesitating whether he should stay, when they both heard the sound of voices outside—voices that might have been angry. A moment later the door opened, and Beatrice Stanmore came in, accompanied by her grandfather.

"Forgive me," panted the girl, "but I could not help coming. Something told me you were in great danger—ill—dying, and I have come."

She had come to him just as she had come to him that night at Wendover Park, and at her coming the power of Romanoff was gone. It was the same now. As if by magic, he felt free from the charm of Olga Petrovic. The woman was evil, and he hated evil.

Again the eyes of Beatrice Stanmore were fixed on the face of Olga Petrovic. She did not speak, but her look was expressive of a great loathing.

"Surely this is a strange manner to disturb one's privacy," said the Countess. "I am at a loss to know to what I am indebted for this peculiar attention. I must speak to my servants."

But Beatrice spoke no word in reply to her. Turning towards Dick again, she looked at him for a few seconds.

"I am sorry I have disturbed you," she said. "Something, I do not know what, told me you were in some terrible danger, and I went back to the restaurant. A man there told us you had come here. I am glad I was mistaken. Forgive me, I will go now."

"I am thankful you came," said Dick. "I—I am going."

"Good-night, Countess," he added, turning to Olga, and without another word turned to leave the room. But Olga Petrovic was not in the humour to be baffled. She rushed towards him and caught his arm.

"You cannot go yet," she cried. "You must not go like this, Dick; I cannot allow you. Besides, I want an explanation. These people, who are they? Dick, why are they here?"

"I must go," replied Dick sullenly. "I have work to do."

"Work!" she cried. "This is not the time for work, but love—our love, Dick. Ah, I remember now. This girl was at The Moscow with that soldier man. They love each other. Why may we not love each other too? Stay, Dick."

But she pleaded in vain. The power of her spell had gone. Something strong, virile, vital, stirred within him, and he was master of himself.

"Good-night, Countess," he replied. "Thank you for your kind invitation, but I must go."

He scarcely knew where he was going, and he had only a dim remembrance of refusing to take the lift and of stumbling down the stairs. He thought he heard old Hugh Stanmore talking with Beatrice, but he was not sure; he fancied, too, that they were close behind him, but he was too bewildered to be certain of anything.

A few minutes later he was tramping towards his own humble flat, and as he walked he was trying to understand the meaning of what had taken place.

Olga Petrovic had been alone only a few seconds, when Count Romanoff entered the room. Evidently he had been in close proximity all the time. In his eyes was the look of an angry beast at bay; his face was distorted, his voice hoarse.

"And you have allowed yourself to be beaten—beaten!" he taunted.

But the woman did not speak. Her hands were clenched, her lips tremulous, while in her eyes was a look of unutterable sorrow.

"But we have not come to the end of our little comedy yet, Olga," went on Romanoff. "You have still your chance of victory."

"Comedy!" she repeated; "it is the blackest tragedy."

"Tragedy, eh? Yes; it will be tragedy if you fail."

"And I must fail," she cried. "I am powerless to reach him, and yet I would give my heart's blood to win his love. But go, go! Let me never see your face again."

"You will not get rid of me so easily," mocked the Count. "We made our pact. I will keep my side of it, and you must keep yours."

"I cannot, I tell you. Something, something I cannot understand, mocks me."

"You love the fellow still," said Romanoff. "Fancy, Olga Petrovic is weak enough for that."

"Yes, I love him," cried the woman—"I admit it—love him with every fibre of my being. But not as you would have me love him. I have tried to obey you; but I am baffled. The man's clean, healthy soul makes me ashamed. God alone knows how ashamed I am! And it is his healthiness of soul that baffles me."

"No, it is not," snarled Romanoff. "It is because I have been opposed by one of whom I was ignorant. That chit of a girl, that wayside flower, whom I would love to see polluted by the filth of the world, has been used to beat me. Don't you see? The fellow is in love with her. He has been made to love her. That is why you have failed."

Mad jealousy flashed into the woman's eyes. "He loves her?" she asked, and her voice was hoarse.

"Of course he does. Will you let him have her?"

"He cannot. Is she not betrothed to that soldier fellow?"

"What if she is? Was there not love in her eyes as she came here to-night? Would she have come merely for Platonic friendship? Olga, if you do not act quickly, you will have lost him—lost him for ever."

"But I have lost him!" she almost wailed.

"You have not, I tell you. Go to her to-night. Tell her that Faversham is not the man she thinks he is. Tell her—but I need not instruct you as to that. You know what to say. Then when he goes to her to explain, as he will go, she will drive him from her, Puritan fool as she is, with loathing and scorn! After that your turn will come again."

For some time they talked, she protesting, he explaining, threatening, cajoling, promising, and at length he overcame. With a look of determination in her eyes, she left her flat, and drove to the hotel where Romanoff told her that Hugh Stanmore and Beatrice were staying.

Was Miss Beatrice Stanmore in the hotel? she asked when she entered the vestibule.

Yes, she was informed, Miss Stanmore had returned with her grandfather only half an hour before.

She took one of her visiting cards and wrote on it hastily.

"Will you take it to her at once," she commanded the servant, and she handed him the card. "Tell her that it is extremely urgent."

"But it is late, your ladyship," protested the man; "and I expect she has retired."

Nevertheless he went. A look from the woman compelled obedience. A few minutes later he returned.

"Will you be pleased to follow me, your ladyship?" he said. "Miss Stanmore will see you."

Olga Petrovic followed him with a steady step, but in her eyes was a look of fear.

Chapter XXXIX
The Triumph of Good

Beatrice Stanmore was sitting in a tiny room as the Countess Olga Petrovic entered. It was little more than a dressing-room, and adjoined her bedroom. She rose at Olga's entrance, and looked at the woman intently. She was perfectly calm, and was far more at ease than her visitor.

"I hope you will pardon the liberty I have taken," and Olga spoke in sweet, low tones; "but I came to plead for your forgiveness. I was unutterably rude to you to-night, and I felt I could not sleep until I was assured of your pardon."

"Won't you sit down?" and Beatrice pointed to a chair as she spoke. "I will ask my grandfather to come here."

"But, pardon me," cried Olga eagerly, "could we not remain alone? I have much to say to you—things which I can say to you only."

"Then it was not simply to ask my pardon that you came?" retorted Beatrice. "Very well, I will hear you."

She was utterly different from the sensitive, almost timid girl whom Dick Faversham had spoken to at Wendover. It was evident that she had no fear of her visitor. She spoke in plain matter-of-fact terms.

For a few seconds the older woman seemed to be at a loss what to say. The young inexperienced girl disturbed her confidence, her self-assurance.

"I came to speak to you about Mr. Faversham," she began, after an awkward silence.

Beatrice Stanmore made no remark, but sat quietly as if waiting for her to continue.

"You know Mr. Faversham?" continued the woman.

"Yes, I know him."

"Forgive me for speaking so plainly; but you have an interest in him which is more than—ordinary?" The words were half a question, half an assertion.

"I am greatly interested in Mr. Faversham—yes," she replied quietly.

"Even though, acting on the advice of your grandfather, you have become engaged to Sir George Weston? Forgive my speaking plainly, but I felt I must come to you to-night, felt I must tell you the truth."

Olga Petrovic paused as if waiting for Beatrice to say something, but the girl was silent. She fixed her eyes steadily on the other's face, and waited.

"Mr. Faversham is not the kind of man you think he is." Olga Petrovic spoke hurriedly and awkwardly, as though she found the words difficult to say.

Still Beatrice remained silent; but she kept her eyes steadily on the other's face.

"I thought I ought to tell you. You are young and innocent; you do not know the ways of men. Mr. Faversham is not fit for you to associate with."

"And yet you dined with him to-night. You took him to your flat afterwards."

"But I am different from you. I am a woman of the world, and your Puritan standard of morals has no weight or authority with me. Of course," and again she spoke awkwardly, "I have no right to speak to you, your world is different from mine, and you are a stranger to me; but I have heard of you."

"How? Through whom?"

"Need you ask?"

"I suppose you mean Mr. Faversham. Why should he speak to you about me?"

"Some men are like that. They boast of their conquests, they glory in—in——; but I need not say more. Will you take advice from a woman who—who has suffered, and who, through suffering, has learnt to know the world? It is this. Think no more of Richard Faversham. He—he is not a good man; he is not fit to associate with a pure child like you."

Beatrice Stanmore looked at the other with wonder in her eyes. There was more than wonder, there was terror. It might be that the older woman had frightened her.

"Forgive me speaking like this," went on Olga, "but I cannot help myself. Drive him from your mind. Perhaps there is not much romance in the thought of marrying Sir George Weston, but I beseech you to do so. He, at least, will shield you from the temptations, the evil of the world. As for Faversham, if he ever tries to see you again, remember that his very presence is pollution for such as you. Yes, yes, I know what you are thinking of—but I don't matter. I live in a world of which I hope you may always remain ignorant; but in which Faversham finds his joy. You—you saw us together——"

In spite of her self-control Beatrice was much moved. The crimson flushes on her cheeks were followed by deathly pallor. Her lips quivered, her bosom heaved as if she found it difficult to breathe. But she did not speak. Perhaps she was too horrified by the other's words.

"I know I have taken a fearful liberty with you," went on Olga; "but I could not help myself. My life, whatever else it has done has made me quick to understand, and when I watched you, I saw that that man had cast an evil spell upon you. At first I felt careless, but as I watched your face, I felt a great pity for you. I shuddered at the thought of your life being blackened by your knowledge of such a man."

"Does he profess love to you?" asked Beatrice quietly.

Olga Petrovic gave a hard laugh. "Surely you saw," she said.

"And you would warn me against him?"

"Yes; I would save you from misery."

For some seconds the girl looked at the woman's face steadily, then she said, simply and quietly:

"And are you, who seek to save me, content to be the woman you say you are? You are very, very beautiful—are you content to be evil?"

She spoke just as a child might speak; but there was something in the tones of her voice which caused the other to be afraid.

"You seem to have a kind heart," went on Beatrice; "you would save me from pain, and—and evil. Have you no thought for yourself?"

"I do not matter," replied the woman sullenly.

"You think only of me?"

"I think only of you."

"Then look at me," and the eyes of the two met. "Is what you have told me true?"

"True!"

"Yes, true. You were innocent once, you had a mother who loved you, and I suppose you once had a religion. Will you tell me, thinking of the mother who loved you, of Christ who died for you, whether what you say about Mr. Faversham is true?"

A change came over Olga Petrovic's face; her eyes were wide open with terror and shame. For some seconds she seemed fighting with a great temptation, then she rose to her feet.

"No," she almost gasped; "it is not true!" She simply could not persist in a lie while the pure, lustrous eyes of the girl were upon her.

"Then why did you tell me?"

"Because, oh, because I am mad! Because I am a slave, and because I am jealous, jealous for his love, because, oh— —!" She flung herself into the chair again, and burst into an agony of tears.

"Oh, forgive me, forgive me for deceiving you!" she sobbed presently.

"You did not deceive me at all. I knew you were lying."

"But—but you seemed—horrified at what I told you!"

"I was horrified to think that one so young and beautiful like you could—could sink so low."

"Then you do not know what love is!" she cried. "Do you understand? I love him—love him! I would do anything, anything to win him."

"And if you did, could you make him happy?"

"I make him happy! Oh, but you do not know."

"Tell me," said Beatrice, "are you not the tool, the slave of someone else? Has not Mr. Faversham an enemy, and are you not working for that enemy?"

Her clear, childlike eyes were fixed on the other's face; she seemed trying to understand her real motives. Olga Petrovic, on the other hand, regarded the look with horror.

"No, no," she cried, "do not think that of me! I would have saved Dick from him. I—I would have shielded him with my life."

"You would have shielded him from Count Romanoff?"

"Do not tell me you know him?"

"I only know of him. He is evil, evil. Ah yes, I understand now. He sent you here. He is waiting for you now."

"But how do you know?"

"Listen," said Beatrice, without heeding her question, "you can be a happy woman, a good woman. Go back and tell that man that you have failed, and that he has failed; then go back to your own country, and be the woman God meant you to be, the woman your mother prayed you might be."

"I—I a happy woman—a good woman!"

"Yes—I tell you, yes."

"Oh, tell me so again, tell me—O great God, help me!"

"Sit down," said Beatrice quietly; "let us talk. I want to help you."

For a long time they sat and talked, while old Hugh Stanmore, who was close by, wondered who his grandchild's visitor could be, and why they talked so long.

It was after midnight when Olga Petrovic returned to her flat, and no sooner did she enter than Count Romanoff met her.

"Well, Olga," he asked eagerly, "what news?"

"I go back to Poland to-morrow, to my old home, to my own people."

She spoke slowly, deliberately; her voice was hard and cold.

He did not seem to understand. He looked at her questioningly for some seconds without speaking.

"You are mad, Olga," he said presently.

"I am not mad."

"This means then that you have failed. You understand the consequences of failure?"

"It means—oh, I don't know what it means. But I do know that that child had made me long to be a good woman."

"A good woman? Olga Petrovic a good woman!" he sneered.

"Yes, a good woman. I am not come to argue with you. I only tell you that you are powerless to hinder me."

"And Faversham? Does Olga Petrovic mean that she confesses herself beaten? That she will have her love thrown in her face, and not be avenged?"

"It means that if you like, and it means something more. Isaac Romanoff, or whatever your real name may be, why you have sought to ruin that man I don't know; but I know this: I have been powerless to harm him, and so have you."

"It means that you have failed—*you*!" he snarled.

"Yes, and why? There has been a power mightier than yours against which you have fought. Good, GOOD, has been working on his side, that is why you have failed, why I have failed. O God of Goodness, help me!"

"Stop that, stop that, I say!" His voice was hoarse, and his face was livid with rage.

"I will not stop," she cried. "I want to be a good woman—I will be a good woman. That child whom I laughed at has seen a thousand times farther into the heart of truth than I, and she is happy, happy in her innocence, in her spotless purity, and in her faith in God. And I promised her I would be a new woman, live a new life."

"You cannot, you dare not," cried the Count.

"But I will. I will leave the old bad past behind me."

"And I will dog your every footstep. I will make such madness impossible."

"But you cannot. Good is stronger than evil. God is Almighty."

"I hold you, body and soul, remember that."

The woman seemed possessed of a new power, and she turned to the Count with a look of triumph in her eyes.

"Go," she cried, "in the name of that Christ who was the joy of my mother's life, and who died that I might live—I bid you go. From to-night I cease to be your slave."

The Count lifted his hand as if to strike her, but she stood before him fearless.

"You cannot harm me," she cried. "See, see, God's angels are all around me now! They stretch out their arms to help me."

He seemed to be suffering agonies; his face was contorted, his eyes were lurid, and he appeared to be struggling with unseen powers.

"I will not yield," he cried; "not one iota will I yield. You are mine, you swore to serve me—I claim my own."

"The oath I took was evil, evil, and I break it. O eternal God, help me, help me. Save me, save me, for Christ's sake."

Romanoff seemed to hesitate what to do, then he made a movement as if to move towards her, but was powerless to do so. The hand which he had uplifted dropped to his side as if paralysed; he was in the presence of a Power greater than his own. He passed out of the room without another word.

The next day the flat of Countess Olga Petrovic was empty, but no one knew whither she had gone.

For more than a month after the scenes I have described, Dick Faversham was confined to his room. He suffered no pain, but he was languid, weak, and terribly depressed. An acquaintance who called to see him, shocked by his appearance, insisted on sending for a doctor, and this gentleman, after a careful examination, declared that while he was organically sound, he was in a low condition, and utterly unfit for work.

"You remind me of a man suffering from shell-shock," he said. "Have you had any sudden sorrow, or anything of that sort?"

Dick shook his head.

"Anyhow, you are utterly unfit for work, that is certain," went on the doctor. "What you need is absolute rest, cheerful companionship, and a warm, sunny climate."

"There's not much suggestion of a warm, sunny climate here," Dick said, looking out of the window.

"But I daresay it would be possible to arrange for a passport, so that you might get to the South of France, or to Egypt," persisted the doctor.

"Yes; I might get a passport, but I've no money to get there."

So Dick stayed on at his flat, and passed the time as best he could. By and by the weather improved, and presently Dick was well enough to get out. But he had no interest in anything, and he quickly grew tired. Then a sudden, an almost overmastering desire came to him to go to Wendover. There seemed no reason why he should go there, but his heart ached for a sight of the old house. He pictured it as it was during the time he spent there. He saw the giant trees in the park, the gay flowers in the gardens, the stateliness and restfulness of the old mansion. The thought of it warmed his heart, and gave him new hope.

"Oh, if it were only mine again!" he reflected.

He had heard that the rumours of Tony Riggleton's death were false, and he was also told that although he had been kept out of England for some time he would shortly return; but concerning that he could gather nothing definite.

Of Beatrice Stanmore he had heard nothing, and he had no heart to make inquiries concerning her. He had many times reflected on her sudden appearance at Olga Petrovic's flat, and had he been well enough he would have tried to see her. More than once he had taken a pen in hand to write to her, but he had never done so. What was the use? In spite of her coming, he felt that she must regard him with scorn. He remembered what Olga Petrovic had said in her presence. Besides, he was too weak, too ill to make any effort whatever.

But with the sudden desire to go to Wendover came also the longing to see her—to explain. Of course she was the affianced wife of Sir George Weston, but he wanted to stand well in her eyes; he wanted her to know the truth.

It was a bright, balmy morning when he started for Surrey, and presently, when the train had left Croydon behind, a strange joy filled his heart. After all, life was not without hope. He was a young man, and in spite of everything he had kept his manhood. He was poor, and as yet unknown, but he had obtained a certain position. Love was not for him, nor riches, but he could work for the benefit of others.

When the train stopped at Wendover station, he again found himself to be the only passenger who alighted. As he breathed the pure, balmy air, and saw the countryside beginning to clothe itself in its mantle of living green, it seemed to him that new life, new energy, entered his being. After all, it was good to be alive.

Half an hour later he was nearing the park gates—not those which he had entered on his first visit, but those near which Hugh Stanmore's cottage was situated. He had taken this road without thinking. Well, it did not matter.

As he saw the cottage nestling among the trees, he felt his heart beating wildly. He wondered if Beatrice was at home, wondered—a thousand things. He longed to call and make inquiries, but of course he would not. He would enter the park gates unseen, and make his way to the great house.

But he did not pass the cottage gate. Before he could do so the door opened, and Beatrice appeared. Evidently she had seen him coming, for she ran down the steps with outstretched hand.

"I felt sure it was you," she said, "and—but you look pale—ill; are you?"

"I'm ever so much better, thank you," he replied. "So much so that I could not refrain from coming to see Wendover again."

"But you must come in and rest," she cried anxiously. "I insist on it. Why did you not tell us you were ill?"

Before he could reply he found himself within the cottage.

Chapter XL
The Ministering Angel

"Are you alone?" he managed to ask.

"Yes; Granddad went out early. He'll be back in an hour or so. He has been expecting to hear from you."

How sweet and fair she looked! There was no suggestion of the exotic beauty of Olga Petrovic; she adopted no artificial aids to enhance her appearance. Sweet, pure air and exercise had tinted her cheeks; the beauty of her soul shone from her eyes. She was just a child of nature, and to Dick she was the most beautiful thing on God's earth.

For a moment their eyes met, and then the love which Dick Faversham had been fighting against for weeks surged like a mighty flood through his whole being.

"I must go—I must not stay here," he stammered.

"But why? Granddad will be back soon."

"Because——" Again he caught the flash of her eyes, and felt that the whole world without her was haggard hopelessness. Before he knew what he was saying he had made his confession.

"Because I have no right to be here," he said almost angrily—"because it is dishonourable; it is madness for me to stay."

"But why?" she persisted.

He could not check the words that passed his lips; he had lost control over himself.

"Don't you understand?" he replied passionately. "I have no right to be here because I love you—love you more than my own life. Because you are everything to me—*everything*—and you have promised to marry Sir George Weston."

"But I've not." She laughed gaily as she uttered the words.

"You've not promised to——But—but——"

"No, of course not. How could I? I do not love him. He is awfully nice, and I'm very fond of him; but I don't love him. I could never think of such a thing."

She spoke quite naturally, and in an almost matter-of-fact way. She did not seem to realise that her words caused Dick Faversham's brain to reel, and his blood to rush madly through his veins. Rather she seemed like one anxious to correct a mistake, but to have no idea of what the correction meant to him.

For a few seconds Dick did not speak. "She is only a child," he reflected. "She does not understand what I have said to her. She does not realise what my love for her means."

But he was not sure of this. Something, he knew not what, told him she *did* know. Perhaps it was the flush on her cheeks, the quiver on her lips, the strange light in her eyes.

"You have not promised to marry Sir George Weston?" he asked hoarsely.

"No, of course not."

"But—he asked you?"

"That is scarcely a fair question, is it?"

"No, no, forgive me; it is not. But do you understand—what your words mean to me?"

She was silent at this.

"I love you—love you," he went on. "I want you to be my wife."

"I'm so glad," she said simply.

"But do you understand?" cried Dick. He could not believe in his own happiness, could not help thinking there must be some mistake. "This means everything to me."

"Of course I understand. I've known it for a long time, that is, I've felt it must be so. And I've wondered why you did not come and tell me."

"And you love me?" His voice was hoarse and tremulous.

"Love you? Why—why do you think I—could be here like this—if I didn't?"

Still she spoke almost as a child might speak. There was no suggestion of coquetry, no trying to appear surprised at his avowal. But there was something more, something in the tone of her voice, in the light of her eyes, in her very presence, that told Dick that deep was calling unto deep, that this maiden, whose heart was the heart of a child, had entered into womanhood, and knew its glory.

"Aren't you glad, too?" she asked.

"Glad! It seems so wonderful that I can't believe it! Half an hour ago the world was black, hopeless, while now— —; but there are things I must tell you, things I've wanted to tell you ever since I saw you last."

"Is it about that woman?"

"Yes, I wanted to tell you why I was with her; I wanted you to know that she was nothing to me."

"I knew all the time. But you were in danger—that was why I could not help coming to you. You understand, don't you? I had the same kind of feeling when that evil man was staying with you at the big house. He was trying to harm you, and I came. And he was still trying to ruin you, why I don't know, but he was using that woman to work his will. I felt it, and I came to you."

"How did you know?" asked Dick. He was awed by her words, solemnised by the wondrous intuition which made her realise his danger.

"I didn't know—I only felt. You see, I loved you, and I couldn't help coming."

Another time he would have asked her many questions about this, but now they did not seem to matter. He loved, and was loved, and the fact filled the world.

"Thank God you came," he said reverently. "And, Beatrice, you will let me call you Beatrice, won't you?"

"Why, of course, you must, Dick."

"May I kiss you?" he asked, and held out his arms.

She came to him in all the sweet freshness of her young life and offered him her pure young lips. Never had he known what joy meant as he knew it then, never had he felt so thankful that in spite of dire temptation he had kept his manhood clean.

Closer and closer he strained her to his heart, while words of love and of thankfulness struggled for expression. For as she laid her head on his shoulder, and he felt the beating of her heart, his mind swept like lightning over the past years, and he knew that angels of God had ministered to him, that they had shielded him from danger, and helped him in temptation. And this he knew also: while he had been on the brink of ruin through a woman, it was also by a woman that he had been saved. The thought of

Beatrice Stanmore had been a power which had defied the powers of evil, and enabled him to keep his manhood clean.

Even yet the wonder of it all was beyond words, for he had come there that morning believing that Beatrice was the promised wife of Sir George Weston, and now, as if by the wave of some magician's wand, his beliefs had been dispelled, and he had found her free.

An hour before, he dared not imagine that this unspoilt child of nature could ever think of him with love, and yet her face was pressed against his, and she was telling him the simple story of her love—a love unsullied by the world, a love unselfish as that of a mother, and as strong as death.

"But I am so poor," he stammered at length; "just a voting machine at four hundred a year."

"As though you could ever be that," she laughed. "You are going to do great things, my love. You are going to live and work for the betterment of the world. And I—I shall be with you all the time."

He had much to tell her—a story so wonderful that it was difficult to believe. But Beatrice believed it. The thought of an angel who had come to him, warned him, guided him, and strengthened him, was not strange to her. For her pure young eyes had pierced the barriers of materialism, just as the light of the stars pierces the darkness of night. Because her soul was pure, she knew that the angels of God were never far away, and that the Eternal Goodness used them to minister to those who would listen to their voices.

Dick did not go to the great house that day. There seemed no reason why he should. By lunch time old Hugh Stanmore returned and was met by the two lovers.

Of all they said to each other, and of the explanations that were made, there is no need that I should write. Suffice to say that Hugh Stanmore was satisfied. It is true he liked Sir George Weston, while the thought that Beatrice might be mistress of his house was pleasant to him; true, too, that Dick Faversham was poor. But he had no fears. He knew that this young man's love was pure and strong, that he would never rest until he had provided a home worthy of her, and that his grandchild's future would be safe in his hands.

When Dick left the cottage that night, it was on the understanding that he would come back as soon as possible. Beatrice pleaded hard with him not to go to London, but to stay at the cottage and be nursed back to health and strength. But Dick had to make arrangements for a lengthened stay away from his work, and to see some of his confrères, so, while his heart yearned to remain near her, he looked joyfully forward to his return.

"And you go away happy, my love?"

"The happiest man on earth. And you, my little maid?"

"Oh, Dick, everything is as I hoped and prayed for."

"And you loved me all the time?"

"All the time; but I did not know it until——"

"Until when?"

"Until another man told me he wanted me."

Dick was in dreamland as he returned to London. No sooner had he boarded the train at Wendover than, as it seemed to him, he had arrived at Victoria. As for the journey between that station and his flat he has no remembrance to this day.

"Oh, the wonder of it, the glad wonder of it!" he repeated again and again. "Thank God—thank God!"

Then, as if in fulfilment of an old adage, no sooner had he entered his flat than another surprise awaited him. On his writing-table lay a long blue envelope, which had been brought by hand that afternoon. Dick broke the seal almost indifferently. What did he care about letters? Then he saw the name of Bidlake, and his attention was riveted.

This is what he read:

> "My dear Faversham,—Forgive this unceremonious manner of writing, but I fancy I am a little excited. Riggleton is dead, and thus it comes about that the Faversham estates—or what is left of them—revert to you. How it was possible for a man to squander so much money and leave things in such a terrible mess in such a short time it is difficult to say. But there it is. Still, a good deal is left. Wendover Park, and all the lands attached remain untouched, and a good deal of money can be scraped up. Will you call as soon as possible on receipt of this, and I'll explain everything to you, as far as I can.—With heartiest congratulations, yours faithfully,
>
> "John Bidlake."

Again and again Dick read this letter. He felt something like the lad of the Eastern Story must have felt as he read. He would not have been surprised if the Slave of the Lamp appeared, asking what his desires were, so that they might be performed without delay. December had changed into June in a single day.

His joy can be better imagined than described. To know that this old homestead was his again, to realise that he was no longer homeless and poor was a gladness beyond words. But he no longer felt as he had felt when he first saw Wendover. Then his thought had been of his own aggrandisement, and the satisfaction of his ambitions. Now he rejoiced because he could offer a home to the maiden he loved, and because he could do for the world what for years he had dreamt of doing.

But he was early at Mr. Bidlake's office the following morning.

"No, no, there's no mistake this time," Mr. Bidlake assured him. "You can enter into possession with a confident mind. Money! Yes, the fellow wasted it like water, but you need not fear. You'll have more than you need, in spite of increased income-tax and super-tax. Talk about romance though, if ever there was a romance this is one."

After spending two hours with the lawyer Dick went to the House of Commons, where he made the necessary arrangements for a couple of weeks' further absence.

"Yes, we can manage all right," assented the Labour Member with whom he spoke. "Not but what we shall be glad to have you back. There are big things brewing. The working people must no longer be hewers of wood and drawers of water. We must see to that."

"Yes, we *will* see to that," cried Dick. "But we must be careful."

"Careful of what?"

"Careful that we don't drift to Bolshevism, careful that we don't abuse our power. We must show that we who represent the Democracy understand our work. We must not think of one class only, but all the classes. We must think of the Empire, the good of humanity."

The other shook his head, "No mercy on capitalists," he cried.

"On the other hand we must make capitalists do their duty," Dick replied. "We must see to it that Capital and Labour work together for the good of the whole community. There lies the secret of stable government and a prosperous nation."

It was late in the evening when Dick arrived at Hugh Stanmore's cottage, so late indeed that the old man had given up hope of his coming; but Beatrice rushed to him with a glad laugh.

"I knew you would come," she said. "And now I am going to begin my work as nurse right away. You must have a light supper and go to bed at once, and to-morrow you must stay in bed all day."

Dick shook his head. "And I am going to rebel," was his reply. "I am going to sit up for at least two hours, while first thing to-morrow morning I am going to take you to a house I have in my mind."

"What house?"

"A house I've settled on for our future home."

"Dick, don't be foolish. You know we must not think of that for months—years."

"Mustn't we?" laughed Dick. "There, read that," and he handed her Mr. Bidlake's letter.

"But, Dick!" she cried as she read, "this, this is——"

"Beautiful, isn't it?" Dick replied joyously. "Will you read it, sir?" and he placed it in old Hugh Stanmore's hands.

After that Beatrice no longer insisted that her lover must be treated as an invalid. Hour after hour they sat talking, while the wonder of it all never left them.

The next morning broke bright and clear. Spring had indeed come, gladsome joyous spring, heralded by the song of birds, by the resurrection of a new life everywhere.

"Will you go with us, Granddad?" asked Beatrice, as they prepared for their visit.

"No," said Hugh Stanmore; "I'll come across alone in a couple of hours." He was a wise man.

Neither of them spoke a word as they walked up the avenue towards the great house. Perhaps their minds were both filled by the same thoughts—thoughts too great for utterance. Above them the sun shone in a great dome of cloudless blue, while around them all nature was putting on her beautiful garments.

Presently the old house burst upon their view. There it stood on a slight eminence, while behind it great trees rose. Away from the front of the building stretched grassy lawns and flower gardens, while beyond was parkland, studded by giant trees.

And still neither spoke. Hand in hand they walked towards the entrance door, Dick gazing at it earnestly, as if looking for something. When they had come within a dozen yards of it both, as if by mutual consent, stood still.

Was it fancy or was it real? Was it because expectancy was in both their hearts, and their imagination on fire, or did they really see?

This is what both of them told me they saw.

Standing in the doorway, with hands outstretched as if in the attitude of welcoming them, was the luminous figure of a woman. Her face was lit up with holy joy, while in her eyes was no sorrow, no doubt, but a look of ineffable happiness.

For a few seconds she stood gazing on them, and Dick saw the look of love in her eyes, saw the rapture that seemed to pervade her being. It was the same face he had seen there before, the same love-lit eyes.

She lifted her hands as if in benediction, and then slowly the figure faded away.

"It is my mother," whispered Dick. He had no remembrance of his mother, but he knew it was she. He felt no fear, there was nothing to be fearful about, rather a great joy filled his life. God had sent his angel to tell him that all was well.

The door stood open, and they entered the great silent hall together. No one was in sight. He opened his arms, and she came to him.

"Welcome home, my wife," he said.

> [1] In view of the fact that the above incident may be regarded as utterly unbelievable, I may say that an experience of the same nature was related to me only a few weeks ago, far more wonderful than the one I have recorded. Concerning the good faith of those who told the incident, it is above all suspicion, and of its authenticity there seems no room for doubt. I cannot further enter into details for obvious reasons. — The Author.

Printed in the USA
CPSIA information can be obtained
at www.ICGtesting.com
LVHW040053090824
787788LV00007B/118